FOLLY

FOLLY

Laurie R. King

BANTAM BOOKS

New York Toronto London Sydney Auckland

FOLLY

A Bantam Book / March 2001

All rights reserved.
Copyright © 2001 by Laurie R. King.

Library of Congress Cataloging-in-Publication Data
King, Laurie R.
    Folly : a novel / Laurie R. King.
        p. cm.
    ISBN: 0-553-11103-5
    I. Title.
    PS3561.I4813 F6 2000
    813'.54—dc21   00-60824
                          CIP

Published simultaneously in the United States and Canada

Bantam Books are published by Bantam Books, a division of Random House, Inc. Its trademark,
consisting of the words "Bantam Books" and the portrayal of a rooster, is Registered in U.S. Patent
and Trademark Office and in other countries. Marca Registrada. Bantam Books, 1540 Broadway,
New York, New York 10036.

PRINTED IN THE UNITED STATES OF AMERICA

BVG   10   9   8   7   6   5   4   3   2   1

For my Rod and staff—all the hands at Buckholdt's Builders, living proof that honest craftsmanship is not lost: Tony, Raymundo, Tom, Steve, Ian, John, Ryan, Mauricio, Cindy, Antonio, and in memory of Pablo.

Thanks, guys.

With thanks to the following individuals who shared their various technical expertise with a writer, and who are not to be held responsible for what she did with the information.

Rod Buckholdt
Bruce Decker, for the Freon smugglers
Michael Gray
Joyce Nordquist
Heidi Smith
The San Juan County Sheriff's Department
All the brave men and women who wrote of their experiences with severe depression and mental illness

And with apologies to the geography and population of San Juan County in Washington State, for that same writer's impertinence in adding one island and an assortment of troublesome individuals to an already perfect corner of the globe.

Folly (from OF, *fol,* fool):

1. lack of good sense or normal prudence and foresight
2. a foolish act or idea
3. evil, wickedness; criminally or tragically foolish actions or conduct
4. an excessively costly or unprofitable undertaking
5. an often extravagant picturesque building erected to suit a fanciful taste

(from *Webster's Ninth New Collegiate Dictionary*)

Preface

The gray-haired woman stood with her boots planted on the rocky promontory and watched what was left of her family pull away. The *Orca Queen*'s engines deepened as the boat cleared the cove entrance, and its nose swung around, a magnet oriented toward civilization.

Go, she told them silently. *Don't slow down, don't even look back, just leave.*

But then Petra's jacketed arm shot out from the boat's cabin, drab and shapeless and waving a wild adolescent farewell. Rae's own hand came up in an involuntary response, to wave her own good-bye—except that in the air, her wave changed, the hand reaching forward, stretched out in protest and cry for help, as if her outstretched fingers could pull them back to her, as if she were about to take off down the beach, scrambling desperately over rocks and water to call and scream *Don't leave me here, I'm so afraid* and— She caught the gesture before any of the three people on the boat could notice it, snapped the offending arm down to her side, and stood at rigid attention. The boat rounded the end of the island, and was gone.

Thank God they didn't see that, Rae thought. *The last thing I want is for Tamara to think I don't know what I'm doing.*

So why do I feel like some ancient grandmother in one of those harsh nomadic tribes, left behind on the icy steppes for the good of the group? I chose this. I wanted this.

The engines' growl softened with the distance, grew faint, then merged into the island hush. No low mutter of faraway traffic, no neighbor's dogs and children, not even the pound of surf in this protected sea. A small airplane off to the north; the rusty-wheel squeak of a bird; the patter of tiny waves; and silence.

Alone, at last. For better or for worse.

Solitude, and silence.

Silence was not an absence of noise, it was an actual thing, a creature with weight and bulk. The stillness felt her presence and gathered close against her, slowly at first but inexorably, until Rae found herself bracing her knees and swaying with the burden. It felt like a shroud, like the sodden sheets they used to bind around out-of-control mental patients. She stood alone on the shore, head bowed, as if the gray sky had opened to give forth a viscous and invisible stream of quiet. It poured across her scalp and down her skin, pooling around her feet, spreading across the rocks and the bleached driftwood, oozing its way into the salt-stunted weeds farther up the bank and the shrubs with their traces of spring green, then fingering the shaggy trunks of the fragrant cedars and bright madrones until it reached the derelict foundation on which fifty-two-year-old Rae Newborn would build her house, that brush-deep, moss-soft, foursquare, twin-towered stone skeleton that had held out against storm and fire and the thin ravages of time, waiting seventy years for this woman to raise its walls again.

Or not. This could easily prove a farce, a tragic folly demanding the effort and expense of a moon shot without a board ever going up. That garish blue tarpaulin covering her pricey lumber might prove her memorial, and Folly would have another chapter added to its already colorful history.

Rae found that her right hand had wrapped itself around the opposite wrist, its thumb tracing the crisscrossed scars on the tender and vulnerable skin. She tipped her palms back and let the sleeves fall away, and studied closely the raised lines as if a message might be read there.

One pair of scars had lived on her wrists for thirty years, but she could still recall the rich well of blood, the overwhelming relief, and the astonishing absence of pain. The slightly longer pair that overlaid them were ten years younger, not much pinker, and less clear in her mind. But on top of that set, the most recent cuts were still bright and sharp. Almost exactly a year old, those.

The scars held a macabre fascination, even during those blessedly long periods in her life when Rae had no desire to add to them. The intriguing dichotomy of the toughness of human skin and its defenseless parting, the body's grim determination to heal itself, the physical proof of how painful life could become, all drew her gaze. Most of all, though, she was constantly astonished—and even more, grateful—that in all that self-mutilation, she'd never managed to slice through anything essential to the working of the hand.

Perhaps there was a message to be read on the skin: Next time, use the gun, stupid.

At that reminder, Rae dropped her hands and raised her eyes to the campsite, searching for the green knapsack that held, among her other most secret and treasured possessions, the wood-grip revolver that had been the reason for her recent long drive up the coast: As Tamara had pointed out more than once, a plane flight would have been easier on everyone else—but they don't allow guns on a plane.

She spotted the lump of green nylon on top of the heap of possessions that had come with her on the *Orca Queen* out of Friday Harbor, piled there by Petra and Tamara and Ed De la Torre, left for Rae to sort and arrange. In those haphazardly stacked boxes were tools and toilet paper, canned goods and dry socks, everything a marooned sailor—or woodworker—could ask for. At least the tarp that protected them from the drizzle, strung between tent and trees as an impromptu outdoor room, was a drab and inoffensive brown.

Rae's gaze continued on, traveling from the shiny new camp equipment arranged at one side of the clearing to the two stone towers struggling out of the vegetation two hundred yards away. The towers were the only visible parts of what had once been a house, and they seemed to tug at her mind and at her hands, willing her to draw near.

A house is an exercise in controlled tension, she mused. Who had said that? Whoever it was, they'd slightly missed the point: A house, she reflected, is more an exercise in using tension to control compression. It's not tension that needs controlling, lest it pull a house to pieces, but gravity that threatens to push a building apart, its compression buckling walls and cracking foundations. Without the tension of a structure's key elements—collar ties to keep the roof rafters from splaying, floor joists to transfer the compression of sofas and grand pianos and running children and lovemaking couples into the tension along its lower edge—the house curls up in a heap and dies.

The Hunter must have come up with that idea of house as a symbol of controlled tension, Rae decided. The succinct but inaccurate phrase had all the earmarks of one of the woman's psychiatric aphorisms, applying the gravity of a thoughtful statement to counteract the stresses threatening to pull a patient to bits. Rae herself would have put it, *A house is an illustration of the power of tension.* Take a saw to the bottom edges of that floor joist, remove the tension of stretched fibers below and leave only the compression of gravity above, and the piano or the sofa or the lovemaking couple drops through into the cellar.

The use of tension, after all, was precisely what Rae was doing here, on this last island before an international border, a middle-aged woman with too much scar tissue and too long a history of psychiatric fragility, a madwoman with a canvas tent, a supply of food, a bag of pills that would stupefy half of Seattle, a huge tarpaulined heap of building materials, and one small boxed collection of simple hand tools with which to tame it. No assistance, no neighbors, no electricity. No telephone, to cry for help.

And a massive sodden blanket of solitude dropped across her shoulders, threatening to flatten her if she dared move.

The Hunter called it depression and prescribed pills and talk.

But it was compression. Its huge weight had crushed a marriage, ruptured the relationship with a daughter, and accompanied Rae to the doors of death three times. She knew, in her bones and with thirty years' intimacy with clinical depression, that for her, the only way to counteract it was to use tension—psychic collar ties—to keep the weight of her life from splaying her out and collapsing her in a heap. Fear was the only tension powerful enough to counteract the weight of the illness: not happiness, not work, not even love, but fear confronted, fears real and imagined. It had been the pursuit of fear that brought her here, to the ends of the earth, where it was going to be easy, so infinitely easy, just to step off.

Here on the edge of the world, on a narrow precipice above the final abyss, Rae Newborn had come to make her halfhearted stand. No safety net, no other to take responsibility, just Rae and her ghosts and demons. She had come here because she was tired, not of life itself, but of living between. She had come to a place whose very name was Folly, as a way of forcing the issue.

Rae had come here to meet her fear, to welcome it, and, if possible, to use it. If that high-strung tension failed to balance the weight of life, if she was pulled to pieces or crushed flat, well, at least a decision would have been reached. The relief from the uncertainty would be considerable.

She hadn't told Dr. Hunt any of this, of course. The Hunter had problems enough with Rae's loopy self-diagnosis and had vehemently disapproved of her patient's self-prescribed plan of treatment, which amounted to recovery through hard labor. After all, Rae had entered the hospital in a state so low that she'd had actually to improve before she could attempt suicide. And although Dr. Hunt had seen the *symbol* of house building (when it appeared in Rae's therapeutic sessions halfway through the year of her hospitalization) as a sign of great hope, when it had dawned on the good doctor that Rae intended an actual, physical act of construction, she had been, professionally speaking, appalled. Was this not just another attempt at suicide, a substitution of lumber on a lonely hillside for sharp blades in the bath?

Rae did not argue with The Hunter. How could she? At the same time, once the hospital staff agreed that she was no longer a danger to herself or to others, neither did Rae back down from her decision. Planning and gathering her strength, she waited out the remainder of the winter in the house of her combination nurse and baby-sitter. Then, when spring began, she packed her bags, ordered her lumber, arranged for her baby-sitter to drive her north, and prepared to step into the renovation process that a far different Rae Newborn had begun several years before.

Although the process now had two enormous differences: She was on her own, not one of a family of three; and in her knapsack she carried a gun.

A beautiful gun, with a worn rosewood grip that endeared itself to Rae's hand, as old as the hills but impeccably maintained, solid and efficient as its six trim bullets. Not that she would need more than one. Blades, she had decided, those exquisitely sharp and sophisticated scraps of steel that dominated her working life, did not belong here. Too, there would be no slow seeping out of life with a bullet. Final, like the solid slam of a well-hung door. The elegant old handgun lay at the bottom of the frayed knapsack that had belonged to Alan (and which still gave out the occasional grain of sand from one or another of the beach treks of his youth), wrapped inside one of Alan's flannel shirts, nestled beneath a portable tape player (which the then eleven-year-old Petra had produced when she discovered that her grandmother was hearing voices) and a couple of paperbacks Rae didn't know if she would ever get around to reading, under the leather-bound journal that was intended to be her substitute for psychiatric honesty, the white paper bag of substances intended to be her substitutes for psychiatric balance, and the plastic zip-bag of soil and ashes that contained the remnants of her life in California. On the very top of the knapsack's contents rode her much-used carpenter's apron, the leather tool belt that Alan had given her, half-joking, for their first anniversary nine years before.

For some minutes now, Rae had been standing in the mistlike drizzle, her face turned to the building site but her eyes and mind far away. A distant boat horn blared, and she twitched. With a deep, long drawing-in of breath such as that taken by a waking sleeper or a diver preparing to go under, she turned her head to look back at the heap of her possessions, and moved at last. She made her way along the rocks, past the tarpaulined lumber and through the campsite, to duck under the brown tarp and stand before her pile of boxes and cartons. She stretched out her hand, and laid cold fingers on the bindings of the green knapsack.

Part One

CLEARING
THE GROUND

Anger did not begin to describe it. Rage, perhaps. Or fury—yes, like a furious sea, pounding against his very bones. It surged and rocked him, this outrage at having what was his—his!—stolen by another. Outwardly, he appeared calm—lashing out from time to time, but no more than usual. His mind was in full control, plotting cold revenge and the retrieval of what belonged to him. The Thief would have to flee a lot farther than some obscure island in the far reaches of the country to find any real refuge.

Vengeance is mine, saith the Lord.

One

In fact, Petra had not been the only passenger of the *Orca Queen* to look back at the sole resident of Folly Island.

Petra Collins, last scion of the once-illustrious Newborn line, certainly looked the longest and waved the hardest at her beloved, bereft grandmother standing alone on the receding shore. The gel that spiked Petra's dark curls felt frozen onto her knit cap, and the puffy coat wrapping her slim, hard body was not really adequate. *Poor, poor Gran,* the child thought; *she looks so lonely Oh man I wish I was as brave as she is all alone on an island with nobody to talk to except the seagulls, not even a dog, I mean I might think about it if I could take Bounce along like that book we read a couple years ago about the boy who runs away to go live in a dead tree in the woods and makes friends with a raccoon and a falcon, I wonder if Gran's island has raccoons? A falcon'd be so cool, though Oh poor Gran, I wish I could stay with her a while Oh jeez it's cold I wish I'd bought her that other hat, five bucks more but it would've been warmer for her she looks so old and cold and Bye Gran. Bye. Bye.*

The thoughts rattling through the mind of Tamara Collins were even less coherent than those of her thirteen-year-old daughter. She was struggling irritably to get her cigarette lit against the wind that flung the lighter's flame wildly about. On the way over, that wind had made her eyes water so badly she was now without any mascara, and she knew she looked a sight—not that there was anyone to see her in this godforsaken hole. She finally got the cigarette going, and an instant before the boat rounded Folly's southeastern point, Tamara glanced involuntarily over her shoulder at her mother, standing proud and straight-backed on the promontory. A pang of sympathy, even pity, sneaked in before her mind came back on-line with *Damn it, how long can it be before we get a call from the police or a hospital asking Do you know a Rae Newborn she was found— pick one or more of the following—a) raving at passersby b) starving to death c) bleeding to death Oh God maybe Don was right and we really ought to do something about her but that psychiatrist of hers said Mom has the right to do things that look crazy so long as they don't endanger her or anyone else but how can this not be considered dangerous? I mean, in this day and age what's to stop some nut—some real nut, some* violent *nut—from walking onto the island and Oh this is going nowhere, I'll have to have another talk with that psychiatrist Hunt, Dr. Hunt and tell her exactly what the situation is here, she can't have any idea Yes Don is right there's too much at stake and I never should have allowed Petra to skip a day of school to come on this fool's errand she's too young to understand and it's a mother's responsibility to protect her daughter just because my mother never did that doesn't mean Oh be fair she couldn't help herself, she never meant to abandon But if she's not responsible for her actions if she wasn't responsible thirty years ago and she wasn't last year either then why should she be allowed to do this completely irrational I mean they'd restrain some delusional person setting off for China in a rowboat how is this any different but No, Mom's not insane and certainly not like that just because she has been in the past but this really is crazy Well not crazy-insane but surely nuts and especially when there's so much at stake Don was right about that and would it really be so bad if we were to take the reins like he says take the reins of the estate and give her a monthly allowance and for sure keep a close eye on her I mean what if she decided to give it all away or something what about Petra? And there Mom stands straight as an arrow all pride and stubbornness and Damn it why do I always have to pick up the pieces for her she's the mother for Christ sake it drives me No it doesn't drive me crazy it makes me so angry something's got to be done here it's just too much it's just—* With that, the tree-covered island rose up and swallowed her mother, and Tamara was looking at nothing more exasperating than island and sea. She did not even know if what she felt was relief or sorrow.

The third party on the *Orca Queen* was its owner, Ed De la Torre, waterborne taxi and delivery service, amateur philosopher, jack-of-all-trades—particularly those trades frowned upon by the law. Ed was more or less impervious to the cold, his skin so toughened by sun and wind it wore like leather. Even the long, white mustaches, startling against the deep brown of his face, seemed barely to move in the gusts. Impervious, that was how Ed saw himself. And with that thought Ed, too, cast his sea-blue eyes back for a final glimpse of the odd figure he'd deposited on the shore of the uninhabited rock, a figure so lanky and so bundled up against the cold that a *man couldn't even be sure of its sex. All alone with no boat and fast-moving water all around, and what would that be like, living with nobody but the birds, no roof but the sky? Old Henry David would've understood, but then he could walk into town, talk to his neighbors, even had family practically within shouting distance. Hell, I've lived on the* Queen *for weeks at a time, but I can't remember ever going more'n two or three days without stopping in at a bar or a marina or something. Thomas Merton, now maybe there was a man who'd explain the attraction. It's been a while since I read Merton, maybe I'll dig him out again, see what the crazy monk has to say about solitude.*

'Course, even Merton didn't do that great with solitude. It distracted him, made him forget about the possibility of bad wiring in Third World appliances, so he got careless and electrocuted himself.

You could say his solitude killed him. God knows it'd kill me.

Alone, at last.

Rae stood beneath the sagging tarpaulin roof, the knapsack gaping open in front of her, and raised her head, abruptly aware of the sheer size of all that solitude pressing in on her flimsy shelter. For the first time— the first of many, she well knew—cold fear trickled into her heart. *What the hell am I doing? I mean, I've done a lot of loony things, but this really takes the cake. I should've been locked up, they should've thrown away the key, how can I possibly—*

She brought herself up short. This was no way to begin. She'd known it would be hard, but hard was the only solution.

Distraction, Rae. Keep moving. Like the old World War I song said, bristling with dark trench humor, Keep your head down, boys, and sing. *Stop to rest, pause to straighten your back, and a sniper will get you for sure. So keep your head down, Rae, and work.*

First things first. She reached into the knapsack and pulled out the topmost object, her tool belt, stiff with long disuse. Absently, automatically, for the first time in a year and a half her hands wrapped the belt around her waist and buckled it, and only when she noticed what she had done did Rae pause to reflect that, although her first thoughts on the island had been of self-destruction, her first act seemed to be one of building. Dr. Hunt would approve.

The psychiatrist might not, however, approve as wholeheartedly of Rae's next action, which was to take out the self-sealing sandwich bag filled with dark soil that she had collected from the center of the redwood cathedral where Alan and Bella's ashes had been scattered. The gray ash of them was no longer visible among the duff; Rae couldn't even make out any of the fragments of cremated bone that she knew were there, but sight did not matter. She went to the front of the tent, studied the possibilities for a minute, and then walked through the sodden grass of the clearing to the wide-spreading madrone tree that marked the eastern edge of clear ground. With the heel of her boot, Rae pounded a shallow depression into the damp soil, and there she emptied the contents of the bag. When every grain was gone, she kicked the mixture of island sand and half-rotted madrone leaves back over the foreign soil, then squatted down to smooth and pat it with her hand. To have come here without something of them would have been unthinkable. But they were here now; one responsibility that she was free of.

Rae felt as if she should say something, if only to give a welcome, but with all the words that had been said over those two, it seemed unnecessary, and at the moment more effort than she could summon. It had been a long two days' drive up the coast with her nurse-cum-baby-sitter, and an even longer seven hours in the company of her daughter. Rae still did not know why Tamara had gone to all that trouble, involving their crack-of-dawn flight to Seattle, a two-hour drive to Anacortes in a rental car, the ferry crossing and then Ed's boat, an hour unloading and standing around in the rain, and now the same journey in reverse, and for what? Because Tamara felt she was saying a final good-bye to her mother? And if that was the case, why didn't she at least hug Rae back, there on the dock? Rigid and unyielding, that was Rae's daughter's attitude toward Rae, had been since Tamara was tiny. Rae knew she was to blame, for abandoning the child to a rigid and unyielding grandmother and . . .

And why had thoughts of Tamara intruded on a memorial for Bella and Alan? Because Rae was tired, she supposed. She had done nothing in particular to wear herself out, mostly sat and stared at a lot of scenery, but she felt absolutely exhausted.

She also felt vaguely aware that she had eaten nothing that day other than a dutiful piece of toast on the ferry. Food, however dismal the prospect, might be a good next step. Food was a habit—without savor and unworthy of any more consideration than shoes on her feet or a daily swipe of the toothbrush—but a recognized necessity, something to put in the stomach to delay the grave for a few more hours. Starving herself to death had never appealed.

She went back to the tarpaulin-room and the knapsack, drawing out the box of matches Tamara had given her (Tamara was smoking again, but Rae had not commented) and the Seattle newspaper that she had picked up on the ferry, and went to fight silence with fire. First construction, now warmth, she thought; surely these were both positive symbols. And if Rae's eyes lingered on the newsprint, first an article about a deadly crash and then one concerning a missing girl in Spokane, she caught herself before she could start to obsess over the sick fascination of other people's catastrophes. She briskly crumpled the pages into the center of the circle of ancient, fire-blackened stones that Petra had regrouped for her and arranged a handful of kindling on top. A match to the corner, and the daily news began to burn.

Once the fire was going, Rae placed the heavy iron grill on the stones. Pawing through the box labeled "Food," she came up with a can of chili. "Utensils" gave her a saucepan, can opener, and spoon. She scooped the beans out into the pan and set it on the grill, which promptly tipped, spilling half the pan's contents into the flames. She rescued what she could, seated the grill more firmly on the stones, replaced the saucepan over the flames, and then carried the kettle over to her water jug to fill it. She brought the kettle back to the fire, and as she was lowering it over the hottest part of the flames, a blue jay screamed directly over her head. She jumped violently: a gout of water shot across the carbonized beans, nearly extinguishing the fire. Rae suppressed the high keen of frustration growing in her throat, and gathered together a second batch of kindling.

While her unappetizing meal warmed, Rae took out a plastic trash bag and began to clear away the litter she'd spotted, spoor of illicit picnickers and campers over the years. She used a rubber kitchen glove to pick up the beer cans and food wrappers, but at the sight of a diet Coke can, she was suddenly seated on the ferry again, across the wide table from Tamara. Neither woman noticed the heavy rumble of the boat or the appearance and retreat of the mist-shrouded islands of the San Juan chain, for Tamara had brought an oversized manila envelope from the shoulder bag she carried and emptied it out with a jerk onto the worn plastic surface.

"These should be the last of the receipts," she told her mother. "Anything else that arrives I'll just readdress to your lawyer. And we sent her a notarized letter to say that we were no longer responsible for paying your bills. Here's your checkbook. You're sure you don't want me to hang on to it for you, in case?"

Tamara could not have caught the brief, cynical question that passed through her mother's mind as Rae took the checkbook, speculating about how Don would lay hands on the family monies without it. Then she corrected herself: Outright theft was not Don's way. Whatever was missing, a careful adding up of numbers would not reveal it.

"I'll leave you as a signatory on the account, but I don't think you'll need to do anything. I really appreciate all you've done, Tamara. I know it's been a pain."

"We were happy to do it." It was always "we" with Tamara. She began to slide the papers back into the envelope. "Was the drive up okay?"

"Long, but good. It's beautiful countryside."

"You should have flown."

"I had too much stuff," Rae told her, giving the ready excuse. *Too much stuff, too many phobias, too great a need for a firearm* . . . "How is Don?" she asked dutifully.

"He's fine. There's a new health club opened up that he joined, he says he's getting out of shape." The thin horsewoman picked up her diet Coke and took a swallow.

Rae would have been just as happy were Don to be struck down by a massive coronary, but again she took care not to show the thought. Before she could dredge up another topic of conversation, however, Tamara went on, looking over the top of the can at the shivering figure leaning on the boat's rail outside the window.

"I think it's Petra driving up his blood pressure, myself."

"Are they having problems?"

"Oh, you know. Teenagers. Don was talking the other day about a special school, one of those highly structured environments. I told him this was a temporary thing—her best friend just moved away and she's upset. Petra will settle down."

Rae chose her words with care. "My father was sent off to military school when he was eight. For some boys it may have worked fine, but he never really got over it. Those schools have a way of making things worse. You might find you've alienated her completely." Then, before Tamara could react to the unasked-for advice, Rae continued, "What about another round of therapy? She might just need someone outside the picture to talk to."

"I was thinking about that," Tamara said—an enormous admission, considering her loathing of anything connected with the taint of mental illness. "The problem is, we're going through a tight spot, and the insurance is—"

"Let me cover it." Rae flipped open the checkbook and took out a pen, adding enough zeros to the sum to shut up Don's talk about private schools (which they couldn't afford anyway, by the sound of it). She tore the check out and put it down in front of Tamara, thinking, *Well, that answers my question about how Don will manage without my checkbook.* Petra tapped on the ferry's salt-smeared window then, gesturing to Rae about the passing scenery, and Rae had folded the oversized envelope into a jacket pocket and gone to join her granddaughter on the wind-blown deck.

But she remembered Tamara's face as she'd reached for the check. It bore the same expression, that of defiance glued thickly over a vestige of shame, that Rae knew it must have borne as the *Orca Queen* rounded the island to the open strait. The same expression Rae had seen for the first time six months before Petra's birth, when she had gone to visit the new-lyweds, and set off an explosion.

She could no longer reconstruct what the original disagreement had been about, what precise words had passed between her and Tamara. What she did remember, vividly, were two things. The first was an emotion, the despair of realizing that Tamara was truly lost to her, that all hope of a mature restoration of some mother-daughter openness had vanished. The second memory was visual: Don standing in the doorway of the decrepit apartment with his arm around Tamara's shoulder, holding his new wife close to his side. Tamara looked terrible, her hair limp and unwashed, blotches of pregnancy-generated acne accentuating the flush of the recent argument, and a gauntness to her that testified to living on saltine crackers and herbal tea. Don, on the other hand, was bursting with health, and his gaze held Rae's in an unequivocal challenge, as if he had said aloud, "She's mine now; you'll only have her if I let you."

And so it had proven over the years, with Tamara and, even more so, with Petra. Tamara had never given Rae an opening; that relationship was apparently beyond recovery. Petra, however . . . Within weeks of her birth, Petra became the battleground for a grim and completely unacknowledged struggle between an amused Don and a desperate Rae. Tamara, to give her credit, stayed out of it, but Don had mastered the art of using Rae's love for the child to keep his mother-in-law in her place.

Tamara's rigid spine and Petra's waving arm on board the *Orca Queen* said it all. And for that wave, Rae would give everything.

The new resident of Folly looked down and realized that she had continued picking up garbage unawares, and that her glove was currently gripping a flaccid, mud-caked condom. With an exclamation of disgust she flicked it into the bag, then stripped off the glove and threw it in after. With fastidious fingers she tied shut the top of the bag, dropping it in the lee of the lumber pile, and went back to the fire to scrub her hands with a lot of soap. Then she returned to her interrupted meal.

The chili was scorched into the bottom of the pan.

As Rae scraped the edible portions onto a plate, her awareness of how alone she was continued to grow. She began to feel like a pea on a platter. As she turned to carry her dinner over to the chair, the corner of her eye caught on a motion and she jerked upright—but it was only the wavelets on her beach, no cause for her heart to race so wildly. She sat with her back close to the tent wall and picked at the scorched red mess, feeling invisible eyes crawling up and down the back of her neck like some many-legged creature. Or like a man's fingers. She put her head down, forced her hand to lift the fork, forced her attention to remain on the food, demanded that her mouth eat it and her stomach receive it. Most of it. She was scraping the uneaten remnants into the flames when the dish slipped from her nerveless fingers into the coals; in snatching it up, Rae brushed her hand against the searing metal grill.

With a sob of fury she hurled the plate into the bushes and cradled her hand to her chest, eyes tight shut. The drugs in her knapsack called to her, but she had other plans for them. Instead, she rummaged furiously through the boxes of equipment piled near the tent until she came to the heavy leather brush-clearing gloves. With her blistered thumb in her mouth and the gloves in the undamaged hand, Rae stalked up the hill to her foundation.

Two

Desmond Newborn's Journal

June 27, 1921

There are times, rare and precious times, when we lowly creatures are vouchsafed a glimpse of Providence at work, the sure knowledge that there is a machinery connecting the disparate fragments of our lives, binding ugly to lovely, despair to rejoicing.

How else to explain the train of events that brought me here? Overheard snatches of conversation in a bleak railway yard, my very presence there traced directly back through the events in Boston to the hell of the Western Front, and before that the strange urges that drove me to uniform in the first place: all linked, all the decisions, foolish, well intentioned, and wicked alike, all the accidents, both the sweet and the bitter, leading me in a most circuitous pathway to this place.

I stood today with my boots planted on the rocky entrance to a piece of land rising from an amiable sea, and I began to feel a most peculiar sensation, as if I were waking following a long and terrible dream. Or it may be that I am, in truth, sinking into a midsummer night's dream on an enchanted isle.

If that be so, I pray God I may never wake.

Three

The house that had once stood on these stones was built by Rae's great-uncle in the 1920s. Desmond Newborn, younger son of a wealthy Boston family, had read the poetry of Wilfred Owen and Rupert Brooke, embraced their romantic idealism of protecting England from the Kaiser, and sailed off to London in the summer of 1915 to enlist in the British Army. He even went as a common foot soldier, without the officer's rank his education and privilege would have bought him. He survived nearly three years of the carnage to be shipped home, alive but profoundly damaged, at the age of twenty-seven years. He was by then far, far older in spirit.

Rae was nine when she discovered that Grandfather William had once possessed a younger brother.

Had somebody merely told her, she would have laughed aloud at the very idea—a person might as well suggest that God had an auntie. Instead, Rae had compiled the unavoidable evidence on her own, beginning one morning when she was, as Cook called it, moping around the house. As often on days when she was left to her own devices, this spindly girl with sleeping problems and a habit of silence, she was drawn to Grandfather's study. The warm, busy life of the house, particularly for a solitary child, might lie in the kitchen, but the true center of power was Grandfather's study. If Rae were to be caught there, she knew the punishment would be severe, but it was worth the risk to stand in possession of that room, with its smell of cigars and strong drink and William himself.

It was not that there was much to do or see in the study. The books on the shelves were too thick to be of interest, the papers on the big desk incomprehensible, the two paintings dull. But climbing into Grandfather's leather-upholstered desk chair was so daring it sent her heart racing, and a glimpse of the world from his side of the desk made her see herself differently.

Usually, she just touched his pen (careful never to move it), dandled her feet for a minute, tugged automatically at the locked drawers without expecting them to open, and crept away again.

Only this day, one of the drawers was open. Not much, just enough that the desk's central latch had not caught it. Rae shot a glance at the door, then dropped to her knees to ease it all the way out.

More papers. How disappointing—but wait. Underneath the files was a lump, and lifting the edge of a slim ledger she saw a wood-handled revolver and a flat leather box. The gun she left in place, but the box was too intriguing to ignore. She took it out to lay it on the carpet, fiddled with the latch, and swung back the hinged top.

The box held a piece of metal with some faded ribbon attached, the sort of thing she'd seen Grandfather's friends wear on their uniformed chests in the Veterans Day parade. And folded small, a piece of paper, some kind of official form, with spidery writing and the word "Enlistment" at the top. None of the words meant much to her other than "Boston, Massachusetts," but she was greatly puzzled by the name it bore: Desmond Newborn.

There was nobody by that name in the Newborn family.

Studying the paper gave no further clues, so after a minute she folded it away, closed the drawer as it had been, and slipped out of the room.

Through judicious questioning, she found out from Cook what Enlistment meant, but there was only one way to learn who Desmond Newborn was. Years later it occurred to Rae that, given a more normal home life, she would have asked her parent; at the time, she never even thought of approaching anyone but Grandfather; William Newborn was, after all, the source of all power, every decision, all authority. And if the question was as important as she felt it might be, everyone else would consult William before answering her anyway.

She knew the risks, or thought she did. It was never an easy matter to approach Grandfather, no knowing if he would respond with his standard brusque but dutiful paternalism or something darker or more violent.

In this case, his reaction was violent indeed; in fact, she had never seen him react as he did to her innocent question. No sooner had she pronounced the strange name than William rose to his terrible height and stormed around the desk to roar down into her face, lashing her with a fury of words more terrifying than any blow from his hand.

"Desmond, is it? Who the hell's been blabbing to you about that worthless ne'er-do-well? Who? Tell me, girl!"

She pressed back into her chair, as if to make as small a target as possible against his wrath, her body rigid with shock. He continued shouting. "My God, I have no respect in my own house. It was the servants, I suppose, chattering about something that's no business of theirs.

"Not that it's your business either, girl. Desmond Newborn was my brother, a shiftless good-for-nothing who went off and volunteered for somebody else's war, got himself shot up for his pains, came back here and lived off my sweat until he could walk, and then to show his gratitude took to the road like some damned hobo. In and out of jail, never a job. The last I heard of him was a letter two months before the Crash, and that's the last I ever *want* to hear of him. DO YOU UNDERSTAND ME?"

Rae seized this crescendo as a command to depart. She scuttled from the room with as much dignity as her nine-year-old self could muster, wrapping pride around her like armor until she had reached the safety of her bedroom, at which point she crawled into the bottom of her bed and let go, sobbing until she hiccoughed at the terror and fury, the outrage and injustice of Grandfather's response. *I was just asking a question,* she whispered to herself over and over. *I just wanted to know.* By the time Cook came to look for her, Rae's young mind had settled on righteous indignation. She did not speak to her grandfather for two days (which he actually seemed not to notice) and never again dared ask him about his brother, but the sheer unwarranted force of William's reaction guaranteed that Desmond Newborn became a permanent resident in Rae's young mind. Once she had recovered from the shock, she found Desmond lurking in the background, a curiosity and an enigma. He became a sort of imaginary friend, confidant to her secrets and problems, unseen protector and bulwark against God's wrath. He helped Rae keep her chin raised whenever William blew up at her, helped her look her grandfather in the eye when she wanted to crawl away and tremble. By her tenth birthday, Rae desired nothing better than to be a *ne'er-do-well* herself. Whatever that was.

She never again approached William about the subject, never saw the leather box again until she inherited it, but over the years she pieced together a few facts about her secret companion. She chose her informants cautiously, relatives and family employees who would not instantly report her interest to William, and discovered that there had been an earlier war than the one in which Cook's son had died and the young gardener had fought: Desmond's war. When she was twelve she found a book in the public library about the terrible conditions of the soldiers in the First World War, but it only puzzled her the more. Given what she learned, she would have thought that the nobility of Desmond's voluntary enlistment, followed by honorably received wounds, would have made him a shining legend throughout the generations. Instead, before Rae was even born, the family's collective memory had shied away from Desmond, retreating into that vagueness that signals extreme discomfort. His Croix de Guerre was locked away in William's drawer, his injuries referred to so obliquely that, as a child, Rae had believed it to mean that his face was horribly disfigured; as an adolescent, she concluded that he must have lost his genitalia. Only as an adult, after poring over the diary kept by William's wife, Lacy—which was, unfortunately, little more than a laconic record of family events and household expenses—had Rae glimpsed the truth: that what Desmond left on the Western Front was a portion of his mind; that was the shame for which his family could not forgive him.

After Desmond had recovered from his body's wounds, convalescing in the chilly family mansion near Boston where Rae had spent most of her own childhood, the ex-soldier, as Grandfather had said, took to the road. Desmond Newborn would appear on the doorstep of one or another of his widespread relations and roost with them for a few weeks, usually in the cold months when pneumonia or just bronchitis laid hold of his weakened lungs (a legacy of the trenches). Then he would pack up his rucksack and disappear again, quartering the country, heading gradually west. Buried among Lacy's dutiful recording of weather and health, the baby's milestones and monies spent on dresses and gifts, William's wife would note an occasional sum wired to her brother-in-law in Louisville or Chicago or Boise. Once, without comment, her copperplate handwriting recorded that bail had been provided on a vagrancy charge near Houston. Later, in early 1921, more jail monies were provided, only this time not as bail. Rae had never found out why Desmond had spent six months behind bars, but she knew that Lacy had sent money and a parcel of warm clothing, with no information in her diary other than the address of the Yakima jail.

Then, the following summer, the wanderer had washed up in the San Juan Islands in the state of Washington, about as far from Boston as a person could get without crossing a sea or a border; here Desmond Newborn found a home at last. Here he bought an island (a transaction not recorded in Lacy's diary, so it must have come under William's jurisdiction) and built his folly, an oddly elegant little wooden house nestled between two highly idiosyncratic stone towers, here on this string of cold, remote, and at the time sparsely inhabited islands on the crumbling edge of a continent. And here he lived, with the seabirds and the orca whales for company, until the wanderlust grew up again and took him off a few years later. At some point—no one seemed to know just when—the house caught fire and burned to the stonework, and both the island and Desmond Newborn's shadowy legend were absorbed back into the family pool. Since that time the island had remained uninhabited, temporarily deeded to the state as a wildlife sanctuary, with the ownership and Desmond's medals coming to Rae on the settling of her father's estate five years before.

It was this strange, bereft remnant of a house, more than any other thing, that had anchored Rae's climb from madness. Last May, five months after the accident and four after the attack, Rae's mind had begun with great reluctance to unfurl from its tight retreat. In spite of herself, she started to take notice of her surroundings—the noise and disruption of the hospital, the tyranny of the drugs, the press of people and walls and cigarette smoke: a turmoil as great as that inside her mind. She began to seek out the quieter corners of the hospital grounds, craving solitude as a desert traveler thirsts for water. And like that traveler, Rae had eventually glimpsed solitude and, more faintly, purpose—a tool in the hand and the ability to concentrate on its use—flickering and wavering in the distance, as ethereal as a mirage and every bit as compelling. Except that the thought of returning home, the very idea of stepping into her fragrant and expectant workshop attached to a house that reverberated with emptiness, made her shiver with a mixture of desire and terror.

Into this tangle of inchoate yearnings and inexpressible fears had dropped a book, one of those strangely assorted and badly worn paperbacks abandoned by patients or donated by the carton to places such as mental hospitals. It was missing its cover and the first dozen pages, but the remainder fell into Rae's confused and heavily sedated mind like a seed into loam.

A man had built a house. An untrained and remarkably incompetent man (who would have reminded Rae of her first husband, David, except that this man was so cheerful about admitting his incompetence) had made for himself a shelter: a roof, four walls, a floor. In the incestuous manner of writers, his purpose seemed to be not so much the creation of shelter as the opportunities the building process gave for self-reflection—and, it went without saying, the publication of a book about both building and self-reflection—but in reading it, Rae saw only the dream given form, the creation of House out of Thought. She read and reread the book until it went to pieces. She could still recite long passages from memory.

Like a seed—or a lifeline.

Great-uncle Desmond's skeletal home came to her as in a dream. In truth, during those months most things came to her as in a dream, but this one did not fade. Instead, it blossomed swiftly into full potential: She would pull herself together, she would go and rebuild Desmond's house, she would lift his walls and dwell within them quietly all the rest of her days. Everything that House was lay there waiting for her to take it up: House as shelter, House as permanence, House as a continuation and a legacy, comfort and challenge, safety and beauty, symbol and reality joined as one. While Rae's body wandered the hospital halls and grounds, her mind walked through the rooms she had known: the coldly formal dining room of her childhood home and the warmth of its nearby kitchen; the oddly shaped attic room of a bed-and-breakfast she had stayed in near Oxford and the gilded ceilings of the palace at Versailles; the tracery of Gaudí's Sagrada Familia in Barcelona and the cramped door frames of Wright's workshop in Scottsdale. She pictured herself in each one, saw herself in the process of hanging that dining room's awful wallpaper, troweling on that attic's plaster, building those rooms, and eventually, as a logical end point, the remembered and the imagined merged: Desmond, the mysterious lost relative who had intrigued her youth, stood beside her as she laid board upon board, making the house on Folly anew. Desmond, the family's other black sheep and the shadowy companion of her childhood, returned now to muse with her: How to get that roof up, all on her own? How to stand those walls, mount those windows, lay those shingles? Desmond, of whom William had disapproved almost as ferociously as he had Rae, walked with her through Folly, until she could envision each step of the rebuilding process, one following another, no flaws. Desmond, fantasy guardian and companion, would be with her.

It had seemed so simple at the time.

Now, standing at the edge of a Pacific Northwest jungle with the painful throb of a burned finger to distract her, just pushing her way through to Folly's derelict front steps looked to be a challenge. Rae had no intention of beginning the ground clearing at this hour, with the first intimations of darkness gathering in, but she also did not want to go to bed without having at least glimpsed the foundation. Gingerly, painstakingly, she threaded her boots through the wet vegetation—most of which seemed to have thorns—wading her way up the low slope until her toe hit something more solid than stems. She plunged a gloved hand deep into the greenery and tugged blindly. The rich odor of broken plant and torn soil rose up, and she pulled again, and again, until there they lay, looking like a stairway leading through the jungle to a Mayan temple: Desmond Newborn's front steps.

Rae gazed up at the four wide, immobile granite slabs. Stone was a medium foreign to her, a woman who had spent most of her adult life in a dialogue between the organic subtleties of wood and the ever-present danger of wickedly sharp steel, but there was no doubt that rock like this spoke of another world entirely, one of eternity, imperviousness, and utter solidity.

She put a foot gingerly on the lowest step, rocking her weight back and forth; the step did not budge. Scuffling some of the generations of leaf mold to one side revealed a mottled gray surface, finely textured. The next step was equally solid, and the third.

Shoving a pile of rich soil off the end of the third step, Rae's boot encountered something hard among the brambles. She burrowed through blackberry canes as thick as her thumb and rose stems hairy with thorns, and found herself looking at a slab of milled wood nearly two inches thick, dark with age but otherwise well preserved. She ripped and yanked, hesitant to commit her leg to leaving the steps but curious to see what this immense plank might be. After a few minutes, she had cleared one corner of it, a handsbreadth in both directions. The rest disappeared into the mass of vegetation. She grabbed the object and wiggled it from side to side; a lot of the growth moved in response. Without a concerted daylight effort there was no guessing the final measurement, but Rae looked from the steps to the wood and concluded that, despite its inordinate thickness, this was likely to be Desmond's front door, fallen here when the house burned away from it. She knelt on the granite and stretched out to shove the growth from the lumber's upper edge; a foot from the bottom her gloves found an enormous iron hinge.

Rae was smiling when she drew back her arm. Desmond's door; who would have expected even a corner of it to have survived? She yanked off both gloves and pulled the knife from her tool belt, snapped open the blade, and stretched down to shave a thin layer from the door's edge. Her hands seemed certain of the grain's direction even if her eyes couldn't see beneath the dirt, and indeed, as the blade traveled down the plank toward her thumb, the wood curled obediently over it. She caught the wide shaving and held it up to the fading light, noting its red interior, then put it to her nose. Beneath the earthy smell lay the faintest ghost of a tang: Western red cedar. She studied the revealed grain for a moment, caressing its fine dry texture, then slipped the curl into her shirt pocket before standing up and giving the protruding corner a last speculative glance.

Then she retreated. Back at the fire pit she threw some wood onto the coals to heat water for the dishes, retrieved her dinner plate from the arms of a bush, and washed up, taking care to lock away all traces of food. She was still hyperconscious of the unaccustomed noises around her, aware of the twitchiness of her muscles and every motion of the waves, but it was not as bad as it had been earlier. Perhaps uncovering the stones had helped: nothing like a ton or so of granite to lend a touch of reality to an enterprise. Maybe the unexpected glimpse of Desmond's own woodwork steadied her. Or it might have been just the consumption of food that brought her down to earth. Whatever the reason, she now felt strong enough for the next step.

She picked up the green knapsack and took from it a mashed white paper bag with the name of a pharmacy printed on the front. The sky had cleared while she wasn't looking, particularly out toward the western horizon; the undersides of the clouds now glowed rosy with the angle of the sun. Sticking the flashlight into an empty loop of the tool belt, she carried the paper bag down across the beach to the rock promontory— and nearly leapt into the cove at her left when a pair of heavy objects splashed into the open water to her right. She peered, trembling, at the water, and a moment later burst into nervous laughter as two drowned-looking heads popped up from the water: harbor seals, disturbed from their perch by her passing. They looked up at her reproachfully with their liquid eyes.

"Sorry," she told them. The two gleaming heads sank back beneath the surface, and Rae somewhat nervously continued on down the promontory. She reached the end without further mishap, chose a rock facing due west, and settled down to watch the sunset paint the sky.

Desmond Newborn, she mused, might have sat on this same rock, watched that same sun go down in a blaze of oranges and blues. Well, perhaps not this very rock—adding boulders to the promontory had been one of the few actions Rae's father had taken during his twenty-year stewardship of the property, to keep the point from eroding and opening up the island's only cove to the sea. And Rae felt quite certain that Great-uncle Desmond had not sat down here in order to open a paper bag and take out six giant plastic pill bottles. Sleeping pills, tranquilizers, mood regulators, megavitamins (on the off chance that theory was not entirely bunk)—she lined them all up on a rock between her feet. The sleeping pills first. She wrestled off the childproof cap and slid a forefinger in to pull the first tablet up the side of the bottle, held it for a moment between finger and thumb, then flicked it away into the water. It disappeared with a small *plunk* and a sinuous spread of concentric circles, as did the next, and the one after that.

It occurred to her belatedly that heavy-duty tranquilizers might not agree with sea life. Oh well; maybe they would dissolve before the fish found them. In any case, tonight the fate of the local wildlife was not her main concern.

When the last sleeping pill had been swallowed by the sea, she screwed the cap back on and returned the bottle to the bag (wholesale poisoner of fish she might be, but she was not going to be accused of littering) before reaching for the Prozac. Those pills made a slightly different sound, more of a *plink*. And the giant megavitamins made a *plonk*, but they, too, vanished beneath the gentle undulations of the water, and they and the rest were all gone before the last banner of orange had faded from the horizon.

Now she possessed nothing more lethal than a hundred aspirin tablets and a bottle of very old Scotch, two things any normal woman might have. *Pretend normality* was Rae's current credo. She was sick to death of pills and control exercises and dream analyses and the overriding magnifying-glass approach of psychiatry. She'd come to envision psychotherapy as first cousin to the debriding horrors of the burn wards, taking control of the healing process by ripping away the body's attempts at scar tissue, no matter how excruciating. Demons needed confronting, yes, but not every hour of the day. Avoidance was, after all, a coping technique; so, now, she would treat her problems with a healthy dose of avoidance, even if Psychiatric Truth declared: *You can't hide, you can't ignore.*

Bullshit. Normal people did, every day.

The rebellious thought made her a little happier. The absence of pills frightened her a little, but that was only to be expected. Fear was normal, too.

Beneath a sky of deepest indigo, with the full moon rising and her pharmacological boats sunk behind her, Rae took out the flashlight and picked her way back to the tent along the unfamiliar shore.

Four

Rae's Journal

I wonder if anyone but me has caught the significance of this date? Not only the night of the full moon, when Luna-cy is at its fullest, but the eve of April Fools' Day as well. The Hunter surely would have been on it in a flash, but as far as she's concerned, I left California on the Ides of March, which carries a very different sort of symbolic content. Give her credit, though—she might even be encouraged if I'd told her I was aiming for this date to begin my folly—a sense of humor indicates a healthy degree of perspective. But I haven't told her anything of substance for weeks now. Poor well-meaning woman: I must send her a postcard.

The date is a private joke. Alan would have appreciated it, if he were here, but then Alan living would drain the joke of meaning.

I first saw the island five years ago, a few months after my father died. When his estate was divided up between myself and various distant relations, for some reason he had specified that the island be left to me. I knew vaguely that there had once been a house here, built by my mysterious Great-uncle Desmond, but no one I knew had ever seen it. So that summer, Alan and I decided to take a look at what I had inherited before putting it on the market. It was actually more an excuse for a holiday than anything else. Bella came with us. She was four and a half then, and I was just back from London, triumphant and exhausted. I know I must have looked as tired as I felt, because while we were here three different people referred to Bella as my granddaughter. Alan was livid, but really, how many women have babies at the age of forty-two? Talk about an April Fool . . .

Anyway, we hired a boat in Roche Harbor to bring us out here. It's called

Sanctuary Island on all the maps and deeds, and that's the only name I had ever heard for it, but when I told the old guy in the boathouse where we wanted to go, he scratched his head for a minute and then said, "Oh—you mean Folly."

Alan was delighted. He'd once spent a summer with a college friend whose family had a Victorian folly in the grounds of their country house, a fake ruin, forlorn and more than a little ridiculous, but appealing. The island's nickname came from the house that once stood here, although I've never known if it was because the house had something quirky about it, invisible in the only photograph I have, or because in ruins it looked like the fake in the garden of Alan's friend. More likely the latter. But in either case, Folly it was called, by the locals and, from then on, by us.

The house—the folly—that I intend to rebuild, those stones that I plan on reclothing with wood and plaster, was built and burned in the Twenties, and was long since jungle by the time we saw it. We came, Alan and Bella and I, and we saw, and we fell under its lonely spell. Our planned quick survey of the island stretched far into the afternoon, cut short only by Bella's hunger. We hiked around the surprisingly large island, found a beach and a fresh, clear spring and eagles' nests and trees and even a sort of mountaintop (well, hilltop) clearing where the world stretched on to infinity.

No, we determined, we would not be selling off this part of my inheritance. When Bella was a little older, when Alan and I had less pressing schedules, it would be a retreat, not only a glorious summer holiday place but a building with personality, a folly in its truest sense of extravagance and irrationality (madness in one of its more amusing manifestations). We began the lengthy preliminaries—legal wrangles, engineer's inspections, restoration permits.

Three and a half years later, before we could return to the island, they were both dead.

I am here instead.

Newborn's Folly.

Only Alan would appreciate the joke.

Five

With reluctance, Rae closed the leather covers of her journal and laid it to one side, next to the old revolver and its six bullets arranged tidily on the corner of the makeshift writing desk, that they might keep her company as she wrote. She leaned back against the reassuring lumps of the tool belt, taken off only when she sat down at the desk, then rubbed absently at the surgical scar along her left forearm, over the metal plate that made her arm ache when fatigued, when cold, and whenever else it damn well felt like it. She took her hand away and gathered up the bullets. The six of them fit neatly into a fist; six bullets that made a lovely dull metallic rasping sound when rolled around in a closed hand, like a mouthful of wet pebbles. She poured them into her other palm, and picked one out. Soft, warm, gray lead at one end, cool brass jacket flaring into the base at the other. A simple thing, really, awaiting a tap in just the right place. She wondered if she shouldn't number them, carve Roman numerals in their soft nub ends so she could tell them apart, but that seemed too much like the list making that marked her worst periods, so she warmed them some more and then arranged them back in their triangle, three on a side, good little soldiers.

The tent surrounding her was brand new, ordered from a catalogue along with half the kitchen equipment and waiting for her in Friday Harbor. Petra had helped her raise it, making it clear that this was about the coolest thing ever, while Tamara looked on in growing disbelief that anyone could possibly consider it shelter. The air inside smelled of waterproofing chemicals and the wrinkles in the canvas and the mesh windows were still crisp from the packing box. Rae had been glad to find all the poles in with it.

Rae Newborn's family was not the sort to indulge in a camping holiday. The closest she'd been to the tenting life was a week with Alan in a canvas-roofed cabin in Yosemite. It had been cold. It was cold now. The walls shifted of their own accord, shivering when the air brushed against them. All the flaps were tied snugly across the windows, but the door was still crimped in spots, and lay against the opening unevenly. Someone outside could, by a stealthy approach and sinking to his knees, peep in at her where she sat at the desk.

Rae reached behind her to pull the hammer from its belt holster, placing it squarely on the desk in front of her.

There's no one out there.

The canvas shivered again; a twig or pinecone hit the peak of the roof with a slap. Rae's body tightened against the noise. She started in on the breathing and visualization exercises that would encourage the muscles to relax, wondering all the while *Why did that twig hit the tent? Was it a twig or was somebody throwing something, and will the next step be a branch scratching the wall even though there aren't any branches for six feet in any direction and after that a knock or a noise like a key tapping on glass only there's no glass window in a tent maybe the Watchers'll just lean against the canvas lean in and push against my space here pushing in on me until the aluminum tent poles bend and the walls—*

She stood up so abruptly the chair toppled over, then reached for the control of the hanging kerosene lamp. Its bright glow faded, the shadows grew soft and then dimmer, until with a small *pop* the light died.

This had always worked at home, the cocooned feeling of being in the dark so those Watchers in the light couldn't see in. What she had failed to take into account was that her campsite had no floodlights, no means of throwing up a barricade of light in the compound outside. Just the moon.

That was stupid, Rae, she berated herself. *Now you'll have to wait until Ed comes to get enough lights to hang up outside, half a dozen ought to do it, but not kerosene, that wouldn't be too safe. Propane ought to be better although what a racket they'll make, and how long does a lamp burn on a propane canister, anyway? No good if I had to go out in the dark and change the canister, maybe the lamps could be put on one of the big canisters like I'm using for the stove, harder to hang but—*

"You're not going to do that," Rae said aloud. The tent seemed to agree, relieved that it was not about to be set beneath a spotlight. Ridiculous—trees strung about with dangling propane tanks. Everyone in the islands would come to see it. Planes would divert to look down at her.

It's dark. Get used to it.

Rae felt her way over to the cot, and from there to the bedside table (two crates of builders' reference books) that held clock and flashlight. She picked up the heavy metal tube, but instead of thumbing it on, she stood in the dark tent, listening and watching. The moon was still too low in the sky to illuminate the tent, which meant that it was also no protection against any Watchers trying to creep up on her. She clicked the flashlight on to check the door, immediately clicked it off again. On, off; which was worse? She wanted nothing more than to sit at the desk and write in her journal for the rest of the night, concentrating hard on ink and paper behind the shelter of the canvas walls until the darkness had been gotten through and dawn allowed her to buckle on the tool belt again. But writing was no solution. She turned on the flashlight, took Tamara's matches out of her pocket, and lit the lamp again.

She glanced down at the small battery-run clock beside her neatly arranged cot, and saw with despair that it was barely nine. Camp was set up, dinner dealt with, the tent's sparse furnishings arranged and rearranged, tea made and drunk so slowly the dregs had been stone cold, the journal written in; still it was only nine o'clock.

Keep busy; but doing what?

Standing beneath the whisper of the kerosene lamp, Rae became aware of a rustle in the front pocket of her shirt. She worked a hand under her fleece pullover and pulled out the curl of red cedar she'd taken from Desmond's front door. It was a lovely wood, with the tight grain of virgin growth, and sure to have been taken from very near here. She turned it over in her fingers, and put it down on the desk, on the opposite corner from the wood-handled gun. Then, taking a deep and steadying breath, Rae turned her gaze to the tent's zipped flap. Her heart began immediately to race, her lungs seemed to tighten, and even sitting she began to feel dizzy. Doom filled the air, the sense of imminent disaster built and grew in her very bones until she'd have been certain she was having a heart attack had she not been through this a hundred times before.

Not outside. Oh, no. Not at night.

Yes, outside.

I can't. I'll—
You have to. It's why you came.
But if someone's there—

Stupid, stupid. A canvas tent is no refuge, Rae told herself ferociously, and took a deliberate step so that her shadow fell on the tent wall, its curve of fabric strangely motionless now despite the rising tempest. The darkness outside the screen pulsated with a throng of Watchers, whispering and waiting to grab at her as soon as she emerged, to seize her and press themselves against her and pant obscenities in her ears; she could feel the bristle of unshaven cheek scraping against her neck, hear the cheerful monologue of a dead child playing in the shrubs— She seized her hair with both hands.

I am fifty-two years old, she shouted silently against the rushing noise filling her ears. *I am the mother of two daughters, the survivor of more than my share of hell; the earth is not about to crack open, there are not two men breathing down my neck, my heart is not about to stop, and I* will not *be reduced to cowering imbecility by a panic attack.* I will not!

Rae grabbed her heavy jacket from the makeshift hook on the tent's internal frame, wrestled open the door's long metal zipper with icy fingers, and stepped out into the nonexistent tumult with the effort of an Arctic explorer entering a blizzard. Abandoning the revealing circle of light, Rae Newborn stumbled out into the darkness.

She tripped twice, nearly sent sprawling by unseen obstacles on the uneven ground, before she found the soft trunk of the fallen cedar that drew a line between her living quarters and the island's forest. There she huddled, head down, fighting to wrap the feeble breathing and visualization exercises around the attack, waiting for the great body of the wave to break over her and retreat.

It did, eventually. The sensation of being a small candle in a gale slowly gave way to steadying reason, the blood ceased to rush so furiously through her veins, her vertigo ceased its whirling, and she did not faint. The groans in her throat stayed behind her teeth. After a time, Rae sat up, bone weary, and dashed both hands against her eyes. The urge to run blindly into the forest (or the sea, or traffic), to abandon the burden of rational thought for pure, mindless panic, was at times close to overwhelming, if for no other reason than the chance it offered for being knocked into blessed unconsciousness. It was to avoid the temptation of oblivion that she'd stopped driving. She well knew why the sensation of panic—demeaning, unpredictable, and completely pointless—was named after Pan, flute-playing tempter of the woods and meadows.

Still, when the attack passed, it was over until the next time, leaving the victim languid and relieved and ready for sleep. Like a recurrent fever, she thought; like some mirror image of sex. And with that, Alan was there at her side.

Rae grieved for Bella and she ached for Alan, every day. Losing them had left two gaping holes in her, one bearing the outline of Bella's vigorous little body, the other Alan's solid bulk, holes of whistling emptiness with the chill of utter vacuum. Bella's joyous greeting *"Mommy!"* was so thoroughly a part of her that she heard it still, heard it with the same conviction that causes a woken sleeper to lie straining for the echo of the disturbance, knowing without question that the sound was real, not a dream. *Mommy!* with its nuances of excitement or alarm or sheer ecstasy would shoot through Rae's hearing while she was reaching for a newspaper, pouring a cup of coffee, turning a page, dropping off to sleep.

And, of course, overhearing the actual cry of a living child to its mother shuddered through Rae like an electric shock.

With Alan, the loss was both more pervasive and less immediate. It came to her as the impulse to turn and tell him something, or the need to be held by his arms or buoyed by his infectious laughter, as the skin of the hand recalling his tight cap of curls and the coolness of his long, fine fingers. Every day for the last fifteen and a half months, the loss of those two people had continued to ambush her, knocking her to her knees with stark, ever-fresh disbelief, and although the sharpness and the duration of these ambushes was fading, that was, in its way, almost worse. Alan and Bella were no longer moving easily through her mind. Once, she could have conversations with Alan, play games with Bella, more or less at will (or with as much will as a mental patient can muster). Now when they appeared in her thoughts, they were oddly static, frozen in attitudes she had once loved; even their outlines were pale. She was losing them for good, and she did not know if she could bear it.

Another reason for the gun in her knapsack.

Two wary people, Rae Newborn and Alan Beauchamp, both long divorced when they met, both parents of grown children they felt they had failed, yet despite their wariness, the bond between them was instantaneous and permanent, a jolt of current that crackled between them when—of all clichés—their eyes met at a gallery opening for a painter friend of Rae's. They left the gallery together. Four days later, Alan proposed, and they were inexorably embarked on The Conversation. Rae had been cold with apprehension, but she had no choice: Alan had to know what he was facing.

"Monopolar depression," she told him. "Not bipolar—that's manic depression. Mine is just the downs. Melancholia was the old name. Winston Churchill called it his Black Dog. It's scary, Alan."

"I can imagine."

"I mean for the people around me. For me it's like being suffocated and having to act like everything is fine. From the outside I begin to look like a zombie. Flat affect, they call it: food, sex, beauty, anger, life, work, everything goes dead. Inside, it's pure agony, unrelieved, pins-and-needles grimness. Physical pain is nothing by comparison. It's why so many depressives commit suicide, because the pain gets to be more than you can bear. I . . ." She cleared her throat, and forced it out. "I've tried to commit suicide twice."

"Jesus, Rae. Isn't there medication?" he'd asked helplessly. "Prozac, that sort of thing?"

"Sure. Some of it even does some good. But they all need a long time to take hold, weeks even, and when they do, I turn into a nice cheerful vegetable. Even relatively mild drugs like Prozac work in the brain by suppressing dopamine, which is linked to creativity. A whole side of me goes numb."

"I see." Rae had heard the brief phrase, and knew with a terrible conviction that what she was telling Alan was too much, that Alan wanted out of the conversation, out of the whole brief, magical, doomed relationship. She made herself go on calmly, although she wanted to rage and weep.

"But the worst part, for me and everyone around me, is the transitional times. I hallucinate. If you imagine depression like a part of the body going to sleep—your hand, say—I go through these times that are the equivalent of the tingling before and after the numbness sets in. It's like my mind tingles. I hear snatches of voices, I glimpse movement that isn't there, I smell things, my fingers imagine strange textures."

"What . . ." Alan looked lost, casting around for the proper response. And being Alan, he retreated into ideas. Rae heard his strategy as a death knell. "I'm sorry, I don't know much about the disease. What do they think causes it?"

"A mix of chemistry and life. The tendency is often inherited. Early life experiences affect it—losing a mother when you're young is common among depressives. And growing up in an atmosphere where no one approves of anything you do, that doesn't help. But basically, nobody knows."

Alan had gone home not long after The Conversation. Rae heard the door close, reached for her glass, and drank herself into oblivion, absolutely certain she would not see him again. The next morning she forced herself out of bed, forced herself to eat and shower and behave as if she still had a life. She was sitting staring miserably at a slab of teak when his knock came on the door.

He had a piece of paper in his hand. He thrust it at her, and asked, "Is this what you mean?"

Confused, she took the paper and read what was written on it:

In the middle of life's journey, I found myself in a dark wood, where the straight way was lost . . .
. . . as one who has escaped, labored of breath, from the deep to shore, turns to those dangerous waters and looks back . . .

"What is this?" she asked him.

"Dante. The *Divine Comedy.* I thought it sounded like what you say you go through."

A dark wood, where the straight way is lost. "It sure does."

"Well, if Dante can survive it, so can we. A *folie à deux.*"

They were married two weeks later, and in the nine years and twelve days of their life as husband and wife, no argument persisted overnight, no parting went without a phone call, and neither of them was ever bored in bed. Even Rae's pregnancy, discovered a scant three months after the wedding, took them quickly from shock through tentative acceptance and into a deep sense of their daughter as a gift, as precious as she was unexpected. Rae's daughter Tamara might have been from another species to her mother; Alan's son Rory was so incomprehensible to his father that the two saw each other perhaps once a year (and always in Los Angeles, on Rory's ground); but with Bella, the fates got things right. Their family was small, but complete unto itself.

And Rae still woke at night with her hand questing blindly along

Alan's side of the bed, still heard his voice murmuring in her ear, felt his fingertips brush her hair, though he and Bella had been cold, scattered ash for four hundred and seventy days.

While Rae sat hunched over on the soft-barked tree holding the hand of Alan's memory, her eyes had adjusted to the dark. Not that much adjustment was required; the full moon was above the trees now, and the clouds had cleared away. She'd forgotten how bright moonlight was, away from the city; she could have read a newspaper by the stark light that bathed her clearing, she could have sewn a seam or worked a piece of inlay—assuming that her hands could remember how to hold the tools. The lowest branches of the trees near her tent were lit by the diffuse warm light of the lamp, but their upper reaches formed intricate black silhouettes against the pale sky.

The night was still, no breeze stirring the branches. Rae shifted on her perch, faintly uneasy. Somewhere across the water, far away on a neighboring island, a dog barked four or five times and then went quiet. A tiny bat flitted through the clearing. A raucous night bird screeched (making Rae twitch), the coals in the fire pit hushed into ash, and a chorus of tree frogs somewhere off in the woods behind her croaked out their availability. A pair of owls hooted at each other on high and low notes. Soothing noises, all of them.

So why was Rae's heart thudding so?

And then the chorus of frogs cut off abruptly. Rae's head came up fast to listen, but the faint, even susurration of water on rock, tiny wavelets pawing at her beach, was the loudest sound in all of creation.

Cold sweat broke out along her scalp, and the breath through her nostrils filled the night, heavy breaths that seemed to come from just in back of her shoulder, and in an instant hands would grab her from behind and the slow-motion nightmare would play all over again and the—

No! she broke in desperately. *This is not fear. Fear has an object; fear makes sense. This is anxiety; anxiety means choking; it feeds on itself, you know that; anxiety has no rhyme or reason. There is nothing to fear here, there's no one behind me, there's no reason to strangle on anxiety. Solitude is not only what I want, it is my natural state. Anxiety is beside the point; fear is—*

The litany stopped as Rae's loud breath froze in her throat. A sound had come to her over the night air, a slow, distant throb, rising and falling, too indistinct to be called a noise. Dear God, she thought hopelessly, is this some new kind of hallucination? Voices in the walls and the touch of imaginary hands are not enough, I now have to draw up the sound of distant drums in the jungle?

She caught the idea before it could feed further into her anxiety, and squelched it hard. *This is a new country to you,* she lectured herself. *This could be an actual, true-to-life, audible-to-sane-ears noise.* No—not *could be;* it *was:* Without a doubt, this sound would prove to be some odd natural characteristic of the San Juans. Mating calls of the whales, or a relative of those seasonal noises north of San Francisco that used to drive people nuts until they were identified as some kind of shrimp or mussel. Although it did, admittedly, resemble the haunting voices of months past, those endless nonexistent sounds bumping against her eardrums, even if there were no words in this sound, and no emotion.

Then a small branch cracked nearby, and Rae's entire body jerked around to face her attacker. Her heart leapt like a wild thing trapped inside her chest as she waited, head raised and jaw slightly open, for a repeat of the noise; when it did not come, the very silence seemed to nestle up to her and pluck at her skin. Her throat choked shut at the looming sky and the towering treetops, the uncanny hugeness of the tent, the sheer massive size of all the world's things. In a minute, she would be a cowering mouse beside a gargantuan Olmec head. In a minute, everything around her would take on the tingling wrongness of Picasso's thick-limbed women thudding along the beach, that smothering expansion of everyday objects that since childhood had sent her cowering beneath folded arms.

There is nothing to fear here, she told herself; *it's a raccoon; it's not going to attack me; everything is normal.* She said it aloud: "There are no attackers here. There are no Watchers in the woods."

Over and over she repeated the words, and she might have made it, might have convinced herself and gone nervously to bed, but before her pulse could return to normal, a third noise came, the sound she dreaded most in all the world, reaching out to plunge her into abject terror: a boisterous young male voice shouting over the roar of a motor. A boat, clearing the next island as a couple of her neighbors headed home, but all Rae heard was Young Male. Her nose was suddenly filled with the stench of young sweat, a ghostly hand insinuated itself through the front of her shirt, and thought fled; Rae broke and ran, straight into the arms of Pan.

Or, straight into one of the panic god's trees. Agony jolted through her as a branch snapped back against the exquisitely sensitive scar tissue on the left side of her body. The pain rattled her from teeth to toes, and she folded up, to lie curled tightly around herself on the cold, damp, soft ground beneath the tree, hugging her pain until it died away and the sounds she made shifted from sharp, urgent gasps to moans, deep and despairing.

Oh, what was she doing here, what the *hell* was she doing here, when a couple of kids in a passing boat could send her off the edge by a shouted phrase? How could she possibly think she could do this? Just take the damn gun and put an end to it, Rae. Oh God, she groaned. Oh shit. Oh hell.

The thing about madness was, it just took so damn much energy, and it was so thoroughly tedious in the meantime.

Perhaps she would just lie here, in the nice, quiet shelter under the fragrant, drooping branches. She would lie still, hidden from sight, feeling the moss grow up over her, pulling itself up one gentle spiky tendril at a time, until it covered her like a blanket and turned her into a soft, green, passive, Rae-shaped mound. What a lovely idea.

The idea was lovely, but the ground was hard beneath the decaying leaves, and her middle-aged bones too stiff to put up with the position. Reluctantly, ruefully, she got to her feet and pushed her way out of the low branches, grateful to find that the only damage resulting from her flirtation with Pan were a lot of bruises and a bash on her face that had missed putting out her eye by inches. Shaken and aching, she picked her geriatric way over the uneven ground toward the calm and disinterested glow of the tent. She did not even pause to check that the male voices were gone.

She crawled into her sleeping bag and lay curled there, slowly warming and feeling, if not safe, then at least not actively under threat for the first time since she'd stepped off the *Orca Queen*. She studied the leisurely drift of the moonlight across her roof, and imperceptibly slipped away into sleep.

Dawn had not come yet when she woke, but it was not far away. The ceiling of the tent was a gray presence overhead, the TICK . . . TICK of the small travel alarm on its bedside crate the only fissure in the stillness. Her bleary gaze rested on the clock's face, its luminous hands faintly visible in the growing light, and then she frowned and worked one hand out of the warm cocoon of her sleeping bag (wincing at the awakening aches) to bring the clock up to her face. Seven hours? She hadn't slept a seven-hour stretch in years, even with drugs.

She put the clock down and drew her arm back inside, and lay in her snug sack while the tent's furnishings slowly took shape around her. A dark blob indicated the kerosene lamp hanging from the ridgepole; a monolithic square represented the stack of plastic storage chests that functioned as a combination bedroom closet, toolshed, and pantry, with the smaller shapes beside it of her locked trunk, the big metal toolbox, and the wooden box that held her fine woodworking tools. The top of the desk seemed to float off the ground, the slats of her wooden chair becoming visible against it. Soon, she could make out the drape of her carpenter's belt, slung from the back of the chair as if a gunslinger had dropped it there. The head of the hammer began to gleam dully; her bladder decided it was time to get up.

The inside of the canvas was beaded with condensation, her boots were as cold and rigid as ice cubes, and she was very glad she had gone to bed more or less fully clothed. She worked a fleece pullover past the layers of polypropylene and cotton flannel she already wore and tugged the knit cap Petra had given her over her short hair. Her fingerless gloves were in the pockets of her heavy jacket, somewhat protected from the cold, and she put them on before reaching for her old friend the carpenter's belt, solitary companion on this mad quest.

With all the clothes she wore, buckling the belt took some attention, and it rode nearly at her waistline instead of down around her hips. Still, the accustomed weight, the rattles and creaks of tools and leather, the pat of the hammer against the outside of her right thigh and the press of the three-quarter-inch tape measure against the small of her back all made her feel more herself than anything in the world.

The hammer at her right hip was one of the few things that connected the Rae who stood on the island with the Rae she had once been, thirty-two years before, when Rae had discovered in herself an unexpected taste for the physical act of building. A pregnant twenty-year-old, married to a man who hid his own manual incompetence behind a scornful derision of those he referred to as "rude mechanicals" (Shakespeare never having changed the oil in a car), and faced with a set of shelves that needed putting up, Rae had marched (or rather, by that point in her pregnancy, waddled) down the street to the hardware store and asked the salesman what she needed for the job. The cheap drill and screwdriver that she had bought that day had long since been given over to landfill, but a month later, looking at a slightly more ambitious project involving a piece of furniture in the baby's room, and with a husband even more vocal about people who do-it-themselves instead of leaving it to the experts (all of whom seemed to be on long jobs or on vacation), Rae found herself defiantly buying the most expensive hammer in the shop.

It was a framing hammer, its short, strong claws nearly flat compared with a standard claw hammer's long curves, twenty-one ounces of drop-forged steel that was "too much hammer for a woman," according to the store owner. Rae, however, was a big woman, tall and broad-shouldered. Besides which, she liked the way the hickory handle fit her hand, liked the way the exploratory swings woke up the muscles all along her right side, from fingertip to jaw and down to her hip. By now, the hammer, like its owner, had seen hard use. Ten thousand nails had worn down the face and left a fine network of scratches over the head, but it still gave her strength, this tool that had stayed with her longer than anything, or anyone, else in her life. Husbands left or husbands died, daughters married avaricious jerks or daughters died, one's very mind wandered in and out of control, but two handles later the twenty-one-ounce hammer still fit her hand, still nestled reassuringly along the line of her pelvis. She smoothed her thumb along its icy steel head, pulled on her jacket, and let herself out of the tent.

She stretched and yawned and scrubbed at her face, waking up and taking in her surroundings. This would be the view that greeted her, every morning she lived in the tent: close at hand, her kitchen (fire pit, storage boxes, camp stove) and living room (canvas-sling chair and two tree sections that could function as dining tables, footstools, or chopping blocks), the fallen cedar on her right that kept the wilderness at bay and drew a line down to the promontory; the clearing to her left, a rough oblong too scruffy to be called a meadow, its borders defined by the cove before her, the old madrone tree some forty yards from her left shoulder, the burnt-out, overgrown foundations uphill from it, and, behind the back wall of the tent, a barren, sharply rising rock slope. Beyond those, water all around.

This morning the sky was a depthless expanse, high mist or low clouds. No birds sang, no wind moved; the strait beyond the promontory was the undulating gray of antique window glass. Rae's breath was loud in her nose; when she moved, the scrape of the fabric jarred the air. As if in response, a quick scuffling noise came from behind the tent. Rae slapped her hand onto the holstered hammer, then stopped, forcing herself to listen attentively to the actual sound rather than her body's reaction to it. A scuffle. Not footsteps. A bird? She edged around the front of the tent to peer at the shrubs, and an explosion of brown wings shot out from under the fallen cedar, followed instantly by a scrap of angry red fur scrambling up the nearby tree to the safety of height, where the squirrel sat scolding her furiously. Rae closed her eyes and took a calming breath. This so-called solitary life was going to take a lot of getting used to.

The angry squirrel continued its imprecations, and Rae was aware of its eyes on her as she picked up the kettle from the fire pit and filled it under the tap on her water jug before putting it on the burner of the propane cookstove. She then used the enticement of coffee to get through the brutal cold of a trip to the privy, and was relieved to find the treetop scold gone when she came out. By the time she had dressed all over again, buttoning, zipping, and fastening clothes and tool belt, a geyser of steam was shooting from the kettle's spout into the frigid air. The stove was a luxury here; its tanks bulky and in need of frequent replacement compared with the old pump-style stoves of her childhood, but it was fast, and a great improvement over having to build a fire just for a cup of coffee.

Rae took out the glossy brown bag of coffee grounds and spooned some into the ridiculously fragile glass French-press coffeemaker—another luxury, one she would no doubt regret when it cracked and left her straining coffee grounds through her socks, but she had justified it in her mind by contemplating the wasteful alternative of all the paper filters she would have either to bury or to compost. The deciding factor, however, had been the vision of that sleek and gleaming symbol of modern sophisticates perched incongruously on a stump in front of a dusty canvas tent. Humor was a rare commodity in her current life, to be seized and hoarded whenever it ventured within her grasp.

She poured the water over the grounds, stuck the plunger in place, and carried the sculptural object over to the fallen cedar trunk, where she balanced it carefully before taking a few steps back, narrow-eyed as a critic at an art show: delicate glass suspended in a silver frame; soft, dull bark heavily worn by time and foraging woodpeckers; three small hemlocks, two cedars, a fir, and an assortment of bushes whose names she did not know as a backdrop; ugly folding aluminum cook table with plastic water jug to set it off; big, high-walled tent to one side evoking a family campout in the Fifties.

Yes, she decided approvingly, nodding at the arrangement; some things are worth the trouble.

This morning she even had milk, half frozen in the cooler box. Later in the year she would be lucky to have the fresh stuff once a week, following the visits of Ed the boatman, since the island lacked electricity and she had not yet decided if she wanted refrigeration and lights badly enough for the interminable bother of solar panels or generator. The idea of living in a primitive dependence on the sun was, temporarily at least, appealing. Either that, or the back of her mind had recognized the futility of making those decisions when it was far from certain that she would still be here to lay the power in.

Today, however, she would enjoy her coffee with milk.

She poured and sipped and stretched her spine and looked down at the mist that lay across the glassy water of the cove, a study in morning gray. She felt remarkably well, as was often the case after an attack like that of the night before. Her mind seemed to switch in and out of the panic mode cleanly, almost as if she had a short somewhere in the wiring of her brain: When connections were normal, everything worked at full strength; when the connection crackled and fizzed, under extra burden or just the vagaries of biology, she was gone.

In part it was the simple fact that nights were bad and things invariably looked better in the morning. Under that pearly dawn light, the texture of the island's hush was benevolent, alive with promise instead of crawling with threat. She was eager to begin work, but put it off to walk out along the promontory to greet the day. She braced herself as she approached the place where the harbor seals had been lying, but there were no splashes; they were already up and away. Instead, she startled, and was startled by, a gray heron brooding over the shallow cove waters. The flaps of its wings cracked the air as it took off, the underside of its body mirrored perfectly in the smooth surface below.

Rae continued out to the end of the floating boat dock and sat down cautiously on the splintery boards, where she sipped from her steaming mug. When the ripples of her passing had calmed, she bent slowly forward to peer down at the water. A woman looked back at her, thin of face, brown of eye, with a fringe of salt-and-pepper hair (mostly salt, now) sticking out from under the garish knit cap and a dark smear down the left temple. She frowned and pulled off the hat to see the mark, then reached down to brush her fingertips in the water and wipe at the trickle of dried blood. When the ripples cleared, she was looking down at a face far more self-assured than it had any right to be. It looked strong and competent and not in the least fragile, its eyes calm, with no trace of wariness, not a nightmare in sight. I have Grandfather to thank for the construction of that façade, she thought bitterly: impervious-looking but frail as lace. God, how looks deceived.

A ghostly hand brushed across her hair and Rae whirled, but it was just the breeze, rising with the sun and ruffling the water along with her hair, stirring the branches in the corner of her eye. The touch woke the thought of Watchers, invisible in the woods, and she was searching for them, staring deep into the bushes, when her eye caught on a flicker of movement up high. She waited, and when it moved again she saw it, a speck of shining beauty even on this dull morning: a kingfisher. The tiny bird with the vivid plumage bobbed on the twig, watching not Rae, but the water. In an instant, it dropped, swooped, and sliced the water, rising with a flash of silver in its strong beak. It dashed down the length of the cove, dipped around the opposite bank, and was gone.

Rae had never seen a kingfisher before. They were magical creatures, she had heard, and now understood why. She climbed to her feet, rubbing the dregs of tension from her neck, and concentrated on a series of long and deliberate breaths of the fragrant sea air.

Birds were waking, a thin invisible warble coming from the shore; farther along the bank perched a black bony hunter of a bird she thought might be a cormorant. Ask Ed to get you a bird book, she suggested to herself; that'll give you something to do other than imagine ghosts. She turned and went on to the end of the promontory.

On the outer side of her rocky protector, small waves teased at the boulders. In the distance, the rising fog revealed a low dark shape in the water, a freighter heading up Haro Strait toward Vancouver or Juneau. An engine around to the northwest whined and cut off, sounding close, a reminder of how readily noises traveled on the water. From the offshore rocks west of where Rae stood, unseen harbor seals coughed and grumbled at each other, and the air seemed to gather itself in preparation for the day. The sun rose through the vapor on one side, the ghostly moon retreated on the other. The mist solidified for a moment, and Rae felt a faint, thin frond pushing to uncurl inside her: hope, perhaps, or even life.

Then the morning mists bowed to defeat and the first direct rays of the sun hit the water, transforming it into a shimmering expanse of light, a visual hymn of rejoicing, a paean to the intimate magnificence of the San Juans.

Rae Newborn's first morning on Folly.

Six

Letter from Rae to Her Granddaughter

April 5

My dearest Petra,

Well, as you can see, I made it through my first days on Folly without freezing to death or falling into the sea and getting eaten by an orca or being abducted by ransom-seeking kidnappers or coming down with ptomaine poisoning or any of your mother's other ghastly scenarios. The only thing that happened to me was I walked into a tree on my first night, giving myself a nice purple bruise and a cut I didn't notice until the next day. Thank goodness I don't have visitors—they would have taken one look at my filthy hands, wild hair (from that super hat you gave me—warm, but it does leave your hair a bit mussed), and the great smear of dried blood down the side of my face, and had me locked up again before the sun set.

Daily life here is settling down into uncomfortable, but not impossible. I never seem to get really warm, since there's no safe way to heat a tent and a campfire only warms one side of you at a time, but if I keep busy enough, I don't notice being cold. Much. One nice thing is that I can eat huge meals and know I won't gain an ounce—between work and keeping warm, I burn it all off.

As for the house, I'm still on the ground-clearing stage, which will take me another week before I uncover the foundation completely and begin to get a sense of the place. Very little of the walls survived, and those hunks are completely buried in nettles and blackberry vines. (I don't think I showed you my blackberry gloves—they're called gauntlets, because they come to the elbow, and they're so thick I believe you could drive nails with them!) There are saplings growing in the foundations too, of course, some of them pretty close to being trees, like the eight-inch-thick maple growing smack in the middle of where my living room is going to be, and although I agree it would make an interesting center-piece, it'd be hard to keep the rain out. Down it comes!

One thing I can tell you already, even with a lot of the blackberries still in place, and that is, Desmond Newborn had a real knack for stonework. The two towers haven't so much as a loose stone, as far as I can see, even with all the plants growing around them, and his founda-tion is nearly as secure as it was seventy-five years ago when it had a house on it. This is a great relief to me, as you can imagine—I was definitely <u>not</u> looking forward to digging and pouring a new footing for my house. (It also means, of course, that I could actually have taken you on a proper tour when you were here, but at the time your mother was right, the stones could have been dangerous. And by the way, I hope your trip home went smoothly.)

Well, shall I tell you about the house-to-be? I don't know if you're the least bit interested in the details, so please let me know if you aren't and I'll write instead about the island and its wildlife.

Perhaps I ought to begin with the name itself. You may know this already, but "folly" is a name given to objects or acts marked by extrav-agance and irrationality. It is used in scorn, but also in awe, at the sheer, preposterous exuberance of a thing ("Seward's Folly" was the name given to the purchase of that vast and "useless" tract of land we now call Alaska). Folly indicates the very opposite of sober restraint, and has come to mean in architectural terms a useless building stuck out in the land-scape for no good reason but that someone thought it would look nice there. Foolish, but fun. I may discover why it applies to this island as my building progresses. However, the island is also known as Sanctuary, and I believe it was given that name before there was a bird refuge on the north end.

You saw where the house used to stand—and will again stand, God willing. It's a boxy shape sort of tucked into a steep patch of hillside as if it had its back to the wall, with one stone tower at the right-hand cor-ner of the rear wall (looking from the front) and another on the left-hand corner of the front. The two towers, with a dark chimney behind them at the back (which will be hidden by the roof), are tied together visually by the height of the stone foundation. It should look odd—I suppose it does look odd, or else why would the people here call it a folly?—but going by the picture I have of it, it won't look as unbalanced as it sounds. The house itself, even without the towers (which aren't much taller than the roof, actually, and sadly enough aren't big enough for rooms at their tops, only windows), is high enough up on the hillside and angled so that it has a view which, while not exactly breathtaking, is definitely satisfying. The clearing where you helped me put up the tent and the rocky point that wraps around to form the cove just seem to open out when you're above them, and draw the eye out, out into the strait and the islands (and—when the mist clears off, which it does occasionally—the northern coast of the Olympic peninsula). In other words, people passing by might not notice the house, but from the house you feel that you can see the world. I like this combination very much.

Speaking of breathtaking, I don't know if I told you (and it was too foggy for you to see) but I have my very own mountain. Well, a tall hill, really, on the northeastern corner of the island, but it has an almost completely bald top, and from there a person can see the world. When I came here before, with your stepgranddad and auntie, we hiked to the top. You probably know that Washington State has a whole string of (we hope) dormant volcanoes, in addition to the not-so-dormant Mt. St. Helens? Well, you can see both Baker and Rainier from my hilltop, as well as the line of snowcapped peaks of the Olympic range. Plus Haro and Juan de Fuca Straits and Vancouver Island to the west and a lot of islands to the north. Somebody once put a little building on the bald hilltop, to see the view. It could even have been the government—I know that during the Second World War the army (navy? air force??) had hidden lookouts all up and down the Pacific coast, watching for the Japanese invasion that never came.

The next clear day I have, I'm going to climb up there with my camera and have a look. It won't be a holiday, really, because I do need to trace the water supply before too long. Might as well do both, wouldn't you agree?

Well, my sweet Petra, I need to end this, because my hands are tired and cold and I need to sleep. Boatman Ed will be here tomorrow, to bring me milk and bread and to pick up my laundry and a sample of water to be tested, so I'll give him this to mail.

Give my greetings to your parents. Tell them I'm well.

Love, Gran

Seven

Rae looked at the sealed envelope, stamped and addressed to Petra Collins, and scratched vigorously at her hair with both hands, as if the gesture might relieve the unending twitchiness and tiredness that seemed to crawl into her scalp at the end of the day. The letter was too cheerful to be believed. If she'd written those same words to, say, Dr. Hunt, all kinds of alarm bells would have gone off. But the truth of the matter was, a person simply couldn't write the sort of brutally honest letter Rae felt like writing and send it to a beloved thirteen-year-old grandchild, no matter how mature, intelligent, and just plain wise the child might be. Rae wanted to complain about how sore her back was from all the bending, and how the pain shot up and down her left arm and shoulder, and how her fingers ached so that even moving a pen was a trial, how alarmingly little mental and physical strength she had and how frightening it was to contemplate the specter of age looming on the horizon. She craved the relief of confession—of the unending jumpiness that rode her every waking minute and many of her sleeping minutes as well, of how she spent half her working time glancing sharply over her shoulders at nonexistent Watchers, looking up from her labors among the stone towers, certain she would see a strange man striding up the promontory or stepping out from behind a tree. Of how the night before she had been jolted from a dream about being washed out to sea, saved only by a boulder on the promontory, and had woken to find her arms around her pillow and Petra's face fading from the dream rock. And of how the island silence, long desired, was proving so oppressive that she had dug out Petra's tape player and let it spin its tinny Oldies into her ears (and of how she had laughed herself to hysterical tears at the first song, which, through some peculiar twist of fate, was Martha and the Vandellas singing "Nowhere to Run"). Rae seemed to cry all the time, in fact, from nervous reaction or from loneliness and fear—fear of strangers, fear of voices, fear of weakness or illness or injury, fear of fear itself. This afternoon she had found herself sobbing with infantile rage when she could not move a fallen stone, kicking the mossy boulder like a three-year-old and screeching at the heavens until her knees gave out and she sat hunched over, weeping in self-pity until her head ached.

She could write none of this, not only because of Petra's age, but because if Petra's mother found such a letter (and knowing Tamara, she was unlikely to allow her daughter so dangerous a privacy as a personal correspondence with Rae), she could not miss seeing what lay at the base of such pure honesty: a deep and straightforward affection such as Rae had never given her own daughter, a hunger for companionship that Tamara could not satisfy—or that Rae would not permit her to satisfy.

Rae's relationship with her elder daughter had been doomed from the beginning. After Tamara's birth, postpartum depression had slid, slowly but inexorably, into a full-scale breakdown, Rae's first. When Rae came out of the hospital, three months later, she had neither husband nor child. It took her four years to regain access to Tamara, four years to prove that she was not about to slit her wrists one day while Tamara was playing in the next room (a vivid suggestion made in court by David's lawyer). By that time, Tamara was well and truly indoctrinated against her. The child screamed when David walked out the door of Rae's apartment, leaving his ex-wife and daughter to their first weekend alone. Tamara screamed all weekend.

For the next five years, Rae and David shared custody—or rather, David's mother shared it grudgingly with Rae, since it was to his parents' house that David took the child. Then, a month short of Tamara's tenth birthday, Rae's second break occurred. Much of that winter was lost to Rae, but clear images lingered, seared into her visual memory by the same mechanism that had carved Bella's happy cry of *Mommy!* into her hearing: the sight of Tamara frozen in the doorway of the living room, her blond hair hanging lank and unwashed in the week she'd spent in her mother's care, staring openmouthed as Rae stripped naked, earnestly lecturing her daughter on the need for doing so—although that reason, rooted in the logic of dreams and madness, was lost in the mists; the image of Tamara being driven away by David's enraged mother, the way her white Cadillac skidded to one side before its tires regained the road; the pattern of the blood, spreading out in the bathwater, delicate scarlet blooms curling against the white enamel. That she remembered, although nothing of the ensuing noise and tumult of David's entrance or the paramedics. Nothing of either hospital. Nothing but muttering darkness, punctuated only by her father's face, looking as much lost as it did angry, telling her that her grandfather William had died at the age of ninety-four, enraged to the last. Rae still believed that her second breakdown had led to William's fatal stroke. Her father had tried to reassure her, but she knew better: The knowledge that his only granddaughter was a mental patient had killed William.

After that, Rae had not fought David for custody of Tamara.

Only in the years of her marriage to Alan had Rae begun to feel able to look Tamara in the eyes without a cringe, and even then, more often than not, she was visited by a quick, terrible memory, of a thing she had never revealed in thirty years of dealing with clever psychiatrists. A thing she had told only one other person in her life: Alan.

The memory was visual, of Tamara as a tiny infant, old enough to have lost her umbilical cord but too young to have any strength in her neck—perhaps a month old. Lying on her parents' bed shrieking with colic or hunger or wet diapers or just the jangled nervous system of the newborn, and Rae had tried everything. She'd nursed her daughter, walked her, changed her, bathed her, patted her, sung to her; nothing worked. Rae laid Tamara on the bed—gently, with immense care—and stood looking down at nine pounds of squalling, red-faced fury. Rae was not far from screaming herself, and her eyes were drawn to the shelf on which she had left twenty-one ounces of drop-forged steel framing hammer. She looked at the tool, and her gaze lowered to her own two hands, then back to the inconsolable infant. It was hard to breathe; the lusty screams seemed to fade in her hearing.

Rae turned and left the house.

And David got home before she did. When Rae walked in, Tamara was peacefully asleep on his shoulder.

Rae had never told David that, instead of raging and ranting at her for this extreme irresponsibility, he should have gone down on his knees in gratitude for her self-control. She had never told anyone of her urge, not even after she had discovered how many other women went through the same thing, particularly those who were young (she had turned twenty the month before the birth), who'd undergone hard births (hers was a thirty-hour labor), who had uninvolved husbands (David worked long hours), and who had no support system (all her family and friends had been left behind on the East Coast). All Rae knew was that she couldn't be trusted with her own daughter, who hated her anyway. It was a feeling she had never shaken off.

She had spent the last thirty-two years, the sane and the mad, knowing that her daughter was afraid of her.

Alan was the only one who had known the whole story behind the estrangement, Alan who saw the fear growing with her second pregnancy and kept digging until she told him the last shameful detail, Alan who took a quarter's leave to be home when she needed someone there, for Bella, in case . . .

Only there was no "in case." Bella was an easy baby, as Rae was a different person from the twenty-year-old who bore Tamara, and the weird chemistry of the depressive mind stayed in abatement. Guiltily, Rae would watch Tamara for signs of resentment at Rae's ease with Tamara's half-sister, but for some reason it never surfaced. Tamara liked—no, Tamara loved—Bella, in spite of resentments past and the embarrassment of Rae's age as a new mother. She had even begun to trust Rae with Petra, until the accident.

Until a month after the accident, when Tamara and her daughter had stood in the living room doorway staring down at Rae in horror.

When Rae came out of the mental hospital in December, she had fully expected that Tamara would never let her near her granddaughter again, and had been reduced to weeping gratitude when her daughter brought Petra for a visit to the informal halfway house where Rae was living. Tamara had watched her every move, but she had come, and she made no overt move to keep Rae and Petra apart. She disagreed with Rae's decision to come to the island with a chill disapproval, but she nonetheless offered to usher Rae from the mainland over to the island, with Petra. And on the ferry over, Tamara had even permitted her mother to be alone with Petra on the outside deck, had not followed to keep them in sight when Petra wandered away down the boat. Rae was grateful, although she couldn't figure it out.

And she had no wish to push matters. Her letters would remain light and chatty and as boringly sane as she could contrive to sound. She would make no reference to the voices that whispered beneath the rain, or to unstoppable tears, or to booting moss-covered boulders and screeching obscenities at their refusal to get up and move.

Picturing herself raging at the rock, Rae was surprised to find a reluctant grin tugging at her mouth. *Jesus, Rae, you must have looked like . . .* Her thoughts paused, and then she chuckled aloud—like a crazy woman.

Still smiling, she tossed the letter to Petra on the table, shut down the light, and crawled into the sleeping bag. A horned owl hoot-hooted up the hill from the tent, a sound comforting in its evocation of her California mountains. Even Bella hadn't found owls a threat.

It's only been five days, she told her fears. *Muscle builds slowly in middle age, whether it's on the arms or in the mind. Look: You stood up and turned off the lamp without even thinking about the shadow on the wall, didn't you? There's progress. Okay, life here isn't a barrel of fun. In fact, it's pretty damn miserable, especially when you're trying to move rocks in the rain.*

But look at the plus side, she added, her eyelids drooping. *You sure don't have any trouble falling asleep.* Staying asleep might be more than she could ask, but surely a day's hard labor was a small price to pay for the delicious luxury of unconsciousness.

The next day was Tuesday, Ed's day. Ed De la Torre was a resident of Friday Harbor, her nearest proper town. Ed acted as unofficial mailman, taxi driver, news service, repair consultant, and delivery boy for the handful of island residents willing to pay. Eventually, Rae supposed, she would buy a boat of her own, but she had not operated any heavy equipment, much less a car, in a year and a half, and for the time being, even a small skiff with an outboard motor seemed so . . . extroverted. And a small skiff with an inexperienced person at the controls would be risky in the fast waters that curled around her island, which meant a larger and more powerful boat, which would require lessons, and complicated maintenance, which in turn meant an even greater commitment to the outside world. Rae wanted to be left alone, but she was not willing to forgo milk and eggs, toothpaste and clean socks. So, she had Ed once a week—and truth to tell, although she cringed at the very idea of visitors, the knowledge that she was not utterly alone in the world was reassuring. In the far back of her mind lay the hidden knowledge that if Ed were to come to the island one day and find her note on the tent saying, "Ed, don't come in, call the police," the discovery would not cause him much grief.

She had been led to understand that most of her fellow island hermits who used Ed's delivery services had cell phones or short-wave radios to call and ask him to bring along a steak or some toilet paper or the part they'd forgotten to order for their sump pump. Rae refused to entertain the idea of a cell phone, declaring to others that it would be an unbearable intrusion, while admitting to herself that she detested the things for their role in the death of her family. Her flat refusal had driven her daughter wild ("What if you get sick?" Tamara demanded. "What if you fall down?"), but Ed had just commented that a cell phone probably wouldn't work there anyway, and instructed her to hang a white shirt or something out over the peeling No Trespassing sign on the end of the promontory if she found she needed him to stop by on one of his other days. He was often passing, he said, or one of her neighbors would get word to him.

So Tuesdays were Ed days, sometime before noon, he had told her, depending on the tide. By eight o'clock that morning Rae was up, her body bathed and her hair washed with laboriously heated water, the dry crescents of dirt pried out from under her fingernails, a small duffel bag of dirty laundry packed and ready, a precise list of the next week's supplies written down.

Now what? she wondered. With her first visitor due, she wasn't about to go and get stuck into the filthy demolition work that awaited her. If Ed was to be her sole link with the outer world, she wanted to start off with a good impression, and although when he had brought her to the island the other day he had seemed so phlegmatic as to be half asleep, she couldn't take a chance. Best to do something not too physical while waiting for him—and not too far away: If she missed him, she'd be condemned to beans, rice, and dried milk by the end of next week.

She carried duffel bag and grocery list out of the tent, zipped the door shut to keep out the slugs and her red squirrel neighbor, and put the two essentials for Ed on her folding canvas chair. The clearing itself was as tidy as a trampled meadow dominated by tarpaulin-covered building material could get, and most of the projects that awaited her were major. There was one, however, that shouldn't take more than a couple of hours and involved a minimum of grime.

One thing Rae would require fairly quickly was a sturdy, all-purpose workbench. She had already decided where she wanted it: tucked into the trunk of the forty-foot-tall, high-branched madrone at the east side of the clearing where she had buried the ashes. The ground was flat there, and lightly shaded, but mostly she wanted her workbench there because from one side she would be looking up at the house, and from the other down at her cove. Too, Alan and Bella lay close by.

Rae caught up her carpenter's belt and snugged it over her hips. The morning was warmer than the previous few, with a promise of sun, and she had traded the fleece pullover and jacket for a lightweight vest that had been Alan's. The tool belt fit normally now, the hammer's handle bumping its customary spot on her leg as she walked over to the madrone.

She had thought to build the workbench out of 2x4 lumber, of which she certainly had plenty, but there in the clearing with the stacks of building material at her back and the only human intrusions decidedly temporary—tent, fire pit, canvas-sling chair, and folding cook center—she realized that a crude, functional block of a table would be, quite simply, an eyesore. Of course, building sites and works in progress usually were eyesores, but something in her drew back from the idea of placing one, deliberately, here.

She shifted around to fix her gaze on the shore, and a picture came suddenly to mind, of a staircase she had once driven two hours to see, a wide descending curve of mahogany and birch, elegant, clean, and vastly expensive, its gorgeous, gleaming sweep of laboriously polished handrail supported entirely by . . . rough, peeled branches. The house's owner had possessed the good sense to leave the stairway alone, not gussy it up with carpeting and pictures along the wall, and the high windows in the curving wall had set off the staircase as if it were a piece of sculpture. Rae had always coveted that sweep of stairs, had often thought about ways to use the beautiful incongruity of natural and worked woods. This might be the time. Not that she was about to dive into the woods and hack away at young trees. For one thing, such green wood was useless for building, and beyond that, she could just imagine the furious argument she would have with the people who had preserved this island over the years. But live trees were not her only source of wood.

Some of the driftwood on her beach was bound to be too rotten to support anything greater than its own weight, but if she could find some pieces that had been in the water just long enough to be worn down, but not long enough to have gone spongy . . .

It took her an hour and cost her a bashed shin and a leg wet to the knee, but she collected a sizable tangle of silvery wood, each piece as thick as her wrist and interestingly twisted. She carried the wood up the hill, dumping it at the foot of the madrone tree, determinedly ignoring the ache down her left arm, and then she stood with her hands thrust into her back pockets, trying to call the structure into being before her eyes.

But the safety and comfort of work was broken. More than that, standing over the wood in that position made her feel uneasy, made her aware of a cold trickle of sweat between her shoulder blades. She became conscious of a powerful desire to hurl the silver wood back into the sea and dig out the 2x4s.

The problem was, building a workbench that was more than a mere functional arrangement of milled lumber called for a commitment Rae did not know if she was able to make. Once upon a time, back in another life, Rae had been a woodworker, a woman whose hands and heart transformed dull, dead trees into glorious pieces of usable furniture, teasing the material into stunning, one-of-a-kind tables and cabinets and dining room chairs. Once upon a time, Rae had stood with her hands in her hip pockets, leaning forward over the exciting potential in a slab of walnut or oak or ebony, planning, thinking, shifting the cuts in her mind. Once upon a time, Rae Newborn would have leapt at the chance to wrap a driftwood-based worktable around the madrone, playing lightheartedly with nature's Art Nouveau shapes of gray, sea-soaked wood against the crisp, cinnamon-colored shavings curling off the velvety green inner bark of the living tree. Once upon a time, sixteen months before, in another lifetime.

Before the phrase "drunk driver" had ripped through Rae Newborn's life. Among the myriad reasons for her being on Folly was the sense that building a house would be a way of putting her empty hands to work that did not require much participation of heart. Woodworking was an intimate relationship; house building was just a job. Rae was not ready for another intimate relationship.

Or so she had thought, until she found herself standing, hands in pockets, a tangle of driftwood at her feet.

But damn it, she needed a workbench.

What did it matter which wood she built it from?

She nudged a branch over to one side with her boot, and noticed an interesting arrangement of knots. Then she saw another, down at the bottom of the heap, that seemed to mirror the angles of the first one, and she knelt down to slide it out. She placed the two together, running her hands up and down them with the same motion her daughter used to feel a horse's leg. She reached out for another branch, then another, and soon she was shifting her entire collection back and forth, seeing how the strengths of one upright blended with the intricacies of another, balancing curve and straight, playing with the wood until she was satisfied not only that her bench would stand even if she set an engine block down on it, but that it would please her when holding nothing more than a mug of wildflowers.

Then Rae went to the tent, and for the first time in seventeen months, she snapped open the clasp of her big, heavily dented metal toolbox. She took from it a crosscut saw, a set of rough chisels with their mallet, her old-fashioned bit brace hand drill and its box of bits, and the sleek aluminum spirit level. Laying the tools down near the driftwood branches, she reached behind her to flick the tape measure from its pouch at her spine, and bent to work.

Weaving a selection of sea-worn driftwood into the strong underpinnings that she needed was no easy task. Each piece had to balance and lock into the next, resisting the tension and compression that would make the bench twist and collapse. By drilling and chiseling a hole to feed one branch into, by trimming and angling and sinking cross-supports, she could link the parts up into an airy yet solid whole. The sawdust smelled of brine, the wood was tacky to the touch and oddly unlike the tree it had been, and Rae was completely lost in her miniature silver forest when the voice boomed from behind her.

"Mornin' there, Mizz—"

The words strangled in the boatman's throat as Rae shrieked and jumped backward, her hammer leaping of its own volition into her hand. He reacted in kind, braced for a vicious fight, and they stared at each other across the upright snarl of partially attached driftwood, the wild-eyed woman and the equally startled man who had come up behind her back. Ed recovered first. With a visible effort he wiped the tightness from his face and straightened, taking off his baseball cap and running a hand over his mahogany-colored tonsure. When his arm went up, Rae glimpsed a band of geometric tattoo around his wrist, oranges and lapis blue.

"Sorry to surprise you like that," he was saying. "I guess I sorta figured you'd heard me. My boat engine and all."

Rae gulped in a breath. *Humor disarms* was one of the vital lessons she had learned in her laborious climbs out of madness, second only to *Pre-*

tend to be normal, and you will be. She, too, stood up straight, gave the hammer a puzzled glance and dropped it back into its holster, and rubbed her hands together to hide their trembling. She cleared her throat.

"Guess I was a little preoccupied," she told him, and stretched her mouth into what she hoped resembled a smile. "I didn't hear you coming up on me."

"So I noticed. Next time I'll toot the horn to warn you. Sorry," he said again. He was watching her warily, as if aware that he was standing across from a woman who heard voices in the empty spaces behind her ears. Given her means of greeting him, Rae thought his reaction understandable. Fear was contagious.

"You've got nothing to be sorry about," she said, making an effort at easing the tension in the air. "I, er, don't get a lot of visitors."

Ed seemed to be thinking. And he was, but not about her words. He was reflecting, *So, this really is a woman I dropped off here—Rae, not Ray—and not at all a bad-looking one, who's trying hard to hide how spooked she was when she turned around and all of a sudden there I stood. Just like all the other single women on the islands—no matter how brave they look, they're scared shitless and needing a man around.* Which thought put a broad smile between his roguish white mustaches. "Yeah, the islands are like that in winter. Come summer, you could walk to Roche Harbor on the boat decks, but the rest of the year it's quiet. 'Course, you'll never get much traffic here, between the currents and the shoal and being a preserve and all."

"I hope I don't," she said fervently, then realized how unfriendly that sounded. "Look, I was just going to make some coffee," she lied. "Would you like a cup?"

"Oh, I won't trouble you."

"The only trouble is putting four scoops of coffee in the pot instead of two. I think I can manage that much."

Ed relaxed a notch more: *Humor disarms.* "In that case, thanks, I'd like a cup."

It was more than Rae could do to walk across the clearing with a perfect stranger at her back, particularly one who'd eyed her appreciatively, so she stretched out her hand in an "After you" gesture, and they walked across the clearing together, side by side though well apart. At the campsite, she filled the kettle and put it on the stove, then ducked into the tent for the wooden chair. She set it down a distance from its canvas-sling cousin, then picked it up again to shift it half a foot closer. In a practiced move she unbuckled the belt and slung it over the slatted back, then went to rinse out the coffeepot.

Ed had set two bulging paper sacks from the Friday Harbor grocery store on the aluminum cook table; she sorted through them until she found her milk for the week. She opened the bag of coffee grounds and spooned some in, checked to see that the mug she intended for her visitor was more or less clean, and then turned to ask if he took sugar. Ed was perched on the edge of the canvas chair with her hammer in his hands, running his blunt fingers over the satiny finish of the handle. She shuddered, as if he had been caressing instead the back of her neck, and her hands yearned to snatch the tool away from him.

"Sugar?" she asked through clenched teeth.

"No, thanks. What kind of wood is this?"

With that opening, Rae was freed to go over and draw the tool gently out of his hands, smoothing her own thumb over the dark rich amber handle that she had turned and shaped to fit her palm and fingers like a custom-made glove. "It's Honduran mahogany. I had a piece left over, I needed a handle, so I thought, Why not? I don't think it's really strong enough for the purpose, but time will tell."

"Left over. Like from remodeling your kitchen or something?"

Rae had a brief vision of a kitchen clothed in that rich wood—like drowning in melted chocolate. *No; left over, as in a peace offering that didn't work,* she nearly told Ed, but said instead, "I made a little end table for my daughter."

His face closed in slightly. "Would that, er, would that be the daughter I met?"

"The one and only," she told him. Now. She watched his face, and this time her smile, though slightly sad, came more naturally. "She's a piece of work, isn't she?"

He looked up, surprised either by the phrase or by the fact that it had been the woman's own mother who said it.

"I . . . well, I guess."

"Bossed you all the way back to Friday Harbor, I'll bet."

"You're right about that." One mustache hitched upward in a rueful grin.

"And then she asked you to keep an eye on me." It was a guess, but not too far-fetched; Tamara had paid neighbors before.

Ed went still, and Rae moved to reassure him. "Don't worry about it. I figured she'd find someone who could check to see that I wasn't lying dead under a tree or going nuts and talking with the birds."

She watched him closely, saw his sea-colored eyes skitter sideways, muttered a curse under her breath, and continued, "I bet she told you I'd been in a mental hospital." His eyes became very interested in his frayed canvas shoes; answer enough. Shit, Tamara; why do you do these things? Well, if old Ed knew that, he probably ought to know the rest—or as much of the rest as Rae cared to tell. She couldn't afford to have all of Friday Harbor thinking of her as the madwoman of Newborn's Folly. Even if it's what she was.

"Did Tamara also tell you I was badly injured in an accident that killed my husband?" She couldn't think for a moment why she had failed to mention Bella. No, giving him Bella would have been too much: Sympathy for a loss was one thing; the extreme pity for loss of a child quite another. "No, I didn't think she'd mention the accident. A person's likely to be a little depressed for a while, after that."

She gave him back the hammer, the wood slapping against his callused palm, and turned to make the coffee. "You take milk?"

"No, just black. Look, I'm—"

"Ed, it's really okay. I'm afraid that my daughter's just a manipulative bitch. I'm only sorry you have to be dealing with her."

"Oh, hey, no, I'm not going to be dealing with her," he asserted, although Rae thought his righteousness did not ring entirely true.

"Why not? Report to her how I'm getting on, take her money, we're all happy. If it isn't you, she'll find someone else. Don't worry about it."

"You sure?"

"Sure I'm sure. I'd rather you than some stranger hanging off my shore with a pair of binoculars."

Normal, all very normal. Who wouldn't be a little depressed after what the newspapers would call a "tragic accident," huh, Ed? And so maybe since you didn't like Tamara Collins all that much anyway, you'll take what she said with a whole shakerful of salt and say the hell with her and all her talk about Mother's need for sedation and Mother's raving about voices and watchers, and you'll just decide that Mother is actually a nice normal crackpot of a female who just decided to come live on a deserted rock and rebuild a weird shack, for the fun of it. You take Tamara's money (no, my money, Rae supposed) and don't bother to keep quite as close an eye on things as you tell her you're doing, and we'll all be happy.

Besides, someone rich enough to own an entire island in the San Juans is bound to be a little flaky anyway.

In any case, the discomfort of talking about Tamara had distracted Ed from the possibility of another attack, and when he finished admiring the unusual handle on her hammer, he stretched out to drop it into its loop—even pointing the head in the right direction, either by intent or by accident.

"So, you build a lot of stuff?" he asked with a dubious glance at the strange-looking object (modernistic sculpture? clothes dryer? alien antenna?) that had so occupied her she hadn't heard his boat approach. Rae thought she knew the source of his discomfort; it was something she had been dealing with all her adult life, since that first hardware store owner had tried to talk her into a lighter hammer.

"I'm a furniture maker. Tables and desks, storage chests and chairs, sometimes kitchen cabinets if people want a custom job. I specialize in inlay work."

This last was the deliberate addition she used to nudge people away from the mental image of badly designed coffee tables with uneven legs and into the realm of the true craftsman. People who knew their stuff would at this point ask her name, and recognize it. Others like Ed would not know her from Joan of Arc, but would nonetheless grant her the aura of Artist. Ed was nodding wisely.

"We got a lot of people up here who paint, do pottery, that kind of stuff. Guy on Lopez, sells his pots in Seattle for three, four hundred dollars each."

Rae did not tell Ed that her small pieces went for five figures in New York and Los Angeles, and figured that he wouldn't be too impressed that one of her more experimental armoires was owned by MOMA, but he seemed happier now that he could think of her as one of those artistic types. Artistic tendencies explained a lot—even, it would appear, threatening your deliveryman with a hammer.

"Another coffee, Ed?"

"Oh no, thanks, Mizz Newborn."

"Mr. De la Torre, anyone who nearly gets clobbered by a woman's hammer and still agrees to carry away her dirty laundry ought to be able to call her by her first name. It's Rae."

He ducked his head in embarrassment—not just, it seemed, at the indelicate subject of dirty underwear. "Yeah, it's funny. I first heard your name in the boathouse . . . short hair and heavy coat and all—it was kind of confusing when your daughter called you 'Mother.' Wasn't till you spooked when I came up behind you just now that I was sure you weren't some kind of trans—whatever. You know, like you read about. Always thought it must be confusing for their families, and . . . Well, anyway. Next time I'll toot the horn," he said, wrenching the subject violently back to the very beginning of their conversation. "Good thing you didn't happen to have a shotgun leaning against the tree. I'd have sure got a surprise then, wouldn't I?"

Rae had been under the strong impression that a move on her part, back under the madrone, and he would have gone for her throat, but she assured him that she rarely blew away her delivery boys, and went to help him unload the rest of her provisions from the *Orca Queen,* then cast off his line from her ramshackle floating dock. As the engine caught in a cloud of blue smoke and he turned for open water, she thought about his words, and it dawned on her, with some amazement, that never once had she envisioned the old wood-handled revolver as a weapon of defense.

Eight

Rae Newborn's Letter to Dr. Roberta Hunt

April 6

Dear ~~Dr. Hunter~~ Dr. H,
   I know you will be wondering how your client on the island is ~~holding out~~ coming along, and I wanted to ~~reassure~~ let you know ~~that all is well~~ ~~that I'm doing well~~ that the experience is proving

April 7

Dear Dr. H,
   Well, still alive here on

April 8

Dear Dr. H,
   My boatman comes in two days and

April 10

Dear Roberta,
   You being the good and caring therapist you are, I have no doubt that your mind has followed me north any number of times over the last month, wondering, wondering. Having been here on the island for ten days now, I can say that I believe it will prove in the end to have been the right decision.

I will freely admit that the first few days were hard. Very hard. Partly that was because of coming cold turkey off the meds, and yes I heard voices and yes I saw ghosts out of the corner of my eye. And when Ed De la Torre, the man in charge of bringing my mail and keeping me supplied with bread and propane, first appeared last week he startled me quite badly. Fortunately, he spoke up rather than tapping me on the shoulder or—well, nothing happened, and Ed now knows to give me fair warning.

Actually, you'll be pleased (I think) to know, the reason I didn't hear him coming was that I was completely wrapped up in building a piece of furniture. That's right, although what Gloriana, my New York gallery owner, would make of it I can't imagine. It is, to put it in its most pedestrian terms, a driftwood-based workbench, but it is actually a far more intriguing medium than I would have imagined possible—the pale driftwood rises up out of the earth (it's sitting on the open ground under a tree—yes, and just think what Gloriana would say at that! Although come to think of it, MOMA might be pleased at the <u>plein air</u> concept). Anyway, the branches rise up like a thicket of waving arms, intertwined to support each other and the heavy slab of the top. And you know what that top is? The front door of Great-uncle Desmond's house, which turned up in the ground-clearing process. The door is solid cedar, which explains its longevity, and badly charred and full of nailheads or something on what used to be the inside, but I turned that side down, planed down the good side (removing the door latch first, naturally—this is a workbench, not a work of conceptual art), and it really is a remarkable piece of usable sculpture.

And the very first thing I did with it was to unwrap one of the glasses you gave me and set it on the middle of the bench, full of my first wine on the island. Magnificent. I even took some photographs of it—I'll ask my granddaughter Petra to develop them and send copies to you, after I've finished the roll.

The table took up the better part of a working week, a ridiculous waste of time considering that I'm living in a tent and winter is only six months away, but it served its function, a restorative one you could say, reminding me of who I was before (a person you never knew, but may have glimpsed) and allowing me to focus on what exactly I am doing here, restoring this wreck of a house.

(Do you notice, by the way, that this letter is heavily laced with

what my old junior high English teacher would disapprovingly call run-on sentences? Think of it as stream-of-consciousness at work, a continuation of our sessions. Better you should think that—bill me, even, for reading this!—than just think what lousy grammar Rae Newborn has.)

One bit of business. You may be—may already have been—contacted by my local sheriff's deputy, who came growling up (his boat, not him—everyone zips around here in a most amazing variety of watercraft, most of them powerfully engined. Sort of like a wilderness Venice. In fact, my island being in a quirky twist of current, when—not if, but when—I finally give in and get a boat, it'll have to have a big motor. Your secret Freudian side can make what it will of that statement). Where the hell was I? Oh right, the deputy. Bobby Gustafsen, a real sweetheart of a man (Oho, says Dr. Hunt; Oh no, says Ms. Newborn: a much married, father-of-twins sweetheart of a man in his early thirties) who eyed me warily as if I was about to leap at him. Deputy Gustafsen came by, mostly to make contact with a new resident (it's that kind of a place, despite the watery distance between neighbors) but also to bring me a photo my local department down there sent him, asking if I could identify the man as one of my attackers. It didn't look much like either of them, but it's nice to know the department down there hasn't written it off completely. Anyway, I gave him your number, as a character reference more than anything. If he calls, reassure him that although I may occasionally imagine little green men, in this case they were just a pair of human (?) creeps. Scumbags, as Sheriff Escobar called them, and I can only thank God yet again for my neighbor Joseph, not only for happening along when he did, <u>and</u> being willing to intervene, but for simply being able to back me up: that on this one occasion, despite all my false alarms and fantasies, I wasn't hallucinating, and I didn't beat myself up. If Joseph hadn't come, you and I would still be having our thrice-weekly sessions and I would have long since come to believe that those two bastards were every bit as incorporeal as the eyes at my windows and the footsteps on my deck.

Instead of which I am here, I am working, breathing a whole hell of a lot of fresh air and eating vast quantities of fairly monotonous but terribly healthy food, and at the end of the day I'm far too tired to listen for voices in the tiny waves that brush on my rocky beach or to look for eyes watching from the rapidly leafing-out bushes around my tent.

58   Laurie R. King

So, dear Dr. Roberta-my-shrink, let your mind cease its fret over this wayward and unreasonable client—for the moment anyway. It is all proceeding in the right direction, and if I slip, if the voices begin to reemerge in the night, I promise I will resume my meds. Much as I love you, I am becoming attached to my hundred-fifty-acre rock, and I would not wish to trade it for the pale green confines of the hospital. Except, perhaps, for the relative comfort of the beds.

With hopes for your physical and spiritual health (for of the mental, I have no doubts) and with all affection,

Yours,

Rae Newborn

Nine

Not too many lies in that letter, Rae thought that night as she addressed the bulky envelope (aside from the impossibility of resuming meds when they lay on the ocean floor). No need to lie, really, and best not to if she could avoid it.

She picked up the glass of wine, the glass so delicate as to be ethereal, and drained the last swallow of California Merlot. The Hunter's farewell present—a gift that could only have been from one friend to another rather than from doctor to client—had been two of these lovely long-stemmed things; a pair, the psychiatrist had told her firmly, not so that Rae could save them until she had a guest, but so Rae wouldn't be tempted to leave them on the shelf in the category of Things Too Precious to Use. If she broke one, well, she had a replacement; if she broke that, well, it was only the surviving member of a pair.

Like much The Hunter told her, there seemed to be a number of levels to the explanation, but Rae suspected that deep down, this petite, urban, Armani-clad woman couldn't bear to picture her client swilling down wine from a tin mug as she crouched by the fire, a horny-handed daughter of toil. Wilderness might be unavoidable at this point in Rae's life, but Civilization must not be abandoned completely.

Besides which, they both knew that wine tasted better from good crystal.

Rae was satisfied with the day's work, which had seen a finish to the simple task of making a workbench, a task that had so rapidly become something far greater. On the one hand, to have wasted so many days on the painstaking artistry of the thing, down to the thread of inlay twining up one silvery leg that called forth the clear glistening cedar of the top and tied in the red-brown in the overarching madrone, was as she had told Dr. Hunt, a ridiculous waste of time. She had far too much to do in site clearance and wall raising, to say nothing of water-supply checking and septic-tank digging, to spend four and a half days on a frivolous structure like that.

On the other hand, that very concentration on frivolity was what marked her as an artist and as a person. Drawers joined by tight and tiny dovetails, cabinets with inlay on the inside, for heaven's sake, hand-forged brass hinges that echoed the design of the piece, and layer after layer of laborious French polish—ridiculous. Unnecessary. As crazy as deciding at the age of forty-two to keep the unexpected baby that would mean giving up, for the health of the child, two years of working with half the glues, stains, and finishes she depended on, and at a time when she was on the edge of becoming Big. But these kinds of decisions were the very center of Rae Newborn. For the first time in forever, she had begun to remember that.

Rae went out of the tent (an action which, after ten days, still raised her pulse, but it was getting easier) to rinse the glass under the tap of her plastic five-gallon water jug. She wondered if Ed would bring the test results of the water sample she had sent to the lab—it would sure be nice to use water from the spring rather than this flat-tasting stuff, which had the flavor of its container. She set the glass upside down on the towel that served as a dish drainer and crossed the dark clearing to say good night to her completed workbench.

Tonight's quarter moon cast no more light than a candle, but Rae found that if she stood to one side, the glow from the tent was sufficient to illuminate the pale tangle of legs beneath the eighty-year-old slab of cedar. She had been astonished, as the door emerged from the concealing growth, to find it largely intact. The edge resting against the ground had needed trimming, and the hinged edge and part of its inner surface had been, as she wrote the psychiatrist, charred by the fire, but aside from a couple of holes in the inside (coat hook nails? Drilled holes for something mounted there?) the rest was solid. Massive, even. For some reason, it had been hinged to open outward, which she would have thought awkward over steps, but Desmond probably valued the space inside over the convenience. Rae had vacillated between trying to restore Desmond's door to its place and using it as the bench top, but she decided she had made the right choice. The past was to be built upon and used, not to be ruled by. She would make her own door, not quite a twin of his, building her new on top of the transformed old. She might even be able to use the original latch, or have it duplicated at a forge.

The bench's builder ran her palm over the dim surface. The wood was smooth, despite the slight variations left by the plane—smoother certainly than the skin of her hand, which was rapidly resuming its old work-roughened, blistered, cut, and abraded state. Rae rarely sanded a flat surface, preferring the clean, cut finish of the plane to the soft nap left by even the finest-gauge sandpaper—although some woods, and many shapes, called for grit over blade. She even preferred the very act of planing, the all-encompassing dance of motion, the long, slow strokes, feeling the grain of the once-living tree beneath her hands. It was a bit like giving a massage, with every muscle called into play and the body's weight balanced on the balls of the feet, her whole person working together at the service of the mind's eye. She relished the slow rip of the steel blade slicing strongly through the wood fibers, and took pleasure in the rain of fragrant curls. She even enjoyed the preliminaries—tuning the plane, setting the blade, honing it to a razor's edge. All in all, vastly preferable to clouds of fine sawdust.

If only life could be smoothed as easily, she thought.

Now, however, came the question of the bench's finish. Oil would darken the wood and leave it duller than a waterproof varnish would. On the other hand, an impermeable finish always looked artificial, riding the top of the wood like the layer of plastic it was, to say nothing of needing to be stripped and replaced every few years—or more often, given this damp climate. What if she—

A sharp *crack* rang out from the hill behind the tent, and every muscle in Rae's body lunged instantly for shelter. One moment she was meditating on her bench; a split second later she was cowering on the far side of the madrone, her face pressed against the cool inner bark, putting tree, workbench, clearing, tent, and fallen cedar between herself and the source of that broken branch.

It was not repeated. Bile tasting of sour wine crawled up the back of Rae's throat, her head swam, the old, familiar roaring arose in her ears. She turned and sank to the ground with the tree trunk at her back, dropped her head to her knees, and grappled with despair.

How could a person live like this? she wondered. A raccoon steps on a dead branch, and that innocent noise acts like an electric prod? It was more than a year since those two bastards had driven up behind her on the road, and in all that time, all those months in the locked ward and under The Hunter's care, rationality still hadn't managed to drive a wedge between perceived threat and the body's response.

Her predecessor here, the builder of Folly, would have known all about the lasting effects of stress, even on a normal mind. The man who had painstakingly assembled that cedar door could have told her how long it took before shell shock began to fade away, before a backfiring car ceased to hit the brain like artillery fire and send the ex-soldier diving for cover.

But then again, maybe Desmond couldn't tell her how long it took; maybe for him, the visceral response had never lessened. Perhaps that was why he stayed here, far from civilization's loud noises.

Or was it not just civilization's backfiring motors and clashing machinery? Did Desmond, too, panic at a mere crackling in the shrubs? Did his poor battered mind, too, read the noise as threat—the Kaiser's soldiers creeping across no-man's-land, perhaps? Is that why he had made a door heavy enough to withstand mortar fire?

Rae wondered if Desmond Newborn had also kept a gun in his knapsack, just in case his nerves got too frayed to bear.

Whatever it was, she was so very tired of carrying the loathsome burden around with her. It was not depression, it was not delusion, it was just the bone-weary sense of the futility of living. Who the hell cared if Folly got rebuilt? Who cared if Rae pulled herself together yet again, or if she swam off into the horizon? A lot of people would be relieved, in fact. Dr. Hunt would feel a pang of guilt—and, to be honest, Tamara would as well. But Rae's only true mourner would be Petra.

Petra whom she craved, Petra whom she was not allowed to embrace for fear the grandmother's madness would prove either dangerous or contagious.

Petra.

Rae was sick of the burden. Sick and tired of the past constantly getting in the way of whatever future she might make, sick unto death of creeping around and jumping out of her skin at every little sound, filled to the brim with revulsion at her own timidity.

She'd had enough, by God.

Before she could pause to reconsider, she was on her feet, storming around her workbench, stumbling into the bright area around the tent, and when she was standing square in the shaft of light that fell from its open flap, she raised her arms and yelled at the dark wall of trees, "All right—here I am! Take a good look, damn you! I'm. Not. Going. To. Hide. Any. More!" And to emphasize the vow, she bent to snatch up a length of firewood, then hurled it into the trees with all her strength. It hit, anticlimactically, on a branch barely ten feet away and dropped straight down, tumbling and ripping through the greenery. The thud of its landing was followed by a thin squeal and a brief, tiny scuffle in the leaf mold, after which a terrified silence fell over the clearing.

Rae stood there panting, running that frightened squeak through her mind. What poor little creature had she just scared half to death? Innocently going its furry nocturnal way when this monstrous noisemaker leaps up out of nowhere and the sky comes crashing down.

And if there really had been someone watching from the shadows, what on earth would he (not she, surely) have made of her actions? What if Alan, for example . . . ?

She began, reluctantly at first, to laugh. Alan *knew* his wife was nuts, even in ways not covered by mental illness; he had more than once said that was why he married her in the first place, but this would have taken even that much-forgiving man aback. Picturing his expression, the curious raised eyebrow above those gorgeous yellow-brown eyes, made her laughter come harder, until she plunked down into the canvas chair and bellowed aloud—startling the island wildlife still more, she had no doubt. Rage and despair and grief and manic humor all welled up together, and she raised her face to the moon, that source of all lunacy, and howled and laughed and wept until the tears were gone.

Then she rose up again, drew a great breath, and shouted at the top of her lungs, "Alan, I miss you like hell, you fucking bastard, Alan! Why the *fuck* couldn't you have been more careful, you murdering shithead, oh Alan, oh, God damn it." Her voice trailed off to a mumble, and then she closed her eyes and stood swaying gently, feeling empty, utterly, weightlessly empty. Even so, when the crackle repeated itself from the hillside, farther up this time, she flinched: only a twitch, but still a reaction.

Even that was too much. "Oh, God," she moaned aloud, although she could not have said if it was a curse or a prayer. In either case, the reaction was the same. She yanked her sweatshirt off over her head and bent to unlace and step out of her boots, and then she turned and walked downhill, away from the light, bruising her stockinged feet and wrenching her ankle as she picked her painful way to the water.

One step, and two into the bone-chilling water, then to her knees. When the level reached her thighs, she began to have trouble catching her breath; at waist level she thought she would be forced to retreat. The water was black against the black land—creepy to venture into, and impossible to see the sandy patches in—and her rapidly numbed feet came down on rocks slick with eelgrass and no doubt a variety of squiggling creatures, but she struggled on until the icy swell of water reached her chest. She remained upright a moment longer, quailing, and then she dropped, surrendering to the frigid benediction of the night sea . . .

. . . To come up moments later with a whoop, spluttering and coughing and shouting incredulous curses at the temperature of the water and at the sharp and exhilarating wash of fear when the weight of her sodden clothing threatened to pull her down. She splashed madly for shore and sprinted clumsily for the comparative warmth of the tent, where she stripped off and toweled dry, her teeth chattering uncontrollably. She dressed in many layers of warm things, dove into her bed, and pulled the sleeping bag up over her wet hair.

That night, Rae dreamed. In one episode, something huge and amorphous but not unfriendly heaved itself up out of the cove to talk with her about Chinese cooking. In the next, a lovely green twinkle that she somehow knew was an elf floated above the rock top of the island, telling Rae that he was with the U.S. Coast Guard and wanted Rae's permission to set up a spy satellite tower here to watch for Japanese submarines. Another time, Rae reached down to pull her hammer out of its loop and came up with one of Dr. Hunt's elegant glasses in her hand, to her annoyance. And then a final dream, just before her true wakening, more fully remembered if no more fully understood:

The house called Folly stood completed on its foundation, graced with the two towers, quirky and delightful and perfect in its proportions and its location between rock and water. It was nighttime and the house glowed with light, warm yellow illumination pouring from its windows, casting a path down the hill from its open door and streaming out of the high narrow windows at the tops of the towers, turning them into lighthouses, twin beacons of guidance and comfort shining out in the wilderness.

As Rae drew nearer, she could see and hear that a party was going on inside, an elegant formal dance with a string quartet and a thousand candles in a ballroom far larger than any fifteen-by-twenty-four-foot cabin had a right to be. Beautiful young women in sparkling gowns whirled and dipped, tall young men in the stark dignity of black and white accompanied and gazed with appreciation, glasses of champagne quenched thirsty throats, and the party was being judged a success. Then the picture seemed to tremble, and the brightly gowned women began, one after another, to stretch their arms up over their heads, sway, and suddenly transform into flame. The ballroom cheerfully caught fire and began to burn.

Rae woke in the cool gray light of dawn with those rich yellow flames in her mind's eye.

Hardly surprising, she thought over her first, meditative cup of coffee. (The squirrel sat on a branch directly overhead, calling down curses; Rae did not wince.) The burning of Folly was very much in her thoughts these days.

Before the construction of the workbench had sidetracked her into four days of messing around, Rae had made the first forays into the jungle around the foundations. It was a little like Sleeping Beauty's overgrown castle—assuming the castle had burned to the ground while the inhabitants slept.

Rae could not remember when she had first heard that Desmond's house had burned. Certainly she knew before she, Alan, and Bella came for their visit, because the bare, scorched stones of the towers and chimney had not surprised her. As soon as she'd reached the stone steps and seen the charred and crumbling threads of sill plate atop the foundation stones, she knew the fire must have been thorough. What it had not consumed in the first white heat, it had weakened, to fall and smolder gradually into ash—other than the door, which had fallen outside the burn zone.

So the dream contained a trace of history—though just a trace, Rae reflected as she rinsed off her cereal bowl and went to collect her tools: She did not expect to find a silver chandelier and dozens of champagne bottles as she cleared ground.

For seven decades the healthy vegetation of the Pacific Northwest had done its best to obliterate Desmond Newborn's labors. Vine maple, red alder, huckleberry, and madrone had found footholds in the rich humus that resulted from the return of a wooden building's component parts to nature; nettle, blackberry, thistle, and wild rose wrapped affectionately around the towers and tore at Rae's skin and clothes; half a dozen kinds of fern had rooted between the stones; a veritable garden of wildflowers sprang up between the woodier plants—delicate white poison camas and yellow desert parsley were already in bloom, interspersed with blue larkspur and purple clover. Rae had brought a brush hook to the island, thinking the machete-like tool might come in useful; she had never thought that she would be swinging it for days on end.

She was ruthless, hacking beauty and pest alike—with a few exceptions, such as the delicate shooting star that was just opening up among the skeletal remains of some floorboards. That, and a few like it, she dug carefully out and relocated farther along the hillside. Most of them would curl up and die, she knew, but they would have more of a chance than if they remained in the places they had chosen for themselves.

So today, with the bench complete, Rae would return first to the ground clearing and then to her excavation of the foundations. Ancient cities, the archaeologists had found, were often slapped down on the remains of previous generations of buildings, but Rae intended to begin at bedrock. Grimly, she pulled on her thorn-proof gauntlets and reentered the fray.

It was slow, sweaty work, hazardous underfoot because there was no way of knowing what the vegetation concealed, whether it was packed soil or a thinly covered scrap of rotted wall held together by air. She inched her boots ahead in cautiously tested increments until she had firm ground to stand on, tugging and unwrapping the vines and shrubs, spending most of her time dragging vast heaps of dying plant life over to the site of her future garden. She felt alone while she was working, but having a focus helped. Sometimes her body forgot to wince at sudden noises; occasionally she would go as long as an hour without a sudden conviction that someone was watching her.

It took another two days to strip the ground bare, long, brutal hours of needle-sharp thorns and burning nettles, a wrenched knee from a piece of solid ground that wasn't, and one terrifying close call when the heavy blade, which she had been too tired to notice was growing dull, bounced off a woody branch and sliced through the air half an inch from her hand.

Two further days to remove the vegetation and reveal the thick decomposed layer of floorboards, siding, shingles, furniture, and whatever else Desmond had in his house when it burned.

Two days of hacking, and now her real work could begin.

Ten

Desmond Newborn's Journal

November 11, 1918

They tell me today that the Great War is over.

The church bells rang out, the streets filled with shiny, upturned faces, and I had to walk and walk to find a place where I could stand beneath a tree and scream and scream and scream.

Was I laughing? Was I weeping? I do not know.

But I do know that the war will never be over. Never.

November 28, 1918

Thanksgiving Day. Why?

I left the house and found my screaming tree again, but it seemed to me the rivulet at its feet was too shallow to drown a man.

December 3, 1918

I arrived home one year ago today, and I still feel less than half a man, my arm baby-weak. And my mind.

The influenza is in the city. My brother's wife Lacy goes out to nurse the sick, pleading with me to stay inside and dry, lest all her nursing of a torn-up soldier be for naught.

I expect tomorrow's newspaper will report a sighting of the Beast of Baby-lon, or at the very least a rain of frogs.

December 11, 1918

William, of all people, has come down with the influenza. How does it dare? Curiously, I find I do care, and would prefer that my brother not die. Would that a dose of mortality might humble him, at least in his treatment of his wife. Lacy is at his side at all hours. I fear she will be next, although in truth, she is nowhere near as delicate as the name she bears.

December 25, 1918

The anniversary of Our Savior's birth, although what that carpenter's son did to deserve the title I do not know. Surely, there is little evidence of salvation in the world today.

William has turned the corner and will recover. Lacy is wan and gray, but as yet not ill.

Two Christmases ago I crouched in a flooded trench, pinned down by a sniper who entertained himself pinging rounds through our peepholes and picking off all periscopes raised above our bags. Like a duck-shoot at a fair, except that it meant two of us didn't make it home. Mrs. Banner received a good if belated Christmas present, though, her sergeant husband with his blighty. True, we sent him to her minus an eye, but even His Majesty's Army has to admit that a one-eyed sergeant may be excused from further service. The rest of us might well have traded in an eye for the chance of missing the remainder of the fighting. We might well have done so for the opportunity of missing the remainder of that day, frozen rain drooling down our necks, icy mud to our knees, made all the more bitter for knowing that the Germans were snug and dry a bare two hundred yards away—we'd briefly held their magnificent, strong, deep trenches some weeks before. Just before the afternoon stand-to (as if the enemy was about to spend his holiday coming across that mud and wire plain at us!) I caught the odor of goose roasting. The captain swore I was imagining it, and he was no doubt right, but it was sore cruel, that whiff of sage and crisp fat skin teasing its way among the thick stench of unburied bodies and eternal mud and flooded privies. Two years ago today.

But I swore an oath that I would write no more about the war, when I put the journal of those months overboard in the middle of the Atlantic Ocean. Why do so today? Because of the rain, I think.

Merry Christmas, Sergeant Banner.

December 27, 1918

Had to leave the house—the smell of roast goose made my insides rage and gibber. Spent the night in a barn somewhere. Lungs don't like it.

February 2, 1919

A long bout with congested lungs, I do not know why they don't just pack it in. I ought to take care of it once and for all, don't know why I don't, except it seems ungrateful to have been brought this far only to throw it in. Perhaps that's why I go out in all weather, tempting fate. People are dying all over the city, why does my body have to be so d——d healthy?

Life here, despite the joys, is proving increasingly uncomfortable. When spring comes I shall have to take to the road.

Part Two

LAYING THE
FOUNDATIONS

Building a well-constructed revenge, he reflected, is like building
anything else: The groundwork supports it, and also shapes it. He
had business that would take him to Seattle in two months, so that
is when he would act. He, himself: It would be too dangerous to
depend on subordinates for something as delicate as this.

Eleven

The only surviving picture of Desmond Newborn was also the only photograph of his house: a creased snapshot of a man in a dusty suit and cloth hat, standing in front of a sturdy-looking wooden building with two stone towers, a six-paned window, and four steps leading up to the door. There must once have been other pictures, from the requisite studio portrait of a child in lace and curls to a confident young man in a stiff new uniform, but all of them had vanished, into time or an impulsive clear-out or the flood that the paternal mansion had sustained in the Forties.

She had found the survivor in the bottom of the flat velvet-lined box that held his medals and enlistment paper, and had taken it to the photo lab to be blown up to the largest dimensions possible before the details began to blur, which turned out to be eight inches square. One copy she had framed, and hung it on the wall of her house in California; the other she had taken to be laminated. This she retrieved now from one of the plastic storage crates in the tent.

Rae studied it, as she had a score of times already. Mostly, in the past, she had pored over the details of the house, calculating its dimensions, sketching the roof angle and the style of window frame. With her eyes shut, she could have drawn its front wall, the arrangement of window and door on the lower floor, the smaller four-paned window in the triangle of the upper level. Another man, with winter coming on (but why did she think that?—oh yes, the fallen leaves from the vine maple, scattered across the steps near Desmond's boots) and a door being needed, would have settled for butting together his lumber and bolting a Z of one-bys on either side. Desmond, working under fairly primitive conditions, had produced a door bonded together with little more than sheer skill. The two holes that she had discovered on the door's inside surface had some kind of metal buried at their base—nails perhaps, melted in the fire and fused into mere lumps; she had left them in place, facing the ground now through a sea of driftwood legs.

Rae planned on tacking up the laminated photo to the madrone over her workbench, whether as decoration or inspiration or an evocation of the island's guiding spirit she did not know. She now noticed, however, that what she always assumed to be the doorknob did not match the mechanism she had removed from the charred door a few days earlier. She looked more closely, and saw for the first time that although Desmond was in the full sun and threw a clear shadow behind him, the knob cast none: It was not a knob, but a hole. And further, while she had always been struck by Desmond's body language—an easy stance with both hands resting loose at his sides, content without fidgeting—she saw now that the right hand, in the shadow of his leg, was actually holding something, some dark shape very like the latch that was now lying, drenched in oil, in a plastic bag on the workbench. What Rae had taken for a photograph showing a self-contained man of few demands was in truth that of a man interrupted in a task, allowing a brief delay before he knelt down on his threshold to make his house secure. It slowly dawned on Rae that this black-and-white image she held in her hand was not a photograph of Great-uncle Desmond and the house he lived in; it was a picture of Desmond Newborn and the house he was on the very brink of completing.

She lowered the picture to look past the top of it, comparing the monochromatic past with the present reality. Some of the trees were missing, she saw, such as the vine maple and a cedar that had stood too close to the house, even their burned stubs rotted to nothing now. The young hemlock that had been protected behind the left-hand tower was now a mighty grandfather, and the thick green shrubbery of the present hillside had, sixty-odd years ago, been cleared away to an airy display of rock and tree trunk.

Of Desmond himself the picture gave away little, for all that it was clear and precise in the way old photographs always seemed to be. Stance, clothing, and half-shaded face, he seemed to her largely a slate on which future generations might draw their own conclusions. The set of his wide shoulders and clean-shaven jaw, the noncommittal expression in his dark eye, the generous mouth that seemed to have tasted pain—or was that the viewer's hindsight? Perhaps even a projection, based on her own history?—when taken together could indicate stubbornness, or the lack of affect in a damaged mind, or the rigid control of a man in chronic pain. It might even be a patient disinterest in the process of picture taking—or in the person taking the picture. Whoever that had been.

Come to think of it, who had it been? Every indication was that Desmond Newborn was not a man to entertain casual visitors; however, his dress, despite the latch in his hand (and she was fairly certain that's what it was), indicated the formality of welcoming visitors. Even in the Twenties, she didn't imagine that men donned suits and stiff collars to do carpentry. Unless this photograph was taken to commemorate a symbolic occasion, the mounting of the front door latch—in which case, why not make a bigger deal of it, positioning the builder at his creation, or at least displaying the metal shape to the camera? Desmond simply looked as if he was waiting for a mildly unwelcome visitor to work the shutter and then leave, so he could peel off his collar and get back to work.

"Uncle Desmond," Rae addressed the picture, "you are a puzzle."

She dipped the fingers of her left hand into the nail pouch on the front of her belt, as she had done a thousand times before, forgetting that she had not yet opened a box of nails of any size or shape; still, her fingertips encountered a sharp point down in one corner, and she fished it out.

A roofing nail. One and a half inches long, galvanized, flat-headed like a giant thumbtack. Digging back into the pouch, she found, ironically enough, two more like it. She knew precisely what she'd scooped those nails into the pouch for, seventeen months earlier.

It had been on a Sunday morning in early November, a crisp, clear Northern California weekend between the rains. Rae had just returned from a hectic two weeks in Japan, leading a workshop that coincided with the opening of a group show in which she had three pieces. Unwilling to be parted so soon after her return, she, Alan, and Bella had driven up to see Petra and Tamara (and Don, if he had not found an excuse to be away), only to find that Tamara had either forgotten or not wanted to think about the visit, because when they arrived she was in the process of herding her family into the farm's oversized pickup, attached to a loaded horse trailer. Petra, then just short of her twelfth birthday and not yet launched into grungy jackets and bouts of adolescent surliness, had a horse show an hour north of the ranch. Rae took one look at Tamara's mood and said that, much as they'd love to see Petra compete, she rather thought she, Alan, and Bella would laze around and wait for the family to return. She'd even cook a pot of spaghetti or something, so that dinner would be waiting.

Tamara made no attempt to hide her relief, just gave her mother the house keys and got into the pickup. Don accelerated off in a cloud of dust that had Petra's horse rocking furiously inside the trailer.

Alan and Bella changed into their swimsuits and went to use the small pool behind the house, but Rae, jet-lagged and on edge as usual after an encounter with her elder daughter, put on the comforting tool belt (which she always tossed into the car for these visits, because Tamara always had some urgent undone job at hand and was willing to overlook her mother's unladylike behavior if it meant that the washing line stopped dipping to earth or the gate finally closed cleanly).

Just before Rae had left for Japan, during the forgotten phone call when the arrangements for this visit were made, Tamara had mentioned the bitter discovery of Don's failure to fix the roof on the end of the stables where a lot of equipment was stored, which meant that half the power tools were now rusted into immobility. So the day before, Rae had dropped by the lumberyard and picked up some bundles of shingles and a box of roofing nails. Now she popped open the box with the claws of her hammer, scooped two handfuls into each pouch, and got to work. Halfway through the soothing job, Bella's wet curls appeared over the edge of the roof, with Alan close behind her on the ladder, hammers in hand, to help her. Three sunburned necks and a couple of hours later, the family of amateur roofers climbed down to go for a well-earned swim.

The peaceful interval lasted until after dinner. Rae clearly recalled being up on that low roof, the sharp chemical smell of the shingles, the rough grit digging into their knees and the palms of their hands. Alan's customary vast patience, bracing Bella's hand as her small tack hammer finished driving in the nails Rae had started. Alan's care, always sheltering Bella from the edge, but so casual about it that the child did not notice. The three of them sitting on the peak of the roof when the job was finished, their arms around each other, looking out over the bucolic view, the freshly greened pastures, the grazing horses, the discussion of "When can I get a pony like Petra's, Mommy?"

Sweet, sweet memory.

They swam, they made dinner in Tamara's ornate kitchen, they poured themselves glasses of red wine. Bella found a videotape and fell asleep on the floor with Tamara's standard poodle on one side and Petra's black Lab across her legs. Alan got out some papers he needed to mark, and Rae had a book. The kitchen was fragrant and it was fully dark outside when the lights of the pickup played across the windows.

Don came in first, nodded to his mother-in-law and her husband, and went straight to the freezer for the bottle of forty-dollar vodka. He was wearing dark slacks, an open-necked shirt, and a light wool jacket, somewhat formal attire for the dust of a children's equestrian event.

"How did Petra do?" Rae asked him.

He glanced up from his pouring, eyes narrowing as if this was some sort of trick question. "Fine. Petra did fine."

"Did you stay for the whole thing?"

"Not the whole thing, no. I had a meeting nearby, a group of investors."

As Rae had thought. Don did not share his wife's interest in horses. Neither did Rae, for that matter—Tamara had caught horses from David's mother, who had more or less raised her granddaughter in Rae's enforced absences. When Don did attend his daughter's events, or those of his wife, it was usually because there were contacts to be made, hands to be shook.

Bella woke up at their voices, demanded to know where Petra was, and flew out the door to the stables, the dogs on her heels. Alan had folded away his work into its briefcase and was standing with his back to the fireplace, his posture one of ease but his eyes not leaving Don.

For Alan detested his wife's son-in-law. It was a reaction Rae had witnessed the moment the two men had met, at the party after her wedding to Alan, although at the time she had not known her new husband long enough to be certain what his behavior meant. Only later did she learn that this was Alan's way of demonstrating that inexplicable, hackle-raising dislike some people trigger in others: an exaggerated politeness, unfailing attentiveness, a smile that did not crinkle the eyes, and an inability to relax when Don was in the room. Now, for example, Alan was politely inquiring about the business Don had conducted, the drive he had taken, and some football game that Rae would have bet Alan had never heard of until he brought it up.

Rae had never said anything to Alan about his visceral reaction, since Don was too self-contained to notice and Tamara too busy eyeing her mother for signs of instability, and because Alan never gave the least indication of wishing to avoid his wife's family. Over the years she had come to accept it as a chemical quirk, the precise opposite of the equally inexplicable urge that had bonded her to Alan in the first place. It was, at any event, not a matter that came up more than once or twice a year, since having both men at any gathering was a rarity.

The conversation sounded like a badly written play, formal and of no interest to any of the parties. Rae assembled the salad, Alan stood with his hands clasped behind his back like a soldier, Don dropped into a chair with his second drink, answering their remarks and queries in monosyllables. Alan was beginning to flag when finally the girls burst in, Petra's horse groomed and settled, its human caregivers more than ready for their own feed.

Bella had recently had it explained to her that she was actually Petra's aunt, despite being three years the junior. The discovery delighted her, and as the two girls came in the kitchen door, trailing dogs and wisps of hay and the smell of horses, Petra was good-naturedly calling Bella "Auntie." Then she spotted Rae standing at the stove, and in three giant steps of her riding boots the child's arms were wrapped around her grandmother's ribs. Except for the gray in Rae's hair, the two could have been mother and daughter—the same coloring, same bones, and the child showing signs of adult height. Rae squeezed Petra back, exclaiming that the girl had grown another inch since summer. She had also, Rae saw when they stepped away from each other, the first intimations of maturity in her face, the loss of a layer of subcutaneous childhood as her bones had stretched up.

"You look beautiful," she told Petra, whose face twisted in a scornful dismissal of her grandmother's absurdity.

Bella giggled. "She stinks," she declared loudly.

"She does a little," Rae had to agree with her daughter. "But it's a nice stink."

"Go change your clothes before you come down for dinner, Pet," Don told the young equestrian.

"Yes, Daddy," Petra said, subdued for a moment by his unvoiced disapproval, and told Rae, "Mom says to go ahead and start. She's just putting away the tack. Come on, Auntie Bella, let's go wash our hands."

Bella's giggle trailed out of the kitchen.

Rae did not look at Don. She was afraid that if she did, she would grab him by his well-starched collar and shout in his face, "Everyone in this whole damned family has been raised by disapproving adults. For God's sake don't do it to your daughter, too!" She bit her upper lip to keep the words in, knowing by bitter experience what the repercussions would be, that evening and in the weeks ahead. She would not be the one to set off a violent quarrel this time—and anyway, Don, the actual target, would contrive to slide away, leaving the field of battle to his willing wife.

But Rae's heart ached for Petra's winces, remembered all too well the blindly cruel remarks of authority: Grandfather supposing a B was only to be expected when Rae had been placed in a class of top students; that the son of a department store owner was probably the best Rae could hope for, considering her history; that . . .

To be fair, most of the time Petra got along considerably better with Don Collins than Rae had with William Newborn. She seemed to accept that Don was not to be relied on for much except an amiable and distracted good cheer—except when he was openly thwarted, cornered into a position of having either to give in or to attack. Then he could be vicious—not physically violent, not that Rae had seen, but capable of a clever and devastating revenge. One walked quietly around Don on the rare occasions when he was truly angry.

But Petra seemed to know this, for up to now the child's need to push back had only been directed against her mother. Rae had raged against her father's spinelessness in the face of William's authority; Petra, on the other hand, patted her father on his well-groomed head and went her own way.

Petra was a different person from her grandmother, Rae reminded herself firmly. For which promise Rae rejoiced. She and Tamara both watched the child fearfully for any signs of inherited instability, and the mere fact that neither had glimpsed any reassured neither of them. Adolescence would be the test.

Rae had never asked Tamara why she had named her daughter Petra. She did not really have to: Conscious or not, the choice of Petra's name was a bid for rocklike stability in the next generation, a plea that the house of Collins be built of sterner stuff than that of Newborn.

When the girls returned, glistening and smelling of soap, Rae put food on the table (the scrubbed-pine kitchen table, not the ghastly over-polished mahogany in the formal dining room). She served up and they began eating, with Petra's excitement about the day and the ribbons she had won carrying them on, until the back door opened. Tamara walked in, and ice settled down on the gathering.

One glance, and Rae's stomach clenched. What on earth had she done now, to provoke that expression on Tamara's face? She had no doubt she was the cause; even Don's transgressions did not earn quite that same look.

Tamara passed through the kitchen wordlessly. When she came back, washed and changed, Petra shot her one sharp sideways glance and immediately asked if she and Bella could be excused, please, so she could finish the story she'd been telling Bella. Tamara nodded, and the girls cleared their plates and slipped away upstairs. Rae wished she could be allowed to go with them, but instead she moved the salad around to Tamara's side and, because there was no point in avoiding it, she asked her daughter, "What's wrong?"

The tightening of lips was so like Grandfather it was eerie, the old man's ghost in that thirty-year-old woman. Utter disapproval, in a mere twitch.

"Bella tells me she was up on the shed roof with you today," Tamara said finally, not looking up from the precise transferal of pasta to plate. Rae felt Alan's eyes on her.

"Yes," she said steadily. "She wanted to help. Why?"

"Is that the safest thing in the world?"

"Alan was behind her the whole time. She couldn't have fallen, if that's what you're worried about."

"Alan was with her." Tamara was now concentrating on the sliced bread, choosing a piece with complete attention.

"We were both with her, Tamara. If there'd been a seven-point earth-quake while we were up there, she still wouldn't have fallen."

"I question your judgment."

So what else is new? Rae thought, and if it had been simply a matter of Bella's safety, she would have said it aloud and let Tamara explode in anger. But this was not really about Tamara's half-sister.

"You're talking about Petra, aren't you? Her visit next month?"

"If she comes to visit you" (it was "if" now, Rae heard, although Petra's stay had been settled for weeks) "I don't want to be worrying the whole time."

"Tamara, you'll worry no matter what, but I promise you I won't let Petra climb out on my roof." It was an effort to push the reasonable phrases past the tightening throat muscles, but essential. Insane mothers were not allowed to lose their tempers like other women. Madness was a Pandora's box: Its lid had to stay locked tight. Rae felt Alan stir, but he said nothing. Instead, it was Don who spoke up, dropping a small bombshell into their midst.

"Actually, Tam, I don't know if we're going to be able to afford your thing after all." Typical of Don, to use the offhand term "thing" to refer to a much-sought-after, weeklong Colorado workshop in an arcane variety of horse breaking, a workshop that Tamara's own income-generating summer classes were to be based upon. Tamara turned to gape at him, her fork suspended in mid-air. "I know you've sent in your deposit and all," he went on, "but it looks like money's going to be a little tight just now."

Tamara's "thing" was the very reason she had agreed to turn Petra over to her grandmother's care, since it could not be expected that Don might cope with full-time parenting for seven whole days. Both women began to speak, but their first words were swallowed by the loud scrape of Alan's chair and his industrious and noisy gathering of plates. His face remained expressionless.

Rae glanced at Tamara, saw the rage that she was trying to hide, and started again, trying not to sound desperate. "Tamara, I've been racking my brain for what to give you for Christmas. Let me give you the workshop, please. I know how you've been looking forward to it."

Now it was Don's turn to rise suddenly—not to help Alan, but to go back to the freezer and fill his glass, as if demonstrating how little interest he held in any decision. Tamara wavered. She was hungry to go, and had in fact arranged her spring and summer around the completion of the course; however, she was not only furious at Don, and unable to show it in front of her mother, but furthermore, accepting Rae's money had always been Don's business, not hers; never hers. Still, she badly wanted to go . . .

Rae tried to nudge her gently toward acceptance, without appearing too eager. "Call it a birthday present, too. I haven't given you anything fun in a long time."

It was the word "fun" that did it, Rae decided later. Fun was a commodity the hardworking Tamara found little time for. Tamara gave in, and thanked her with as much grace as she could muster. Don smiled into his glass, Alan slammed the dishes into the dishwasher, and Rae went out to the car for her checkbook.

Alan intercepted her outside the front door on her way back inside. Petra's voice in monologue drifted down from her upstairs bedroom, where by the sound of it she was either telling Bella about the day's events or, more likely, making up a story for her young auntie's entertainment.

"You do know he manipulated you into doing that?" Alan demanded.

"Of course I do, sweetheart. It's what Don always does. And if it makes him feel clever, who am I to argue?" To Don, the cleverness was as important as the money. They all knew that if they had flat out asked Rae for money, she would have given it. But doing so would have left a bad taste in both Tamara's mouth and Don's, for slightly different reasons. "Let it be," Rae said. She kissed him on the cheek, and went back to take her seat at the kitchen table.

"How much is it?" she asked Tamara.

"Nine thousand."

"Nine—"

"And the thousand deposit," Don contributed helpfully, studying the overhead lamp. Tamara opened her mouth to speak. "And airfare," he added. Tamara's mouth hung open for a moment longer, then closed.

At Don's casual words Alan, back at the sink, made a noise that might have been a cough but which Rae knew for a snort. Good; he was able to see the humor in it.

She looked over at Don. "Fifteen thousand ought to do it, then?" she asked sweetly.

Again Tamara started to protest, but Don moved to squelch it. "That'd give her a little to buy books and some of their specialized equipment. Very nice of you, Rae."

Rae had no doubt, from her daughter's reaction, that the original sum Tamara had stated was all-inclusive, and she knew she should be outraged at Don's blatant sticky fingers. Another time, she might be, but today she was merely amused at the transparency of his greed. The man had no shame. Of course, if Don were stingy with Petra and Tamara, she might have put her foot down, but she knew that his self-respect included keeping his wife and daughter in all the comfort anyone's money could buy. There was nothing Rae could say that might make things better, so that was what she said: nothing. She merely wrote out a check for fifteen thousand dollars and slid it across the table to Tamara, taking care not to meet her daughter's eyes lest contact bring forth a confession.

They left shortly after that, since Alan had a class the next morning. When Bella's snores came from the back, Alan, at the wheel, said to Rae, "Are you all right, sweetheart?"

Tears had been trickling down her cheeks for the last couple of miles, and he knew that, although he had not looked away from the road ahead and she had neither sniffled nor wiped her eyes. He always knew.

"It's just so sad, Tamara's situation. Such a lot of games she puts herself through. It takes all her strength to stay convinced that she's not her mother: *I* don't need counseling; *my* marriage isn't in trouble; *I* don't have any problems with my daughter. She learned more than horsemanship from David's mother—denial was that woman's middle name. And I worry about Petra in a few years, when she starts to demand her independence. It won't be long—she's already getting that look on her face when her mother talks to her."

"Petra seems a remarkably well-balanced child," Alan protested mildly.

"So did I at that age," Rae retorted.

After a moment, he intoned, "Said she, ominously."

Rae had to laugh at that. She blew her nose and laid her hand on his thigh, where he covered it for a moment with his own before putting his back on the wheel. They traveled in amity through the night. Ten miles later, Alan spoke again.

"You have to wonder if this mighty effort of the white-coats in mapping the human genome will ever lead to any real understanding of the human being, beyond the mere mechanics. Where do characteristics come from, things like stubbornness and a disdain for convention?"

"Are you talking about Tamara and Don, or Rory?" Alan's son, an enigma to his father: witty, intelligent, enormously energetic when it came to avoiding work, his charmer's sparkle masking his utterly amoral nature. A born con-man, Alan had called Rory once in half-admiring sorrow, just after he'd told his only son that he was no longer welcome in their house. Bella was two, and Rae had caught Rory pocketing an antique silver rattle that had belonged to Rae's grandmother Lacy, an object valuable both in money and in memories. Alan still saw him from time to time, but Rae hadn't laid eyes on Rory since that afternoon.

"Both, I suppose. I mean, say the scientists do isolate the scrap of protein that makes a man a rogue. What happens if you eliminate it? No more rogues, but do we also find we've eliminated ruthlessness in mathematicians and inventors and artists as well?"

It was Alan's kind of conversation, the academic's search for meaning in any field. Rae replied, "I was thinking this evening about how like Tamara is to my grandfather William. Physically she resembles my grandmother, but in personality—talk about ruthlessness."

"And yet Petra shows no sign of it."

"She doesn't, does she? Petra the Rock. Maybe it's like a double negative—when it comes from both sides the two doses cancel each other out."

"And she does have the honest love of both parents, no matter their other problems. Who knows what your grandfather's childhood was like, to shape him that way."

Rae knew full well what Tamara's childhood had been like, and it would support Alan's thesis of nurture's preeminence. "William's mother was indeed a tyrant, by all accounts."

Neither of them made mention of the true subject of their thoughts, serenely dozing in the back.

They drove on through the night toward their hilltop home, deep in the woods. The next morning, with Alan running late (as usual) for his first lecture, she would gather her tool belt up in a hasty armload of damp swimsuits and leftover roofing material and sling it on its hook just inside her shop door. There the belt would hang, gathering dust, three galvanized roofing nails overlooked in its pouch, for seventeen months while Rae's world ended and slowly remade itself.

Three overlooked nails: last remnants of a family's happiness.

Rae looked from the nails resting in the palm of her hand to the laminated photograph of a man with a door latch in his, then up at the tree trunk on which she intended to mount the picture. Instead, she laid the photo down on the workbench and knelt on the ground to drive the three nails in a straight line along the edge of the bench, in the center of what had originally been the upper edge of the door. Their dusty gray finish was oddly similar to that of the driftwood below, three metallic circles surrounded by rich dark wood. They looked like a Braille message, put there for those in the know to decipher, like the dots on an elevator's control panel. She ran her thumb over them to confirm that they were uniformly flush against the wood, feeling the rough surface against the freshly planed wood. Then she went off to find another nail to use in mounting the picture of Uncle Desmond and his house.

Twelve

Desmond Newborn's
Journal

October 22, 1923

To my amusement, I have discovered that I am greatly more suited to the life of a hired man than I am to the role of overseer, my once-soft hands more fitted to the pickaxe than the pen. A university man am I, younger son of a tycoon, who should be growing a belly behind a desk and conversing with Cabots and Lodges, yet here I stand with a mason's trowel in my hand, speaking only to God.

"Stand" is hardly accurate at this very moment, and if I have spoken to the Almighty today, it was in terms so unflattering, He would have to be All-forgiving indeed to have answered me with anything less than a bolt of lightning.

I broke my foot this morning. Not too badly, thank the much-maligned Divinity, but when the swelling goes down I fear one of the bones along the top will creak and groan, and I shall be reduced to a hobble for some time.

My first act, after I had removed the rock from my extremity, cursed God and all his lithic creations, and pried the boot from my wounded member, was to cut a sturdy branch with a convenient crook from the madrone tree and trim it to fit beneath my arm.

Despite this setback, when I took up this journal to write the first entry in months, I discovered that I am quite ridiculously pleased with life.

Some of my happy delirium, I admit, may have more to do with the liquid pain relief of which I have partaken than with my contentment with my current life. Some may even be the spectacular sunset which the Almighty has laid out at my wounded feet, where I sit out on my finger of rock in the sea, and the intoxication of those colors that no painter has captured. But beneath those passing joys lies the deeper one of a man who has discovered his true purpose on this sorry globe.

I am a builder.

Not a builder of grand houses and factories like my brother William, but the builder of a house, this house, as yet little more than wax pen outlines on naked rock. The shape of it was imprinted on me, as if from birth, so clearly has it grown up before my eyes: towers that reach for the sky, a deep foundation that settles firmly into the earth, and a dwelling between, strong yet light, like the trees from which it will be made, like the native peoples who trod softly but firmly on this land before me, leaving behind a few subtle artifacts and images.

And sitting beneath this sky tonight, with the strip of black island to the west to separate the deepening oranges and blues of the sky above from the sparkling oranges and blues mirrored on the water below, I begin to see that my towers will do more than reach for the sky.

Had I not been forced to flee Boston by my sins, had I not gone to soldier, I would never have found this skill in my hands. I would have become my brother, grumbling behind his desk, dying there.

So now I speak to God, not to rail and curse, but to thank.

This is a blessed place, broken foot and all.

Thirteen

With the vegetation decimated and the jungle inside the stones reduced to a trampled expanse of mud, Rae could now begin to dig out the foundation, hauling away seven decades' worth of fallen rock, composted leaves, and the decayed remains of floor and furniture, siding and shingles. It made for a rich soil but brutal work, shoveling the wet debris into her heavy, high-sided builder's barrow and wrestling it out of the foundation and off to the future vegetable patch. It took just a couple of trips for her to realize that she would only be able to manage three or four hours of it before her back started to scream at her and the bone and muscles of her left arm grew too painful. The afternoons she would have to dedicate to other labor.

This morning, once Desmond's photograph was on the tree, she rattled her barrow over to what would be the crawl space beneath the floorboards, then ran it up the bouncing ramp she had fashioned the day before out of 2x10s. Once up and over the foundation stones, she pulled on her work gloves and reached for the shovel, sinking its head deep into an undisturbed heap of fallen rock and the softer stuff below.

One of the questions whose solution Rae had most anticipated was the discovery of just how much Desmond had left behind him in the house, whether he had abandoned a bare shell (the front door, after all, seemed to have no lock) or if she would uncover some remnants of his life there. She could not hope for photographs or papers, and it was doubtful that she would encounter even scraps of his furniture, but the odd coin or cracked Mason jar, or some of those peculiar rusted lumps uncovered in garden beds and displayed in small museums—that sort of thing was surely not out of the question.

With that in mind, Rae had included in her endless lists (compulsive, Dr. Hunt had called them reprovingly—but then The Hunter had never built a house) a quantity of heavy-gauge wire mesh in order to sieve the soil before it went into the future garden—which would also save the future gardener's fingers, since there was bound to be glass and nails aplenty. She positioned the sieve frame over the deep barrow and set to shoveling.

Her first shovelful gave her only rotted leaves, her second a couple of nails, but the third time her blade went into the soil it gave a hollow thump and yielded a six-inch-tall brass vase. The incongruity of the find made her laugh aloud. What on earth was a bachelor pioneer doing with a brass flower vase? It would never hold water again, but with a chemical polish and a bunch of dried grasses in it, she could use it in her house. She set it aside atop the foundation wall, and returned to her domestic archaeology.

Over the next three days she found her coins and her Mason jar, along with a plenitude of peculiar rusted lumps. She also discovered the location of Desmond's kitchen (in the northeast corner between the fireplace and the rear tower, marked by the handle of a spotted enamel coffeepot, one saucepan, a clot of fused silverware, a mass of broken plates, and one cast-iron skillet, red with rust) and the pantry behind it (several canning jars, all of them broken, and the lacelike remains of some food tins). She found his library to have been along the northwest wall, although nothing remained but a few scorched leather covers. He'd had a comfortable chair in front of the fireplace, whose brass feet and iron springs she encountered; the ivory pipe stem buried nearby evoked a homey image of Desmond at rest, reading a book with pipe in hand and a glass of Prohibition whiskey nearby. In the same area she found a fountain pen, cap fused to one end and incongruously shiny gold nib at the other, along with a dented brass candleholder with a loop for the finger, a smashed glass and an intact (but uncapped) whiskey bottle, a handful of porcelain that closely resembled a cup and saucer handed down from her grandmother's wedding set, and the leather scraps of a pair of boots. She began to keep notes of what she found and where, and writing them up one evening decided that the upper floor had held his bed (an entire metal bedframe, matted with the roots of the tree she'd dug out, that had held a pad of some stuff packed too tightly to burn, now thoroughly rotted) and his wardrobe (two more leather boot soles, one gold cuff link, and some horn buttons). Finally, to her pleasure, she found his tool cache, fallen from the upstairs north wall. A badly pitted saw blade came up with one shovelful, and in the next a hammer—just the head, worn and old-fashioned in shape, but making her feel as if Desmond himself had greeted her. She decided to mount both saw and hammer (giving both of them new handles) over her mantelpiece, once the house was restored.

The work itself, aside from the physical demands, she found satisfyingly mindless, a matter of skilled muscles left to do their labor, with the occasional return to full attention when the sieve turned up something more interesting than the ton of thick, viciously sharp window glass or the thousands of rusty, hand-forged square nails she was collecting in buckets. Shovel, sieve; shovel, sieve; and when the wheelbarrow was as full as she cared to handle, down went the shovel while she pulled the barrow back from the sifting frame, ran with it at the ramp to the top of the foundation wall, and then, slowing, let its weight pull her down the other side of the ramp and around the hill on the track she was rapidly beating to the future garden. Every third or fourth load she stopped, eased her spine, and drank a glass of water or cold tea. She would survey her domain, its growing disorder in the piles of soil and the bags of garbage and the raw stones of the foundation that were emerging where nature had once reigned uncontested. When her glass was empty and her vertebrae more or less in line, she would return to her rectangular stone enclosure and to the sounds of shovel scraping against stone, soil raining down onto soil, breeze and waves and birds in the trees and the occasional plane overhead.

The labor was long, mindless, apparently never-ending, and, she was beginning to understand, absolutely vital to her continued presence here. Not only did the day's exhaustion take the edge off the night noises (and why had she ever imagined that the island was empty, or even peaceful? Folly was a 145-acre organism, endlessly restless, its parts snuffling through the leaves and branches at all hours of the day and night), but the work gave her a point of focus, distracting her from the sense of Watchers and the fear of returning voices. Concentrating on the job at hand, in all its filthy tedium, let the edges of her mind grow used to their surroundings, identifying and accepting the night scrabbles of raccoon and mouse, the day noises of drumming woodpecker or screaming raven, becoming aware without being hypersensitive to threat. The low hum of bees working the first madrone flowers, the zip of the hummingbird, even the distant whine of neighboring chain saws were all familiar noises, lulling her into something resembling complacency. The creatures, similarly, were becoming accustomed to her, the red squirrel around her tent no longer scolding every move, the harbor seals no longer bothering to take to the water when she approached.

Yesterday, as proof of her growing imperviousness to intruders, she had taken three trips back and forth to the tent before she realized that there was a Watcher in the vicinity, that she'd been feeling eyes on the back of her neck for ten minutes. The sensation was one she'd felt a number of times over the previous days, albeit briefly, since neither squirrel nor blue jay was capable of looking on in silence for very long. The space between her shoulder blades began to crawl and her hand went to the hammer on her belt, but she did not panic. She searched the shrubs, the bank of dark leathery green near the ground and the delicate unfolding green of the maples above, and found nothing. It wasn't until she had rotated three complete circles and was searching the high ground that she spotted her Watcher: a bald eagle, the world's most glorious scavenger, perched in the upper branch of a cedar, studying her closely. Rae laughed in relief, and turned her back on him without a qualm.

With her fears distracted and under the autopilot of physical work, Rae's mind was free to range at its will, and as she worked she would mull over things she'd been either too preoccupied or too drugged to wrestle with until recent weeks. It was stream-of-consciousness with no therapist to interrupt, no fifty-minute time limit, no external force to interfere with its flow.

Rae picked from her archaeologist's sieve a once-silver spoon—or rather, a twist of blackened silver that had once been spoon-shaped—and wondered what story Petra would spin from it. From there her thoughts went to the letter from the child that Ed had brought her two days before.

She could tell that her granddaughter had worked long and hard on the thing, her clever thirteen-year-old mind shaping an argument as if she might thereby shape her world. Three quarters of the long letter (composed on her computer, as all business proposals should be) concerned a long-term history assignment Petra had for school, which she was thinking of doing on the history of Folly.

Rae had no doubt that Petra's teacher would be overjoyed at the student's initiative. However, at the tail of Petra's somewhat rambling description of the assignment's requirements and how she figured she could meet them, the girl threw in the stinger: She *really* needed to spend some time on the island herself, and although it was too late for Easter vacation, this project could, if the student wished, form the basis for an eighth-grade project. And so a stay over the summer would do just as well.

So could Rae *please* write to Petra's mother and talk her into it?

Rae tossed the spoon-shaped object into the "save" bucket, scraped half a pound of thick window-glass fragments into the bucket marked "sharp," and wondered if army records still existed for that long ago, and if so, who might be asked to lay hands on them. No family letters had survived either from or to Desmond, and as far as she knew, the scanty mentions in Lacy's diary were the only references to Desmond in the handful of family diaries kept by his or his parents' generation.

Had Desmond settled in Seattle, she meditated, there might have been a newspaper reference to him, coming as he did from a relatively well-known Eastern family, but she didn't even know if there had been a local San Juan paper in the Twenties. Maybe Ed would know, or could find out for her.

A Zen koan: A hermit's cabin burns down in the woods; does anyone hear but the trees?

Certainly, Rae reflected as she raised her arms to scrape the shovel blade down along the stones of the northwest corner, Desmond had not stayed on here after the fire, not unless he'd lived back in the woods. There was no sign of any earlier attempt to clear away the fire-blackened remnants and start again.

Desmond had, apparently, taken to wandering again, only to die, friendless and alone, somewhere in the West. That was what Rae had been told long ago, when her continuing curiosity about the family's black sheep drove her to bypass Grandfather William and press her father about Desmond's fate. Although he claimed at first that he knew nothing about it, she kept at him until he admitted that he was not positive, since he'd been away at school at the time, but he thought a last letter had been received from Desmond not long before the Wall Street crash in 1929. After that, of course, everyone had been too busy coping with the disaster to bother with a wayward son, who no doubt now lay in a pauper's grave in New Mexico.

Rae paused to lean on her shovel, hearing the phrase "pauper's grave" clearly in her memory. It was one of the few conversations she remembered having with her father, and it had left her with the vivid image of a fresh, unmarked mound in a dry and dusty cemetery surrounded by crumbling adobe walls and overgrown with prickly cactus and tumbleweeds. It was a vision that had struck the adolescent she was as unutterably tragic, lonesome beyond words. She had, now that she thought about it, been just about Petra's age—and here she was proposing to infect another generation with this tragedy. Maybe Petra should be encouraged to do something else for her school project, she thought. As if Petra could be turned away from anything she'd set her mind to.

No, Petra would research the builder of Newborn's Folly, as Petra would try her damnedest to wangle her way here come June. Certain facts in the universe were unarguable. Rae could only hope that Petra's stubbornness did not backfire, and drive her parents to forbid any visit whatsoever. Or even worse, any contact.

In the unlikely event that Petra managed to cajole, bribe, or manipulate her parents into letting her visit Folly, it would not only affect Rae's plans during her granddaughter's stay but also over the intervening months: Unless Petra's startling new image, which involved near-black fingernail polish and raccoon-mask eye makeup, overcame the primal drive for cleanliness exhibited by every teenage girl Rae had ever met, in less than two months the owner of Folly was going to need a vastly more adequate water source than five-gallon plastic jugs. Roof be damned; what she'd need was a shower.

So between the future possibility of a visit from Petra and the current hard fact of a body that rebelled after three hours of hard digging, Rae decided to dedicate the afternoons to a different set of tools and a different group of muscles, working on the water line.

On Saturday she stopped digging well before noon, telling herself with satisfaction that one more morning ought to see a finish to it. She dumped the day's last load of sieved soil from the barrow, cleaned off her shovel in a bucket of oiled sand, carried the buckets of "sharp" and "save" to their respective caches, and finally went to scrub her hands and make some lunch. After she had eaten, she stretched out flat on the camp bed for ten minutes, rereading Petra's letter and thinking about her answer.

She would have to respond to her granddaughter before the *Orca Queen* came on Tuesday. She would also have to take considerable care with what she wrote.

Over the year of Rae's hospitalization, the balance of Tamara's marriage seemed to have shifted somewhat. Don's real estate deals had been getting even shadier, the expenses of house and stables and the grandiose entertainment of prospective customers and would-be investors had grown so that even Tamara seemed to be concerned, and although they were still holding the line, Rae wouldn't be at all surprised if the enterprise was resting on shaky foundations. Divorce had always been a disaster inflicted by irresponsible mothers onto their innocent families, and was thus for Tamara unthinkable, but frankly Rae didn't see how her daughter was going to continue keeping her life together. One more tremor—Tamara's falling ill, say, or an unfortunate inquiry into one of Don's murkier real estate deals— might well tumble the enterprise to the ground, taking the marriage with it.

All in all, however, Rae thought that the nexus for future problems might well be Petra. Going by their prickly attitudes on the trip here, and by asides in the child's letters, Petra and her mother appeared to be headed toward a difficult patch, going through the inevitable phase of the child's growing desire for independence, magnets in reversed polarity. In the brief time they had been together, from their meeting in Seattle to Ed's taking the other two off on his boat, there had been much rolling of eyes, several pregnant silences, and two brief but vicious skirmishes. Petra's troubles seemed to concentrate on Tamara, not Don— outright confrontation not being his style—but even he had been affected, and seemed unwilling to put up with much more. Tamara had admitted that Don was looking into special schools for Petra, the sorts of places that advertised in magazines as being for "troubled youth." Rae didn't think Petra qualified as troubled, aside from the normal troubles of her years and the state of her hormones. Indeed, considering her parents, and everything that had happened over the last year and a half, Rae thought Petra was doing remarkably well. Her curiosity and intelligence, her ability to rationally consider all options, make up her mind, and stand by her decision, and above all her ability to retain a degree of loyalty in the face of her parents' increasingly harsh, conflicting, and incomprehensible demands, made her a cuckoo in that nest. Sure, she painted her fingernails with colors named after bodily functions and her style of dress was somewhere between that of a street urchin and a skinhead, but she never disappeared without leaving a contact phone number, rarely received a grade below B, and to Rae's knowledge had never made more than the most token objections to the life of a young equestrian, uncool as it might be considered by her comrades-in-grunge. Tamara and Don seemed unable to look beyond the surface, but Rae had long thought her granddaughter one of the most sensible people she knew. During the day she had spent with Petra and Tamara coming here, Rae had caught herself thinking of Petra as the daughter she should have had.

Petra was, quite simply, central to Rae's life. Petra was all Rae had left. The mere suggestion of having to do without her was unbearable. Rae had lost Alan and Bella, she had driven away most of her friends, she might never do any serious work again; to add Petra's loss to that would be the final blow.

All in all, she reflected, little Petra was the meeting point of any number of awkward situations. Even before Rae's last breakdown, Tamara had taken great care to keep her mother from having too much influence on her child. More than once, even with Alan present, Rae had felt as if she were some untrustworthy suitor having to outflank a suspicious and protective family. The whole business of having to buy Tamara (and Don) an expensive vacation in order to have Petra to herself for a few days was typical. Now, moreover, Petra seemed instinctively to grasp the undercurrents; on the ferry, around her mother, she had hid some of the affection she felt for her mad grandmother, as if she knew that an interest in that direction would be considered unhealthy. Rae guiltily discouraged Petra's duplicity, and steadfastly refused to take sides openly against Tamara and Don: She would give the child no conflict to her love for and loyalty to her parents. Nonetheless, Petra's affection—the solid fact that Rae could depend on that affection—created a warm glow within. Yes, in truth Petra was all Rae had left.

And so Rae would have to be very careful what she said in response to the letter.

Rae got up and laid Petra's missive back on the desk, then changed her sweat-soaked T-shirt for longer sleeves that would protect her skin from snatching branches, picked up the other set of tools, and set off to climb the hill she had begun to call Mount Desmond.

The gentle, steady spring that Desmond Newborn had cleverly diverted as his water source was up on the side of Mount Desmond, a third of the way around the island. The cedar water troughs that he had hollowed out, fitted together, and covered had been marvelously tight and had probably carried water to the now-defunct storage tank above the house for thirty or forty years, but after nearly eighty, there was just enough left of the water line to indicate the skill of its builder.

Rae would have dearly loved to repeat his laborious, demanding woodworker's technique—just as she would have loved to build her house by felling her own trees, milling her own lumber, splitting her own shakes. Her original dream, coming like a shaft of light into her deeply depressed mind, had in fact been just that: a log cabin in the wilderness, honest to the point of starkness, caulked snug with moss and mud, hewn with implements that carried weighty and ancient names such as *adze* and *peevee* and *double-bitted axe*. She had pictured a traditional Native American longhouse, low and windowless, built of thick cedar planks, with a carved totem pole standing in front. An ideal place for a potlatch, the ultimate community bond.

Later, weeks later, with shock therapy giving way to long sessions with The Hunter and the bleak and unrelieved terrain of black depression giving way to an interior landscape possessing at least a faint trace of green, Rae had come to decide that such extreme purity of purpose was unnecessary. Human beings are not, after all, dropped down upon a darkling plain with no tools, no companionship, no aid; indeed, working with materials and on foundations made by others was a more accurate description of human progress, individual or collective, than *creatio ex nihilo*. As a woodworker Rae used power saws and mechanical routers, commercial plywood and modern glues and finishes. It would not negate her purpose, using the present to rebuild the past, if she were to use Desmond's site and foundations to support her own creation, or even to top Desmond's mossy hand-laid stones with walls built of commercially milled lumber.

And in the case of the water supply, pipes made of polyvinyl chloride.

Rae climbed back to where she was working the day before, following the black and spongy remnants of Desmond's handiwork. He had been painstaking in his preparation of the ground and his choice of route, and after two days of testing with her spirit level, she had decided to trust to his engineering for the most economical pathway from A to B, source to house—hauling the four-foot level through the trees was a pain. Now she was mapping out her needs, so as to give Ed an order for the PVC pipe and angle joins she would need. Desmond's joins, having all been carved to serve the needs of the moment, rarely agreed with the angles of the plastic fittings available to his grandniece from the plumbing supply shop in Friday Harbor (or anywhere else, for that matter, in this world of uniform sizes) and the most fiddly part of her work would be to compensate for the differences in path this would necessitate, when for example his hand-fashioned join of fifty-two degrees caused the waterway to wrap neatly around a deeply rooted boulder, whereas her standard forty-five-degree-angle joint meant overshooting his path and running over uneven ground until it could be eased back up to his again.

It was not unsatisfying work, however, despite the frustration and the lingering urge to imitate Desmond's techniques and thereby commit herself to a solid six-month job of building the pipeline out of cedar logs. She pushed away the temptation, reminding herself how delicious a long shower would feel at the end of a day of work, and continued with her tape measure and notebook.

A couple of hours later, she ran into the snag she had feared she might the first time she had walked the line. Her rigid angles trapped her between the choice of digging out (or blowing up) a depressingly large rock and having to build a long stretch of raised supports over a deep and treacherous gully. Even the native flexibility of the pipe would not get her around the corner, not without bending it to the breaking point. She finally sat back and studied the jumble, through which the wood-chip trail of Desmond's rotted waterline blithely wove, mocking her attempts at adapting uniformity to a natural phenomenon.

"Hell," she said, and laid down her tape measure. One thing life as an artist had taught her: Sometimes one had to walk away from a problem in order to see it right. She would try, quite literally, to approach this one from another angle.

Rae set off straight up the side of Mount Desmond, shoving her way through salal and huckleberry, watching carefully for insecure footings in the rocky soil. She couldn't remember after all this time just how she and Alan had found their way to the top, but supposed there must have been a path worn by the island's tiny black-tailed deer. The going was not too difficult, and she gained the clear top, blown and sweat-soaked but without having lost too much blood along the way.

The top of the mountain was, unlike most things seen through hindsight, even larger than she remembered it from five years before, a wind-scoured knob bald but for a few stunted trees and tufts of grass. She clambered up the last hillock, and her eyes were suddenly drawn to a slight unevenness in the overall rock, a bump. She had forgotten; how could she have forgotten? *The Peak,* Alan had declared it, years ago. *The Height of Folly.* He'd made a flag to plant on it, with a stick and Bella's handkerchief, propping it upright with a handful of rocks: *We claim this island in the name of King Desmond the First, Lord of Misrule.* The rocks were still there, scattered around the bump. Rae picked one up, cupping it in her hand. Alan. *Bella,* he said, *have you ever played King of the Castle? and the flag came down and the rocks scattered, and we all took turns shoving each other off The Peak, claiming possession of what Alan called the island's moral high ground . . .*

High ground was a lump about a yard square, tilting to a height of about eighteen inches above the rest of the summit. Rae kept her head lowered, looking only at the rock between her feet, and stepped onto the rise. Only then did she throw back her head to look out. There, due east, rising just above Orcas Island's Mount Moran, stood Mount Baker, floating white above the mainland. Farther south loomed the pale bulk of Mount Rainier, vastly superior in all ways and knowing it. Rae turned around slowly, and the other islands came into view, with the edge of Puget Sound over the top of San Juan and the snowcapped wall of the Olympic range rising in the distance like a shark's jaw. Then came Juan de Fuca and Haro Straits, followed by long, dark Vancouver Island, with its smaller neighbors laid across the water as perfectly random as stones across a Japanese pond. Closer to home, Stuart and Speiden, and finally a full circle, with Mount Baker again before her.

This was by no means the highest point in the San Juan chain, but it was the highest this far west. On a clear day like this the dark bulks of the freighters seemed close enough to step onto, and she felt that, had it not been for the unending breeze, she could have heard the slap of the motorboat that was laying a white trail across the placid blue surface. A large bird—eagle? vulture?—cruised the air currents below her, sliding off toward the blue-gray rise of San Juan. A few sailboats had ventured out of Roche Harbor for the day, harbingers of the summer masses.

Rae stood on her height and breathed in her surroundings, rapt with the glory of the day in the exquisite beauty of this place, and with the simple, rare, everyday, in-spite-of-everything joy of being alive. A terrible joy, sweet as the sunshine and cruel as the grave, to stand here with the breeze touching her face, alone, forever. The view at her feet was so beautiful it made the heart ache, and if there was darkness at the edge of her vision, it made the snow and the sea all the brighter. She smiled, sadly, at the echoes of a family's silliness, and after a moment tossed the small stone she held back to join the others. Then she stepped down from her position of superiority to go look for the remnants of the small building Alan had discovered and judged a World War II lookout tower. All she could find were a few scraps of broken board, which surprised her a bit until she thought of the fierce winds the top must see. She'd probably find the wood scattered all the way down the side of Mount Desmond. Too bad; Petra could have used a photograph of the debris for her school project. The mountain itself would have to do.

Rae took a last glance at the Height of Folly and crossed the clear space to the western edge, the wind in her hair and the sun on her face as she studied the descending hillside. The spring was not far from a tall Douglas fir that had long ago been struck by lightning and split, growing again in bifurcation. She ought to be able to see it from here—and there it was, rising clearly above the rest a few hundred yards straight down the hill.

A few hundred yards straight downhill worked out to considerably more in the circuitous route Rae was forced to take, but she never lost the tree completely, and eventually she was standing at its base. She paused to take a drink from the flask of bottled water she had brought, and stood listening for the sound of water. When she could make it out, she pushed through the undergrowth to the spring itself.

The water seepage that made Newborn's Folly habitable was a younger, less saline brother to the warm waters of Salt Springs Island to the northeast. Rae's spring did actually come out of the hill tepid enough for comfortable bathing, and the first of the pools was just large enough for a floating body—had she been willing to hike halfway around the island for the privilege of washing in the same water she intended to drink. If the spring's temperature had actually been hot, she might have been tempted, but she was grateful enough for its steady flow, cool or hot.

The water welled up from a layer of sandstone that rose from the sea at a seventy-degree angle, sandwiched between igneous rock, cross sections of the land's stressful geological history. The more porous stone purified the water, and the first pool, which looked as if it had been enlarged by human hands long before Desmond Newborn came on the scene, was a clear, tepid bowl overhung by branches. There had been a layer of mud on the bottom when Rae first came up here to get a sample of water for testing, and she had slopped some of it out to see if the pool stayed clean. It had.

There was no one clear hole in the source stone, just a series of oozes and trickles that added up to a decent-sized stream, now making its way down to the sea in the old, natural course it had followed before Desmond diverted it. Rae intended to use only a part of the water, since taking all of it off again might kill the strip of vegetation dependent on its flow. It would take a lot of tinkering, but tinkering was one thing Rae Newborn was good at.

She rolled up the sleeves of her shirt and knelt down beside the pool to wash her face and arms. She sat back on her knees with her eyes closed, smelling the wetness, hearing the gentle rhythm of the falling water. It sounded like Bella's breath, that childish half-snore in the back of the throat, more a texture than a noise.

Rae had known a sculptor some years ago, long before miniature fountains had become all the rage for executive desks and middle-class coffee tables, who had used water as a medium to combine the sculptural and the organic. Three of his works—aesthetic experiments, he called them—involved the slow welling-up of water into a bowl with perfect, precision-ground edges. The level gradually rose, to the edges and above, the surface tension holding it, quivering and alive as if it might be a substance far more complex than water, until finally the tension became too great and the liquid collapsed in a gush down the sides of the bowl and the next cycle began.

The spring had no such dramatic climax to its upwelling, but the water seemed every bit as alive as that in the sculptor's artificial pools, and infinitely more mysterious. Moisture oozed, coalesced into drips, joined together in tiny streams along the mossy rock face, and on the far end of the smaller second pool burbled away down the hill between ferns and roots and new spring growth.

It was a hidden place, as springs should be, quiet and secret and gentle, a place of maternal strength. Its only violation until now had been Desmond's water trough, and even that had been shaped by careful hands from wood that grew out of the same piece of earth that the spring did. Her own harsh PVC would have to be buried, she realized suddenly; otherwise she could never bear to come here. Even thinking about her water source—the island's wellspring—would make her feel guilty.

And now that she thought about it, burying her ugly white pipe for the first hundred yards might also solve the problem she had with the incompatibility of her angle joins and Desmond's route, since dropping it even a foot into the soil would mean shifting the route as much as a yard uphill in order to keep the actual level of water in the pipes the same. Desmond's line came off the bottom of the pool; if she drew from farther up, deepening it a few inches with her pick, she could compensate. If, that is, the ground between here and the problematic join proved soft enough to dig.

Laying it out in her mind, picturing the area uphill from Desmond's line, Rae thought it might just work. There was one area of rock, but that was the sandstone, and although it made her shoulders ache just thinking of the job, she thought it doable. Just.

It was ironic, thinking of this place in terms of picks and shovels and plastic pipes. It was one of the most peaceful and undisturbed places she had found, as if the earth's basic purity welled up along with the water. Fern fronds thrust their heads up from a patch of earth, and she knew that salamanders and frogs would be hiding among the stones. Petra would love this place; Rae could imagine her granddaughter hunched over here, tracking the course of a dragonfly, feeling the magic of the place seep into her adolescent bones, giving rise to flights of imagination. Rae smiled to herself, and cupped a last palmful of the untested water from the pool. This time she sucked it in, chewing on the mouthful of liquid as if it were nourishment. It tasted like water used to, laden with minerals and the essence of the earth. She could only hope the flavor would survive the trip downhill.

With a last glance at the bed of soft mosses and taut fiddleheads, Rae laid her wet hand, fingers splayed, on the soft ground preparatory to standing up. That was when she saw it: a sharp indentation no larger than her thumb, directly in front of her fingers, caught in the slanting afternoon sun: a mark that had no business here, gouged into the soft ground at the side of her water source.

The mark of a stranger's boot.

Fourteen

Rae's Journal

Bad.

    Very bad.

    Thorazine, lithium, Prozac, I don't have anything. I looked through the bottles to see but there's nothing, not even powder at the bottom, and alcohol cools the trembling but my pulse is, Jesus, 120? 140? My heart's going to explode or my head is, God I'd take lithium even if it turns my blood to cold mud, makes me slow and clumsy and stupid and defenseless, weak and exposed, old and helpless, dull and

    Oh, bad, bad. Voices scratching at my ears, not the wind, not the waves, not the trickle of dirt from the hill trying to cover up the foundation again, not the worm in the soil or the deer in the brush but voices, nagging and teasing and laughing at me and telling me what they're going to

    bad this time, and cold.

    bad

    cold

    shivering

    drymouthed heartracing

    can't sit still

    skin itching

    bugs under my skin, crawling there

    Oh God, oh Hunter, I'm sorry, this was wrong, I was wrong. I brought along a gun, Hunter, a smooth, well-made

    handgun

pistol
revolver
with a wooden handle stock that is
delicious
smooth
worn
and it's sitting on my desk with me right now, sitting
hard
strong
heavy
next to this journal, the end of the barrel holding the left edge of the
journal open (see the dent?) with my hand
covering it
holding it
warming it
while my right hand writes these words, makes these lists and I list
to the left and I list to the right and to the port and starboard and if I
had any port I'd drink that with my right hand the woodwright/the
wordwright and at my left hand the gun, and between them in a tri-
angle/the top of a triangle formed by right and left and words and gun
stands a tight little forest of six smooth phallic bullets, beautiful smooth
pieces of brass and lead and I'm sorry
Dr. Hunt
Roberta
Hunter After Truth
I'm so sorry but there was a footprint near the spring and I'm tired,
tired and
tired
lonely
alone
afraid
small
weak
tired
tired
tired
afraid

Fifteen

It was Petra, all unknowing and innocently asleep in her bed a thousand miles to the south, who reached out a hand and kept her grandmother from sliding the bullets into their chambers.

I'm sorry, Rae had written, knowing that Roberta Hunt would read the journal, but when she wrote the words, she seemed to hear herself say them, and suddenly she was wrenched back to winter the year before, to the first week of February, looking up into Petra's horrified, tear-streaked face and telling the child, "I'm sorry, I'm so sorry."

The dates had taken on a luminosity in the calendar of Rae's memory, a counting-down of days.

November 1: repairing Tamara's roof with Alan and Bella.

November 25: Thanksgiving dinner at a friend's beach house: children running, fragrant turkey roasting, cold sea air with the taste of wine on Alan's mouth and wood smoke in his hair.

December 3: finishing Bella's present, an intricate inlaid box bristling with secret drawers.

December 11: Alan's last class, his grade sheet turned in, home now.

December 12: the world came to an end.

A middle-aged real estate broker with a cell phone in one hand and the remnants of a well-lubricated Christmas party singing through his blood. Alan was killed instantly. Bella died twenty-four hours later, or so they told her; Rae did not know it for a couple of days. Rae was in surgery for five hours to piece together the smashed left arm, the torn flesh of her left breast and shoulder, the hairline fracture of the left jawbone, all injuries given her—cruelest of ironies—by Alan, some fluke of air bags, seat belts, and the driver's-side impact that had flung her husband's beloved body into her. His glasses had shattered against her chest. His skull had smashed her raised forearm. A later surgeon found a piece of his front tooth buried in Rae's shoulder.

If Bella had screamed one last terrified *Mommy!* it was wiped from Rae's memory. Or perhaps not entirely: Maybe it was the echo of that cry that came to her beneath the rain and in her moments of awakening.

Five days in the alien world of an intensive care ward at Christmas, a place that even Rae's mind registered as bizarre (the grimly cheerful tinsel swags on the monitors still appeared in her nightmares), followed by two weeks in a private room, then nine more days under the care of Tamara's series of round-the-clock nurses before Rae could pull together sufficient energy to throw them out. All these health professionals saw only the expected battering of the bereaved; not one of them looked deep enough to notice the massive weight of melancholia settling in. Sitting in a still house in a dumb haze, Rae knew what was happening. A part of her looked on, that portion of her mind that split away at times like these, to watch with dry amusement as she slumped for six hours in a chair without moving, to observe her friends arriving to take her to the long-delayed funeral and finding her unwashed, unfed, wearing old jeans and one of Alan's plaid shirts, having to brush Rae's hair and get her dressed around the cast on her left arm. Sardonically, the looker-on noted the people, a sea of faces: colleagues, students, friends, touching Rae's good arm, tears on their cheeks; Rae herself was aware only of nothingness. Home again, to a house in which silence dwelt, silence and Rae and the looker-on who had accompanied her into depression each time before, whose grim business it seemed to be to make careful and disinterested note of the number of sharp knives in the kitchen, the length of the cord on the radio near the bathtub, the vent of the propane tank, the proximity of the wheels of passing trucks. Rae had just enough sense to give up driving then, not wanting to take anyone else with her when she went.

It was in the middle of January, five weeks after the accident, that Rae first began to feel the presence of the Watchers. They came at night, picking at the edges of the grim blanket that smothered her mind, small, niggling twitches that could have been life returning to deadened limbs, but which felt more like the threat of a further descent into lifelessness. A sound from the deck that, mere weeks before, would not have had her looking up from her book now drove her to the light switches, off for all the inside lights, on for the outside floods. Nothing was there, just the trees pressing up against the railing, the branches of the winter-dull garden moving gently in a breeze. Nothing there, but still Rae began to retreat into the upper rooms, or to the storage spaces that had no windows. After a few days, she went around with a staple gun and fastened bedsheets to all the uncurtained windows—which, it being a house without neighbors, was virtually every one. This transformed her house into a place simultaneously of refuge and of enclosure, a hiding place and a jail.

Rae started to walk. She would leave the house each morning, trudge her mile-long driveway and several more miles of lightly used public road to the small country market, where she would buy a paper and a desultory selection of groceries. Some days, when she was feeling too ill, she would occupy the bench at the bus stop for most of the day; on others she would wander on, far afield, miles and miles of mindless walking, watching the approach of each car and wondering calmly if this would be the one whose wheels she flung herself under. She could not have said, afterward, where she had been, but always she would return home before darkness fell, pick at some tasteless food, and take out the newspaper she had bought, clipping all the articles about disasters. A drug-related killing. A multicar pileup in the fog. A woman arrested for locking her child in the closet for two years. A massive earthquake in some dry and distant country. Disaster, catastrophe, death, disorder. She began to keep lists: the places struck down, the names and ages of the victims, the cars sought in the hit-and-runs. Lists of words that occurred in the articles, in descriptions of the victims and their assailants, even in adjacent articles, as if the words held some hidden meaning she might understand if she took sufficient care, as if the world might reveal meaning if she paid sufficient attention.

All the while, Rae's own internal Watcher was fully aware that she looked a sight. Unkempt and often inappropriately dressed, she could not summon the energy to care. Friends came and buzzed in her ears with worried offers of driving her to the supermarket or the doctor's; her lawyer came with papers, as if the transfer of Alan's possessions to her mattered; Tamara arrived to tidy the house (although when she attempted to clear out Alan's closet, Rae drove her off in a rare summoning of fury). Nurses, doctors, lawyers, Alan's colleagues—all called or left messages on the machine until Rae just stopped answering.

In the evenings, behind her stapled-up barriers, she sat at Alan's desk or in the beat-up leather chair that bore the clear imprint of his shoulders along its back. The last book he had been reading lay on the table next to the arm, and she read and reread the pages where the bookmark lodged, troubled mightily that she did not know at which precise spot he had stopped reading. The page before the bookmark, so that he might start here afresh? Or halfway through the left-hand page where a section break occurred? Or even all the way to the bottom of the right? Oh, why couldn't he have put the bookmark in at a new chapter? she raged. And why didn't she know him well enough to guess? If she scrutinized the words closely enough, maybe she could feel which words his eyes had passed over, and which remained unread . . .

At night Rae curled up in Bella's bed, where the pillow still smelled faintly of peanut butter and crayons and lemonade, or so she imagined, if she buried her face deeply enough into it. In the morning she put on clothes (baggy sweaters that would go over the cast; mismatched socks) and pushed her spoon around a bowl of cold cereal, staring at the floral and geometrical fabric prints over the windows and trying to convince herself that there was nothing on the other side of them, that if she pulled one aside she wouldn't see a stranger's face looking back at her. The anxiety usually hit before she finished her cereal, cramping her belly and making her pace up and down, hands clenched or wringing each other, until she could bear it no longer and burst out the door to hurry down the gravel drive toward the road.

Once her feet hit the tarmac, the feeling of Watchers would begin to fade. She would sink back into a dull, apathetic state, not caring much about anything or anyone, so long as she could keep moving.

And keep moving she did. She must have put on twenty miles a day during the end of January, rain and shine, up and down the roads with her hands thrust into her jacket pockets, her eyes on the pavement in front of her feet, a quart of milk sloshing beside the newspaper in the green knapsack. Fortunately, it was a mild patch of winter weather, even for California, and only twice did she get truly drenched. But the rain seemed to interfere with the Watchers, because as she splashed up her long, empty drive on those wet days, the back of her neck did not prickle so ominously and the skin of her arms felt merely cold and clammy, without the crawling feeling that usually started up at the first curve in the road. Well worth the discomfort of being soaked to the skin, even if it meant the cast on her arm went spongy for days.

It was just bad luck that on the second of these drenchings the propane tank ran empty less than an hour after she reached the sanctuary of the house. She had neglected to phone for a delivery, or to unlock the gate for the truck. Now her only heat was the open fireplace. She used the last logs before midnight, leaving her the options of venturing outside to the woodpile or going to bed. She did eye the wooden furniture, but in the end took to her blankets.

She awoke to full sunlight, a scratchy throat, and the sound of footsteps walking across her deck. No knock came, no voice, and the sound was not repeated. Cold terror trickled into Rae's veins. Long minutes passed with a whimpering deep inside, until finally she fumbled for the telephone with trembling hands and whispered to the emergency dispatcher that she had an intruder.

The sheriff's deputy took forever to arrive. Red-faced from the stiff climb up the drive from the locked gate, he kept one eye on Rae the whole time he checked the house for intruders; whether he was more taken aback by her appearance or the state of her house would have been hard to say.

He found nothing, and eventually walked off down the hill, shaking his head.

In the week that followed, Rae called 911 twice more, each time with the same result, or lack of result. The third time the sheriff himself, Sam Escobar, strode up the road, walked briskly through her chaotic house, sat her down for a long talk, and left with a spare key to the gate in his pocket. She did not call again, not even when the Watchers took to scratching at her windows with twigs and rattling her doorknobs.

So she huddled into the sofa in front of her fireplace, concentrating fiercely on her newspaper disasters and her lists of related words and events until she could bear the noises no longer. Then she drew a pillow over her head to muffle the scratches and rattles, and she lay through the night, listening to the whispers that rose and fell just below the threshold of her hearing.

Rae's own internal Watcher was aware that her behavior was irrational. As if it were studying a stranger, a woman curled up in the dark and spending long midnight hours poring over endless lists, her inner eye knew there were neither whispered conversations nor heavy-footed Watchers outside of her head, as it was also faintly aware that before too long something would have to be done. However, the truth was, Rae found the unjustifiable terrors strangely comforting. Focusing on them, she had no energy left to think about the impossibility of life without Alan and Bella. Imaginary enemies were infinitely easier to face than real ones.

It seemed, looking back, that this period in her life went on for years. In fact, the downward spiral lasted for just under three weeks, from the funeral to Rae's readmission to the hospital intensive care unit, feverish from a low-grade pneumonia, a rebroken left forearm, a lot of superficial cuts and bruises, and a nasty infection in her left shoulder where what they thought was a bone chip was creating havoc.

The downward spiral's end came abruptly, from two more or less simultaneous directions.

Only many months later did it occur to her that she was an unlikely candidate for rape. Sheriff Escobar's response to that tentatively offered observation, that some animals would rape anything that moved, only served to confirm how unappealing she was at the time: gaunt to the point of collapse, ill-washed, shiny-eyed with fever, racked with a cough, dressed in Alan's baggy clothing, and wearing a backpack oozing the remains of a dozen broken eggs.

Late in the afternoon on the first Tuesday in February, as Rae stepped off the public road to slip through her gate, a big black pickup truck with oversized tires drove up behind her and braked in a rain of gravel. Two stocky young men hopped easily down from the cab, leaving both doors wide open, and strode confidently toward her, joking with each other and looming larger and larger, and only breaking into a run when she turned to flee in slow motion up the drive.

Cats with a mouse, lions with a rabbit. They seemed to be on her in two huge steps, the nightmare panting of their breath sweeping up behind her, their boisterous shouts terrifying in their merriment, and then the carnal rut of sweat and cigarettes filled her nostrils as they pounced, iron fingers yanking her off her feet, leaving a row of black circles in the skin of her shoulders and arm, the first of many. They stank of aggression and they laughed at Rae's feeble efforts.

She fought them wildly, squirming and hitting out in desperate, futile silence. The only sound to escape her was one brief cry when the dark-haired attacker broke her cast as he yanked away her knapsack. Their hands were all over her, wrenching and pinching and brutal; hitting them felt like slapping the sides of the redwood trees that stood quietly nearby. Only one of her blows connected with any force: The blond staggered back, clutching his nose, but struggle as she might, the brown-haired one's arms held her fast. Then the blond was back, angry now, coarse laughter turned to foul curses. Hard fingers tore at her shirt, two arms locked around her from behind to keep her from flinging herself away, a hand, shockingly cold, thrust into the loose waistband of her jeans. She kicked out hard and the hand drew back, but only for a moment, to return with a brutal slap that snapped her head to the side. Half stunned, with the blond man's jaw buried in her neck and his voice murmuring monotonous obscenities while the other one half-carried her toward the bend in the road, she felt the hand come back to insinuate itself between soft belly skin and fabric.

And then a shout, which Rae heard only later, in memory, or in a construct of imagination. All she knew at the time was that the hands in front stopped tearing at her clothes, and then she was flying through the air, arms spread wide, to land with a crash in the bushes.

Joseph Ayala, on his way home from work, dropped into the middle of Rae's assault like an angel on a golden chariot, with a squeal of rubber and a furious blare of the horn of his beat-up Chevy pickup. Thirty seconds later and Rae and her pursuers would have been out of sight, but Joseph glanced up the dirt road as he passed, saw his recently bereaved neighbor struggling against two young men, and rolled down his window to shout, "I'm calling the cops, right now!" He held up a compact black shape to his ear to illustrate his threat. The two young men hesitated, then decided to cut their losses. The taller of the two threw her bodily off the road, and they ran back down the hill for their truck. Ayala hastily slapped his own vehicle into gear and retreated on up the road a bit, but Rae's attackers did not pursue him, merely gunned the shiny black truck and accelerated away in the other direction toward the main road.

Rae, tearing herself out of the brambles, looked up to see a man laboring up the road toward her, a black leather wallet held incongruously in his hand. She snatched together her torn, bloody clothing, grabbed her dripping knapsack, and fled. Her appalled neighbor slowed to a halt and watched her disappear. Then he ran back to his truck and drove fast for home and a real telephone, to phone 911 and gabble about the crime he had witnessed.

In the meantime, earlier that same day, Rae's doctor had called Tamara to say that two appointments had been missed—was Rae all right? When she could not get Rae on the phone, Tamara, disgruntled and dutiful on the surface but queasy underneath with a lifetime of experience, picked up Petra from school and drove down to her mother's house, letting herself in the gate a scant ten minutes after the sheriff and paramedics had done the same. Tamara pulled through the last grove of redwoods to find three official vehicles in her mother's normally deserted forecourt, and a lot of people in uniforms.

In a panic, she rushed in, Petra on her heels. Both of them stopped, aghast, at the sight that met their eyes.

Sheriff Sam Escobar, six feet of broad muscle and tan uniform, was squatting down at one end of a sofa littered deep with scraps of paper, his hand held cautiously out as if to a panicked animal. Which was precisely what Rae Newborn was just then, a beaten, bloody, stinking, half-naked animal in pain, too terrified of assailants both real and imagined to do more than cower in the dark corner between the wall and the sofa, surrounded by a blizzard of her scribbled lists, hidden from the outer world by the bizarrely colorful bedsheets, whimpering in the back of her throat. The paramedics were looking at their watches, the deputy was fingering the lockstrap on his gun nervously, and Rae was hunched up into a ball, one eye on the man in the tan uniform as if judging when to bite his hand.

"Mother?" Tamara gasped. "Oh my God, Mother, not again!"

Rae gave a single sob, a sound of loss and relief, and tried to unfold her stiff limbs from their fetal curl. "I'm sorry," she whispered, but it was not to the sheriff, nor even to her daughter. "I'm sorry," she told Petra, over and over. The child's frightened face cut through it all—fever, terror, madness, pain: everything—and all Rae could think of was that her granddaughter should never have seen her like this. And so, "I'm sorry. I'm so sorry."

"Situational psychosis" was a phrase whose source Rae could no longer remember, but one which she found infinitely reassuring, an acknowledgment that even the strongest mind could give way following a series of blows, blows carefully calibrated and delivered by Fate. Even if she had not been the world's most securely balanced woman before, even if she had gone through periods of grim depression and compulsive behavior and attempts at suicide, even if she had known panic attacks long before they had a name, it did not mean she was always and irrevocably crazy. It just meant that she had a weakness, no more of a moral flaw than her mother's bad knee or her uncle's trick back.

Situational psychosis. Clinical depression. Nervous breakdown. Shell shock—all names for the neurological fault line that gives way under severe pressure, a shattering, devastating internal earthquake that leaves raw and gaping scars across the lives of everyone in the vicinity. This time when Rae was taken into the hospital, there was no overlooking the patient's deeper problem. This second time in the ICU, the nurses were watchful, omnipresent, and meticulous about never leaving sharp objects near her bed. This time, once the antibiotics had done their work on her lungs, when the arm was reset with a plate on the bone and the cast replaced, when the fragment of Alan's front tooth had been taken from her abscessed shoulder and most of the gravel from her hands and knees, she was transferred not to an open ward, but to a locked one. It was there, ironically enough, that some weeks later Rae managed to pull her wits together enough to make her third suicide attempt. Unlike the earlier two, this time she was by no means halfhearted. She wanted seriously to be dead, and she went about it with a determination every bit as grim and narrow-focused as her world had become. Only because of a fluke bed check was she caught before the blood loss became too great.

That was rock bottom. After that, she gave up. The soothing, mindless routine of the hospital took over; gradually, it began to do its work. Rae's surroundings became a place of asylum, not just a madhouse. Swaddled tightly in the security of having absolutely no choices, seesawed by drugs, and seared by shock therapy, she found that in spite of herself, the scope of her vision began slowly to expand. The inescapably dreary hopelessness of the universe thinned a fraction, Rae's field of awareness spread to include things outside her own uncomfortable skin, and then one day she suddenly became aware of the smell of popcorn being prepared in the staff room. She didn't even care much for popcorn, but the odor drifted down the institutional halls like an angel choir. Then came Dr. Roberta Hunt, bearing the first glimmer at the end of the tunnel, lighting up the long road home.

Only, home was a place now shut up and silent, the furniture draped with sheets against the dust (the same sheets she'd stapled up to the windows, in fact). Or was home now this island, two broken stone towers at the base of a hill that was trying to bury them?

The question really only mattered if the six bullets remained in their neat pyramidal arrangement on the corner of her desk. The definition of home would hardly matter to a dead woman.

Most of the night Rae sat at her desk, picking up the bullets and playing with them, caressing the gun's worn rosewood stock with her thumb, loading and unloading the chambers. Most of the night she listened to the low exhalation of the kerosene lamp and the shifting conversation of the two horned owls, torn between peaceful oblivion and the look it would bring onto Petra's face. Toward morning, undecided still, Rae lay her head down on the journal. *How different the arrangement of bullets look from this perspective,* she thought. After a while her eyelids fluttered closed. Toward morning the lamp faded, and died.

It was light outside when a sound woke her. She tried to sit up, grunted at the protest of her cramped neck and spine, and peeled herself off the desk.

The sound came again. A woman's voice, this time, and inexplicably calling Rae's name. A dream, Rae knew. In the dream she stumbled to her feet and pushed her way out of the unzipped tent flap, where her eyes were met by the fairy-tale vision of a family of castaways deposited on her shore, a family of three coalesced out of the mist that swirled and glowed around their remarkable figures. What a peculiar dream. The father resembled Sheriff Escobar in his tan uniform (though taller and lighter of skin), the mother looked like a fairy without wings, and the boy was neither dark frizzy Petra nor blond curly Bella, but pale-skinned and red-haired like the mother.

The dream-family's reaction was even more startlingly bizarre than their presence: The redheaded woman took one look at Rae, snatched up the child, and curled her body over his in a gesture of urgent protectiveness. What the man did was even more hallucinatory: He dropped into a crouch, drew out a gun, and lowered it at Rae.

Sixteen

Letter from Rae to Her Granddaughter

April 12

Dear Petra,

Before I left California, I ordered a couple of books on the history of the San Juans, since it occurred to me that I ought to know something about my new home. I suppose you've been doing some research too—let me know what you've discovered.

Now that I've had a chance to read them, I've been amazed to find that, for such a nice, peaceful landscape (even the water here is ridiculously calm compared with the Pacific—I've known lakes with bigger waves), there's sure been a lot of wild goings-on here. During Prohibition (have you studied that yet in school?— the period when first the state and then the U.S. as a whole outlawed alcohol, making the Temperance Union happy and lots of criminals rich) the San Juans were a hotbed of rum-running, followed by marijuana in the Sixties and I'm sure other substances today. McConnell Island, west of here, was the home of an early racketeer. To the north, a man who called himself Brother XII fleeced a congregation of wealthy people on Valdes Island by setting up a sort of New Age church called the Aquarian Foundation—in, if you can believe it, the late 1920s.

Skull Island, Victim Island, and Massacre Bay (where a local deputy lives) commemorate Native American raids. Closer to Folly, and just around the time you were born, a drug smuggler set up shop on a little island in a deserted bay, only to find six months later that *it became packed with summer tourists. Who, naturally, noticed his enterprise. The island was confiscated and is now a wildlife refuge named, appropriately enough, Justice Island. We even had an international incident on nearby San Juan: The so-called Pig War started over an English pig that strayed into an American farmer's potato patch and got shot. That was in 1859, when the U.S. and England were arguing over the boundaries and both claimed the island. We nearly went to war over a pig, if you can believe it.*

So, how do you like your grandmother's nice, peaceable new neighborhood?

> *Love,*
> *Gran*

Seventeen

The gun, like the man behind it, was huge and steady and utterly terrifying: the dream's nightmare phase. "Drop it!" the man barked.

"Wha—?" Rae looked down at her left hand and saw that she had come out of the tent carrying her own weapon. "It isn't loaded," she told the man in the tan uniform, holding the gun away from her body by the tips of her fingers as if to repudiate its very existence.

"Place it on the ground, Ms. Newborn. Now."

Rae started to obey, then hesitated. "Would you mind if I put it on the table instead? Sand is really hard on the works."

By all rights, the man should have bellowed at her for instant obedience. Instead, after a hesitation of his own, Rae's intruder nodded; in a way it was even more daunting than shouting would have been. "On the table, then. Move slowly. Now, come away from it, and keep your hands out from your sides. Okay, now turn around."

Footsteps approached behind Rae's back, and she braced herself against the inevitable rush of fear, but the man's hands as he patted her down were brisk and surprisingly gentle. "Okay," he said, which she took for permission to turn around. She watched as the man backed toward the cook table, his gun still out although it was pointing at the ground between them. He picked up Rae's wood-handled revolver, spun its chamber to check that it was indeed empty, glanced at it more closely, and laid it down.

"Nice weapon," he said. His gruff voice gave no hint of his thoughts; he might have been about to arrest her, or to invite her for tea. "Looks antique."

"It was my grandfather's," Rae told him. She felt awake, but the conversation was doing nothing to convince her of that. "I was . . . about to clean it last night, and I fell asleep. Sorry to come out waving it around, I forgot I had it in my hand." In the real world, the uniformed man would now ask if she had a permit, and when she didn't, the gun would be confiscated. But he did not ask about permits. Instead he studied her for a minute, then gestured across the clearing at her workbench.

"The table's new. You build it?"

"Yes, last week. I needed a place to work on." Had she broken some mysterious San Juan law? Did she need a permit for gathering driftwood, like she did for shellfish?

"Pretty fancy workbench. Looks good there, though. I take it you are Rae Newborn?"

The sheriff looked at the tall, strongly built woman a little older than himself, the lines of great strain alongside her generous mouth and the round red blotch on one cheek the same dimensions as the button on her cuff. There was intelligence in that face, and bravery despite the circumstances of the day and what he knew of her past. She looked at him evenly.

"Yes, I'm Rae Newborn."

The big man seemed to come to a decision. He slid his considerably sleeker, flatter gun into its holster and snapped the strap over it. "I'm Jerry Carmichael, San Juan County sheriff. Welcome to the San Juans."

"Thank you," Rae managed.

"This is Nicola Walls," Carmichael then told her, taking a step back to clear her view of the woman and child, who had moved apart and were now standing side by side, paler than ever and looking a little shaky at having been greeted by a gun. The child's face was pressed against his mother's waist, and her right arm was draped in loose protection around his shoulders. "Nikki's with the Parks Department," the sheriff said.

Not a wife; a girlfriend, perhaps, in spite of the age difference—the woman's early thirties to his late forties.

"Morning," Rae said to Nikki Walls. The child peered one eye around his mother's jacket. Nikki bent to say something to him, and after a minute, he nodded and consented to being led forward, clinging to his mother's hand. He appeared to be about five, though small for his age, and Rae was already bracing herself against the first time he called the woman "Mommy." When they had worked their way up to the campsite, Nikki extricated her hand from her son's and held it out to Rae. It was warm and slightly sticky, not much larger than a child's hand itself, and Rae had to fight an urge to wipe this tactile memory of childhood from her skin. Her mind gave up trying to suggest this was an elaborate hallucination: The touch of Nikki's child-warmed hand was real.

"Rae Newborn," she forced out.

"I know," Nikki surprised her by saying. "When Jerry told me he was coming out here I asked if I could tag along and meet you."

Good heavens, thought Rae; *who'd have expected a woodworking fan out here?*

"This is my son Caleb," the young woman continued. "Caleb, say hi to Ms. Newborn."

The boy's hand was clenched into the hem of Nikki's coat, his face turned away.

"Good to meet you, Caleb," Rae told the side of his head.

Mother and child were extraordinarily beautiful, but not by any conventional standard. Theirs was the beauty of a giraffe crossing a plain, or a flamingo wading through a marsh, or an alien on an otherworldly terrain: Human measurements of loveliness seemed inappropriate, somehow. The jeans they both wore and the red knee-high boots the child had on looked as unlikely as hats on a pair of kittens. They were too ethereal to be mere mortals, with pale red curls, delicate bones, and white freckled skin: like something out of an Irish folktale, perhaps, wood nymphs and sprites. The child's thick frizz of hair stood out in finger-length red dreadlocks; the mother's had been gathered into a pair of tight French braids along the side of her head that ended in a snug bun at her neck, which was probably the only way she could keep the curls under control. Despite the troubling handshake, Rae felt a vague desire to touch the two, to reassure herself that they were corporeal and not some trailing remnant of her fitful sleep. She caught the impulse, and pulled herself up sharply.

"Coffee," she stated, and went to make it.

"I should apologize for disturbing you so early, Ms. Newborn," the sheriff said. "Ed De la Torre told Nikki that you were usually up with the sun, so we thought it'd be okay. Even though the sun isn't exactly up."

"It's fine. I am usually awake at dawn, but I had a sort of disturbed night, and I seem to have slept in. I would've been awake as soon as the blue jays started up, so don't worry about it."

The detached and unreal sensation persisted; coffee would help, she told herself. Strong coffee. She dumped in another large spoonful. And

Folly   117

food: Was there anything to eat in her pantry? By Sundays her fresh food was generally gone, although she still had five eggs and plenty of butter.

"Have you had breakfast?" she asked her as-yet-unexplained guests.

"We brought a picnic," Sheriff Carmichael replied, which was both a relief and a further source of confusion. Did people in the San Juans habitually drop in on each other, food in hand? Somehow, learning the habits of a new community had not entered in during her planning.

"Caleb," the sheriff said. "You remember where you put that big bag?" The boy nodded. "Think you can get in and out of the boat all on your own, to fetch it?"

Before Nikki could protest, her son shot off down the hill and onto the promontory. All three adults watched the small figure dart across the floating dock and clamber over the side of the sheriff's launch. A drift of fog threatened to vanish the child, boat and all, back into the nether-world from which he had come, but after a minute, the luminous head reappeared on deck above a bag so tall his arms could barely contain it; Rae could see the cause of maternal concern. Caleb sidled up to the high side and peered down at the dock below. The boat shifted, the dock was unsteady; the bag was large, the boy small. Nikki drew breath to call out instructions, but the sheriff spoke up quietly.

"See if he can figure it out," he told her. Rae wondered at the under-currents of that mild command, which bore the marks of a long, close rela-tionship. It was not quite that of an older brother bossing his sister around, neither was it that of a husband. The nearest Rae could place it was that of a divorced couple who remained very close, or that of an uncle who had helped his niece grow up and was now doing the same for her son.

"He'll drop the bag in the water," Nikki protested, although Rae did not think it was the bag that worried her.

"So we'll have soggy croissants."

Now it was Rae's turn to stifle a protest. Fresh croissants, in the water?

But the child had it now. He rested the bag on the edge of the boat, stretched up to grab the bag's top edge, and let it swing down onto the wood. The balance was precarious and Rae braced herself for the splash, but Caleb saw the danger and, leaning farther out over the side, swung the bag securely away from the gap and let it go. He then climbed back up and over the side, gathered up their breakfast, and marched proudly up the dock and the rocky spit to the waiting adults.

Rae pushed down the filter plunger on the coffeemaker, aware that two years ago, if confronted with a shy child, she would have suggested he push the plunger for her. Now she made no effort to bring Caleb out of himself. When she had produced the other chair and distributed plates, she asked Nikki what her son wanted to drink instead of addressing the child directly. She talked, in fact, mostly to the sheriff, avoiding those two glowing heads as much as possible.

"You settling in okay?" the sheriff asked her.

"I guess." "Settled" was not the word for the last eighteen hours, but a full explanation was too daunting a prospect. She gave him an artificially wide smile. "It took some time to get used to the night noises, but I've gradually sorted out the raccoons from the deer from the mice, and they don't keep me awake now." A blatant lie, but he couldn't know that. Or could he? Those steady brown eyes in that sun-darkened face seemed to see a great deal. "Coffee?"

The croissants were gorgeous, flaky outside and chewy within. There were also three kinds of muffin, a big plastic container of fruit salad, some tubs of flavored yogurt, and another plastic box of still-warm spicy link sausages. When the time came to toss wrappers into the fire pit and rinse out the cups, Rae found that she had eaten three of the croissants as well as half a dozen sausages and a blueberry muffin the size of a softball. Combined with her share of two pots of coffee, her eyelids were so wide open now the lashes might have been glued to the lids.

She also found that, while she was devouring all that food, she had without realizing it been the object of a subtle bit of questioning on the part of the sheriff, who now knew rather more about her and her family than she thought necessary, particularly with the ranger and her son listening in. She poured steaming water over the mugs and knives in the dishpan, put the kettle back on the fire, and sat down to confront the sheriff.

"So tell me, do you normally come out and break bread with every newcomer to the islands?"

Sheriff Carmichael turned slightly in his chair. "Nikki? Maybe you and Caleb . . ."

Nikki reluctantly got to her feet and addressed her son. "Caleb, let's go down and see how many crabs we can count on Ms. Newborn's beach."

The sheriff's eyes lingered on their retreating backs, and when they were out of earshot, he turned back to Rae and drew a sheet of paper from the breast pocket of his shirt. He unfolded it, and got up to hand it to her.

"Does this man look familiar to you?"

It was a faxed photograph of a square-jawed, wide-necked man with close-cropped blond hair and a curl to his lip as he stared down the camera.

"He looks like a Nazi," she said.

"That's what I thought. But do you know him?"

"He doesn't look familiar. Is this another mug shot from Sheriff Escobar? This one's even further from the description than the one your deputy brought out the first week I was here."

"Escobar told me he didn't think this was the guy, but he asked me to bring it out anyway, see if it rang any bells."

"I see. No, it wasn't this guy." She glanced up. "He told you I'd been . . ."

"Attacked, yes. The general outline, not the details."

"Well, this isn't one of them. One of them was blond, but a darker color than this. And his neck wasn't as thick. This guy looks like a weight lifter." If she had been attacked by this muscular Nazi, Rae was thinking, she might well not be here to look at his picture. She handed the photo back, and Carmichael fed it into the fire.

"It was a long shot. They picked the guy up for a similar assault; Escobar thought it was worth a try."

"Sorry."

"He said I should tell you they are still working on it."

"I can see that." *Probably the main reason he had Carmichael trudge out here, to let me know he's working hard.*

"You want to tell me what's happening out here?" he asked, his voice and expression unchanged. Rae assumed he was talking about the mug shot.

"You said he told you about—"

"I mean here, on Folly. You obviously had a bad night, you fell asleep with a gun in your hand, and you're jumpy as all get-out. I *am* the sheriff here, after all. If you're having a problem, I'd like to know about it." And if she was about to go nuts and start shooting at night noises, he'd need to know that as well, she thought. Still, it was nice of him to put it as concern *for* her rather than *about* her. Who knew—it might even be true.

Where, however, to start?

"Before you begin," he said, "you should know that your sheriff gave me a certain amount of background. I know that you were in a bad accident and lost your family, spent some time in the hospital, and then no sooner did you get out than two men attacked you. You spent the next eleven months in a psychiatric hospital. Escobar told me that because I had to know, but maybe I should make it clear that as far as he's concerned, that hospitalization wasn't that out of the ordinary, considering what happened to you. He's really glad you're doing better.

"I'm only telling you all this so you realize that neither of us hold anything against you. I grew up with a cousin who developed schizophrenia in his late teens, so I've seen at first hand the stigma attached to mental illness. So that's not part of the picture. Now please, what is going on here that you're not happy about?"

Rae had to stand up and move away. If she hadn't, she would have burst into tears. As it was, her eyes filled and the salal bush in her vision wavered, but she could at least keep her voice steady.

"I do, occasionally, have . . . well, hallucinations. I hear whispers, smell things that aren't there. If I take medication, they fade, but the meds make me feel so awful I'd really rather have the odd voice than drug myself. It's just . . ." She stopped, drew a deep breath, and went on. "Yesterday I was up at the spring, around the side of the island, and I thought I saw what looked like a footprint. In the mud near the pond. It wasn't mine."

"Like Robinson Crusoe, eh? Only you'd rather Friday stuck to his own island and left yours alone."

"I know it probably wasn't a footprint. I thought at the time that it looked like one of those lug soles on a hiking boot, but there was just a little corner of it, and thinking about it, the mark could as easily have been made by a couple of deer. I just . . . lost it, that's all."

Then came the sound of the wooden chair creaking.

"Let's go see," he said.

Rae was so startled she raised her face, without a thought for the ravage of tears.

"Why?"

"Why?" he repeated. "Because I'm the sheriff of San Juan County, and if someone's trespassing on a designated wildlife refuge, I should know about it."

Rae squinted up at him. "Tell me—do you also sit by the roadside waiting to catch people littering?"

The slightly forbidding lines of his face relaxed for a moment. "Only in the wintertime, when I'm really bored." He half-turned to call over his shoulder, "Nikki, will you and Caleb be okay here for a while? Ms. Newborn needs to show me something."

"Sure," Nikki shouted back. Caleb's jeans lay folded on a driftwood log while he went wading in the cove, the top of his boots a fraction of an inch from being inundated, his small body bent over so that his nose almost touched the icy water.

"Lead the way," the sheriff suggested.

Rae hesitated, then started up the hill in front of him, but the sound of his boots close on her heels proved more than her nerves could take. She stepped to the side and gestured up the hill.

"You go first. The path is fairly obvious."

Now it was the sheriff's turn to hesitate, but only briefly. Rae trailed behind, and it soon occurred to her that law enforcement personnel probably had their own reasons for not wishing to turn their backs on strangers.

The trail was narrow and Carmichael set a brisk pace, so they spoke little on the way up. Halfway up the hill the sun began to strengthen and Rae shed her jacket, leaving it on a branch to collect on the way back. Before long she was wishing she'd left her long sleeves behind as well. When they got to the lower pool she knelt down to splash her face with water and run wet fingers through her hair. The sheriff stood for a long moment looking at the view, which was framed by branches but none the less dramatic for it. The rocks in the water off the island made for a lot of turbulence in the surface, and buoys marked more hidden dangers. This particular bit of water looked to Rae more like the wild water off Big Sur than the calm friendly coastline of the San Juans.

"Too bad your man didn't build his house up here," the sheriff said. "Great view."

"Bit of a trek to carry groceries, though," Rae countered, and walked up to the higher pool. "It was over here."

The fern fronds had uncurled a fraction more, the moss was just as green, the intrusion of two large humans seemed to jar the placid air, and the boot mark was still there.

If it was a boot mark. The ground had softened even more during the night; had it looked the day before like it looked this morning, Rae might not even have noticed it. She told him so.

He was bent over the indentation, as intent as young Caleb had been with his undersea creatures. After a couple of minutes, during which he'd done everything but stand on his head and sniff the soil, he rose, brushed off his hands, and placed his own boot a foot or so away from the mark. He bounced up and down a couple of times, then took a step back. Now they were both staring intently at the ground.

"It could be a Vibram sole like mine," he said finally, "but you're right, it could be a number of other things as well." The mark his boot had left in the tender moss was unpleasantly close to what she had seen the previous afternoon. But then, the strike of a mallet would look much the same, or the scratch of a hoof or something dropped from a great height or—

"I'm afraid we're not going to be able to figure this one out today," Carmichael said regretfully. "If it was summer, I'd guess you had a trespasser, but this time of year it's not as likely. And it's rained since Easter vacation, when we had the last big bunch of tourists around. Besides, you were on the island for most of that vacation; you'd have noticed someone walking through your campsite."

"I wouldn't have seen them if they came from the other side of the island," Rae pointed out.

"That'd be one determined trespasser."

"Why is that?"

He looked around at her in surprise. "Haven't you ever seen your shoreline?"

"Bits of it, between the cove and here, and the other side from a distance when I was here five years ago. I do understand from Ed that the currents are difficult to navigate."

"Typical Ed De la Torre understatement. The little cove where you've made camp is the only beach on the whole island, and just offshore from the spit is the only really safe mooring. You've either got cliff faces down to the sea or reefs like sharks' teeth. Plus that you're smack in the middle of the worst set of currents in the San Juans, Speiden Channel meeting Haro Strait. Riptides, eddies, you name it. You'd have to be a cross between Captain Ahab and a mountain goat to climb onto Folly anyplace but through your front yard. I know—I've sailed these islands all my life and I've only known two idiots who would try it on a bet, and one of those lost his boat in the process."

"I didn't realize. It's reassuring to know that I won't have to keep throwing people off my property."

"Put up a big new No Trespassing sign with a picture of a shotgun, you won't have too many problems. In fact, you should talk to Nikki about that. She's actually the one whose job it is to worry about trespassers on a bird sanctuary." He cast a final look out over the water, and turned away to retrace the path down to the campsite. Rae made to follow him, then turned back to kneel and scoop some water onto the twice-dented moss.

She was not sure if she was attempting to speed the moss's recovery, or trying to cover over the mark of Jerry Carmichael's boot.

Carmichael led more slowly going downhill, stopping to study Rae's work on the water line, asking intelligent questions about the original construction. When they came to a bend, Rae picked up a scrap of the old cedar line and gave it to him. He turned it around in his big hands, his fingers exploring the shape, and listened to her conclusions about the changes that burying the line would make to the configuration.

"Quite a project you've got here for yourself" was his only comment.

"You're not going to tell me it's too much for a woman?"

"I wouldn't dream of it, even if it showed some signs of being true, which I can't see that it does. Actually it's been my experience that when women get into a thing like this, they run into fewer problems than men do, because their expectations are more realistic. And you've obviously got experience." He tossed the scrap of wood into the bushes and started down the hill again.

His last comment had sounded faintly like a question, so Rae gave it an answer.

"I've done a certain amount of building over the years—everything but the wiring. Electricity makes me nervous. I even spent a couple of summers with a building crew when I was young, rough-framing tract houses. By profession I'm a woodworker."

"I know. One of my deputies recognized your name." Too much to ask, Rae supposed, that the Big Man himself would know her reputation. The sheriff, oblivious, went on. "You might want to get that No Trespassing sign up pretty soon, you know, unless you want your neighbors lined up outside your cove. It's kind of surprising that they've held off this long."

"Oh, I hardly think I'm *that* famous," she protested.

He stopped to look back at her. "Here? You've got to be kidding. You're a local celebrity."

Rae, astonished, stared at him, but before she could begin to preen at the idea of having been dropped into the midst of an entire community of woodworking connoisseurs, he went on. "Everybody on the islands knows there's someone come to restore Folly."

Rae deflated rapidly, and then, to her own surprise as much as his, began to laugh. "Is that why Nikki wanted to meet me?"

"Sure. Although she knows your work, too."

That was something, anyway. "Who is Nikki?" she asked.

"Nikki? A park ranger, didn't I tell you? Oh, you mean in relation to me?" He turned back to the path, speaking to her over his shoulder. "She's a friend, although she's also a sort of distant cousin by marriage. Most of us on the islands who aren't newcomers are somehow related. Nikki's my older brother's ex-wife's younger sister. She's a single mom— married a guy who turned out to be abusive, stuck with him until he hit Caleb, when she came back here. They're doing fine now, but it's hard for a woman to raise a boy on her own, so I take her and Caleb out sometimes. A boy needs men in his life, seems to me. Nikki—well, you saw with the boat, she tends to be a little overprotective."

Rae did not think the young woman had demonstrated an overly protective attitude toward her son. Nor was she convinced that the sheriff's interest in the redheaded pair was as strictly avuncular as he would have it.

"By the way, I was just joking about the shotgun," he told her. "Not the picture of one—hell, a little threat never hurt anyone—but I'd hate to see you actually use one. Or even that pretty revolver of yours. Have you thought about getting a cell phone?"

"I don't think they work here, not at the cove anyway."

"The satellite kind would. They cost an arm and a leg, but—"

"No."

"Okay. What about a radio?"

"I thought I'd try to do without one, for a while," Rae told him.

"At least get yourself a flare gun. That way, if you start having problems, you can shoot it off. If one of us doesn't see it, your neighbors will, especially if it's dark. Not as good as a radio, by any means, but it's better than nothing. Ed could pick one up for you in Friday Harbor. Just be sure to shoot it out over the water, so you don't burn up your island. And, er, try not to use it unless you're really sure. That there's some threat, you know?"

Rae smiled wryly, hearing evidence of his conversation with Escobar in his words. "So I don't call out the troops because of bumps in the night, you mean?"

Something in her voice made the sheriff turn around fully to study her. "Ms. Newborn, you were under a hell of a lot of stress when you made those false-alarm calls. I'd hate to think that you'd put off calling for help here because you were afraid to be embarrassed. You of all people should know that just because you sometimes hear things that aren't there, that doesn't mean there's *never* anything there. I'd guess, in fact, that's one of the reasons you're here, to prove that you can tell the difference. Prove it to yourself, if nothing else."

He held her gaze for a long moment, then turned and continued on his surefooted way down the hill, leaving Rae to gape for a long minute at the retreating uniform. Jerry Carmichael would have made one ferociously effective psychiatrist, had he chosen to police humankind's minds instead of its actions.

They walked the rest of the path in silence. At the clearing, Carmichael paused to admire the emerging towers while Rae continued on around the tent to the cooksite. Caleb was sitting in the canvas chair, his legs dangling free of the ground, searching inside the white paper bakery bag. Nikki was bent over the cook table, her back to them.

"Looking for something?" Rae asked.

The young woman jumped as if she'd been stung, dropped the plastic snap-top box of kitchen tools with a clatter, and whirled around, her hand over her heart.

"Damn, you startled me!"

"Did you need something?"

"Well, I was just thinking I might put away those knives and things that we used, but they didn't seem to go in here."

"No. Silverware is in that other box."

"Oh, I see—"

"But don't bother putting them away," Rae told her. "I only keep the can openers and stuff in there because they rust. The silver is stainless."

"Okay. If you're sure."

Nikki abandoned her project with a suspicious alacrity and went to help her son sort through the big white bag for enticing edibles. Without the diffuse light of the morning fog, both looked more substantial, the fairy's wings traded in for a denim shirt. Nikki looked up as the sheriff came around the tent, and grinned at him.

"It's been a whole hour and a quarter since breakfast," she explained. "Caleb thought it was time for a little brunch." She found a rather flat chocolatine, and held it out to her son.

The three adults watched the boy take an enormous bite of the squidgy pastry. His mouth disappeared in a dark smear.

"You like the chocolate ones?" Rae asked the child. More accepting now of her presence, he nodded vigorously. "My—" She stopped short. *My daughter liked them, too.* "Well," she said briskly. "I've got a ton of work to do. Thank you for the breakfast—it was a real treat."

"Nikki," the sheriff said to his brother's ex-sister-in-law. "I was telling Ms. Newborn you people might be able to arrange a big new No Trespassing sign for her before summer. So boaters have no excuse."

"Good idea. It'll take a while to process it, so I'll get it started this week."

"And if you happen to be out here one day, you might swing Ms. Newborn around her island, point out the sights. Since she doesn't have a boat of her own yet."

Rae started to protest, but Nikki's face had lit up.

"I'd love to," she said, practically wriggling with enthusiasm. "And in fact, I'm going to be working around this end of the county tomorrow. Would that be a good day?"

Rae wavered. Put her off, or get it over with? Interest in seeing the full extent of the island overcame her hermit's reticence. "Tomorrow would be fine. Thanks. I'd enjoy that." "Enjoy" was pushing it a bit, but manners never hurt. And then she remembered something else she could ask a park ranger. "Oh, and Nikki? If you have a bird book you could let me borrow, I'd appreciate it. I'd kind of like to know what all these birds are that I'm living with."

Nikki said she had just the thing, and they settled on the late morning, to give the fog a chance to burn off but to miss the afternoon's low tide, then Rae walked the trio down to the dock, where she waited while Nikki cast off their lines. The launch moved into the sunlit bay, and as it turned, the sun's rays caught both red heads. They were, Rae saw, not actually identical: Nikki's was the rich, full color of a ripe apricot, whereas her son's gleamed the precise shade of fresh copper. The child's pale face watched Rae's receding figure, and then a small chocolaty hand lifted over the side of the boat and waved, energetically. Rae's hand twitched up in response, her fingers outspread, then slowly curling shut as the boat's motor deepened and the water behind it began to churn.

When the boat had left, Rae went to see what Nikki might have been looking for, but the box contained only such treasures as corkscrew, vegetable peeler, and shish kabob skewers. The zip of the tent was more or less where she remembered leaving it, and the things inside looked undisturbed.

It was unlikely that the ranger would have conducted an illegal search for drugs or firearms with her young son sitting right in front of her, Rae decided. The young wood nymph was just curious about Folly's owner. That was all.

Eighteen

Letters from Rae to Her Granddaughter and Daughter

April 18

Dear Petra,

Thank you for your letter, which Ed De la Torre brought me last week along with groceries, a gallon of linseed oil for my workbench, and a report from the lab saying that the water in my stream tests "within acceptable limits" on about eighty different things (thank goodness for that). There was also a stern letter from the Parks Department saying that yes, they suppose I do have the right to fix up this "derelict residence," despite the island's being a wildlife refuge, but that I have to agree to go along with this, that, and the other limitation. Of course, I don't have to do any such thing; I know it and they know it. Your great-great-grandfather William built a legal agreement every bit as solid as his factories and office blocks, and he was ferocious about preserving his family's right to do anything they pleased with their possessions. They're just trying to bluff me into agreeing to it. (Has anyone taught you to play poker yet, my dear? If not, remind me the next time I see you.) Actually, I'm not even bound by the original agreement, since the grant's original fifty years expired a long time ago, but to tell you the truth, I'm happy for them to continue using the island as a wildlife sanctuary. I'm all in favor of sanctuaries (which is, you will remember, the real name of this island). Plus, it means that the summer tourists have no right to set foot on it, and this way the government has to enforce the ban rather than me having to do it myself. But anyway, that was my battle for the week.

The message being, I suppose: Always make sure you have a good lawyer at your side.

All of which is by way of an answer to your letter, which I will take in two sections: your school project and your proposal of a visit.

The project sounds very interesting, much more so than the sorts of boring history papers we had to do "in my day" (said in a quavery old-lady voice). Certainly a history of this 145-acre rock covers everything from Native Americans through English explorers (Cook sailed past, and Vancouver and all the rest), the Civil War period (one of the first islands of the San Juans to be colonized, other than by the various Native Americans [who didn't actually live here year-round, just fished and gathered food], was settled by a group of ex-slaves who bought their freedom in the 1850s and came here, a good long way from the South), and the late nineteenth century (when people on the islands smuggled everything from Chinese workers to whiskey), to the early twentieth century (Desmond Newborn, for example) and WWII (those "pillbox" bunkers watching for enemy subs), to the beginning of a new century (yours truly).

It sounds to me like you could have a lot of fun with this project. If it would help, I'd be happy to take photographs, or make you a map, whatever you need. Between your search engines and Internet and libraries and my actually being here, between us we could write a small book. In fact, that's not a bad idea. If you type it up all pretty on your computer, I could have a friend of mine bind it for you, in leather. Shall we put your name in gold?

By a funny coincidence, when Ed brought your letter I was digging out the foundation, after days of cutting my way through the brush like some explorer in a jungle movie, and almost immediately I began to find things in the soil—an old canning jar, a bunch of silver forks, the mostly rotted covers of half a dozen books, various lumps of metal. All of them your great-great-uncle's possessions—I feel like an archaeologist. I cleaned them off and have set them aside for you to look at.

And that brings me to the second part of your letter. Petra—of course I would love to have you come here for a couple of weeks in June or July, but it's not as easy as what either of us want. What do *your parents say about it? When you talk to them (your letter didn't say if you had yet or not) please let your mother read this letter so she knows my reaction. And I am also including a letter for you to give her.*

But to tell you the truth, my dear, you might think long and hard about whether a trip to the island is really what you want right now. It's not a summer camp here, you realize. I sleep on a hard cot, eat dull food, work long hours of dirty, hard labor. You saw my privy—I still don't have a flush toilet or a proper shower. I have to heat water on the stove, so I don't even try to stay clean. There are mice and insects everywhere (and more, come June). I don't have a boat, so you're stuck here. I'd like to say I could take a week off and spend it going on hikes and picnics and swims with you, but I know I'm not going to be able to, and considering the wildness of the island, I can't even say that you'd be free to take off and wander as you like. And, you wouldn't be able to bring Bounce, because, this being a nature preserve, the authorities frown on dogs running around and worrying the nesting boobies or whatever.

Maybe we should think about next summer, when the house is finished and my only work is hoeing some tomato plants? I'd even have a boat then, I'm sure. Or maybe Christmas vacation, which would allow you to use the trip for the eighth-grade segment of the project. Still, it's your decision. Think about it, talk to your parents, give them these letters, and let me know.

> *Love,*
> *Gran*

P.S. I'm sticking in two rolls of film that I've taken here on the island, to see if any of the shots might be useful for the project. Why don't you have two sets of prints made, and keep one for yourself.

April 18

Dear Tamara,

I've asked Petra to give you the letter I wrote her, so I don't have to copy it over again. As you can see, I've tried to discourage her with realism—life here is no holiday, and Petra is not used to roughing it.

Not that I wouldn't love to have her here, but I don't imagine the idea pleases you too greatly.

If the deciding factor is emergency communication, I could find out if cell phones will work here, and would agree to allow her to bring one—if she agrees that it is only for emergency use. If you have other specific objections, ones we could work out, let me know. If your objections are more general, well, I suppose I could understand that. Perhaps in the future we could talk about it again.

I have spent many quiet hours here, thinking about you and all the ways I have failed you as a mother. I hope it is not too late for us to begin again. Yet again.

I love you, Tamara.

    Mom

Nineteen

Rae folded the two letters away, leaving the bulky envelope unsealed. She was not at all sure about the wording, but she was too tired to think about it any more tonight. Tomorrow she would read them both again, before giving the packet to Ed on Tuesday.

An unsettling day. The feeling of having one foot in the waters of sleep had persisted, as had the memory of looking down the beach to see the man, woman, and child materializing from the fog. She had not quite managed to finish the excavation work, because first the wheel had come off the barrow and it took a while to dig up a replacement nut, and then the ramp had fallen apart and she had to remake it. Mostly, though, she'd just been a weird combination of lethargic and jumpy, a sensation that bore a worrying similarity to the beginnings of one of her downward cycles, yet not the same. There were no voices, for one thing.

Yet.

However, even if she was sure that she was slipping, there was little she could do about it. All she could do was wait, and in the meantime, work.

Tomorrow she ought to reach the back wall.

So why had she agreed to spend the middle of the day being ferried around by that young woman?

Rae sat back in her wooden chair and dropped her hands away from her face, and as she did so, her eyes lit on her journal. She pulled it over in front of her and reluctantly opened it to the last entry, a scrawl of mad words disturbingly like the scattered lists that had filled her house and her mind in the weeks following the funeral service. Hundreds of them, there had been. Tamara, taking on the job of clearing the house while Rae was hospitalized, had not known what to do with them; in the end she put them all into a couple of big grocery bags, to be saved or dumped as Rae chose.

Those scribbled sheets of paper, deep on every surface in the house by the time Sheriff Escobar came for her, were as clear a sign of trouble as blown leaves were of a windstorm, a last-ditch attempt to impose order onto her decomposing mental process, as if the definitions of words and the relationship between objects and events might restore meaning to her life.

She might have thought that stability was restoring itself, here in the tranquility of Folly, but she was in truth only a narrow step from quivering mutely in the corner: Last night's journal entry was evidence of that. She reached out to tear the offending pages from the book, and stayed her hand. Psychiatric honesty, she had said, was the journal's purpose, and honesty could not be had through censorship. She looked at the list of words, then ripped the two pages out.

And folded them in half to stick in the back of the journal.

A good hour before dawn, Rae was up and brewing coffee, impatient to finish the clearing. She had slept fitfully, but felt rested, or at any rate felt ready to begin.

However, there was no point in digging and sorting debris that she couldn't see. When the coffee was made, she took it out to the promontory to try and hurry the sunrise.

She'd done this so often, it was becoming a ritual, its varied elements assembling themselves out of the crepuscular light like the individual instruments in a tuning orchestra.

The waves were first. Rae had spent enough hours with them to tell, by hearing alone, which way the tide was moving. This morning the water was crisply nibbling its way up dry rock, so the tide was coming in. Then would come the foghorns—although this morning the sky was clear, with no mist to obscure the warning beacons or the stars, which were fading until only the brightest persisted. The air seemed to change, gathering itself to greet the day; the first birds stirred in the branches, and the early-rising humans. She was coming to know the various engines of her neighborhood: the rough-sounding motor chugging its Roche Harbor–bound owner to work and home again; a small, shy outboard heard only at low tide; a floatplane that passed over regularly; the big commuter ferry to Sidney. She heard the *Orca Queen* plying the nearby waters from time to time, usually at a distance, and although she couldn't have said what was distinctive about its engines, her ears twitched whenever her daughter's paid spy, genial as he might be, passed by Folly.

No motors this morning, though, just a gradual, pleasing discord of smells and sounds, raising her spirits and her anticipation until the crescendo came with the appearance of the sun.

Sunrise was a little after six. At nine o'clock Rae reached the back wall of the foundation, where she made a pair of interesting discoveries that she had no time to investigate because just then a new and unfamiliar engine intruded itself into her consciousness. She stood up and saw a Parks Department launch entering her cove, at its helm a petite figure with a cap of gleaming red hair. Rae looked down at herself, patched clothes caked with dirt, and sighed. Then she looked at the object she was holding and decided that, since the first time she'd met the woman she'd had a gun in her hand, maybe this time it would be better to be empty-handed. She dropped the corroded hunk of metal that had been Desmond's pistol back to the ground, kicked some soil over it, and climbed out of the foundation.

At the tent, Rae stood scrubbing the soil from her hands and watching Nikki Walls approach. She wore her ranger's uniform today, and looked like a pixie with a gun belt; all Rae could think was, How had this enticing creature managed to remain a single mother for as much as two weeks? Nikki was, granted, too fey for conventional beauty—her extraordinary looks, Rae knew, might even work against her, considering what conservative souls men were—but she was also neat, intelligent, and bursting with energy. Rae suddenly felt old and clumsy, like something that ought to crawl back under its rock.

"Morning," Nikki called, and held out a paper bag, its neck gathered in her child-sized fist. "I brought you that bird book you asked for, and also some apples. Last year's, of course, but they've been in cold storage and they're still good. I hope you like pippins. Knowing Ed, he doesn't bring you much fruit." She put the small bag on Rae's table, her quick gaze flicking into the nooks and crannies of the campsite as she did so. "I know I'm a little early, but I got to thinking that I wasn't sure about the depth of your cove, and there's a big minus tide around three. I'd hate to get stuck. It looks really bad when Parks Department employees screw up that way." Nikki's heart-shaped face ended in a pointed chin below a slightly secretive mouth that radiated innocent mischief when she smiled, as she did now.

Rae nodded. "Probably a sensible precaution. Do we have time for me to change?" She wanted to get out of her work clothes, but God forbid she should delay so long that she found the inquisitive redhead trapped on Folly until the next high tide freed her boat's hull.

"Oh, sure. Shouldn't take us more than an hour to make the circuit."

Rae ducked into the tent to drop her filthy clothes in a heap on the grubby canvas, exchanging them for something several degrees less disreputable. She came out to find Nikki carefully scrubbing the apples under the water tap, one of Rae's bowls from her storage boxes sitting ready to receive them, and not one book, but three (birds, trees, and wildlife of the San Juans) stacked to one side. Rae couldn't decide if Nikki was just chronically overhelpful or if she was expressing puppylike devotion to the owner of Folly Island. Whatever it was, it was beginning to make her nervous. Maybe she should have asked Ed to buy her a bird book, instead.

However, Rae had to admit that the apples looked good in the blue bowl; more than that, they looked appetizing, smooth and green and glistening with drops of water. She picked one up as she headed down to the boat, and crunched into it. Almost too tart for comfort and crisp as if it had just come from the tree, the fruit made her whole mouth feel alive. How long since she had tasted something that intense? How long, come to think of it, since she had actually tasted anything at all?

She climbed into the boat after Nikki, most of her attention on the apple. As soon as they were clear of the cove mouth, the ranger opened throttle, and they roared out to sea. Rae sucked the last juicy scraps from the core and dropped the remains overboard.

"Thanks," she told Nikki. "That was good."

Nikki just grinned at Rae, balancing herself on the balls of her feet with the bumps and sway of the boat, openly inviting Rae to make fun of the pride the boat's captain felt over her abilities. And they were considerable—Rae could feel that, even if all they were doing was speeding in a straight line away from the island. Nikki was a natural, an extension of the boat; she would also be absolutely fearless.

"Why'd you become a park ranger?" Rae asked, shouting over the engine noise.

Nikki throttled back a bit and veered the boat to run parallel to the island's shore before she answered. "Basically, for the fresh air. I go nuts if I don't get outside regularly. I was born here, moved to L.A. to go to college, came back when Caleb was little, and swore I'd never live in a city again. I've been posted various places, managed to wangle this assignment a year and a half ago. With Caleb small and needing my family, I could plead hardship. I try not to let them know how happy I am here, or they'll send me to Yakima or Olympia, or have me designing computer programs somewhere. What happened to your arm?"

Rae glanced down at the arm braced against the boat's motion, its sleeve creeping back from the wrist. It was not the three scars on the inside of her wrist that Nikki had seen, but the straight surgical scar along the side. One of the surgeons had suggested plastic surgery to make it and the other scars less prominent, but tidy skin was not at the time high on Rae's priorities.

"I broke my arm a year and a half ago; they had to put a plate in it to hold it straight." Not that it was any of Nikki's business. Then Rae remembered the sheriff saying that Nikki had married a violent abuser. Maybe this was her way of asking if Rae too belonged to that sorority? *No,* thought Rae, *let's nip these personal revelations in the bud.* "Where are you taking me?"

"Just a circle. Jerry said you didn't know why your island is so difficult to get close to. You see those ripples?" She pointed to one patch of rough water among many, this one offshore of some scrawny trees.

"Er, rocks?"

"Bad reef. Great if you're into skin diving, but not if you want to get close in. It wraps around the point up there before going out. The divers anchor offshore, don't try to swim through it. Not more than once, anyway, and they usually only stay a couple hours at a time, around slack water. Current gets strong once the tide gets under way—it'll pull a light anchor right up."

To her passenger's relief, Nikki kept well clear of the reef, and around the point came the other barrier the sheriff had mentioned, a sheer cliff face that dropped like a highway retaining wall into the sea. The boat's powerful engines throbbed at low power as they chugged along against the full flow of the retreating waters, Nikki pointing out landmarks as if she owned them. They saw a bald eagle perched in a half-bare tree over the cliff face, Nikki spotting it as soon as they came around the bend, although it took a while before Rae could make out its white head against the foliage, even with Nikki's massive binoculars. Rae could see the lightning-split tree over the spring, and showed it to Nikki as one of her two contributions to the tour.

The bare cliff face ended sharply in a forested spit that came out into the water like a bent arm, a miniature version of her campsite promontory, only this one was covered with huge, low-limbed cedars that brushed the water. To the right, a delicate waterfall marked the entrance of the spring waters to the sea. In front of the wooded arm, Nikki pointed out another submerged reef awaiting unwary hulls and wetsuits, and gave it wide berth. As they turned to follow the island's north shore, the sun shifted from their backs to their right sides. Rae closed her eyes and raised her face to the warmth.

"I saw that show," Nikki said abruptly. Rae reluctantly turned her head and opened her eyes. "That traveling show a couple of years ago? Women woodworkers, something like that."

"Women in Wood." The summer before the end of things.

"Right. Your big piece just blew me away. The small one, too, but especially the figure. *Lacy* something—*Lacy Runner,* that's it."

Rae had to smile at the subtle difference it made to put the emphasis on the second word, as Nikki had, rather than on the first as Rae herself did. The piece had taken her the better part of a year, and at the end had become something far more than the wooden figure in running shoes that she had originally envisioned. Its very submission into the show had been cause for heated debate and protests by those who saw it as being too close to conceptual art, even containing elements of performance art, for a dignified show of fine woodworking techniques.

The figure was that of a slightly larger-than-life woman in running shorts and a stretch top. She was a portrait of Rae's grandmother, wife of the tyrant William, who had died when Rae was six years old, less than a year after Rae and her newly widowed father had returned to the family mansion in Boston where he had grown up. Rae had rendered Lacy in woods as light as she had been in life, birch and yellowing white pine, with mother-of-pearl for her eyes.

The name of the piece, as far as most people were concerned, came from the arch over the runner's head, an intricate lace table runner that had belonged to the woman herself. Only Rae's family and close friends knew about the play on words, since Lacy's name had not been mentioned in any of the promotional material about the show. Rae had stiffened the lace into rigidity with a plastic resin and curved it on a frame, so that it resembled a garden arch—or a finish line. The key element of the piece was that the woman herself was composed entirely of drawers, large and small, of myriad shapes and angles. With all the compartments in place, the figure was simply a runner with a wide band of lace arched over her upper body. When the drawers were all removed, from the side she remained the same, a running profile veiled by a lace archway, but from the front she was revealed as empty, a ghostly presence made of delicate wooden lace. Some of the drawers also had objects in them, inlaid or fastened down or lying loose—again, several of them had personal meaning for Rae alone, having belonged either to Lacy herself or to Rae's mother. Every day, the gallery would transform the wooden woman at least once, removing and replacing the drawers and changing the objects they contained. A person could see *Lacy Runner* a dozen times and never catch the same exact figure twice.

"I went to see it four times," Nikki told her. "Drove all the way to Seattle twice. I even bought the catalogue, just for that. I . . . well, I'm really glad you came here. And if there's anything I can do, just say. Please."

Good heavens, Rae reflected; *the woman actually is a fan.* And she thanked her.

The northern corner of the island was a less precipitous rock face than the western side; heavy splashes of guano testified to its long history as a nesting site for a dozen varieties of bird. Nikki handed over the binoculars again and described each type of nest, its occupant and the bird's habits. The Parks Department had participated in a banding the spring before, it seemed, and Nikki had been the first to volunteer.

"I hope we can continue to do it," she told Rae abruptly. "I mean, this is your island, no matter what my bosses say—I've seen the legal agreement, and you have every right to throw us off. But I hope you don't. We need every sanctuary we can get. For the birds, I mean." The ranger had the grace to look uncomfortable, aware that the hand of friendship she had extended might well now be seen as the proposed handshake of a business agreement.

"Nikki, I don't intend to throw anyone off, although my lawyer would have a fit if she heard me admit that. There's not enough sanctuary in the world; I'd hate to rob the birds of theirs."

"That's great, especially because there's some very interesting wildlife on Folly—a big pigeon guillemot rookery come June, river otters, and the like. Have you seen the eagle nest?"

"I saw one when I was here several years ago. I don't know if it could be the same one."

"Sure to be. Eagles use the same nest for years and years. Yours was here when I was a kid, though it was probably the current one's parents'. There it is. See?"

They had now reached the western flank of Mount Desmond, its sheer wall rising nearly a thousand feet straight out of the sea. Here and there, trees had attempted a foothold, and on one of the dead snags near the water perched a massive tangle of sticks. Nikki looked at it hopefully, although there was no sign of nesting activity that she could see. A little farther around, a glimpse of the bald mountaintop gave Rae her second opportunity to offer information, because Nikki had never heard there was a hut on its summit, long derelict or otherwise. The ranger thought it more likely to have been a birder's blind than an armed forces watchtower, and Rae did not argue with her, although as she remembered it, the hut had been far too heavily built to be the work of a casual bird-watcher.

Three quarters of the way around the island, rock face gave way once more to forest. Just before the trees began, another water source leaked down, darkening the rock and causing green growth to crop up vigorously on the ledges below. Rae asked Nikki to pause so she could study this seepage through the binoculars, but she eventually decided that the quantity of water staining the rock was much less than that of her primary spring.

"Too bad," Nikki sympathized. "It would be a lot shorter to bring that water over."

"That's what I was thinking," Rae agreed ruefully. "There's even a cave it's started to carve out."

"Probably just softened the sandstone enough to let the rain wear at it. That layer of rock pops up here and there, and often brings water and little caves with it. Soft sandstone between harder stone, you see? That's where the water goes." She powered up the engine again, and in a few minutes Rae's tent came into view.

The tide was still going out, but Nikki nudged the boat up to the rickety dock so gently the fenders barely compressed, and held it there with the casual skill born of a lifetime on water while she and Rae finished their conversation.

"I put in an order this morning for an official U.S. Government Piss Off sign," she told Rae. "'Trespassers on this refuge will be strung out for the eagles to eat,' something like that."

"I appreciate it."

"You will, come summer." Nikki looked up at the stone towers, then blurted out, "I just can't tell you, how fantastic it is to have Folly rebuilt. You know, when I was young, we used to think it was haunted. Kids still think it is. Still, I have to say it's a little hard to visualize how it ties together . . ."

"I have a guide," Rae told her. Nikki looked at her out of the corners of her green eyes. "A picture," she explained.

"Really? A picture of the actual Folly? Oh, I'd love to see that."

"It's on the madrone where the bench is. Do you have time now, or maybe you'd rather get off before the tide goes out any more?"

Nikki practically leapt off onto the floating dock. Rae caught up to her at the bench, where the young woman peered up at the laminated photograph. Rae pulled the picture off its tack and handed it to her.

"When you said 'guide,'" Nikki commented, "at first I thought you meant you'd found someone who remembered it."

"No, just the picture," Rae said. "If I didn't have it, I wouldn't have the faintest idea how to begin." Although she supposed that Desmond Newborn might be called a guide, at that.

"You know, I thought I'd seen all the old pictures of the Islands. But I've never seen this one."

"It's a family snapshot I had enlarged. That's Desmond Newborn."

"Your uncle."

"Great-uncle," Rae corrected her. "My grandfather's younger brother."

"Oh, of course. It must've been taken in, what? The Thirties?"

"Mid-Twenties sometime. Not long before he disappeared, I'd guess."

"I thought he died."

"He must have eventually, but not around here. He was last heard of in the late Twenties; after that, nobody knows what happened to him."

"But there was something strange about his disappearance, wasn't there? I can't remember, just that people used to talk about how he'd no sooner finished building it than it burned and he dropped dead. It added to the mystery of the place."

"Going by what I've been digging out of here, I'd agree that it burned down shortly after he finished it. And considering how long it must have taken him to build, it wouldn't be too surprising that seeing it burn would have driven him away. I know it would dishearten me." That was putting it mildly. How would it feel, to see the labor of years go up in smoke? Something along the lines of seeing a husband and daughter being fed into the flames of the crematorium?

Nikki's inquisitive mind was still chewing on the problem. "But he must've died. The island's been a sanctuary since 1928, and I thought it came to the Parks Department in a will."

Rae shook her head. "My grandfather was the one to turn it over to the state, at first informally and then, when it looked like Desmond was probably dead, on a more permanent basis. The last thing that anyone knows is that Desmond wrote to his brother, my father's father, just before the stock market crash in 1929, from Arizona or New Mexico, I forget which."

"A puzzle," Nikki said, reluctantly parting with the photograph and watching Rae return it to its tack before they turned back to the dock, the ranger's bright head barely clearing the level of Rae's shoulder. "But it is an amazing house. The historical society would love a copy of the picture."

"The negative's in California. I'll see what I can do."

"How long do you think it'll take you to rebuild?"

"Nowhere near as long as it took him. Most of his original labor went into the stonework, and that's still in great shape. The house itself is fairly straightforward. It'll be rough, of course, none of the finish work done, but I won't have any problem in sealing it up before winter."

"You're planning on staying here, then?"

"I was thinking about it."

"The weather's nowhere near as friendly in January as it is now" was Nikki's only comment.

"Well, we'll see," Rae said, and thanked her for the boat tour.

"My pleasure," Nikki replied cheerfully, then clasped Rae's offered hand and trotted out onto the weather-beaten boards. As Rae watched her pull smoothly away, she found herself wondering if the other kids used to call her "Nosy Nikki."

Twenty

Letter from Rae to Her Granddaughter

April 23

Dearest Petra,

I found something exciting to put into your report the other day, buried in the foundation of Desmond's house.

I told you I've been finding things of his in the rubbish under the house—all nonflammable stuff, of course (and nonbreakable, meltable, or rust-awayable). No gold bricks or bags of doubloons, I'm afraid, though there were a handful of coins, along with cook pans and dinner plates, a hunting knife with a blackened bone handle, a few chess pieces (also bone, I think, though it'd be hard to tell black from white now), a string of silver medallions (silver the metal, not the color—they're absolutely black with tarnish!) that might be one of those decorative bands men wear around their cowboy hats, a fishing reel (and all the hooks, fortunately all safely corralled in what looks like an old tin cough-drop box), a thoroughly melted and rusted-away pistol (no bullets in it, fortunately—I seem to remember that they can go very unstable with age), and a lot of other blobs and whatnots I can't identify.

So there I am, scraping the last bit of soil from the rock floor of the foundation, and I notice a hole the size of my fist along the back wall. This is the first gap I've found in Desmond's stonework, and it looks just the right size to let mice and other undesirables under the house, so I get down on my creaky old knees to take a closer look. And I find that it's not a gap where a stone has fallen away, but a hollow in the center of a soccer ball–sized stone.

Great-uncle Desmond found a stone mortar, as in mortar and pestle, the kind Native Americans used to pound nuts and things, and he incorporated it into his foundation. And I would say that it was just another convenient rock to him, but for its placement smack in the middle of his back wall, where the fireplace stands. Nobody but he would have seen it (and now me) but I think he must have come across it on the island—an archaeological discovery just like I've been doing with his things—and mounted it there deliberately. A piece of personal symbolism, tying his house to the people who were here before.

Nice, huh?

I'm afraid it'll be under the floorboards again by the time you get here, but I'll take some pictures of it for you. I'm nearly finished with another roll, which I'll send via Ed either this Tuesday or next. I'm also nearly finished with the floor—I hope to have the building inspector out to approve the foundations soon. Keep your fingers crossed!

I hope Mandy's hoof is better. Horses do seem to pick up a lot of stones, don't they?

    Love,
    Gran

Twenty-one

Why had she neglected to tell Petra (and through her, Tamara and Don) the full story of the soon-to-be-rehidden mortar in the foundation? After all, she'd told her about the old pistol, knowing that it might create an unfortunate subconscious link between Folly and violence in the minds of the child's parents—although she had been careful not to describe how wicked it still looked, pitted and scarred as an old soldier and every bit as deadly. But the contents of the mortar were something else. Rae could not have said exactly why she found them troubling; she simply knew that she did not want Petra handling them. If Petra came, Rae would have to discourage any exploration of the crawl space below the floor: nail down the access door while she was here, perhaps, or at least cover it with a throw rug.

Within the mortar's hollow, protected from fire and debris and a certain amount of ash and dust, Rae had found two objects, side by side: a stone spearhead, as wickedly sharp as the day it had been shaped, and the thumb-sized wooden figure of a man.

It was just a man—no facial details, unfortunately; the cleverness of Desmond's hands had not extended to artistic representation of the human form. Or perhaps simplicity, even crudeness, was his intention. At any rate, human it was, a man fully clothed even to the hat. Imagination might identify this figure's hat brim with the headgear Desmond wore in the photograph, but the face could have been that of any clean-shaven male. Or female, for that matter.

It was the spearhead that disturbed her. What did it signify? Had Desmond merely come across it one day, and placed it in his foundation as a token of the island's previous inhabitants? Or was its significance darker, more totem than token, a warrior's killing talisman buried in the house's foundations to protect the inhabitant from harm? And was the thing as pristine as it looked? Or had it been used, had it shed blood? Killed? And if so, was the blood animal or human? Spears seemed more weapons of war than of the hunt, and even a quick glance at the county map revealed a bloody past, with place names such as Victim Island and Slaughter Point. Had one man killed another with this razor-sharp rock, here on peaceful Folly?

For the time being, Rae left the spearhead where she had found it. That night, sitting by the fire, she turned the small figure over and over in her hands, her expert fingers getting to know it. Her immediate impulse had been to carve her own manikin and lay it alongside the hatted man, back in the depths of the foundation. However, picturing the two figures lying throughout the years in such close proximity, even without the lethal stone blade watching over them, brought with it a more immediately identifiable frisson of discomfort: incest. Desmond Newborn might be her father's uncle, but all her life he had felt like the brother she never had, a shadow twin, whispering beneath the covers, two of us against the world. Months, years from now, sitting in her snug living room in front of Desmond's fireplace and surrounded by the subtle labor of her own hands, knowing that beneath her feet a wooden male lay beside his wooden mate . . . It felt too like a fertility rite for comfort. Had the figure been bearded, hatless, and worn spectacles, she might have found that Alan was moving into its outlines, but no: This was unarguably Desmond Newborn.

She sat with the figurine cupped in her hands, her fingers laced together so that the bulge of its hat rested in the meeting place of her thumbs, the squared-off boots just at the edge of her little fingers. *Well, Desmond,* she told him, *I'll just have to make sure that we look like brother and sister. Or partners.* Surely the creator of *Lacy Runner* was enough of an artist for that.

So it was that over the next few evenings, having spent the mornings clearing off the foundation stones with a wire brush and patching the few places where Desmond's cement mortar had failed, then the afternoons trenching the hill for the laying of PVC pipe, Rae sat by her campfire and whittled a painstaking wooden self-portrait. She chose madrone in lieu of Desmond's cedar, madrone being a harder wood and more accepting of detail, but in all other ways she followed his lead, her character the same height as his, her shoulders as wide, with the same bend to their trousered legs. When she was satisfied with Desmond's companion, she fashioned a cedar base, so that the two guardians of her hearth might stand upright, elbow-to-elbow, comrades—twin siblings, even—with no tinge of romance in their splintery hearts.

She completed the work late Friday night, running tiny brass screws up through the flat base into the feet of the two Newborns. She studied the features for a bit, wondering what first Desmond and then she had intended by this whimsy. Before she went to bed, she carried the linked figures over to the workbench, and there she left them overnight, standing in the open air beneath the stars, in a spot where they would catch the early morning sun as it crept under the madrone's wide branches, fragrant now with masses of tiny white flowers. In the morning she rose and drank her coffee, waiting for the shadows to move across the watchful pair, and when the sun was off them, she blew the figures free of petals and took them over to the foundation, where she trimmed the base until it fit snugly into the hole of the Indian pounding-stone. A carelessly carved man on one side, a meticulously shaped figure of a woman on the other, with a hammer at her hip and boots on her feet, the drape of her shirt, she now noticed, subtly flatter on the left side of her thumbnail-sized chest than on the right—an exaggeration of her injuries, but psychologically true. And what, she wondered in amusement, would the sharp-eyed archaeologist of the next millennium make of that little detail? Amazons in the San Juans?

Then she hesitated. Leave the spearhead, with all its ambiguity—amusing curiosity or double-edged threat—or remove it, to be replaced by the image of herself? She pulled it carefully from the back of the mortar. It was a beautiful thing, to be sure, dark gray with faint light threads lending it texture. And brilliantly shaped, by an artist as well as a craftsman, each side mirroring the other, the undulations of its edge calling for the testing thumb even as it clearly menaced. She held it up by the blunt end, half-tempted to prick a few drops of blood, some obscure instinct for sacrifice. She laid the flat of it against her wrist; it covered all three scars. She pushed down, feeling it cool into the warm flesh. Tilting it slightly would draw blood. Tilting and then drawing it back . . .

Rae snatched the blade away from her lifeblood before it could cut her. After a moment, she reached forward to lay it crosswise in the mortar's depths. In front of it she wedged the two wooden figures; they now stood between her and the sharp blade. Heavy-handed symbolism, she scoffed, but sometimes that was better than the overly subtle.

She brushed off her hands and stood up. Her guardian spirits in place, at long last it was time to breach the vast, ugly blue tarpaulined stack of lumber.

One thing Rae had known from the very beginning was she would build her house with wood of the same solidity that Desmond Newborn had used. Modern lumber is milled far below its nominal size: A "2x4" actually measures one and a half by three and a half inches, a "1x10" is a mere five eighths of an inch thick. Adequate, particularly when sheathed with plywood, but noticeably less solid than the full measure.

Rae would build with full-measure wood. It had cost her a small fortune to arrange for custom milling, but the sight of those authoritative studs was deeply reassuring. Her house would withstand gales.

In part, the decision was wished upon her once she chose to use the existing foundation—narrower wood would have required an endless round of jiggling and trimming to fit. But in the end, it was the sensual satisfaction of the heavy wood that decided her.

With the foundation stones clear and strong, Rae buckled on her tool belt and wrestled back the hateful blue tarpaulin on the first stack of building material, and began to haul out the wood for the sills.

Had Rae been building a modern, engineered, permit-laden structure, she would have begun by drilling holes through the rocks for anchor bolts, to tie top to bottom. Actually, she probably would have begun by bulldozing the entire foundation into the sea or just moving to another location, because the drilling would have been a brutal job, impossible without heavy-duty power tools. This, however, was to be the restoration of a historic building, and as such she had permission to be scrupulous about following Desmond's lead. He had set his sill plate actually into the stones of his foundation, creating a raised stone lip that was not continuous, but which would cradle the sills and hold them in place. As a woman who had spent most of her adult life in earthquake country, Rae was not entirely comfortable with this, but other old buildings were still on their pinnings, so in this, as elsewhere, she would trust Desmond.

She trimmed the sills—cedar, these, like Desmond's, cedar being the Pacific Northwest's native rot-resistant wood—and tapped them into place. They took remarkably little adjustment—the length, of course, and shaving off the odd tight place where it met the stone lip—but Rae was enormously pleased when the last board went in as easily as the first. The foundation was now neatly capped by cedar, all the way around but for where the towers and fireplace interrupted, everything fitting neatly—except for the front. Unlike the other three sides, where the stone lips holding the wood were narrow enough to be covered by the future exterior siding, in the front the stones jutted out a good two inches from the cedar sill. She didn't know if this would prove to be a problem or not, although as it stood, it looked as if it would direct rain-water under the sill plate, and even cedar was not intended to stand in water for long. She would have to take a closer study of the photograph, to see what Desmond had in mind. His attention to detail would not have failed him in such a crucial spot. She hoped.

Other than that slight doubt, the sill plates lay clean and true in the spring sunshine, and Rae was humming as she went back down the hill for the floor joists.

Modern wood-frame building was dubbed balloon construction not just for the openness of its internal space, but because of the speed with which the structure rose up. Drive past a housing development one week and see little more than scattered concrete foundations; the next week the houses are up—or at least their skeletons. One good strong breath, and an architect's dream inflates.

A solitary middle-aged woman may not raise a stick-frame house with the rapidity of a team of union-wage framers, but then Rae's project was considerably smaller as well. She had been on the island for three and a half weeks and had yet to drive a nail into lumber. That was about to change dramatically.

Once she got the damn boards up to the site.

Other than that Desmond had worked with the standard (for his time) full-measure wood, which had been noted in the original engineer's report that she had commissioned shortly after her visit here with Alan and Bella, Rae hadn't known until reaching the back wall during demolition exactly what dimension lumber her predecessor had used—the photograph she had showed nothing beyond the exterior siding. Rae had drawn her own plans with an eye to modern building codes, knowing that her building and his would agree only in places.

Enough had survived of the back wall of the house, to the left of the fireplace as one came in the front door, for Rae to know that Desmond had used the same 2x8 joists at sixteen-inch centers that her plans called for (although his were of cedar, hers the stronger Douglas fir). There did seem to be something odd about the structure near the fireplace, marks of extra boards against the scrap of doubled joist under the wall that Rae hadn't been able to figure out yet, but since it could be anything from a patch around some inadequate lumber to the need for greater support under a proposed upright piano, she decided not to worry about it.

A few boards at a time, Rae hauled her lumber up to the footing: floor joists, rim joists, 2x8s for the cripple wall to lay the floor above an uneven foundation—but at these she paused. That sill had looked nearly level, perhaps close enough to receive the joists directly . . . A careful check with the spirit level confirmed it: After all these years, Desmond's foundation stones stood true. She could get away with minor shimming and trimming; there was no need to frame a separate wall to join floor to foundation—which would also give her more height inside the finished house. Whistling, she measured, marked, and laid the first joist over the sawhorse, leaned on the board with her left hand, drew the teeth of the saw gently up along the pencil mark, then drove the saw down firmly into the wood.

The forgotten odor of fresh sawdust juddered into Rae, as shocking as an open-handed slap, as blindly unexpected and powerfully evocative as the fragrance of Bella's hair or Alan's shirt. This fragrance did not just evoke building, however, or creativity or action or a step toward the future; what jarred Rae's mind was sex. The cedar she'd cut earlier for the sill plates had no such effect, but the more familiar construction softwoods, redwood and especially Douglas fir, Rae had always found more than a little erotic, reaching in to send a thrill up her spine even before the memorable if somewhat besplintered afternoon when Alan had discovered his new wife's little quirk. They had come out of her workshop looking like a pair of millworkers, or snowmen, pale sawdust glued to their sweaty skin and plastered into their hair, and . . .

And if she didn't pay closer attention to the work at hand, her joists would never fit. She corrected the angle of the saw and focused on the clean line of the cut, pushing away the memories it had evoked.

But the memories, once aroused and reinforced all that day by the heady perfume of the sawn joists, did not go away. She had forgotten how frankly sensual the act of building was, particularly at the very beginning.

Alan had come to anticipate the days when one of her projects finally moved from drawing and visualization to the actual laying on of hands upon wood. The exhilarating, dangerous moment of conception invariably transformed her, made her restless and distracted and randy.

Rae didn't have Alan. Even Ed wasn't due for four days, by which time—fortunately—the first flush would have passed. She'd just have to sublimate the urge, turn it back into the building. Cold showers were said to be good; God knew she could have any number of those.

She set the joist up to span the cedar sill, nudged it into place, scooped a trio of nails from the pouch at her waist, and for the first time in seven decades the joyful noise of hammering on Folly Island rang out across the water.

With a break for lunch, Rae had the joists laid down, shimmed level, and nailed fast by the middle of the afternoon, and most of the bridges to tie them were in place before the sun dropped behind the trees and forced her to stop work. Muscles trembling, back screaming, but immensely pleased with herself, Rae hobbled away to her tent to buckle off her tool belt and slide the saw into its place in the toolbox, and then collapsed onto her cot. After a while she forced herself upright, sluiced off hands and face, put some rice and beans on to cook, then poured herself a celebratory measure of wine in one of The Hunter's elegant glasses. While dinner was bubbling, Rae went back to admire her handiwork, in the same way that she used to visit in-process pieces of furniture in her workshop.

Tomorrow was the first of May, she realized, and with a full moon to boot. International Workers would march beneath their red flag, children would pick weedy bouquets and hang them from neighbors' doorknobs (did anyone actually do that anymore?), and New Age Celts would burn the spring fires of Beltane. She had been on Folly for one cycle of the moon, from April Fools' to May Day, and she had a clean, bright, fragrant grid of close-locked boards to show for it. The scorched stones of the fireplace and towers seemed more out of place than ever, uneven and dark against the pale wood, like a couple of wizened old men who had stumbled by accident into a kindergarten room. On a more technological building site, Rae would have hired a power washer to scour the stones; here she had to wait until she had the subfloor down, so she could get at the stones without having to teeter on an ill-placed ladder.

"Don't worry," she told the rising stones. "I'll clean you up in a few days."

The moon rose, gravid with light, pulling itself with ponderous dignity out of the sea, and with the moon rose the noise she had heard on her first night on the island and not since then: drums. This time she was more sure of herself and her surroundings, and did not immediately assume it to be a hallucination, although she was still open to the possibility. She carried her bowl of dinner out to the end of her promontory to listen, eating without tasting until she was satisfied that, somewhere nearby, her neighbors were drumming up the full moon.

It was cool near the water. When the bowl was empty Rae went back to the warmth of her fire pit. She poured herself a second glass of wine and shut down the kerosene lamp, which was attracting moths. Rae sat and drank, her muscles tired but her blood restless, her eyes darting across the unearthly landscape, while the blue light of the moon grew stronger. The directionless drumming filled the air one minute, ebbed into the night the next. Everything around her was stark, black or white, the shiny tops of the madrone leaves contrasting with the dark shadows underneath. Bats flew; an owl called. The waves came and receded rhythmically against the stones, each one curling briefly into the light as it rose to meet the shore.

Rae wondered what it would feel like to lift her face to the moon and howl aloud. She wondered if the drummers on the neighboring island would hear, and if so, what they would think. She tried to imagine what The Hunter would say, and failed. She put down her glass and got to her feet to pace slowly up and down from tent to house and back again, feeling a nameless urge trying to rise up, an urge that felt like fur and smelled of sawdust. She ached with it, her bones and her flesh craving something, craving contact, physical, warm contact. She wanted Nikki here to take her on a moonlight boat trip, Sheriff Carmichael or Ed De la Torre to fill the air with the sound of their male voices. She wanted Bella to hug her, Alan to grab her hair and wrestle her to the floor. It was not a desire for sex—or, not only a desire for sex—but something even more powerful, the desire to wrap herself up in a pair of strong arms, to crawl into an embrace and put her head down and stay there, nestled into a shoulder, warmly clothed in the affection and protection and camaraderie of another human body and soul.

She wanted Alan, and Alan was gone.

It was odd, she reflected, but in the mental hospital it had been Bella she lusted for the most. The maternal drive to wrap her arms around her missing child and comfort her had then been overwhelming, but that urge seemed to have shriveled into insignificance by being so long denied. Since coming here, Bella had faded, and Alan had come to the fore.

Well, she couldn't have either of them. Considering her age and her state, it was all too possible that she would never again know either of those kinds of embraces, sexual or maternal, that the brief, dutiful brush of a daughter's cheek or the furtive hug of a granddaughter would be all she would have, ever after.

Now Rae really did feel like howling at the moon. For a moment she thought about taking the still-empty gun out of the locked storage box and feeling the smooth and comforting authority of its grip against her rough palm, caressing her cheek with its cold metal, holding it between her breasts. Instead, she walked down to her rocky little cove and methodically stripped off her clothing, shirt to shoes, and stood there, clothed only in the cool light of the moon.

She threw back her head, held her bare arms out from her sides, and closed her eyes, feeling the reflected energy that washed over the sea and the land, the beach and the figure that stood there. The night air stirred around her, bathing her face and body, caressing her exposed skin. The night smelled richly of seaweed and sweat, the rocks beneath Rae's feet were hard and round, the branches above her head still and watchful. The warm moist hair under her arms and between her legs shrank at the unaccustomed touch of air, and she shivered, and then for the second time she walked slowly forward into the gently undulating water of the island's cove.

When the freezing water of the cove was lapping at her upper thighs, Rae halted. Eyes still tightly shut, she lifted her hands to her face, and the hard, sensitive skin of her fingertips began to probe and explore. Like a blind woman getting to know a new person, Rae felt herself: the shaggy, wiry tendrils on her head (*I need a haircut*) and the broad stretch of forehead, the bristle of the eyebrows in an arch over the soft hollows of her eyes, lids twitching as if she were dreaming. The warm breath from her nostrils, the dry elastic of lips, strong jaw and vulnerable throat, a full, round breast in her right hand and the poor damaged object bisected by scar tissue in the left, and down.

Oh, Alan, she breathed soundlessly. Oh, oh, Alan.

Twenty-two

Rae's Journal

May 2

I don't remember my dreams being so strange, before. No dreaming at all for a whole drugged year may have something to do with it—like mental chemotherapy, chemical psychotherapy makes a person's dreams fall out. My unconscious has to grow again and catch up, pushing fantasies to the surface, some funny, some frightening, others just odd.

A while ago I had a vivid dream, just before waking, that I was pregnant, huge of belly and full of breast, being told by a doctor (who looked remarkably like Nikki Walls in drag, come to think of it) that it was a healthy baby dolphin. On waking, my first thought was how I was going to adapt the cradle I made for Bella so it would hold water.

Then I dreamed of men marching to war, grim, gray, muddy men with gaiters and greatcoats and rifles slung over their shoulders, marching in unison through a blighted landscape, past smoking tree stumps on which vultures perched, tramping blindly down the road in mechanical precision and straight off the edge of a high cliff, one row at a time, tumbling without a sound. At the bottom their bodies lay piled, like the news photos of mass graves, human beings turned to cordwood. Brrr. I did not sleep much after that one.

But the most convoluted dream yet was last night's, going on and on with a cast of thousands, or dozens anyway—everyone I've ever known or even met seemed to flit through at some point. I forgot most of the dream's details long before I woke up, but one scene lingered.

I was in a cedar longhouse, a dim and smoky space, but cold even with the fire going. Everyone inside the place except me was a man, all the men in my life aside from Grandfather. I've never dreamed about Grandfather directly, although he often seems to lurk in the edges of my vision. But my father was there, and my uncle Gavin (looking even more like my mother than he actually did) and my first husband David and a couple of cousins. Vivian was there in the background, with Alan standing next to him.

They were all dressed in Native American costume, robes and a few bark rain cloaks, and they all wore wooden masks. Most of the masks looked like the person—Alan looked like himself, down to wood-rimmed glasses—except for two figures in the middle of the enormous room.

Their backs were to me. I went forward to see what they were look-ing at, and found them bent over the cherry cot I made for Bella. There was a baby in the cot, a girl baby awake and looking up at the two men. I couldn't tell who she was—it could have been Bella, or Petra, or even Tamara for that matter, although they looked nothing alike even when they were tiny. The baby was a girl, that was all I could tell.

I went around to the other side of the cot and looked at the two men, but these masks were different. You couldn't tell who they were, because the wood had been carved as traditional Northwest masks, a raven and a bear. When they looked across the cot at me, I was fright-ened by the glitter of their eyes, and I wanted to grab up the baby and protect her, but then I thought that might only make things worse, that what I needed to do was draw their attention away from her.

So I put on a sort of mask of my own, and started acting abrasive and confrontational, asking them what the hell they wanted and who the hell were they, anyway?

They stood looking at me, and then one of them held out his right hand with Bella's antique silver rattle in it, and the other held out his left hand holding Desmond's rusty hammerhead that I found under the house. I knew in an instant that I had to get that hammer away from the baby.

"Who are you?" I shouted again. So they reached up with their free hands and lifted off their masks, and they now wore wooden faces with the features of my son-in-law Don and my stepson Rory. And then they reached up again to take those off, and Rory turned into Don and Don to Rory. Then they did it again, and again.

I grew frantic, not being able to tell which of the figures was Don. If he was the one holding the rattle, I didn't think I had too much to worry about, but Don with a hammer in his hand was another thing entirely.

They kept shedding faces and I kept trying to locate Don beneath the masks, and then all of a sudden the baby started to cry, and I looked down to see that the heap of discarded masks had filled the cherry cot to the top, and the child was completely buried.

I woke up then, as frightened as if I'd dreamed a monster.

Dreams tell us truths, but it's often a slim fragment of truth under a load of rubbish. Don is the key to this one, but what fragment of Don? Threat or thief? And if he is a threat, who is he threatening? His daughter? His wife? Bella is beyond his reach—or is it my poor infantile feminine side lying there in that cot, the last of the family at his mercy?

Ironic, considering all the men who have dominated my life, that both my children and my only grandchild have been girls. And that both surviving members are in fact lying there, with me on one side and Don Collins on the other.

Twenty-three

Hanging pipes under the joists took the better part of a day: water pipes and a waste outlet for the shower and sink. She had approval to mount a shed at the side of the cabin for a composting toilet, a complicated mechanism that nonetheless simplified the other septic demands considerably.

Framing and building the access door for the crawl space took a morning. Then she was ready for her first inspection, after which she could begin to lay the subfloor.

The county building inspector came on Monday morning, in accordance with the letter she had sent with Ed the week before. There was something infinitely comforting about a man with a clipboard, the threat he carried both tangible and universal, and therefore welcome. Rae quite looked forward to doing battle with him, and was disconcerted when he proved a jovial balding man on the edge of retirement, who was just terribly interested in everything but in too much of a hurry to do more than a quick run-through today, maybe coffee next time, Ms. Newborn. Even his clipboard was unthreatening, a bright blue plastic affair with a butterfly sticker on the back (his small daughter's addition, he told Rae without embarrassment). Vaguely disappointed, she held her signed permit and watched his boat pull away. Then she went back to her officially sanctioned foundation and let herself down between the floor joists to check on the two carved figures of herself and Great-uncle Desmond. She blew gently to free them of a light drift of sawdust, then pulled herself back up to staple fiberglass batting over their heads.

More boards to haul, this time 1x8s with shiplap edges for the subfloor. They were also mostly warped and knotty, which offended the precise woodworker in Rae even though she knew full well that using clean, close-fitting, kiln-dried boards for the purpose would be a waste both of money and of resources.

Still, her boards would be true, whether they started out warped or not. It pained her to use even a cheap screwdriver as a brute lever to force the boards into alignment before hammering them into place, but she did it, and her floorboards were tight enough to qualify as a finished floor, though they were rough and fastened with common box nails.

Rae drove the last nail in on Tuesday morning, and was trimming the overhang when the familiar cadence of Ed's boat engine reached her ears. As he was easing up to her dock, she sawed through the last few feet, and then she walked across the fresh new floor of her house and stood where her front door would be, taking in the change of perspective that the combined elevations of foundation and floor provided.

The view was good.

Ed threw his rope around the stanchion and looked around for her. She waved broadly to catch his attention, and was amused to see the energy of his return wave. She trotted down her front steps and across the clearing to help him unload.

"Hey, there," he called when she was within earshot. "You got yourself a floor!"

"That I do, Ed. Want to see it?"

He all but ran up the hill, his stocky figure bowling along, mustaches flying. Rae tucked the canvas-back camp chair under her arm and followed. When she joined him on the platform, she set the chair down in front of the fireplace and gestured to it with a ceremonial flourish.

"Please have a seat, Mr. De la Torre. You're my first visitor."

"I am honored, Mizz Newborn." He lowered his backside with an air of ceremony, and tugged at his mustaches in pleasure.

"Call me Rae," she told him, as she'd told him on each of his four previous visits. He merely looked out over the scenery and beamed, as proud as if he'd done it himself.

She was pleased to have him here, an actual visitor without a clipboard, someone with whom she could share her achievement. Ed was growing on her, this genial aging hippie boatman who smelled of marijuana and engine oil, who acted like a resident of Margaritaville, yet in whom she suspected a number of dark corners. She wasn't at all sure how she'd feel if he arrived on the island in the dead of night, but during the daylight hours, he was a welcome if perplexing visitor.

"You oughta have a porch out front," he told her. "With a rocker on it."

"Granny Newborn," she remarked. Ed's suntanned features twisted up and he hastened to assure her that he didn't mean it that way, that he'd never thought of her as— She laughed. "Never mind, Ed. I am a grand-mother, after all. And you're right, it does need a viewing point. The only problem is, the original didn't have a porch, and I'm supposed to be restor-ing a—Hey, wait a minute." Rae squatted down on the front steps to take a closer look at the troublesome lip. As it stood, it was an oddity that threatened the house's fabric, but with Ed's words in mind, she began to smile and shake her head admiringly. "Desmond was going to put a porch on; he just never got around to it," she said. The lip that threatened to direct rain to the sill would be a perfect ledge on which to rest a porch. And—damn! That also explained why the door was hinged as it had been: Standing on a porch, a door opening outward would not be awkward.

She realized that Ed had said something to her.

"Sorry?"

"Who's Desmond?" he repeated.

"Oh. Desmond Newborn, my great-uncle, who built the place in the Twenties. None of the family knows much about him, but I keep finding out things, like this. The only reason to make a foundation this way is if you want to add a porch in the future." Another thought suddenly struck her, and she turned to look at the empty space to the left of the fireplace. Her grin widened. The peculiar framing she had uncovered there would be no accident, either. For whatever reason, Desmond had built a narrow door smack against the stones of the fireplace. Or a window, but why build a window that looked directly into a rock wall? She couldn't wait to tell Petra, her partner in—what? forensic anthropology? analytical architecture?

"Want some coffee, Ed?" she called over her shoulder, but she knew his answer, and was already moving down the steps.

She put on the kettle and helped Ed unload her usual selection of basic groceries, the propane canisters, water jugs, sack of clean laundry, and assorted building materials that she had ordered. The plastic joints for the water line had come, stapled into a heavy-weight plastic bag. Seven weeks, and Petra (assuming she came) would have her shower. Out in the trees, true, but there would be water, and it would be hot.

She gave Ed her laundry sack and shopping list, and then his cup of coffee. She watched, amused, as he settled into his chair for his weekly gossip as if he'd been doing it all his life. Rae had no real desire to know what was going on in the outer world, and it was an interruption, but Ed did usually keep his stay down to a half hour or so, and it seemed to make him happy. If thirty minutes a week would buy her a contented deliveryman, it might prove a good investment, if she ever needed something above and beyond his call of duty.

So she told herself. The truth of the matter was, solitary she might be, but she was discovering that she was not by nature a complete hermit. Part of her enjoyed the human contact with the earthy rogue Ed De la Torre and the otherworldly busybody Nikki Walls. She might not want to see too much of her neighbors, but it was nice to know she had them.

And beyond mere human contact, Rae was coming to have an intrinsic interest in Ed himself.

On his second delivery run, Rae had caught the first hint that the man was more than just a seagoing jack-of-all-trades. She had been relieved to see the wariness fade quickly from his eyes when she met him with a nice, normal greeting, her hammer left behind on the workbench. They unloaded the boat, coffee was offered and accepted, and then Ed tugged his heavy corduroy shirt down over the tattoos on his wrists and asked her, "Do you know anything about Kant?"

Rae nearly choked on her coffee. "Kant? You mean the philosopher?"

"Yeah. Immanuel Kant. I've been reading my way through him and ran up against a couple of things I don't understand. Whenever that happens I just sort of ask around until I find someone who knows the answer. You'd be amazed, the kinds of things people in these islands know."

She blinked. "You don't say."

"Really. There's a guy over in Deer Harbor, wrote a book on Thomas Aquinas. He came in handy, I tell you, whenever I got stuck with the *Summa theologica*. But he's not much help with Kant."

"Well, I'm awfully sorry, Ed, but the last philosophy I read was in a class when I was eighteen. It made my head hurt."

"It does that, all right," he agreed cheerfully.

The weathered features of a sixty-year-old boatman-philosopher crinkled up in a rueful smile, and Rae was blinded by the sudden, sure knowledge that Alan would have loved to meet this man, would have sat forward in his chair to pry out more of his unlikely incongruities, delighted at the discovery of a diamond in the rough. She had had to go and busy herself with the coffeepot to hide her face from Ed.

Now, three weeks later, she handed him his mug and asked him how Kant was coming along.

"Finished him Friday."

"And did you solve the problems you were having?"

"Not really, but I wrote them down to think about. Someday I'll find someone who can answer them. Now I'm working on Confucius."

"That's quite a shift."

"I don't like to get stuck in one place. But Confucius . . . I don't know. Feels to me like a person really has to know Mandarin Chinese to see what the guy's getting at. I know a little Cantonese—enough to order a meal or give directions to a taxi driver, but I can't read it."

"Ed, you are a constant surprise. Where did you learn to speak Chinese?"

"Lived in Hong Kong for a couple of years. Want to see?"

Before Rae could ask what he meant by this cryptic offer, he stood and began to unbutton his corduroy shirt. The T-shirt he wore underneath it concealed his torso, but when the long sleeves came off, Rae could finally see what she had glimpsed at its beginnings: Ed's skin was a solid tapestry of color, starting at the wrists with a pair of similar but not identical bracelets in an African sort of design, and moving up his arms. He pushed up the right sleeve of the T-shirt to reveal a dragon, the tip of its tail just below the elbow, its body a sinuous curve up toward the shoulder, its head doubled around to breathe fire down the back of the arm.

"Hong Kong," he said.

"You mean you had that done in Hong Kong?"

"That one I did, yeah, although most of them I have done by a guy in Vancouver. He's been working on me for thirty-five years now. I give him a design, he figures out how to fit it in. It's my life, all the important things, beginning with these." He clasped his left wrist with his right hand, then the right with the left. "Two years with the Peace Corps in Kenya—I came home and wanted to make sure I'd never forget it. So we started with them, and added on. We figure that unless I get real busy, we won't get to my ankles until I'm ninety-five or so."

His was a truly magnificent epidermis, peculiarly sensuous, a solid plane of shifting, intertwined, richly colored images, indigo and emerald and maroon, with not a scrap of flesh tone to be seen. It was difficult to resist caressing it, so velvety warm did the surface appear. Ed pointed out a leaping salmon along the left biceps (commemorating two seasons on a fishing boat) and a standing grizzly bear on the right (an encounter while working the Alaska pipeline), a whirl of purples and blues (a Caribbean hurricane he'd been through), and a brightly striped balloon (summer employment in the Napa Valley). The shapes were as intricately fitted as a jigsaw, but one shape she puzzled over.

"What's that?" she asked. It looked like a bottle with lines in front of it.

"Ah," he said, looking embarrassed. "I did six months for drunk and disorderly, punching some guy in a bar. He turned out to be a cop."

It *was* a bottle, with cell bars overlaid.

She sat back, sure that if she expressed an interest, he would happily strip off his shirt and show her how far they had gotten. And perhaps more than his shirt. For today, however, she'd had enough revelation.

"So, Ed," she said. "What's new in the outside world?"

What's new in the world was an unending source of interest for Ed, as compelling and instructive as Kant or Aquinas. What's new was also, for Ed, almost exclusively local; his world stretched from the northern end of Vancouver Island to the southern tip of Puget Sound, only occasionally extending to the rest of Washington State. The lawmakers in Washington, D.C., might as well have been on another planet—ironic, she thought, for a man so thoroughly traveled. Today's news bulletins were typical, beginning with the recent near-trauma of a rumored buyout of the local market by a huge mainland chain, a narrowly averted catastrophe that would have brought the islands arugula and fresh mozzarella at the cost of a local institution, and continuing on to a scandal involving a high school teacher on San Juan Island, a dead orca found near Shaw (one with a letter and number designation rather than a name, which meant it was not one of the more prominent island residents, though nonetheless mourned), and finally some complicated fracas on a private beach on Lopez that had Sheriff Carmichael diving into the water, fully clothed, to rescue a drunk girl. Rae listened with half an ear, distracted by the play of Ed's tattoos. A slim rattlesnake had been slipped in between a brown football with a black squiggle on it (a signature, blurred by age?) and a squarish object that looked like a sandwich. What would it be like to go to bed with that skin? she speculated. She had absolutely no interest in Ed, but the skin he wore was another matter.

She realized that her guest was sitting forward, hunkering toward her as if they were in danger of being overheard by the blue jays. Rae tore her attention from his skin to listen, and found herself leaning forward as well.

"You heard about them girls disappearing on the mainland?" he repeated.

"Um, there was a girl in the papers, but that was weeks ago. Rugeley, the name was; Joanna Rugeley. When I first got here." A newspaper story from which she had torn her eyes, crumpling it up for firestarter, but not before the name and photograph had imprinted themselves on her memory. "In Spokane, wasn't it? Has there been another one?"

"Her sister," Ed said, relishing his role as bearer of grim news—even if the news was from the far distant edges of his recognized world.

"The paper seemed to think the girl had run away," Rae remembered. "There was some kind of school the father was going to send her to, wasn't there?"

"Yeah, some reform school in Tahiti or something. Wish someone'd send *me* to the South Pacific to go to school."

"And now her sister's disappeared?"

"Yep. Ellie, they call her. Fourteen years old—walked off to the school bus and just vanished into thin air. They think either some freak's out there, or else the first girl came back for her sister."

"Either way, it's hard on the parents."

"Mother's dead, it's just the father. And yeah, he was on the news, all cryin' and stuff. They had an interview with one of his friends, called him a God-fearing man."

The only God-fearing people Rae had known were, in her opinion, self-righteous, judgmental individuals with good reason to fear divine disapproval. But Rae had not forgotten the scene with Tamara on the ferry, hearing of the growing antagonism between Petra and Don, and Don's consequent investigations of schools for troubled youth. The narrative, typical of Tamara, had been disjointed, leaving Rae to guess what lay between the lines. At the time, she had assumed Tamara was exaggerating, that this was just the latest in a long series of messages, ultimately from Don, asking Rae to contribute yet again to the Collins family finances—surely Don would not seriously consider farming his daughter out just to extract some cash from his mother-in-law. Still, she hadn't been able to call his bluff, not then, probably not ever. Instead, she did as she had for years, more times than she could count—namely, sat and written Tamara a check, this one ostensibly for the child's therapy. But the memory niggled in Rae's mind, and made her answer sharply.

"I've heard about those schools, Ed. Tropical boot camps, all drills and structure and a fair amount of abuse. There's good reason they don't have them in this country—our laws would never stand for some of the things they do to those kids to keep them in order. If I were a teenager, I'd probably be tempted to run away, too."

Rae's vehemence had Ed raising an eyebrow over his coffee mug, but it was a question that made her very nervous. How long would Don be satisfied with the last check? There was no knowing, with him. Should she have paid more attention to what Tamara was saying about the schools? Rae could only hope to God that Petra would back away from open confrontation with her father.

"Hey," said Ed suddenly. "Jeez, I nearly forgot. I got a call from some lawyer down in California, said she'd sent you a letter and would I please wait for you to look it over. She needs something signed, said you'd want me to take it back and overnight it to her so she wouldn't have to wait till next week. It's in that fancy envelope," he said, as Rae picked up the canvas pouch that Ed always brought her mail in. The bag was heavier than usual, due in part to a packet from Petra—the photos, no doubt. She laid that to one side and pulled out the express packet. It was an immensely thick bunch of documents from her lawyer, Pam Church, nearly an inch of paper; when Rae read the cover letter, her heart sank.

"Oh, shit," she said in disgust.

"Problems?" Ed asked, trying not to sound too inquisitive.

"Legal problems," she said vaguely.

"Legal things are a plague," Ed said darkly, grim personal experience clear in his voice. "It's like that story by Dickens—court case goes on and on, people die off but the case lives forever. You ever read that?"

"*Bleak House*? Years ago. I hope to God this isn't that bad."

Rae's normally imperturbable lawyer had been practically spluttering with indignation when she wrote the letter; reading it, Rae could see why: Don—and Tamara, although Rae well knew who was behind it—had filed suit to get his mother-in-law declared mentally incompetent. Not in so many words: The words were all in polysyllabic legal language and therefore barely comprehensible. But there were a hell of a lot of them: LPS conservatorship and Petition for Appointment of Probate Conservator, Capacity Declaration and Springing Power of Attorney were a few of the phrases that leapt off the pages and straight into her brain when she flipped through the immense document. Then a dread word snagged her eye, and she went cold: "Dementia." SPECIAL ORDERS REGARDING DEMENTIA, the official form was titled. The next one read CAPACITY DECLARATION, and then the searing phrase UNABLE TO PROVIDE FOR PERSONAL NEEDS. That form included half a dozen categories of mental disorder from DSM-IV, all of which had been applied to her at one time or another. She winced away from the list, and turned the page, and there she found her case history.

There was page after page of it, a catalogue of Rae Newborn's lengthy experience with mental illness, from her first suicide attempt to the recent year of hospitalization, with a heavy emphasis on the month before Sheriff Escobar came for her. A signed admission form was the only contribution by Dr. Hunt, Rae was relieved to see, but there were also copies of the police reports *(How the hell did Don get those? Did Tamara have them, or were they somewhere in my house?)*, descriptions of her bizarre behavior that led to full-blown psychosis during the weeks after the accident. Delusional, said the admission form. Hallucinating. A danger to herself. "Gravely disabled," someone had typed *(Oh, not Tamara, please not Tamara . . .)*, and her physical state when she had been readmitted to the hospital.

The conclusion was what she would have expected: Rae Newborn's continuing and dangerous instability as demonstrated by her moving to the island, away from psychiatric and medical supervision and into a state of "extreme isolation and primitive conditions unsuited to a woman of her age and psychiatric condition, tantamount to a threat of suicide or a cry for help."

The final piece of evidence was a photograph, dramatically enlarged and without the distraction of a caption, showing her current surroundings. It took Rae a moment to realize that it must have come from the rolls she herself had sent to Petra a bare two weeks before, the very photographs that waited for her in the envelope with Petra's handwriting on it. The picture was of the tent on a particularly wet and dreary day, when her living quarters had looked as wretched and tawdry as a gypsy encampment. Only a crazy woman would live like that.

Damn the man, anyway. She'd sent him enough money to keep Petra in fifty-minute hours for years, knowing that he would suck up most of it. Why wouldn't the bastard stay bought off? And she couldn't confront him, not unless she was willing to sever all ties with the child, which Don knew damn well she was not. All she could do was what she had been doing all along, which was to give him money while more or less pretending that she didn't realize what he was up to.

She found a pen and scrawled her signature on the form, clipped to the document, which in many long syllables reiterated Rae's desire for

Pamela Church to continue acting as her legal representative in this and all other legal matters, and then sealed the return envelope irritably.

"I'll mail it soon as I get back," Ed assured her, then he drained his cup and picked up the laundry bag, his long-sleeved shirt, and her envelope. At the dock, Rae handed over the empty propane tank that she had left there earlier, and thanked him.

The sun was high in the sky now, the still air very nearly hot. Ed cast off with insouciance and accepted her push away. The engine kicked into life and he waved to her, then turned the boat toward the mouth of the cove. As the *Orca Queen* straightened out, Ed took both hands off the wheel and reached down to peel his T-shirt off over his head.

It was, Rae decided with amusement, probably a gesture as much of narcissism, perhaps even flirtation, as it was of comfort: the human canvas proudly displaying its colors. And it was truly an extraordinary sight, a well-muscled, gray-ponytailed man painted from wrist to beltline, glowing in the sun. Most of the shapes were too far away to make out, except one: Ed's entire left side below the shoulder blade was covered with a red patch broken by dark lines, and although she had no idea what the red was, the stripes looked very similar to the bars covering the bottle on his arm, only bigger.

Leaving Rae to wonder if her deliveryman had once worked as a zookeeper.

Or if he'd done serious time in prison.

Rae shook herself to shed her dark speculations, and found that she had held on to Pamela Church's letter. She stood on the undulating boards and read it a second time, becoming aware as she did so of the concern behind the indignation.

Pam was worried.

Damn, she thought. Don Collins had been a part of her life for fourteen years now, and the only good she'd gotten out of the relationship was Petra.

Don had known Tamara in high school, when she was a sophomore and he a senior. They dated a few times, then he graduated and went off to college, leaving his old friends behind, including Tamara. Two years later, when Tamara was a high school senior and Don came home for his spring break, they met again at a party. Tamara went to her graduation pregnant, although none of them knew it at the time—certainly not Rae, who had not seen her daughter more than a handful of times that spring. Rae met Don for the first time at the graduation. She met him for the second time at the wedding, two months later, a formal if hasty affair at the house of

Rae's ex-husband, David, the house where the bride had lived under her grandmother's care for most of her life, the house where Rae was watched like a ticking bomb. Petra had been born the following January.

Long before Petra's birth—perhaps, she suspected, even before he agreed to marry Tamara—Don had discovered the lever to pry a steady supply of cash out of his wealthy mother-in-law: guilt welded to family. Within weeks of the wedding, with Tamara barely in maternity clothes, Rae had stood outside the apartment doorway looking at the newlyweds, Don's arm possessively wrapped around Tamara's shoulders, blatant extortion in his eyes; in that instant, her financial relationship with her daughter and her new son-in-law was set. She wanted the newlyweds to move to a decent neighborhood? Fine, Don told her, but she'd have to help with the rent. She wanted Tamara to continue with her plans for college? Okay, but Don couldn't afford two tuitions plus the cost of child care. An allowance, and an extra sum for health insurance and baby equipment, and the repair bills when the car broke down, and they really needed a computer. Then later—well, of course Petra *could* go to a cheap and basic day care with fifteen other babies, but for a little more . . .

It had been a source of conflict with Alan, who was deeply resentful, not so much about the money as the manipulation. By the time Alan came along, however, Petra was two years old and there was not a lot anyone could do to change the way things worked. The set monthly allowance died away once Don graduated from college and began to earn a salary in his father's real estate firm; instead, Rae's contribution went into a savings account for Petra (although Rae doubted much of it stayed there), to be supplemented by checks to cover the regular catastrophes that plagued the family. The vastly inflated sum for Tamara's horse-training workshop was typical. Rae could not remember how many unreliable appliances she had replaced, how many tuition emergencies she had covered. The one time Don had tried a variation on a theme, asking her to become an investor in one of his schemes, had been the only time she had flat out refused him—the last thing she wanted was to become enmeshed in her son-in-law's business. Even then, however, she had written him a check, to keep him in good temper. Rae had expected that the proposed visit from Petra would follow the same pattern, that permission would be given, followed by a regretful memo in Don's writing to say that he was sorry, but the extra expenses he was incurring meant . . . Rae would then send him a check, and everyone would be happy.

This threatened suit was a whole different matter. Now, it seemed, Don wanted it all. He had probably gotten the idea during Rae's hospitalization, when Tamara had been given a temporary conservatorship in order to pay Rae's bills. That glimpse into Rae's financial status must have set his mouth watering, and given him ideas.

Why, oh why couldn't he have waited a few years to do this? Rae raged, but she knew damn well why he couldn't: Petra. The child was thirteen, securely a minor, with five years to play her in front of Rae as bait and as threat. He knew damn well how much Petra meant to Rae, knew it better than his wife did. If Rae fought back, Tamara would side with him, and Petra would be lost to Rae until the child's eighteenth birthday. A grandparent's legal rights to a child were far from certain.

Damn, she thought. Damn and damn. How much was it going to cost her to buy two weeks of Petra's company next month? She didn't know if this counted as extortion or blackmail, but she did know one thing: For whatever reason, the stakes had suddenly expanded; the pressure would not stop until Petra was legally free to make her own decisions, or until Don got his hands on a lot more of his crazy mother-in-law's money.

Maybe I should have asked Ed to take me over to San Juan and a telephone, she thought. Pamela had not asked for it, but the lawyer quite obviously wished a consultation, almost as much as Rae wanted reassurance.

Not this week, she decided. Maybe next Tuesday she would rent a couple of hours of the illustrated man's time and phone her lawyer, tell her that what she wanted was to maintain the status quo, to avoid outright confrontation, to continue being allowed to buy access to her own family. If it left a bitter taste in her mouth, so be it. She'd eaten worse things than gall, and it was only for a few more years.

But damn, and damn.

To take the taste out of her mouth, Rae sorted through the other letters waiting on her cook table. The thick envelope from Petra was indeed the two rolls of developed film, and Rae ripped it open, then flipped quickly through the photographs, pulling a face at the shot of the campsite that Don had appropriated, remembering with the early shots how new the scenery had looked through the viewfinder, how exotic. Two rolls of thirty-six, and most of them, inevitably, rubbish: a bird on a branch that would only be noticed if an arrow were drawn to it; the subtle colors of a sunrise that came out dull gray on the paper. Some of them, though, were not bad. Two or three, in fact, were first-rate. One of the madrone tree sheltering the new workbench from the rain captured some interesting juxtaposition of the natural and the man-made that seemed to invest the qualities of one in the other: The bench looked like a living thing, emerging from a tree that itself looked far too perfect to be anything but an artist's creation. And one of the photos of the house site before anything had been done to it was . . . eerie. Shot from the promontory in the angled light of early morning, the towers seemed to cry up out of the foliage like a pair of drowning hands. Tennyson, she thought; Tintern Abbey or Glastonbury.

Yes, a handful of the seventy-two were good. Professional, even.

And why did that particular word come to mind?

She pushed the pictures back into their sleeves and glanced at the other pieces of mail, most of them forwarded, most of little interest. But at the sight of one distinctive hand, she smiled involuntarily, then frowned. Vivian Masters, her wood man; more than that, a close friend. He had been, anyway, before Rae had decided that she could not afford friendships, had refused would-be visitors to the hospital, had on her release put herself in the hands of a trained nurse-cum-baby-sitter rather than submit to the loving arms of friends, had hired the woman to bring her up the coast rather than allow a friend to volunteer for the task. Strangers and professionals made no demands other than the financial, and did not grate on the nerves. What did Vivian want?

Dear Rae,

I hope this reaches you; nobody seems to know where the bloody hell you are.

I don't want to bother you, but a couple of years ago you said you wanted a big walnut burl and last year I came across a real beaut. Just your kind of thing, dark and twisted and completely impossible for anyone else to use, but in your hands it'll make the critics bleed. I'll hold it for you forever, you know that, darling, but I just wanted you to know that when you're ready for it, it's ready for you.

No rush, girl. The tree has waited three hundred years for you, it'll wait a few more.

I hope you're better, Rae—last time I saw you, you looked like you'd been through the wars. Guess you had. Take care of yourself, girl, and, write a boy, eh? So we know you're still walking the earth.

Vivian

When you're ready for it . . .

Dark and twisted and impossible . . . Yes, it sounded interesting, it sounded like her kind of thing. *Like my kind of thing used to be, once. Before I'd been through the wars.*

Rae crumpled Vivian's letter and threw it into the fire pit. After a minute, she fed the legal document to the flames as well.

Distracted by legal suits and painful reminders of times past, Rae went back to fiddling with the water line, and spent that day and the next at it. The work was hot and dirty, involving hacking into the ground to form the trench and continually checking the level, and she was overjoyed when, late on Wednesday, she completed the underground section, submerged the collecting end in the lukewarm water of the upper pool, and a few minutes later watched the first water trickle out of the plastic tube a hundred feet away from the spring. The rest of the line, aboveground and following Desmond's path, would go a lot faster.

Thursday afternoon, more than halfway down the hill now between spring and house, with mud to knees and elbows, her back on fire from all the bending, her skin scratched and inflamed from the bushes and stinging nettles she was working her way through, and half her fingers glued together with the plumber's cement she was using, Rae heard an engine. With a grunt and a groan, she came upright and staggered over to prop herself against a nice straight tree trunk until the engine came into sight. Even if it proved to be merely a passerby, any interruption was welcome.

It was not a passerby, it was Nikki Walls, stepping from her boat in a crisp uniform, as lithe as a teenager and nearly as perky. Nikki had stopped in twice since the day of their boat tour two weeks ago, each time bringing food, boundless good cheer, the curiosity and affection of a Labrador puppy, and (Rae had to admit) the good sense to leave before Rae grew too tired of her bounce. Rae pushed away from the tree trunk, discovering in the process that she had been leaning against a large patch of sap that was, now and forevermore, a part of her shirt, and stumped off down the hill to see what the park ranger wanted.

Nikki took one look at the shambling creature that came out of the woods, and left her hand firmly in her pocket. Rae waved a couple of stuck-together fingers at her in greeting and walked straight down to the shore, where the saltwater and sand scrubbed away the more superficial grime and made the myriad scratches and nettle rash sting fiercely. Plumber's cement, obviously, was not designed to be soluble in water, but it would be a waste of time and solvent to scrub down properly twice in an afternoon. Besides, Rae was well accustomed to working with hands glued into mittens by one or another wood glue. It was one reason she almost never worked with Super Glue—getting that stuff off involved skin loss.

She came back from the beach to find that Nikki had already fetched the second chair from the tent and was sitting in it, thumbing through the photographs that Rae had been looking at again that morning and that she'd left on the log table beside the chair.

"These are good," Nikki said, then looked up. "I hope you don't mind—they were just sitting there."

Rae had come to think of Nikki not so much a fairy as a small colorful mammal with the defining characteristics of curiosity and helpfulness. A Beatrix Potter red squirrel, maybe, tail flicking, clever tiny hands sorting through other people's lives and setting them straight. On her third visit, Nikki had arrived with a bag containing a quart of milk and a roll of toilet paper. Milk was a natural enough gift to bring someone who lacked refrigeration, but the other showed not only that Nikki had noticed the absence of a spare roll in the privy on her visit five days before, but that she had also found out that Ed had neglected to bring any on his intervening visit. It should have been oppressive, if not downright creepy, but somehow Nikki's good cheer overrode it all, as if the woman's otherworldly appearance brought with it a natural inability to follow normal human mores. Today she'd brought a jug of fresh apple juice and a tall, tubular object of brilliant orange plastic, which sat by the leg of her chair.

"You're welcome to look at the pictures," Rae told her. "My granddaughter's working on a school project; she wanted some shots of the island. I had her send me duplicates."

"You know, this one of the bench should be in a book."

Rae hoped she did not show the reaction she felt, a reverberation deep inside: She had sat in that chair with her morning coffee, studying that very picture and thinking that very thing.

Rae poured out two mugs of the juice, then dug around in her food storage locker for a package of fig bars and set it on the upright stump. With the formal hostess duties out of the way, Rae dropped into the canvas chair and leaned back gingerly. Even Nikki winced at the clearly audible grinding sounds that came from Rae's spine.

"Thank you for interrupting," Rae told her visitor.

"You sound ready for traction. And you look like you've been mud-wrestling."

"I have been. I am determined to get water down here before Ed comes on Tuesday. I'm sick to death of fighting with those jugs."

"How's it going?"

"I'm halfway down. With the harder part half finished."

"That's great. Do you have a storage tank yet?"

"It'll just have to dribble into five-gallon jugs for a week or two, I'm afraid. But at least we won't have to juggle them off Ed's boat."

"Let me know if you need a hand—with a tank, I mean. I could bring half a dozen guys with muscle up to shift one into place for the price of a six-pack. Each, that is."

"I'll be using three interconnected smaller tanks, instead of one big one, so I think I can handle them myself. But thanks, I'll keep your male harem in mind."

"Family, mostly—I've got dozens of cousins. Most of them male, all of them protective. And three brothers-in-law; the shortest of them is six feet."

"Say," Rae said suddenly, her memory jogged by the picture of a gathered multitude. "Do you know if there's a drum circle somewhere nearby?"

To Rae's astonishment, Nikki's pale skin flushed scarlet beneath the freckles, and she mumbled something about um yes, there was a bunch of people, she had heard, who got together with these drums they had made . . .

"I just wondered. Twice now I've heard this noise, both times at the full moon. The first time I thought I was imagining things."

Nikki looked relieved. "Oh, no, it's a real group. They meet at the mouth of Roche Harbor, which is probably why you can hear it from here."

"Sounds fun. I could take my granddaughter, if she's here on a full-moon night."

Nikki's small mouth turned in, a secret smile full of mischief that made her look more than ever like an Irish wood sprite, and that made Rae wonder if any artist had ever used her as a model. "The first part of the night, she might enjoy."

Which left Rae to speculate about what took place the latter part of the night, and if the activity was the reason for Nikki's sudden blush.

Picturing the tiny red-haired ranger throwing off her neatly ironed uniform for a pagan fertility ritual in the sand, clothed only in her freckles, Rae hid a smile of her own. Nikki went quickly on.

"Anyway, I won't keep you away from your work. I'll be back in a few days with your No Trespassing sign, but at the moment I'm just passing on a message from Jerry Carmichael. He was going to come out himself but he's a little shorthanded, with one guy out with some kind of skin allergy and another on vacation. Okay; here's what it is. Jerry had a conversation with your sheriff down in California—Espinosa, was it? Right, Escobar—who wanted you to know that he'd heard a very second- or third-hand rumor from an informant about a couple of lowlifes overheard in a bar down in Bakersfield, bragging about being paid to rough up an old woman in Santa Cruz."

"What?"

"Rae, this is very, very iffy. Super insubstantial, you know? I told Jerry we really shouldn't bother you with it, because it's just going to make you worry unnecessarily. You don't live in Santa Cruz, you're not an old woman, and it's far too shaky a connection. But Jerry promised the sheriff he'd pass on the message, and I was going to be out here today anyway, so I said I'd tell you. The part I liked was, Escobar wanted to recommend that you, and I quote, 'avoid any deserted roads.'"

The two women looked around at their surroundings: clearing, tent, trees pressing in, boat bobbing gently at the ancient dock. They began to laugh at the same moment—Nikki more easily than Rae, but even Rae had to see the humor in the warning.

"Right," she said. "I'll bury myself in the crowds."

"In a couple of months, that wouldn't be a problem, but even now you'll begin to see the boaters growing every day. Anyway, Jerry sent you this, whether you want it or not." She held out the tubular orange box to Rae.

It contained a flare gun, ugly and orange and very functional-looking. Rae picked it up; it was heavier than it looked. Nikki took the gun, broke it open, and demonstrated how to load it, with cartridges that resembled shotgun shells for an elephant shoot. She ended with "Just point it straight up—although you might check that there's not anything flammable underneath it. Or a person. And I'd send off two or three flares if you really want a response. They burn for three or four minutes, and you can see 'em for miles, even during the day."

"Thank you, Nikki. And thank the sheriff. I'm sure I won't need it, but I do appreciate the thought. I really can't believe that anyone's paid some guys to attack me. And even if someone did, they're not about to come a thousand miles to do it again." Not even her son-in-law Don would do that. Legal harassment, yes, but criminal? And that was assuming that he could come up with the ready cash to hire a harasser. "They must have been just a couple of hopped-up opportunists, like Sheriff Escobar has said all along."

"Tell you the truth, Rae," Nikki said shrewdly, "you don't sound all that sure."

"Don't I? I just—I can't imagine the other." Then she went on, reluctantly. "The only thing that gives it even a trace of believability is that the two who attacked me? They didn't smell like alcohol. It's funny what sticks in the mind, but that's always niggled at me, that they just smelled of sweat and cigarettes. No beer, or drugs. It just struck me as odd, considering."

"Well," Nikki said after a minute, "I don't know just what we can do, other than say that if a boatload of strangers puts in at your dock, don't go down and try to run them off by yourself. Put up a flare and go into the woods."

"The bat-signal over Gotham City," Rae said, more sharply than she had intended. *Why did I tell Nikki about the smell? Little Ms. Innocence here may well be the worst gossip in the county.*

Nikki laughed blithely. "Sheriff Carmichael in his bat-boat. Although Ed's more likely to see it first."

This time when Nikki left, Rae did not stand on the bank to see her off. She turned her back on the uniformed ranger and everything she had brought along with her, and returned up the hill to the task at hand.

For the rest of the afternoon she kept her head down, bent over recalcitrant lengths of white plastic pipe, welcoming the hot and distracting pain in her back, refusing to look up when she heard the occasional rustle in the bushes, shoving away her mind's suggestion of Watchers, balking at the very thought of a plot against her.

Ridiculous.

Her skin crawled and her muscles twitched, but she gritted her teeth and fought against the feelings. She measured her pipes with close deliberation, she sawed with precision, she fitted and glued the joints in place, this slick dead material so unlike her usual wood.

Ridiculous idea. Absurd.

Unthinkable.

Twenty-four

Letter from Rae to Her Lawyer

May 9

Dear Pam,

I trust you received the signed forms. Ed De la Torre, the boat-man, promised to mail them on Tuesday when he got back to Friday Harbor.

Something's come up here that is very troublesome and very dis-tracting. I heard on Thursday that the police have picked up a (com-pletely unsubstantiated, as well as insubstantial) rumor that someone actually paid those two men to attack me. No proof, no indication of who or why. Maddening.

Still, I think that taken in conjunction with Don's competency suit, I'm afraid I have to bow to your long-held recommendation and rewrite my will. I'll say right off, however, that you're not going to like what I propose.

This is what I want to do—and wait until you read my explana-tion before you start shouting at me. I want you to get in touch with Hoskins, tell him I want to liquidate one quarter of my holdings. Let him choose, I don't care in the least so long as it's not real estate, but one quarter of what he estimates is the whole. And divide that into three, with one part each going to Don, Tamara, and Petra. Petra's share will have to be a trust, I presume, held until she's eigh-teen, but I would like for you to administer it, not her parents, *and* to let her know privately that you will hand over money if she *has a reasonable need for it before then. Just so Don can't get his hands on it.*

The remaining three quarters let's leave as it is now, divided up between my various relatives and Alan's family, with percentages and set amounts to assorted charities, but with the following addition: I'd like to add a discretionary fund for Dr. Hunter, to be used for equipment or to cover the costs of some needy loony, mad artist, or the like—word it however you like, to give her the maximum freedom with it. And make it an amount that's substantial without being too intrusive into the whole. Say $100,000? Maybe $200,000 would be better—she could do something with that.

And now for the explanation.

The issue here, basically, is extortion. Don holds the power over something I value, namely my granddaughter and her mother, and is telling me that unless I fork over some cash, to put it elegantly, I'll not see them again. Or maybe this is ransom, I don't know. At any rate, I can't believe Don really thinks he can get me declared incompetent. I think this is his way of saying that he's willing to make life very rough for me, and incidentally to block access to his wife and daughter, unless I open up some funds to him. The stick, you could say, to go with the carrot that is Petra.

Why am I bothering to tell you this? You know the whole story—my chronic willingness, as you once put it, to succumb to Don's manipulations. It's his way of doing business. He sees something he believes he has a right to, convinces himself that its owner is deliberately withholding it from him, and manipulates the situation until it falls into his lap. He did it with Tamara when she was still in high school, whisking her out from under her boyfriend's nose; he did it with the ranch they own, buying it from a woman who hadn't any intention of selling it; he did it with the partnership at his real estate firm, somehow getting the senior partner to retire; and he's done it with me a couple dozen times over the years. To your endless disapproval, I know.

Pam, I don't care about the money. I know it's your job to make me care, but the only reason to have money is to buy what you want, and in this case, I want Petra. There's nothing else that matters anymore. And God damn it, Don knows it.

Call him in, talk with him, make a few of those ladylike threats you do so well, make him see that we know exactly what he's doing and are only willing to go with it so far. Get him to sign an agreement to back off, if that's possible. But do not, under any circumstances, bring Tamara into it. She works very hard to keep from seeing Don's manipulations, but if she's forced to focus on what's going on, she will side with him, I promise you, and Petra will be beyond my reach for the next five years.

As you've said before, I'm letting my feelings of guilt take over. You're right, except that my guilt is not a feeling, it is a fact. I failed my daughter, badly, at two key points in her young life. The fact that it was due to an illness beyond my control—depression—does not remove the effects on my daughter and my relationship with her.

And that's my explanation for asking you to go against your lawyer's principles.

Fiddle with this and talk to Hoskins, send me a draft if you like. Getting a notarized signature might be a problem out here—could we just have it witnessed, by a government employee? My local park ranger is a bit fey, but terribly upright and responsible.

More than you can say for some of your clients, I know.

I'm doing well here—the life of a hermit seems to suit me.

> *Yours,*
> *Rae Newborn*

P.S. I realize I've left dangling the whole question of Don's possible involvement in my attack, but really, what can I say? The police are looking into it, although I somehow doubt they'll prove anything. If Don did instigate it, maybe this financial arrangement will buy him off. If he did, then it would have been just (!) a harassment that got out of hand. I will admit that I could picture Don sitting in a bar with some good buddy over a lot of beers, bitching about how short of cash he is while his wife's mother is sitting on a fortune, and then saying to the buddy, Here's fifty bucks, go make her feel threatened so my wife and I can offer to step in and take over her affairs. And I could well imagine the guy taking the money and bringing in a friend and the two of them getting carried away, going way further than Don intended. What I can't visualize is Don, much as I distrust him, actually going so far as to hire two guys to beat up and maybe rape his mother-in-law. He's manipulative and greedy, but he's not stupid, and seems (I have no proof, you understand) to have a fair amount of success in hiding his shadier deals. If this bar scenario or something like it turns out to be the case, and if (a big if) the police find evidence, then that may well be the end of Don—surely even Tamara wouldn't stick by him after that. And maybe you can throw in some subtle lawyer's phrase to our agreement that gives me a way to remove the money from him if he is convicted of a crime.

    Anyway, Pam, you deal with it. Frankly, I don't care, just so I'm left in peace. A year and a half ago, I might have dug in my heels. Now I know that life is too short for the luxury of pride. Let Don tie himself up in knots—I won't work to do it for him.

    Rae

Twenty-five

Rae had not quite finished the water line by Ed's next visit, but she was close enough to the end that she could continue to work on it without risk of missing his arrival. He gave a brief hoot on the boat's horn as he came into the cove, startling the juncos and the red squirrel, but she had heard the sound of the motor half a mile off and was on the promontory before he had a chance to get the groceries from his cabin.

Ed handed over the bags and then, balancing a five-gallon water jug on his shoulder, swung a leg over the side of the boat and followed her up to the tent, eyeing the building as he went.

"You haven't done too much work this week," he commented with a question in his voice. "I'd've thought you'd have some walls up by now."

Rae laughed, and held out her hands, ingrained with soil and crusted with layers of cement the solvent hadn't quite taken off. "Plumbing this week, Ed. This is the last jug of water I want you to bring me. If I can't get the line finished, I'll just have to go up to the spring with buckets."

"Water's a fair distance, then?"

"Clear around where that big forked fir tree is."

Ed whistled. "Why didn't your man build his house a little closer to the spring?"

"I guess he liked the site over the convenience."

"It is pretty," Ed allowed.

They drank their coffee while he caught her up on all the news, whether she was interested or not: that the two missing sisters in

Spokane had turned out to be runaways, and although they were still missing, the younger had written a letter to a friend, mailed in New Orleans ten days after she disappeared; that someone had burned down a barn on Lopez, and was in jail now with his parents screaming false arrest; that the county Board of Commissioners had discussed rationing water during the summer but decided instead to hand out flyers telling tourists not to sluice down their boats with fresh water and to wait until they got back to the mainland to take their half-hour showers.

It all ran over Rae's hearing like water off a duck's oily feathers, and she couldn't have recalled a word of it (other than the change in status of the missing girls) by lunchtime. She gave him her letters, her lists, and her laundry; he went back to his boat. Alone again.

As she waved good-bye to the illustrated philosopher, it occurred to her that, for a hermit, she was well on her way to becoming a member of a community. No man is an island—nor, it would appear, woman.

The rest of her little community arrived on her doorstep, or her dock, the following day. She had spent the remainder of Tuesday pushing to complete the water line, and late at night, working by flashlight, she glued the final joint, and springwater finally trickled from the end of her circuitous snake of plastic tubes. Rae marked the occasion by a cautious victory dance on the rock slope and a ceremonial glass of the water, which tasted of mud from the pond and petroleum by-products from the pipe, both of which would, she prayed, be gone in a few days. She knelt to bathe her sweat-caked face in the trickle, set a five-gallon jug under the end, and went to bed to the sound of an owl duet.

Wednesday morning, the jug was full to overflowing, the water from the pipe dribbling free and clean. She dumped the jug's murky contents, replaced it under the pipe, and rigged a series of three more jugs, linked together by thin tubes that would allow the water in each jug to settle before moving on to the next. The last one had a spigot at the bottom, to which she attached a common hundred-foot garden hose, which would at least reach the lower tower of the house. Ed would deliver her actual tanks the following week, and civilization would settle over the island.

She was standing at the base of the system, her ears enjoying the musical trickle and her mind turning over the symbolism of water and life and the wellsprings of the island, when a half-familiar and close-by engine intruded itself. She turned around to see the county launch that had rested at her dock on the peculiar morning when the "family" had walked out of the mist. They were here again—minus Caleb this time, to Rae's mixed relief and disappointment.

Sheriff Carmichael had not gotten any smaller in three and a half weeks, nor had Nikki grown any less ethereal—although being dressed in jeans and a short-sleeved T-shirt and struggling beneath one end of a large flat object brought even that sprite closer to earth. Rae trotted quickly down to join them, and found herself supporting one end of a large, sternly lettered sign declaring:

NO TRESPASSING!
Nature Preserve Includes Cove

The posts holding the old sign were sturdy enough to hold this one up for a few more years, and the sheriff had brought a portable electric drill, so installing the new declaration was a matter of a few minutes. Since standing back to look at it would have required that they walk on water, they settled for perching with their heels in the water and looking up at the sign outlined against the sky.

As a gateway to a home, it was neither aesthetic nor welcoming. Next year, Rae thought, she would build one of her own that was both. A series of posts, she mused, some natural, others carved, iconic in nature: a modern interpretation of the local totem poles. Like that Brassil installation with the pilings. Not consciously artificial like Nils-Udo or Goldsworthy, or as polished as Murray's things, but— She caught herself, and began to laugh: First build your house, then think about the gateway.

"Thank you," she said to her two companions.

The sheriff scooped up the remnants of the old sign and carried them along the promontory to the campsite, where he tossed the boards onto her pile of firewood. He straightened, brushing his hands, and lifted his chin at the building on the hillside.

"You've got a lot done since I was here."

"The subfloor's finished and the water supply's complete."

"Mind if I look?"

"Help yourself. I was just going to scramble some eggs. The least I can do is give you breakfast. Or lunch."

"Why don't I do that," Nikki offered. "I saw the subfloor when I was here the other day."

"Well," Rae said, "okay. Eggs are in the cooler; there's some bacon, too, if you want. Bread in the wooden box." Nikki, however, already knew where everything was. She even managed to light the stove without an explosive puff, which Rae only did about half the time. Rae gave in and turned to join Sheriff Carmichael.

As they approached the heap of studs piled by the stone steps, Carmichael stopped. "Those aren't two-by-fours."

"Actually, they are. Full measure two-bys."

"Why?"

"Because Desmond used them. And because they're sturdy."

He said nothing, but once up on the flat, clear floorboards, he bounced, and when his considerable weight caused not the slightest shift, he nodded. "Sturdy's the word. I helped some friends put up a post-and-beam house a few years ago. It felt like this."

"I'd have loved to do this as a timber-frame house, but I just couldn't."

"It does take a fair number of people to get those beams up," he agreed.

"That, and I feel that if I'm following in my great-uncle's footsteps, I have to follow his style of building. And not only because I'm supposed to be restoring the building, but because it needs to be the way Desmond Newborn built it."

"You're a woodworker, I hear. Cabinetmaker, furniture maker, whatever you call it."

"Used to be."

"So tell me, do all woodworkers wrestle with two-by-fours on their off time?"

"Like an artist doing housepainting during the holidays, you mean? No, not all. It's about all I'm good for anymore." She halted as the words sent an echo through her, and Carmichael paused by her side questioningly. She laughed, a little sour sound. "I told my husband that same thing, when our daughter was small and I couldn't find the energy for creative work. He gave me a carpenter's tool belt. As a joke." And a pair of three-hundred-dollar chisels. As a serious response.

Carmichael glanced at her, but did not comment. Instead, he went over to each of the stone towers, leaned inside to look up to the circle of open sky, then stepped down from the platform to take a closer look at the impromptu water system behind the house. After a minute, she followed.

"Things going better now?" he asked as they picked their way back down the steep rock slope. "No more strange footprints?"

"Things are fine, Sheriff. I—"

"Call me Jerry. Please."

"Jerry. And I'm Rae, with an e. Though you already know that. Yes, things are going well."

And they were, she realized. Her nights were invariably broken and her days filled with a thousand startling noises, but she hadn't had a full-out panic attack in a couple of weeks. Too tired, she guessed, and found herself smiling. "Yes. Very well indeed."

"I'm glad to hear that. I called Sam Escobar this morning before we came out, but he's got nothing new. They can't even find the guy who told his informant he'd heard two people talking about being hired to attack you."

"Or somebody who may not have been me."

"You're right. A rumor of a rumor. I'm glad you're not fretting about it."

Back at the campsite, Nikki deftly divided the contents of the pan onto three plates and held one out to Rae, who perched on the cedar tree, leaving the two chairs to her guests, and dug her fork into the soft curds appreciatively. The Irish wood sprite could certainly cook an egg.

"Is it okay?" Nikki asked.

Rae looked up questioningly, then realized that manners might be a good idea.

"It's great. I was just thinking that it's been—oh, months since I ate something I didn't cook myself." Since her discharge from the hospital, in fact. The dutiful casseroles Tamara had brought were probably still in the deep freeze, and the nurse-cum-baby-sitter Rae had lodged with on her release had been a firm believer in the tough love policy, requiring Rae to forage and clean for herself. Everything else, with the exception of several cups of coffee bought on the drive up from California, had either been eaten straight from a package or peremptorily stirred together by her own hands. The unexpectedness of another person's simple but utterly different cooking style made the sloppy omelet a feast. She felt as if she should say grace over it.

"Oh," said Nikki. "I nearly forgot. Caleb sent you something." She fished a piece of paper out of her shirt pocket, then handed it to Rae. Rae balanced her half-empty plate on the tree trunk and took the offering. Unfolding it, she found that Caleb had drawn a portrait of her standing in front of her tent. At least she supposed it was she: a tall stick figure in brown with a frizz of gray hair. As flattering a representation as any five-year-old could manage, she figured.

"What are those around my feet? Rocks?"

"Crabs. We counted twenty-three the day we were here, and Caleb put in every one."

"I see. Tell him thank you," Rae said, and folded the drawing away. She returned to her meal with a lump in her throat.

When they had finished all the eggs (Rae's supply for the week, unfortunately) and half of her bread, Nikki moved to clean up, but Rae took the dishes out of the young woman's hands and put them in the plastic dishpan. "It'll make a nice change to wash up an actual pile of dishes," she told her guests, and herded them down to the boat.

On the way past the stack of lumber (little diminished, despite the numerous trips she had already taken) she remembered something.

"I wonder if one of you could do me a favor? I forgot to tell Ed that I need a couple of heavy plastic sheets—they don't have to be big, twelve by sixteen is fine, but they should be thick. Maybe six mil."

"Better ask Nikki," Jerry Carmichael suggested. "Ed and I don't exactly see eye to eye."

Nikki's mouth quirked into her elfish smile. "Jerry caught Ed red-handed smuggling a load of Freon a few years back. Ed kind of holds him responsible."

"Freon?" Rae asked, thinking she must have misheard.

"Freon," Jerry confirmed. "You know, the stuff they use in refrigerators and air conditioners. A canister that costs maybe thirty bucks in Mexico goes for eleven, twelve hundred here, because of the EPA regulations. So old Ed thought he might just as well pay for his winter in Baja by loading up on the stuff and bringing it to Seattle. It was really a Customs problem, but I stumbled across it, so I had to arrest him. Canisters up to the gunwales, and he thought I ought to look the other way."

"I see."

"Mostly what he didn't like was when I suggested he might be able to whittle down his sentence if he turned in the guy he was selling to. The arrest itself didn't bother him, but ever since I asked him to 'rat out,' in his words, he looks at me like I'm a cockroach."

"He went to jail?"

"Prison. It was a lot of Freon, and not exactly his first offense."

"That explains the big tattoo on his back," Rae said, half to herself.

Nikki halted to stare at her. "Ed showed you his tattoos?"

"That one I saw by accident, more or less. He did show me his arms. They're amazing."

Nikki and Jerry Carmichael looked at each other, but Nikki said only, "Ed is kind of like a cat. He doesn't take to a lot of people."

"Look," Rae said abruptly. "Should I be concerned about Ed? I mean, I know he's a rogue, but can I trust him?"

"Oh sure," Nikki answered immediately, as if the idea of Ed De la Torre being cause for worry was laughable.

Jerry Carmichael, though, took his time in responding. "I'd say Ed has a sharp eye for the quick buck, but he has his own sense of morality. He might sell a little marijuana to his friends, maybe a few mushrooms, but he'd draw the line at anything harder. And he'd never steal from a friend, although it's not always easy to tell if you're a true friend or just someone he's setting up. 'Rogue' is a good word for him. But if you're talking about violence, to my knowledge he's only aggressive when he's been drinking. And he's been off the bottle for years. The one thing I would say you ought to watch for is, he's got a reputation with single women. Especially women over forty."

"But only consensual," Nikki hastened to add.

"That's true. I've never heard a whisper of Ed's forcing himself on anyone. Seduction, that's Ed's game."

The smile Jerry Carmichael gave Rae had more than a trace of the seductive itself. It startled her, until he then turned it on Nikki as well. Ranger and sheriff climbed onto the boat and cast off. As Jerry steered toward the open water, Nikki leaned into him to say something over the noise of the boat. Rae watched carefully, but she could tell no more about the nature of their relationship from that piece of body language than she had learned from seeing them together. There was depth there, that much was obvious, but in what direction was impossible to tell.

She shook herself. It was none of her business. Jerry Carmichael was not her concern.

So it was that more than a week after trimming the boards from her sub-floor, interrupted by water systems, No Trespassing signs, and visits from her community, Rae was free to return to the actual work of raising her house. First, though, she washed the breakfast dishes and pulled on her swimsuit for a brief (a very brief) dip in the frigid cove. Finally, she strapped on her tool belt and resumed her proper labor.

With the floor in place, Rae could now reach the first section of stonework without risking her neck on a ladder set on uneven ground. She filled a bucket from the end of the hose beside the house, spread out a plastic tarp to save the floorboards from a drenching, and set to with a heavy brush and soapsuds.

Desmond's fireplace and towers had been built out of water-rounded stones ranging from fist-sized in the fireplace to watermelon-sized in the towers. The effort he had gone to was enormous, boggling to contemplate. Furthermore, as the day went on and the stones emerged from their thick layer of moss and char, it became apparent that Desmond had chosen them for more than size.

At first Rae thought that she would never rescue the stones from their patina, that all the elbow grease and harsh cleansers in the world would never make the fireplace stones anything but black. Then, standing critically back from the fireplace to evaluate her progress, she realized that although the stones themselves were indeed unremittingly dark, the mortar between them was not. As an experiment, she took her bucket and brush over to the adjoining tower, and quickly discovered that the rocks there were considerably lighter. Desmond had selected his stones from the beach below (and, very probably, from a lot of other beaches as well) with an eye to their color. The fireplace was black, the wet stones as glossy as if they had a layer of wet ink over them, but the tower was, for lack of a better word, orange. Translucent agates the size of a teapot, iron-rich metamorphic boulders, mottled sandstone with infinitesimal seashells embedded in it, all of them in shades ranging from yellow to pale brick, giving the overall impression of a warm, glowing orange. New, and in the full sunlight, it must have been an extraordinary sight.

Unable to resist, she crossed the platform to the other tower, scrubbed for a few minutes, and found there not orange, but greens and even blues. She had never seen anything like it.

"Uncle Desmond," she said aloud, "you're a wonder."

She dove back into the work with renewed vigor, scrubbing at the stones, gouging away at the engrimed mortar, starting at the floor and working her way up.

Late that night she finished the rough scrub of the first dozen feet of the fireplace. She stood across the bare platform where the door would be, trying to imagine coming into a room with that at the end of it. It rose like a living thing, primitive and massive and at the same time sophisticated, with faint traces of pale gray threads here and there in the darkness of the stone that echoed the web of the mortar. She would, she decided, replace all the visible mortar in a dark gray color very like the present stained tone. And to the left she would build a storage wall, more Japanese than Shaker in its simple elegance, of some slightly cool wood, birch perhaps, or spalted maple, to repeat the dark lines, formal against the rising tower of stone, with the least touch of ebony inlay to tie the two shapes together.

Yes; oh yes.

The next day, Rae found the bullets.

She was on the stepladder, scrubbing patiently at an especially ragged bit of mortar when a chunk of the stuff the size of her thumb came away in her hand. She fumbled and caught it, turned it over curiously to see why this particular bit had proven more unstable than the rest, and found embedded in its base an odd gray lump.

Her first thought was that a stone had slipped past Desmond's screen when he had prepared the sand for the cement. She pulled off her thick rubber gloves and picked the lump out with a thumbnail, then frowned at the soft, slightly flat object in the palm of her hand. It was like no stone that she had come across; more like a piece of metal. Had Desmond perhaps driven a nail between the stones to hang something on, and it had melted into a lump with the heat of the fire? How hot would a fire have to be, to do that? And why would that careful workman have bashed a hanger into his nice neat stonework a scant two feet from the ceiling? It was as odd as the pair of holes she had discovered in the smooth inner surface of his front door.

She buttoned the lump into her shirt pocket and went on with her work, thoughtful.

Rae broke off that afternoon while it was still light and tugged on her damp suit for a swim. The water was not warming up much with the weather, but it seemed that a person could grow accustomed to anything, because after half a dozen such dips she no longer felt as if her heart was about to stop every time she submerged. After all, it seemed wasteful to be the owner of a nice clear bay and not make use of it. And Nikki's books were proving more interesting than she could have anticipated; Rae now knew the names of all the commonest plants and sea creatures around the cove, from Acorn barnacles to Yellowlegs (greater and lesser) and their habits and characteristics. She did not know why it seemed important to know these things, but it did, as if she was learning the names of neighbors and what they did for a living.

She pulled herself out at the dock and picked her way barefoot over to the stove, where she set the big pan of water on to heat for a proper shower. Then she took an old narrow-bladed chisel from her toolbox and the big flashlight from beside the bed, and crossed over to the workbench.

Getting at the underside of the bench through the forest of driftwood legs was no simple matter, but Rae managed to find a slot where she could thread her head in. It was damnably awkward and she only managed to shine the light into one of the holes, but it was enough to confirm that, half an inch beneath the surface of what had once been the inside of Desmond's front door, not far from the place where the latch had been mounted, there was a spot of gray metal similar to those she'd found in the fireplace. She drew back and, working mostly by touch, gouged and pried at the wood surrounding the holes, only slicing into her fingers two or three times.

The thing seemed to have gone in at an angle, Rae was thinking when something dropped from the wood into the sandy soil. She retrieved it: a gray, misshapen lump a little bigger than a pencil's eraser. She placed it on the workbench above her head, and went to work on the other hole. It was higher up on the door, buried at a slightly more oblique angle, and its lump proved to be even more completely preserved, with a rounded head and blunt end.

Bullets, all of them.

No doubt about it: Three bullets had gone flying through the air of Desmond's Folly to lodge in its walls. At least three, she corrected herself, and in two opposite directions.

She set all three lumps on the workbench while she went to bandage her fingers and make her dinner, but when she glanced over at the three gray objects and noticed how they echoed the three roofing nails that she had driven into the wood, the duplication made her uneasy. She walked across the meadow to retrieve them, and buttoned them into her shirt pocket.

After dinner, over coffee, she lined the three objects up on a tree-stump table and sat back to contemplate them.

Bullets didn't necessarily have to mean that someone got shot. Maybe Desmond just liked to fire his gun. If Sherlock Holmes had enjoyed blazing away at his living room wall until the queen's initials were pocked out of the plaster, why not Desmond Newborn? Maybe the man had gotten drunk. Maybe he had an attack of the jitters on Christmas Eve and hallucinated German soldiers coming down the chimney.

On the other hand, she wondered if there was any way of finding out if the three lumps of lead had come from the same gun. It would be something, anyway, to confirm that two different weapons hadn't blazed across the room at each other. Maybe Jerry Carmichael could submit them to a police lab for her—but surely he would consider it frivolous, a waste of taxpayers' money.

She wondered, too, how many more such lumps she would find, were she to pick closely through the great pile of unidentified objects the sieve had separated out for her.

Oh come on, Rae, she chided herself. *Is life so dull you have to manufacture a melodrama, a furious gun battle in a small wooden room?* Still . . . How long after those bullets hit the wall had the place burned? And how long before Great-uncle Desmond disappeared, fleeing the San Juans for the wilds of Arizona?

For a week, Rae pondered these things. While she finished cleaning and mortaring the stones of the black fireplace, then moved her plastic sheets over to the orange tower and cleaned that, and finally set to work on the blue tower, she turned the implications of the three bullets over and over in her mind. The moon went dark and was reborn. Pleasure boats drifted past. Nikki stopped by to say hello, Ed came and went, leaving behind some heavy tarps and three green plastic water tanks, and Rae said nothing about gun battles to either of them. She was still wondering about the three bullets when she finished with the higher reaches of the stones, cleared away the protective plastic from the floorboards, and carried the last of the wall studs for the first floor up to the site.

On Thursday, Rae framed out the wall to the left of the fireplace, vaguely recalling Desmond's peculiar doubled supports at the spot. She secured the two-bys with a temporary brace, turned the corner, and fastened down the top plate. That night, she retrieved the problematic chunk of Desmond's wall from the dump pile and carried it over to the lamp by the fire.

Sill plate along the bottom, upright 2x4 studs, held together by a couple feet of scorched, half-rotten, still-attached siding. For two weeks now she'd been convinced that there was a purpose to Desmond's doubled studs, that the wall above had been breached by a door or window. She had no way of knowing how wide the opening had been—if there had been a second support, it was not in the eighteen-inch-square segment of Desmond's wall she possessed.

She turned the problem over in her mind as she lay listening to the noises of the night, the owls and the bats, her resident raccoon, a plane and a ferry and the tide going out. At the tide's lowest mark, a quiet engine puttered by and, looking at the lightening canvas, Rae decided that it was close enough to dawn to justify rising. She made coffee, drew on her belt, and in the pearly light of a misty dawn walked the beaten path up to the house. She set her mug down on the floorboards in front of the fireplace and went over to the section of wall where Desmond's doubled support had been, adjacent to the fireplace. There she leaned out between her fresh new studs to look down at the sharp slope of the rock face into which the house was nestled.

There was a lot of soil out there, rock and debris under heavy vegetation, as would be expected when the burning house collapsed, some of it falling outside the foundation. However, there should have been little woodwork on this side, other than the roof overhang, since the chimney and tower together made up more than half the wall—and yet the level of accumulated soil appeared more or less continuous. During the night it had occurred to her that some wooden extension of the house might have rested on the stones behind the fireplace. If so, and considering the location of the doubled 2x4, Desmond's framed hole might well have been for access to a wood box, a place to store firewood that was convenient to the fireplace and avoided the debris inevitably left behind when wood is carried through living quarters. And although getting at such a woodbin from the outside and filling it with logs would be a job—one that in her opinion would benefit from climbing ropes to help the householder work his or her way around the steep west wall—the idea might be worth adapting with, say, an exterior set of steps.

Rae eased herself out between her studs and onto the treacherous surface of the rock face. She had not cleared any of the debris here, since her policy was to create a secure footing before venturing into hazard. This was the closest she had been to danger her entire time on the island, and she was all too aware that if she fell, Ed would not find her for four days.

She tugged cautiously at the ancient burned fragments of wood, which crumbled in her hands, and at the vigorous tangle of blackberry vine that covered the back of the fireplace. She shoved and yanked and fought to keep her footing, she sweated and burrowed into the unexplored wasteland behind the tower wall, she cursed and thought of turning back, after just a bit farther.

In no time at all, she found Desmond Newborn.

Twenty-six

Desmond Newborn's Journal

Ten thousand miles and eight years separate me from the trenches, but the ghosts visit me still, dart away from the corners of my eyes, moan beneath the sound of the wind, reach out from the stench of a rotting seal carcass on my shore. Yesterday I looked up from my work on the rear tower and there was Harper standing among the trees. "You left me to drown in the mud," he told me. And indeed, I did so. He was alive when the wiring party crawled past him, buried past his waist in the eternal muck, and he was dead, toppled forward until only the back of his head was to be seen, when we came back fourteen hours later. We had spent the day ourselves in a shell-hole only marginally drier than his, pinned down by a Maxim gun. "We had orders," I told his ghost. "No stopping to rescue the wounded. We tried to pull you, and five of us couldn't break the mud's hold. Digging would have meant the wire didn't get laid. Going back for reinforcements would've meant a bullet from the Sergeant. You know that." "It is an evil way to die, alone and drowning in the cold mud." "I am sorry," I told him. "I am sorry."

He faded away after a while, leaving me with a half-set bucket of mortar at my feet. A stuff, incidentally, that brickmasons call "mud."

We're all mad, I believe, all of us who came out of the trenches. A twenty-three-hour stretch of earth-quaking, bone-rattling, sky-splitting hell from the big guns, and even the most solid nerves dissolved. And that was only one bombardment. Georgie Abbot, a cattle farmer, a man

191

who went out to pull a friend back from no-man's-land under a murderous line of fire, a man who made a game out of how many rats he could impale in a day on his trench knife, a man who was always one of the first up the ladders, singing under his breath a rude version of a hymn called "Onward Christian Soldiers"—this same stolid farmer broke under one prolonged shelling. He began to giggle, helpless as a tickled child, then he shed his helmet, dropped his rifle into the mud, and before anyone could stop him, over the top he went. He walked out into no-man's-land with his arms outstretched as if to greet a loved one, striding as strongly as he was able over the pitted ground. He made it nearly to the wire before the disbelieving Germans had to dispatch him.

I saw Georgie, too, one day last month, flickering through the bushes down near the water. He looked happy.

The ghosts are not threatening. Now that I have come to accept their presence around me, they even make for a peculiar sort of companionship. I find myself talking to the aptly named Mason, the cleverest trench builder I ever saw, who made his living laying dry-stone walls in Yorkshire and who is as helpful with my own tower as ever he was with sandbags in the French soil. And evenings I often call to mind Jimmy Hurlstone, older than any soldier in the company but with a younger man's face that got him past the enlistment sergeant. Jimmy was a slow and deliberate teller of deliciously ridiculous stories, who would keep us entertained on the most miserable of nights. I would never mention it to another soul, but in truth, some of the tales Jimmy tells me here on my island I would swear that I have never before heard.

They keep me company, my ghosts do. And I think perhaps they need me as well, to help them live out their days. I do not mind sharing my life with them; for every ghostly wail that comes to me out of a storm, jerking me straight back to the night after a battle with the piteous, hoarse screams of dying men reaching out of the dark, there are ten hearty, crude, cheerful, courageous men, lending me their memories.

One thing can be said for an experience like the Western Front: There's little to be dreaded about death afterward. I do not fear death, although I will regret if I be alone when it comes for me, and I can only pray that it be not an unquiet end, that my shade does not have to travel the earth in search of a vessel to help it live out the fullness of its days.

All I ask is a continuation of the peace I have found here.

Part Three

BUILDING
WALLS

There was an unexpectedly intense pleasure to be had in delaying revenge, he reflected; anticipation of The Thief's face, on realizing that the time of reckoning was suddenly at hand. All alone in the middle of the deep blue sea, mad Thief and cool Victim meet, and balance would be restored.

Twenty-seven

As far as Rae could figure, the heap of rotted wood and ash behind the house meant that Desmond had possessed a fairly well-stocked wood-shed behind his house, in the L-shaped structure that filled the gap between the back wall and the rock face, wrapping around the fireplace to the rear tower. The rotted material would need rakes and buckets to remove, which Rae had planned to do once she had a second story on which she could fix a boom-and-pulley system—a minor building project that would save her hours of scrambling, to say nothing of twisted ankles and imperiled bones.

Now, however, she was concerned only with tracing the outlines of this peculiarly Desmond-esque wood storage box, to see if she could understand why he had gone to the effort of building an elaborately enclosed space when a six-by-six-foot lean-to would have done. She stepped down gingerly from the rock face to the soft soil, hoping to avoid the worst of the buried nails, and found the surface firm enough that her boots only sank in a couple of inches. She pushed with the head of the hammer against the nearest brambles, and when they were bent she systematically crushed them flat under her boots before tackling the next patch.

The narrow space ended in a dank corner where the moss-covered orange stones of the rear tower joined the rock face to Rae's left and the black fireplace to her right. Approaching the end, hedged around by rock walls both natural and man-made, Rae felt as if she were wading into the bottom of a well.

Although the soil had looked uniform in depth and quality, she found that the farther back into the well she pushed, the shallower the layer of organic matter grew. Low light and solid rock at their roots made the plants thin and lank. The L-shaped woodbin must have been more fully loaded just behind the access door, which made sense—who would need a filled bin the width of the house? Maybe Desmond had envisioned an East Coast blizzard out here, Rae speculated sourly as she peeled the claws of a Nootka rose out of her jeans. Arctic snowfall that would have buried him inside for weeks, forcing him to tunnel through the access door into the depths of the—

Wait a minute. What was that?

Her tugging at the spindly bramble had loosed a small rockfall from the hill above, scarcely an arm's length from the corner of chimney and tower, but instead of tumbling down to bury the toe of her boot, the scree had simply vanished. She scraped at the rock face with the side of the hammer's head, then shifted it around and drove its strong, straight claws into the soil, and pulled. A bushel or two of rock and dank soil came down across her feet, but Rae did not notice.

There was a hole, into the rock.

Scraping with the hammer could only do so much. Rae, suddenly impatient to find what Desmond had been hiding behind his woodpile, waded back over crushed vegetation, broken rock, and black humus and through the newly framed wall. She dropped her tool belt and went to fetch a shovel, a couple of buckets, and the big flashlight.

She shoveled at the place where the rockfall had disappeared, and in the end did not bother with the buckets, simply heaving several cubic yards of greenery and soil away from the tower and concentrating on the hole. For hole it was. More than that, a small cave—or at any rate, a cave with a small entrance.

When she had scraped the vegetation and soil clear, Rae was standing in front of a neat hole in the rock face slightly more than two feet in height, somewhat less in width. A chisel had bitten into the stone all around the edges—a heavier tool than anything Rae used, but its mark instantly recognizable. She picked up the flashlight and went down on her knees.

The beam shone back into the hill, Rae was not surprised to see. Indeed, it extended so far that the back wall was only palely illuminated. She hesitated, but could think of no reason not to go inside. If the cave's roof hadn't collapsed by now, odds were pretty good it would go another day—if she avoided bumping into anything she shouldn't, or making a loud noise.

Rae took a breath, and crawled forward into the belly of the island.

This was, she realized, the same stratum of sandstone that dove and warped its way through the harder stone of the island. Elsewhere it carried water; here it carried . . . what?

Air, perhaps, though stale and utterly without motion, even three feet inside the opening. And water somewhere, since the air felt moist and every few seconds she heard a *plunk* of falling drips. The floor and walls here were dry and smooth, and she inched forward down the uneven tunnel, looking for the source of that noise.

She did not find it, not that day. What her flashlight beam found instead, tumbled together at the end of a short side passage that came in from the left, was a heap of dust-colored clothing draped across a collection of pale bones: long shins, curling rib cage, naked wrist, grinning skull.

The next twenty seconds decided the question of the cave's stability against loud noises and sharp jolts. For three of those seconds, Rae froze there on her hands and knees, gaping back at the naked skull, and then all the hair on her body rose up and she shrieked, dropped the flashlight, and scrabbled her way to the entrance, tumbling out into the soft pit she had dug and clawing her way between rock and fireplace, through the studs as if they had been a doorway, sending her abandoned coffee mug flying as she leapt across the floorboards and down the hill to the safety of her workbench. She slapped her hand on the surface with the gesture of a medieval felon claiming sanctuary at an altar, leaping around to its far side and gaping at the house as if awaiting pursuit. She gulped three enormous breaths; then she clapped her hand across her mouth and started to laugh, halfway to hysteria.

The emotional storm blew through, leaving her light-headed and trembling, and she tottered across to the canvas chair to sit before her legs gave out on her. First, though, she turned the chair so that she had a clear view up the hillside.

She lowered her head nearly to her knees and waited for the world to stop swimming, glancing up at the two towers every few seconds. Nothing moved. The adrenaline faded, and she began to feel distinctly queasy. After a while, she stood up on a pair of legs that didn't feel like hers to make herself a cup of tea (no milk, it being Friday). She drank it, and began to feel less shaky.

Well, she told herself, at least she no longer had to feel haunted by the vision of poor Great-uncle Desmond lying in an unmarked and cactus-covered grave in Arizona.

But what the hell had happened to the man?

For the first time since moving to the island, Rae wished she had a phone. A seventy-year-old skeleton hardly seemed to justify emergency flares shot into the sky, but she knew that even a skeleton long stripped and dry had to require some kind of official treatment. Maybe not paramedics and one of those black, zippered body bags so beloved of television programs, but surely somebody with a truly authoritative clipboard and maybe a video camera would want to come out and put the bones in a box, to send them off to a nice sterile lab somewhere to be poked about and stared at for a while.

She looked up at her waiting house and thought, *This might be as good a time as any to break for lunch.* She dug out a can of tuna and made herself a couple of sandwiches, and took herself down to the water for a while to think.

What she found herself thinking was *Myself, I'd hate to end up in a nice sterile lab somewhere.*

After a while, Rae forced herself back up to the building site to work on the walls. It wasn't as hard as she anticipated. She cut and nailed studs, laying headers over the window and door holes, waiting for the symptoms of added stress—the jumpiness and sudden shortness of breath, the shadowy hearing and seeing of things that were not there, the brutal dive of a panic attack swooping out of the blue—but they all failed to arrive. Twitchy, yes, and she did keep a very close eye on the wall beside the fireplace, but her breath, once it had returned to normal, remained there; the breeze through the fragrant blossoms of the madrone was just the sky's breath; the constant gentle motion of the wavelets remained a reassuring tempo and not a continual corner-of-the-eye threat.

She got through the rest of the day; she ate her evening meal; she slept—not a lot, and the gentle rainfall that started around midnight brought disturbing possibilities of restless skeletons outside the canvas walls, but in fact her sleeplessness was due more to the intensity of her contemplation than to any real fear. The more she thought it over, the less she liked the idea of just turning over Desmond Newborn's mortal remains to the unheeding hands of the law, to be bundled up willy-nilly into a box. She was quite certain they would not allow her to just leave him where he was; nor was she sure she would want that, if for no other reason than he would always be in the back of her mind, unfinished business, an unrecognized death. Even the long-imagined unmarked grave in an arid cemetery would have been recognition that someone, however nameless, had passed on. She could perhaps ask that the bones be brought back here for a proper burial—or was there some law about consecrated ground? If so, she would have what was left of him cremated, and bring his ashes back to the island to join those of Alan and Bella. In either case, she couldn't help thinking it a jarring way to treat the old gent, jerked from his peaceful rest like that.

No, she would not leave him in his natural tomb; she would send word to Jerry Carmichael and allow the law to have its way with Desmond. First, however, she would go to him herself, and break it to him gently.

It would not, after all, be the first conversation she'd had with the dead.

The rain cleared by mid-morning. When the sun was as close to upright in the sky as it would get and the shadows behind the house were at their narrowest, Rae took up the smaller of her two kerosene lamps, along with a set of spare batteries and a bulb for the flashlight, and returned to the cave. The heap of thrown-about dirt behind the house was muddy; the plants were wilted; the hole was still there.

When her upper body was just inside the cave's narrow entrance, Rae became aware of the silly urge to clear her throat, as if warning someone of her approach. She eased forward until she could reach the flashlight, which had rolled against the cave wall, and pulled it apart to replace its batteries. The bulb, she was pleased to find, had not broken in the fall. Her hands were remarkably steady. She shoved the flashlight into the back pocket of her pants and lit the lamp, turned the shield so it cast its light in front, then worked her way down the tunnel until she reached the small side cave where Desmond Newborn's remains lay. There she turned the lamp around to illuminate the space.

And let out a breath she hadn't known she was holding; he was still there. God only knew what her reaction would have been if he'd been missing, she reflected a touch wildly, and then made herself settle back against the wall to face the bones of the man who had made his home on Folly.

"I love your house, Uncle Desmond," she told him.

Her voice rang oddly flat in the cave, and Rae abruptly felt ridiculous sitting and talking to a pile of bones and rags. Respect for the dead was one thing, but if Great-uncle Desmond was anything like the man she had come to imagine, he would either break down laughing or walk away in disgust.

What could she say to him? *Desmond, I've imagined meeting you ever since I was nine years old, when I found your medal in Grandfather's drawer? Desmond, fellow wounded black sheep, you helped me survive my childhood, you were my guide through some very dark days?* What could she say to him that he did not know?

So instead of talking to the shade, Rae simply sat with him for a while.

Then she got back to her knees and, scooting the lamp before her, went to examine the rest of his tomb.

The cave's narrow opening grew wider and taller, until finally she could stand, if cautiously. She did not know what to expect of Desmond's cave, although she would not have been surprised to find crates of smuggled goods—rum, or bathtub gin perhaps, it having been Prohibition when he died. Actually, she halfway thought she might find some hidden treasure or other, and was disappointed when the cave opened up to reveal nothing but a set of nearly empty shelves.

The main cavern was a lopsided egg perhaps fifteen feet long and ten wide, with a drip down the back wall falling from a calcified point into a pool of water no larger than a soup bowl. The back wall had crumbled and slumped any number of times over the years; short of attacking it with pick and shovel, Rae could not tell if the debris concealed another low passage leading farther into the depths of the hill. From the looks of the rock, she doubted there had been a further cave; certainly not in the last hundred years.

This room had been used by Desmond for storage, possibly while he was building the house, but little remained. Even the shelves he'd built were so rotten that she hesitated to touch them. A crate of wine bottles rested on its side on the cave floor, the bottle necks too thick with dust for her to guess at any contents. Half a dozen canning jars sat on one shelf, equally obscured by dust and the rust that bubbled out from their lids, and with them a few odds and ends—a trowel missing a handle, some antique seed packets, a pile of rusted-together chain. And, a rectangular object slightly larger than a cigar box.

She reached for the box. Although metal, it was light enough to be empty, except that something inside shifted. Where it had lain there was now a sharply defined rectangle of startlingly bare wood, and she nearly put it back in place, thinking of the accusing questions of the officials who would come here to collect Desmond's bones. But this was her land, was it not? Why shouldn't she take her relative's strongbox with her? Defiantly, she picked up one of the wine bottles as well, brushing against the lower shelf as she did so; the shelves teetered and nearly collapsed. *That would take care of any accusing mark in the dust,* she thought, but instead of giving them a firm push, she settled for moving the seed packets and dead tools around a bit to confuse matters, then blowing gently against the top of the strongbox to transfer its dust back in the direction of the shelf. The outline was obscured: good enough. Tucking the box under her arm and picking up the bottle and the lamp, she turned to make her way back to the cave opening, then froze.

She stepped away from the wall, holding the lamp up so it cast a more oblique light; no, it was no mistake: There was a petroglyph carved into the wall of the cave, an arching shape with swirls across its body and a high, proud dorsal fin. She traced the orca's outline with a reverent finger, then turned her lamp attentively to the walls as she made her way back down the lowering passage, but it had no companions.

Rae paused at the opening to the side cave that held Desmond's sad and dusty remains. She tried to think of something to say that was neither inappropriate nor embarrassing, and failed, so she crawled on toward the circle of light with her booty.

The narrow opening was an awkward space to work through. Rae let the wine bottle and the strongbox slide down gently into the dirt outside, leaving the flashlight and lamp, both of them shut down, in the cave behind her feet. She squirmed out of the opening, more or less falling forward into the soft soil outside, soft soil that hid something hard and viciously sharp.

"Shit!" she yelped, continuing her fall until she fetched up on her back against the black stones of the fireplace, grasped her right hand, and saw the line of red well up from the brown crust of mud. "Damn." She struggled to her feet, reached for the neck of the wine bottle with her left hand, and went rigid at the sound of a familiar voice echoing across the rocks: Nikki Walls. "Damn," she said again, and snatched up the metal box to send it skidding back into the cave, then turned to flounder through the damp mud and beaten vegetation before the friendly busy-body of a ranger could find her. Rae did not stop to think why she didn't want Nikki to see the cave yet; she only knew that she wasn't ready for it to become public property. So she waded frantically through the mess and ducked between the studs, tracking great clots of muck across the floorboards.

Nikki was halfway up the hill to the house when she was greeted by the sight of what looked like a newly dug-up corpse, covered in dirt from head to toe, hurrying down the stone steps. A newly dug-up corpse with an equally filthy wine bottle in her left hand and a lot of white teeth showing out of a wide-stretched grin.

"Nikki," said the corpse. "Just the person I needed to see. Did your ranger training include first aid, I hope? 'Cause if not, you're going to have to sit there and watch me try to put a Band-Aid on with my left hand." She thrust out a hand that was dripping gore and covered with mud. Nikki took a sharp step back, then turned and followed Rae back down the hill, eyeing her closely all the way.

"Er, Rae? Have you been drinking?"

"Drinking? God, no, why—oh," Rae said, looking down at the bot-tle she'd forgotten she was carrying. "No, it's not even open," which did not exactly answer Nikki's question, although the ranger was reassured by Rae's usual crisp diction and her unhindered coordination.

They reached the tent, and Rae put the wine bottle down at the side of the folding metal cook center, half concealed behind its legs. She turned to the tent, and stopped, looking down at herself. "Good Lord," she said, and laughed merrily. "I look like a golem."

Nikki Walls did not know what the Lord of the Rings had to do with anything, but she decided not to ask, merely held back the tent flap so Rae could maneuver her way through without brushing either dirty body or bloody hand against the canvas. Rae came out a minute later with a large metal first-aid kit.

"I think I'd better clean this off a little before we bandage the cut," Rae told her apologetically. "Otherwise I'll just get it wet again."

"Good idea." Nikki thought Rae would go over to the shower she'd rigged, a bucket with a shower head attached to it, but instead Folly's owner pinched up a towel between thumb and forefinger and marched down to the cove. Nikki's eyebrows went up as she saw the woman bend to unlace her mud-caked boots. Nikki still occasionally took quick dips in the fifty-degree water, but she'd been doing it since she was a kid, and she was half this woman's age. *This is one tough old lady,* she reflected.

Not so old, she corrected herself, as Rae's firm back emerged from shirt and pants. Underwear but no bra, Nikki noted, and then turned away to put on a kettle of water. She couldn't help glancing back at the cove twice in the next few minutes. The first time she saw Rae calmly floating in the icy water as if she were lying in a hot tub. The second time, checking that the splashing noises meant it was time to pour the water on the coffee grounds, she caught Rae just as she was rising up in the shallow edges of the cove. Nikki's eyes narrowed at the jagged red marks down the woman's left arm and chest. She had seen the neat scar on the back of Rae's forearm where the plate had been implanted, but she hadn't known the woman had been so torn up as that. She looked as if she'd fallen into a piece of farm equipment.

Rae came back to the campsite, clutching the inadequate towel around her, teeth chattering and gory right hand held out from her side.

"Thanks for putting on the coffee," she said, and ducked into the tent. When she came out she was wearing jeans and a sweatshirt, with a clean rag around her hand. She began to work at the first-aid box, oblivious of Nikki's stare. After a moment, the ranger went over and took the kit from Rae's hand.

"Let me."

The cut was not deep, a slice across the outer side of the thumb's pad. If they had been closer to town Nikki would have urged stitches, but it was not a cut that justified a boat trip into Friday Harbor, and neither woman suggested it. Nikki bathed the hand with antiseptic, dried it and tugged a trio of butterfly bandages across it, then covered the whole with gauze. The bleeding had nearly stopped already.

"How did you do it?" she asked, repacking the kit.

"Fell," Rae said. "Onto dirt that must've had a piece of glass in it. It's nothing, and I had a tetanus shot before I came out here."

"You won't be able to use a hammer for a couple of days," Nikki advised.

Rae laughed and held out her left hand for Nikki's examination. Her fingers were a network of scars, small shiny lines of many clean cuts, quickly healed. "Chisels," she said briefly. Nikki's eyes flickered a few inches farther up, to the three long, straight scars that crossed the pale skin of Rae's inner wrist. She said nothing, just got up to pour the coffee.

"Is that where you found the bottle?" Nikki asked.

"Bottle?" asked Rae, after a brief but telltale hesitation.

"Of wine. That you were carrying when you came stumbling down the hill looking like my little brother when he tried to dig to China."

"Oh, the wine. Yes, it was up behind the house. It must've belonged to Desmond. I don't suppose it could still be any good."

"Was it lying on its side? If the cork stays wet, wine lasts a long time."

"It was, yes."

"Is it red or white? Red lasts longer." She glanced at Rae. "I have a brother-in-law who's into wine. 'Raspberries in the nose' and all that. Drives us crazy at Thanksgiving."

"I don't know—what color it is, I mean. Let me look." But Nikki was already holding the dusty bottle up to the light.

"It's red," she pronounced. "And the cork looks fine. Are there any more? They could be worth something."

"I don't know," Rae said again, and then kicked herself for not saying, No, that's the only one. Nikki was on it in an instant.

"Let's go look," she suggested, all but wagging her tail in eagerness. "That would be cool, to find a stash from the Twenties. The historical society would love it. You could—"

"I'll let you know if any more turn up."

"But I'm—"

"Nikki."

The ranger broke off, belatedly aware that the easygoing owner of Desmond's Folly was sounding remarkably like Nikki's ferocious and generally disapproving old grandmother, the Irish matriarch who ruled the clan's holiday dinners with an iron tongue.

"I'll let you know," Rae repeated, now that she had the other woman's full attention. "This is my treasure hunt, not a community project."

Chastened, even hurt, and looking very like her small son, Nikki put the bottle down and subsided into her chair. "Okay. Sorry."

"Hey. I know you're just trying to help out, and I appreciate that. But at the moment, I'd rather do it myself. I don't want to give your bosses the least reason to poke their noses in." It was a feeble excuse, since Rae had full faith in her lawyer's ability to keep governmental hands away from Folly, but Nikki was nodding sadly. "Thanks anyway, for the offer. And for the doctoring." She held up her hand. A spot of red had come through the bandage, but it was not spreading very fast. "By the way, was there anything you wanted here? I never did ask if you had some reason for dropping by."

"No. Just in the neighborhood, and I wanted to see how far you'd gotten on the walls."

One of the drawbacks of being a part of the community, Rae reflected, was that you had the responsibility to respond to your neighbors. You had to allow them to intrude, to nibble at your time and attention, even when your temptation was to throw them off the island. So when she got to her feet, to indicate that the visit was at an end, she also gave Nikki a smile, albeit a rather forced one. "That's fine. Don't think you have to bring me a bag of food as an excuse to come."

Nikki returned the smile. She allowed Rae to walk her back to the boat, but once aboard, she turned for a parting shot. "I hope you at least think about the historical society," she urged. "With the wine, I mean. They'd love to add a bottle of Folly wine to their display."

Twenty-eight

Desmond Newborn's Journal

August 22, 1921

For two years and four months I was a sojourner across the face of the land, from the still night I crept away from my family home until the glorious morn eight weeks ago when I set foot on this island. For eight hundred and fifty-two days I was a man without a home, a vagabond whose worldly goods were on his back and in his pockets, one untrustworthy, unsavory figure among the many who move on the fringes of society.

I belonged with those other outcasts, too. I felt at home with their rootlessness, felt relieved that they demanded no more of me than a handful of half-spoiled vegetables for the communal pot and a pair of watchful eyes against the railway guards. Not that I was always comfortable with the degree of drunkenness and crudeness and the constant peril from the truly insane, but the simplicity of the demands made by the homeless brotherhood is soothing to the troubled soul. If I cried out in my sleep, my neighbor would do no more than curse me and kick my leg to silence me; he would not make earnest inquiry into the troubles I bore, for they were much the same as his.

Still, even before the violent episode in Yakima, I was growing fatigued of the life, restless in a manner that wandering could no longer assuage. Returning to Boston might be impossible, but the thought of returning to the confines of any city at all made it difficult to breathe. And yet I found myself stopping to admire the lines of houses, the solidity of their stones, the promise they held of shelter and permanence, a stage on which the future of one's life might be lived out. Hovel and redbrick mansion alike, all spoke to my growing desire for walls and a roof, to stand between me and the elements.

Memories of childhood summers by the sea, long sun-drenched hours of freedom and companionship, no doubt drove me ever farther west, until I ran out of land—and even then I continued, across these lovely, blue, scattered islands in a gently flowing sea.

It comes to me that this is an ironical enterprise, when one considers William's chosen manner of expanding the family fortunes by building houses and factories, railway stations and huge blocks of offices for others. He would laugh at his younger brother's idea of "building."

Foolishness, perhaps, but my only other choice is to continue moving west, either on the sea or into it. Here I will stop, here I will build and live. And God willing, after finding peace, here I will die.

Twenty-nine

Forty-eight hours went by, the remainder of Saturday and all of Sunday, while Rae came to terms with both the physical bones and the reconstruction of her past that they entailed.

Not that she spent the days staring off into space; far from it. Saturday she worked on her boat dock, keeping busy away from the house and the cave, thinking of nothing in particular but the job at hand. Saturday night she constructed a squirrel- and raccoon-proof food safe out of scavenged branches, deliberately rough-looking but tight enough to thwart the increasingly clever hands of her furry neighbors. And Sunday, although she returned her attention to the house, she was mostly hauling lumber and framing the first-floor walls, mechanical labor made awkward by the bandage on her hand.

All the while, however, the back of her mind was occupied with her options concerning Desmond's remains. Gradually, the choices came together, and the decision was made.

On Monday morning, fresh coffee to hand, Rae sat down and wrote a letter:

Dear Sheriff Carmichael,
    I am asking Ed De la Torre to drop this by your office when he gets back to Friday Harbor. If he does so late in the afternoon, or if you get it late, please do not imagine there is any urgency in the matter.

Waiting a day (or two, or six for that matter) is much preferable to having you rush out here in the dark.

I have found some old human bones in a cave behind the house. I believe they are the remains of my great-uncle Desmond Newborn, who disappeared in the late 1920s. I don't know what one does with bones that ancient, but I imagine there needs to be some sort of official examination before I can have them buried or cremated.

I will wait until I've heard from you before I do anything with them, but honestly, there's no need to rush over and hold my hand. I am far beyond the stage where a few dry bones keep me from sleep.
Rae Newborn

It was, she decided, looking over the fifth and final attempt at the letter, nothing more than the truth. If anything, in the three days she had lived with the knowledge of her cave's remains, she had come to think of them as a larger version of Desmond's crude wooden figurine in the foundation. Were she any less automatically and unfailingly law-abiding, were she not certain that sooner or later she would break down and admit to Nikki or Petra or someone else that she was concealing human remains, Rae would have been tempted merely to cover them over and leave them there.

Still, secrets had a way of coming out at the most awkward moment possible. Besides which, other than the temporary upheaval of her daily rounds, she did not see what harm would come of bringing Jerry Carmichael in.

Having written the letter, however, there was something Rae needed to do before she placed it in Ed's hand the next morning. On Monday night, the first floor framed in and her hand nearly healed, she ate an early dinner and then, when she was certain that no one was going to drop in on her unannounced, she walked in twilight up to the house and through the stud wall, entering for the third time Desmond Newborn's final resting place.

She had not been back to the cave since Nikki's precipitate arrival on Friday morning, although looking back, she thought that her mind had been on little else. Images and questions and decisions had all whirled their way around and around, and one of the decisions she had reached was that, of the myriad questions about Desmond's presence, there were few that she would care to share with outsiders.

The questions all boiled down to one: *Why was he here?* How Desmond had died, when he had done so, and the reason why his family had believed him to be in Arizona—all these puzzles fell into line behind the one big question: How had Desmond Newborn come to crawl into the earth, there to die?

Rae had no doubt the coroner would have some idea what had killed Desmond, even if it was just old age. But tonight would be her last chance to have him on her own, to allow his remains to tell her what they would. She felt strongly, for reasons she could not have explained even to herself, that she owed him that chance: She owed the builder of Folly the opportunity to speak privately to the one person who might hear. She had never had a last moment alone with either Alan or Bella. Both of them had been whisked away from hospital to morgue to crematorium before Rae knew what she wanted. With Desmond, she would take her time to say good-bye.

Plus, she had to know what was in the metal box that she had flung back into the darkness.

The spare lamp and the flashlight were both where she had left them, just inside the narrow entrance. She lit a match and set it to the mantle, which thankfully lit without the small puff that invariably proved fatal to the delicate membrane. Instead, it began instantly to glow, filling the passage with light. She replaced the glass hood, and shuffled forward on her knees down the stone floor.

Hello, Desmond, she said silently. *Not long now.*

From here on, whatever she did would be obvious to the police. There would be no way to conceal her passage into Desmond's cubbyhole, no way to replace the disturbed dust on his clothing. Well, she would face that problem when she came to it. It wasn't exactly a crime scene she was disturbing, after all.

Unless . . .

Only one way to find out. She didn't know if she should reassure the spirit that she was about to lay the body to its long-delayed rest or apologize for disturbing its peace, but she pushed forward until the knees of her jeans brushed the delicate foot bones, scattered on the ground like some ancient runic consultation of the oracles. Then she sat back on her heels and raised the lamp, sending weird shadows fleeing across the rock.

After the house burned, enough debris had covered the cave opening to allow only the smallest of scavengers access. Nothing larger than a rat could have reached the body, which meant that Desmond was more or less intact, if somewhat . . . relaxed. However, she doubted very much that even a large rat would have taken away articles of clothing, yet Desmond had nothing on his feet, not even stockings. His leg bones disappeared up into a pair of dust-draped trousers of some heavy black fabric. Good, thick woolen cloth, she judged, rather than workman's pants. He wore neither jacket nor waistcoat, only a long-sleeved shirt that was white beneath the stains, with the sort of neck band designed to button into a high, stiff collar. The collar itself was missing, as was his necktie, but behind the shirt she could see the neck band and a few inches of under-shirt, draped across the breastbone. The lower section of the undergar-ment was ragged, either rotted or chewed away. He also wore a pair of suspenders, but not over his shoulders: Both sides were down around his waist, one actually looped underneath his thighs. Most telling of all, the buttons down the front of his shirt were all undone, obvious even con-sidering the amount of nibbling something had done to the garment.

With absolutely no experience in the habits of a body in dissolution, Rae could not be certain what the relative position of the various limbs meant, but if she imagined it as a melted ice sculpture, it appeared as if the figure before her had expired in a somewhat slumped position, its—his—head resting against a slope to his right, his right leg slightly drawn up, his left leg outstretched. The bones of the left arm had slid out of the sleeve onto the ground, but the right sleeve remained folded against the body, its cuff tucked inside the remnants of the shirtfront.

Along with the bones of the right hand, she saw when she shone the flashlight down into the jumble of ribs and vertebrae.

The bones inside the shirt (and Rae couldn't help wondering if this lit-tle exploration was going to give her nightmares) were cleaner, more pro-tected from dust. Taking the edge of the shirt between her fingernails, she drew the fabric back, casting the powerful beam in among the bones to study what lay beneath: curving ribs, the knobs of the spinal column, flat pelvic bones, a lot of leathery scraps she didn't care to think about, and sprinkled among them the small bumpy bones of the disintegrated right hand. And among these, an unnaturally smooth shape little larger than a pencil eraser. She wouldn't have seen it if she hadn't been looking for it. Rae screwed up her face, which was inches from Desmond's leather-draped skull (he'd had good teeth, she noted), and gingerly snaked two fingers in behind the waist of his trousers to retrieve the object.

A bullet. And not a smashed leaden blob as the others had been, but a clean, only slightly misshapen bullet. She put it in her chest pocket and buttoned the flap over it. She started to withdraw, but when her light came up, it illuminated an unexpected bulge on the back of the left shoulder blade. A second bullet, but this one had once been nearly the size of her little finger, though it was now flattened and half buried in the bone. At the thought of prying it out, her nerve finally failed, and she sat back to catch her breath; after perhaps five seconds she leaned forward again, to look more closely at the shapeless wad of metal. The bone around the bullet showed clear fracture lines, but no movement. The shoulder blade had cracked, but not fallen apart.

No, she corrected herself: The bone had fallen apart, and had then regrown, trapping the bullet in place.

She was looking at the work of a German sniper, whose shot had gone through Desmond's shoulder and smashed the bone a decade before the smaller bullet that had killed him.

Enough—she couldn't face any more. She had what she came for, the bullet and the metal box, and she moved to pick up the lamp and go. At the mouth of the side cave, however, one last oddity niggled its way into her mind: the weight of the dusty shirtfront as she had pulled it back. She took up the flashlight again, straightened out the fold of the shirt-front, and saw in the breast pocket the edge of a small leather-bound book the size of her grandmother's New Testament, barely larger than her palm. She eased it out, letting the neck of the shirt fall back across the pocket, and glanced at the pages. It took a split second to realize it was not a Bible: The pages were covered with handwriting.

A diary.

Without hesitation, Rae flipped through to the final entry, twenty pages or so in from the end. There, on the twelfth of September, 1927, Desmond had written a brief entry.

My brother comes tomorrow, to talk me out of my folly. Let him try. Although I freely admit, to myself if none other, that the thought of seeing his face fills me with a terrible dread.

Thirty

Letter from Rae to Her Lawyer

May 25

Dear Pam,

 You're going to think I've well and truly lost my mind this time. All I can say is, I wish it were that simple.

 I want you to find a private investigator who has access to a forensic lab, and give him the enclosed packet. Do not open the packet. Do not report any of this to the police, do not let the lab report this—I swear to you it would only get them excited for no purpose. I'll explain it all once I know what it means. Please, trust me.

 I need the lab to give me a complete analysis on the five objects I am sending, comparing them for similarities and differences. I want to know absolutely everything about each one, and I don't care what it costs.

 I may be returning to civilization for a few days; if so, I'll phone and let you know where I am.

 Sorry for the mystery. I'll explain when we talk. Promise.
   Rae

Rae was up that night until well after three o'clock, straining her eyes to finish Desmond Newborn's diary; the hoot of Ed De la Torre's horn before eight the next morning caught her still in her sleeping bag. She threw on some clothes, doused her face with cold water, and made coffee, drinking it with her mind far removed from Ed's informative philosophic monologue. Eventually, he tired of her unresponsiveness, and stood to go. Rae hastily got to her own feet.

"Can you wait for just a minute, Ed? I need you to mail something urgent for me." Without waiting for his response, she ducked inside the tent, took the note she had written to Pamela Church, and packaged it up with the five separately wrapped and numbered lumps of lead. She filled out the mailing label and sealed it, then took it and the letter to Jerry Carmichael and handed them to Ed. He seemed less than thrilled about having anything to do with the sheriff's office, but made up for it in his hearty reassurances that the overnight package to the lawyer would make it into the box for the afternoon pickup.

When he left, Rae was tempted to climb back into her bed, but she had things to do before the machinery of the law began to turn and deposited Jerry Carmichael on her shore. She heated water and showered, tidied her tent and the space around it (which looked more than ever like a gypsy camp, with 2x4s propping up the sagging blue tarpaulin and various branches of the fallen cedar turned into pan hooks and drying racks), then slid the things she did not want anyone to see into the bottom of her knapsack and piled clothes, shoes, and a toilet kit on top. Her locked trunk was all well and good, but some things she needed to keep with her.

When the sheriff arrived, she was ready. More than ready: She was, for what felt like the first time in her life, impatient, eager to move. Her campsite was spotless, every fire-blackened pan was gleaming, tent and tarpaulin were snug, the ground looked as if she had swept it. She heard the boat before she could see it, and was waiting on the dock with her knapsack at her feet. At nearly noon, the low tide had long since turned, and there was no hesitation as he came into the cove.

The sheriff was alone.

"Nikki's bringing the others" were his first words to her. "We've got a woman from the university flying in later, to look at the bones, as she said, 'in situ.' This is all going to be very disruptive for you." He looked at her with a mingled apology and question in his face.

"Actually," she told him, "I was thinking I might just use this as an excuse to go over to Friday Harbor for a day or so. If I can trust your guys to keep an eye on the place, so the passing tourists don't walk away with all my things."

He looked surprised, and it occurred to her that he had been preparing an argument to persuade her to leave the island, for a few hours at any rate. But she knew full well how disruptive this was going to be, and wanted no part of it—besides which, she did actually have business on San Juan Island. If nothing else, between her hard labor and Ed's commercial laundry (both of which appeared to involve pounding clothes on rocks) she was running short of things to wear.

She led him up to the house, where she had left both flashlight and kerosene lamp, and then back along the gap between rock wall and stone fireplace to the cave entrance. "He's in there," she said, pointing at the hole. "Do you want me to show you?"

"Is there anything tricky about finding him?"

"Not at all. He's just sitting there."

"Then if you could just wait here for a minute, I'll check it and be right back."

Carmichael looked too large to get through the entrance, but he did not get stuck, merely wriggled his shoulders a few times before his feet were disappearing. She followed the sound of his passage, heard him pause as he spotted the bones, then he turned and came back out.

"Well," he said, "I've seen a lot of things in this job, but never anything like that. It looks like a movie set. Spooky."

Rae thought it an interesting reaction: She didn't think the bones spooky, just sad.

"I've got a generator and spotlights," he said, and Rae made a face at the thought of the racket. Yes, far better to retreat, not to witness the invasion.

"Is there someone who could run me over to Friday Harbor?" she asked. "Or if you could radio to Ed and have him come pick me up."

"Do you mind waiting for Nikki?"

Rae did, but didn't tell him that. However, she also did not help him unload all the equipment he would use to illuminate and record the bones before their removal. She went into her tent and took up a book, turning her back on the entire proceedings. When the other boat arrived, she presented herself promptly to the ranger.

"Can I just go see the cave?" Nikki pleaded. Rae did not trust herself to speak, just nodded and retreated into the tent.

Nikki was back inside of ten minutes. Rae was wearing the good khaki pants that she had preserved, a cleanish T-shirt, and city shoes. She picked up her green knapsack.

"Shall we go?"

"Jerry says he'll need you to make a statement, when things settle down a little. I saw where you found that wine, by the way." She arched an eyebrow at Rae, to chide Rae for her lie, but Rae refused to be penitent.

"And if any bottles are missing, or if anything in the tent is disturbed without a warrant, my lawyer will raise holy hell." Rae held the younger woman's eyes to make it clear that half a dozen friendly visits did not mean a friendship without limits, ignored the hurt look that came over the ranger's face, and turned to zip the door all the way around, then tie down the flap. Head down, ears shut against the cacophony of the generator, she followed Nikki to the boat and sat down, leaving the ranger to cast off. She heard Nikki talking on a radio, no doubt conveying Rae's threat of legal wrath descending on the county, and then they were in open water.

Rae was far enough from Nikki to make speech difficult; neither of them said anything. After a while Nikki pointed out a splash and a fin a mile or so away and shouted at Rae that it was a minke whale. Rae nodded, and that was all.

You can't hide, you can't ignore.

Maybe not. But as far as Rae was concerned, beyond a certain point the continual picking open of wounds was torture for its own sake, pointless and even hindering to healing. There were times when a person had to hide; there were things it was best to ignore. She had stopped arguing with the professionals about it, since it just worried them and, in a hospital situation, a worried psychiatrist made for a hefty barrier between patient and outer world. Still, she had long ago come to the conclusion that sometimes, things actually did go away—or rather, a person could cover enough ground to leave the problem behind, and when it did catch up again it was apt to be weakened by the journey. Sometimes, pretending things—bravery, wholeness, humor—made them so.

Right now, she was content to close off the image of what was happening on Folly. She would not think about the violation of her privacy, not picture what they would do with Desmond Newborn, not even think about the old, stained leather diary with the brittle pages that lay in her knapsack. She would instead reduce herself to a small and intense point of focus, pretend this was an outing she had chosen; she would take care of the tasks she had set herself, then she would go back to Folly in the serenity of her chosen ignorance, to take up her hammer anew.

Her resolve was shaken when Friday Harbor appeared through the boat's windshield. A forest of masts grew from the water, behind it a far more bustling town than she remembered. A ferry horn blared massively, and Rae twitched. Nikki glanced over at her, then returned to her task of threading the boat through traffic.

"It's really a pretty quiet little town," she said reassuringly. "And I called my aunt, who has a small inn a couple of miles outside town, and she says she has a room free for tonight. If you like it, that is."

No town was quiet, compared with Folly, Rae thought, but she told Nikki that would be fine.

"I'll just put in to the dock and run you up to—"

"No need for that," Rae interrupted. "You have work, and I have things to do in town." She met Nikki's green eyes evenly. It was like being mean to a kitten, seeing the faint hurt in the wrinkles on Nikki's pale brow, but at the same time, Rae knew that if she didn't cut this tie of responsibility here and now, she was in danger of becoming Nikki Walls's property for life. After a minute Nikki shrugged her narrow shoulders and reached into her pocket for a pencil.

Rae took the address, thanked her, and was off the boat before the second line was secure. Nikki called that she was welcome, and Rae walked away before the ranger could offer to pick her up the next day.

Rae strode briskly up the street, excruciatingly conscious of the number of strange men behind her back. She made it a couple of blocks, and then ducked into the first likely place to buy a map, taking her time before forcing herself back out to the street. She traveled a little farther, then retreated to a coffee shop, where she ordered a sandwich she didn't want for the privilege of sitting at a table with her back to a wall, the map and a phone book borrowed from the cashier on the table in front of her. She located the bank, the newspaper office, Friday Harbor's historical society, and then asked the waitress for a good place to buy some blue jeans. First of all, though, the bank.

She ate half the sandwich, leaving the waitress a nice tip by way of apology, and made it as far as the bank in one try. There she introduced herself to the manager as the owner of an account set up in February by her lawyer in California. She received her ATM card and took out some cash with it, then rented a safety deposit box large enough to hold Desmond's strongbox and his diary. Before she put the battered tin container away, she lifted the lid to take another look at its enigmatic contents. She'd had to break the lock to open it, but the treasure it held was not the sort to require guarding. A smooth gray pebble, a small shell, and two pieces of twig had been placed in the box, along with a pearly button, a bit of green ribbon, a three-inch maroon tassel, and the program for a concert that gave neither date nor location. The only understandable item among all these mementos—if mementos they were—was a handsome gold locket on a heavy chain, containing a lock of a dozen or so long blond hairs pressed into one side and a thicker lock of short brown hair on the other. Blond and brown touched when the locket was shut. She put it back and closed the tin box, locked the bank box, and thanked the manager.

On the street again, she rested her shoulders against the brickwork while she checked the location of the post office on the map, then set off to identify herself to the people there as well. It was getting easier, she found to her relief. No one here crowded her, no footsteps speeded up, and there were plenty of open doors waiting to rescue her, many honest citizens ready and willing to come to her aid.

The post office held three letters for her, one from Pamela concerning a bill, and one from Gloriana, the owner of the New York gallery that sold Rae's smaller pieces, saying, Please, please, *please* get in touch. The third was from Petra. Rae stood outside the post office, tore it open, and fumbled to catch the note that fell out from between Petra's folded pages. It was from Tamara, and in growing amazement, Rae read:

Dear Mother,

I have given Petra my permission, conditional to her good behavior in the meantime, to spend a week with you on your island. Considering the complicated travel arrangements necessary, Don and I have agreed that we will need to bring her to you. We will only stay a few days, and if Petra chooses to do so, she will remain with you. We can arrange the details of her return later. I propose that we spend the Fourth of July weekend with you, arriving on July first.

Love,

Tamara

Rae went through the note again, this time reading between the lines. "Don and I will need to bring her to you" meant that Rae could not be trusted to be at the airport to meet Petra's plane, and Tamara did not wish to risk a stranded thirteen-year-old. "If Petra chooses" to stay meant if Tamara and Don approved of Rae's state of mind and her living circumstances.

Rae had to give Petra credit for getting even so conditional an approval, but the more she considered Tamara's letter, the greater grew her astonishment—not at Petra's manipulative skills, but at the sheer, brazen effrontery of Petra's father. She shook her head in wonder: *First he instigates an incompetency case against me, then he has the nerve to expect me to welcome him as a guest.* As she had so often before in her dealings with the man, Rae wavered between disgust and admiration: She felt she ought to embrace fully the outrage Don inspired, yet she was also constantly in awe of his utter self-interest, his easy assumption that things would go his way simply because he wanted them to.

Amazing, Rae thought, coming down as always on the side of bemusement. But it might also be a form of unstated challenge: Don saying, *I'm grown-up enough to compartmentalize my life; are you?* Very well—as a challenge, a means of letting him know how she felt without saying it directly, she would allow him to set his Gucci loafers on Folly. As proof of her own mental resilience—to herself if no one else—it would be without parallel.

Petra's letter was a relief, chatty and meandering, giving mere glimpses of the battle that had raged before Tamara had written her note, including the brief but ominous admission that she'd "never seen Dad as mad as he was" when his daughter refused to accept his decision of "no." Tamara had had to step in and soothe the waters, and Petra went blithely on, assuming that all was well again. Rae was not so sure, but despite her concern, the letter's childlike glee was contagious, and Rae reread some of the lines to make the impending visit more real in her mind. Some minutes later, with a smile on her face, blissfully unheeding of the threatening presence of other people all around her, Rae looked up to find a sheriff's car sitting at the curb in front of her. A fresh-faced young man in a crisp new uniform was looking over the top of the car at her.

"Mrs. Newborn?"

"More or less."

"Um. Sorry?"

"Ms. is fine."

He blushed, both cheeks taking on red circles like clown paint. "Ms. Newborn, right. Um, you are her?"

"Yes."

"Oh, good. The sheriff wants to talk to you."

For a moment Rae thought in disgust that she was about to be hauled back to the island to answer questions, and watched the boy deputy get back in the car, but he then fiddled with a car phone for a moment before lying flat across the front seat to open the passenger-side door. Sitting upright again, he held the phone out in her direction. She slipped her knapsack from her shoulder and sat on the edge of the cruiser's front seat to take the phone, leaving the door open and one foot on the ground.

"Hello?"

"Ms. Newborn?"

"This is she."

"Jerry Carmichael here. It's about the dirt in the area behind your house."

"Yes," Rae responded, mystified.

"Well, it's just that we really ought to sift through it, just to be thorough, and it occurred to me that if you were thinking about moving it out of there anyway, my guys could as easily dump it where you like rather than putting it carefully back where we found it. Up to you."

"That's very thoughtful of you, Sheriff. No, I certainly don't want it there. I was planning eventually on putting it over with the other soil I excavated, around the hill a ways. If you'd shift it anywhere in that general direction, that would be helpful."

"I did see that place. And I noticed that you'd been collecting the stuff you sieved out into a pile nearby. You want us to do the same?"

"It would be too much bother, Sheriff."

"None at all. Uh, would you mind if we borrowed your wheelbarrow?"

"Any of the outdoor tools at all, help yourselves," she replied, with the stress on *out*. Although if it meant getting all that soil out of there, she might even lend him one of her rattier chisels.

"Thanks, that'll speed it up."

"But watch out for the glass and nails. I cut myself on something in there the other day."

"Will do. See you later, then."

The phone went dead and she handed it back to the young man, then asked him, "How did you find me?"

The pink bloomed on his cheeks again. "Sheriff said watch for a six-foot-tall woman with short gray hair and a green backpack. Didn't take long."

She thanked him, then watched the cruiser drive away. Back to research.

She discovered that the historical museum was not open until the following afternoon, so she went on to the newspaper office instead. This occupied a building with a flat gray false front, like something from a Western, but the cowboys inside were of the cyber variety, and back issues were available for perusal. The mid-1920s? the woman asked. No problem; the *Journal* had been in print since 1906.

Rae found the article about the "fiery destruction" of the house on Sanctuary Island, also known as Newborn's Folly, in September 1927. It was front-page stuff, jockeying for space with a political scandal in Olympia and a rash of burglaries in the county, in which the stolen items included half a dozen laying hens, a skiff, a buried Mason jar filled with cash, and the engine out of someone's Model T. The flames had been seen from Roche Harbor, at the northern end of San Juan Island, by an early-morning fisherman in the wee hours of September 14. The date jolted Rae, and she had to drag her attention back to the article and read on. By the time firefighters could get a boat out to Sanctuary, they found the house burned to the foundations, and although they had stayed on to search by daylight, no trace was found of its eccentric builder. Since his rowing skiff was also missing, it was thought that he might have left the island in the wake of the fire.

The following issue saw an article about Desmond Newborn, who by now, since he had not appeared in Roche Harbor or any of the other island towns, was presumed dead, "consumed by the fierce flames." He was, the editorial noted, from a prominent Eastern family, but of his past, little was known. Residents and visitors to the islands knew him by the work of his hands, the twin-towered structure that had been dubbed The Folly by locals. The editor went on to say that Desmond Newborn was familiar to the residents and businesses of Roche Harbor—to which he was in the habit of rowing every week, in any but the stormiest of weather, to pick up groceries, newspapers, building supplies, and the rare piece of mail—as a polite, quiet man with a "wry" sense of humor.

That last interested Rae: She had somehow not thought of Desmond Newborn as having a humorous side, wry or otherwise. Certainly the diary showed little of that, although she supposed that the house itself argued for a quizzical worldview.

There were no illustrations to the articles, and nothing in the next few papers, but a month after the fire Desmond's name appeared again, this time paired with that of his brother.

FOLLY GOES TO STATE

Mr. William Newborn, of Boston, Massachusetts, has granted to the State of Washington the island on which his brother, Desmond Newborn, built the house known throughout the San Juan Islands as "The Folly," a sobriquet attached to the structure with a view to its colorful twin stone towers front and back. Mr. William Newborn, appreciating the affection his brother (presumed dead in the fire that consumed "The Folly" last month) felt for the islands and the wildlife, has granted the State the use of the entire island as a preserve for resident and migrating birds. The grant covers a fifty-year period, and applies until such a time as any direct relative of Mr. Desmond Newborn (he leaves no descendents) wishes to take up residence on the island.

Folly is currently home to two nesting pairs of bald eagles as well as two or three juvenile birds, a colony of auklets, and a sizable heron rookery. San Juan County is pleased to know that such a jewel is to be held safe for the heritage of our children.

Nikki had been right, Rae reflected: The island had been park domain by the beginning of 1928, a good year and a half before Desmond's last letter.

Desmond's purported last letter, Rae corrected grimly. She turned to the next issue of the *Journal*.

During the spring, a scant handful of mentions caught her eye. The county wished to remind boaters that Folly was off limits for the gathering of wood or shellfish. An arrest had been made of a pair of boys for poaching eggs during nesting season. And in March the sheriff announced that the ashes of Desmond Newborn's residence had been probed, and judgment reached that, unless Newborn had been in the hottest portion and thus totally consumed, he had not been there at all. Therefore, the sheriff asked anyone with information on Mr. Newborn's whereabouts, particularly in the middle of September of the previous year, please to come forward.

After that, nothing. On the anniversary of the fire a brief article appeared, as well as on the subsequent few anniversaries—due, she figured, to the romantic images the two ruined towers evoked for passing boaters.

At five o'clock Rae was thrown out of the newspaper offices. Bleary-eyed after two stints of difficult reading in twenty-four hours, filthy of hand and crook of back, Rae tottered out onto the street and tried to orient herself to the modern world. She dug out her map and looked for the inn run by Nikki's aunt, and thus missed the sudden pause and subsequent acceleration of a passing sheriff's car. She set off in the right direction, and had just begun to find her stride when another car belonging to the San Juan County Sheriff's Department drifted over onto the shoulder of the road ahead of her and stopped. This time, the sheriff himself emerged, dressed, despite the official vehicle, in jeans and a clean, freshly pressed chambray work shirt. He closed the cruiser's door and came around the back of the automobile to join her.

"Ms. Newborn," he said. "Could I by any chance interest you in a bite of dinner?"

Jerry Carmichael moved quietly, Rae noticed, as some big men do, so as not to frighten lesser humans—or to step on them by accident. Alan had moved that way. Alan had lived that way. And why was she thinking about Alan?

"I'm pretty tired," she answered. "I was heading for the inn Nikki Walls arranged for me. She said it was quiet."

"Is that the one her aunt owns? It's a good two miles out, and she doesn't serve dinner. We could eat and I could drop you there in the time it'd take you to walk it."

If his attitude had been even faintly pushy, Rae would have said a polite thanks and continued on around him, but Carmichael seemed content to go by her decision, offering an alternative rather than coaxing. She found herself folding her map away.

"I'd like dinner, thanks."

It did not occur to her that "dinner" meant anything but a quick burger, so it wasn't until they were inside the door of the restaurant that she came to a halt.

"I'm not really dressed—" she began, but was cut off by the approach of a young blond woman with a gold loop through her left nostril, a wide smile on her face, and a pair of menus in her hand.

"Good evening, Sheriff. Two tonight?"

"Thank you, Sara. That corner table'd be good."

It was early, so only three or four of the twenty or so tables were taken. Rae wavered, on the brink of demanding to be taken elsewhere, then decided that at this hour, it was not likely that anyone would look askance at a woman who was dressed for a hike in the woods sitting down to white linen and sparkling crystal. She did, however, excuse herself to scrub irritably at the day's accumulation of dust, salt spray, and newsprint. When she got back to the table, the sheriff rose, an old-world courtesy that also reminded her of Alan. She plunked down in her chair, yanked her intricately folded napkin onto her lap, and told the attentive Sara, "Wine. Red."

The waitress was new enough to the job to blink at Rae's brusqueness, but the man seated across from Rae suggested a variety and a maker, and Sara went off to fetch it.

Rae applied herself to the menu, aware of the gaze of a pair of all-seeing eyes on her, but unwilling to be drawn out of her sulk. When the wine came she swallowed two large gulps without tasting it. This had been a long day filled with unaccustomed demands and revelations, following a sleepless night, and she could feel the restless stir of energies, pushed deep down. She needed quiet and solitude; she'd told the sheriff as much, yet he had still brought her here; let him deal with a difficult dinner companion.

What she failed to reckon with was the sheriff's long experience with hostile witnesses. After a moment, she became aware of a large, callused hand with nicely shaped nails being held across the table in her direction. She looked up.

"My grandmother would turn me over her knee for my manners. I believe you've met my alter ego, Sheriff Carmichael," he told her. "My own name is Jerry, Jerry Carmichael." Rae looked at the extended hand, and her mouth twitched, not so much at the humor of the introduction as at the picture of any woman turning this man over her knee. She took his hand over the table, and felt her own work-hardened hand completely enfolded in the delicate grasp of a vise, a vise of great precision as well as strength.

"Rae Newborn," she said in response, and he let her go.

"Nikki tells me you're a woodworker," he said as he picked up his menu. "Furniture and tables and things." They seemed to be starting from scratch—not only with new introductions, but they'd covered the question of her profession at least once already. She took another swallow of wine, thought, *What the hell,* and responded in the same way she had two weeks before.

"I used to be," she corrected him. However, Carmichael seemed to be more interested in the choices before him than in her faults and failures. She lowered her own eyes to the menu, and was suddenly ravenous. He made comments about a couple of items, suggesting an appetizer that sounded unlikely but that, in his words, "went down a treat."

Rae made her choice, Sara materialized and took their orders, and

Rae reached out for her glass, which had somehow been refilled while her attention was on the menu. The sheriff raised his glass to her, and sipped.

"You seem to come here a lot," she commented.

"Oh, I own two of the tables."

"You own . . . ?" Was this some kind of San Juan tradition? she wondered, but suddenly his habitual expression of quiet watchfulness gave way to an eye-crinkling smile.

"When Rafe and Sally were first starting the place, I put up ten percent of their costs, and told them I'd take repayment in meals. I think I'm down to about one and a half tables now. Rafe's my cousin."

"Everybody on the islands seems to be related," Rae commented. "Talking to Nikki, she has a brother or an aunt or someone she went to school with in every corner."

"Well, Nikki probably does. She's one of nine kids, and her parents between them have . . . oh, let's see, twelve, no—thirteen brothers and sisters."

"They must have to go off the islands to find a spouse they're not related to."

"Yeah, most of 'em have found someone at college. We bring 'em in during summer vacation, you understand, when the weather is good. That way, by the time winter closes in, they're already hooked."

"And you—were you hooked, or born here?"

"Born and bred on Lopez. You been there?"

"When I was here a few years ago. They wave," she recalled suddenly. "All the drivers who go past you, they wiggle their fingers to say hello." As an anthropological phenomenon, it had entertained her and Alan for hours, and Bella had adopted the custom, waving with enthusiasm at puzzled Californian passersby.

"The Lopez wave. It'll probably die out in a few years, but yeah, it's a rural community. You assume it's your neighbor going by."

"Even if the car has California plates."

"Yeah, well, we're willing to let county borders stretch a ways."

Rae was startled to find herself laughing along with him. Laughter over a glass of good wine with a . . . well, a handsome and intelligent man was probably the last thing she would have expected of this tumultuous day.

"Are you married?" she asked, then realized how abrupt it sounded, and how intemperately she'd been drinking. She changed the question to "I mean, did you go away to college and hook someone home yourself?"

"I found a native," he said. "But we moved off the islands, lived on the mainland for nearly ten years before she died and I came back."

"I'm sorry."

"Long time ago."

"Does that matter?"

"Sometimes," he replied, gazing down into the depths of his wineglass. "Sometimes it matters. Mostly when I try to remember what she looked like."

Rae felt the tears prick at her tired eyes. "There are times I can't remember my daughter's face," she admitted, and was abruptly appalled. She pushed away the glass and grabbed for a less loaded subject. "Other than that ten years, you've lived here your whole life?"

"College, the army, and a few years of living far from the water was enough. I've got the sea in my blood. Spent my childhood in a boat, practically. In fact, I spent a lot of it right on your island."

"Folly? What, living there?"

"Oh no, just picnics and the occasional campout. Exploring the woods, fishing and digging clams for dinner, picking berries. Mountain man stuff, great for a kid—although you can't let kids have that kind of freedom these days."

"Did you have your fire pit in the same place mine is?"

"The very same."

"My granddaughter tidied it up a bit, but it looked like people had used it over the years."

"Not for a while. Truth to tell, my family once owned Folly, long time ago. It was called Minke then."

"Really? When was this?"

Jerry looked uncomfortable, as if regretting that he'd told her this, and reached for the bottle to refill their glasses. "My granddad sold it in the Twenties. Must've been to your great-uncle."

"Good heavens. I had no idea."

"Yep. I always had the fantasy of rebuilding it myself, when I was young. My dad tried to buy it back, but of course by that time it was a sanctuary and nobody could quite sort out who owned it. Not that he would've had the money, of course."

He had not looked up from his glass and plate during this entire tale.

Was he embarrassed at the regret, and the tinge of resentment, that edged into his voice? Or did he fear that his audience might be embarrassed at the revelation? Rae couldn't decide.

"My grandfather would have owned it," she told him. "From the late Twenties until he died."

"Yeah, I know. Dad tried to get a court case up, but again, it was too much money." At last he raised his head, a crooked smile on his mouth. "So as you can see, I have a proprietary interest in the place."

"Well, any time you want to camp in the clearing and dig clams on the beach, feel free."

"So," he said. "Tell me about woodworking."

"I used to be good," she said, as if speaking of someone else. "I'm more of a rough carpenter now."

"That workbench of yours testifies to the fact that you're more than that."

"Turned out okay, didn't it?"

"That little shaving of cedar you put into the one leg. Did you do that because it's the same color as the madrone bark overhead?"

"You have a good eye, Sheriff." The detail had been fairly subtle; most people who noticed it would take it for an echo of the bench top.

"You going to do some stuff like that in the house itself?"

And so Rae began to describe her plans for the inside of Newborn's Folly, the Japanese (or perhaps Shaker) shelf-wall next to the black fireplace, the floating steps winding up the two towers, the bedroom and work areas on the upper floor with the incomparable view, the balance between drama and comfort and the difficulty of restraint. At some point Rae suddenly realized that a magnificent entrée was lying half eaten on her plate and that she had been talking earnestly about the personality conflicts between teak and zebrawood to a man whose idea of wood was probably limited to logs for the fire or 2x4s for the wall. She flushed.

"Sorry to get so carried away."

"I'd say—not sure, you understand, it's just a guess—but I'd say maybe you could still call yourself a woodworker."

She felt herself returning his slow smile. "I'd say maybe you're right."

Thirty-two

Letter from Rae to Her Granddaughter

Dear Petra,

I wonder if you've done any research yet into the far-off, distant past of our island? Before the peoples came here, before the nomadic tribes crossed the frozen Bering Strait or paddled with the Pacific currents, when the land itself was being laid down?

A person sees everywhere the immense pressures and incomprehensible tensions that accumulated here, shoving and wrenching the landmasses around like a pizza crust. There's a layer of light-colored sandstone that runs through Folly, folded back on itself in some places, twisted in with the darker bedrock. How much pressure must it take to <u>fold</u> rock? Can you begin to imagine something like that? I can't.

The other huge force acting on this placid-looking group of islands was ice. The last glaciers began to retreat up the Georgia Strait to the north around 13,000 years ago, scouring the strait, grinding and eroding the crests of the folded rock, but when they passed, the layers of sandstone and bedrock underneath them rose, jutting up into the air sometimes nearly perpendicular to the current sea. When the weight of 3,000 feet of ice—three thousand!—lifted, the release of pressure caused some of the land beneath to, as they call it, rebound. Incredible to think of, the earth <u>bouncing</u> back after that, isn't it? But the unevenness of the postglacial rebound, following the grinding of *the glaciers, broke Folly and her neighbors away from the larger landmasses, crumpled them as they rose, and twisted them into the shapes of islands.*

Huge tensions, incomprehensible pressures, ripping and heaving at the land; such sweet beauty at the end.

Love,
Gran

Thirty-three

As she sat in Jerry Carmichael's cruiser outside Elaine Walls's neat two-story inn, it occurred to Rae that Carmichael had never said why he had hunted her down in the first place.

"Jerry, I appreciate you taking me out to dinner and carving another few inches out of your two tables' worth of investment, but did you have something you wanted to talk to me about?"

"Yeah, I did, but I could see how tired and hungry you were, so I figured I'd just soften you up and come back in the morning. I'll need a written statement about finding those bones."

"It's not that complicated. I could do it now."

"Morning's fine. In fact, Elaine makes one of the best breakfasts on the islands. Your being here would give me an excuse to add myself to her table."

"Dear God, after that dinner, how can you even think about food?"

"Come morning, her huckleberry waffles will have you drooling."

He retrieved her knapsack from the trunk of the car, handed it to her on the steps leading to the rose-lined walkway, and accompanied her to the inn, where he joked familiarly with Elaine Walls and warned her that he would be back for breakfast. Then he wrapped Rae's hand in his giant grip again, wished both women a good night, and left. The inn's small foyer seemed suddenly large in his absence.

Elaine Walls was very obviously her niece's relative, from the frizzy red hair (in her case paling toward gray) to the perky speech. She kept up a string of friendly inconsequentials all the way up the stairs, peppering her remarks with everything from instructions for using a key if Rae needed to go out at night to the doleful state of the television reception downstairs.

"I start serving breakfast at eight," she said at the door to Rae's room, "but if you want coffee earlier or a cup of tea during the night there's makings in the common room, and since yours is the room above, you don't even need to worry about making noise. Good night, and if you need anything, just go through the kitchen and knock on the door."

Rae closed the door on the woman's retreating footsteps, and stood for a long minute with her hand on the knob and her forehead resting against the door. Alone, at last. Christ, what a day.

Standing there, feeling the cool painted wood against her warm face, the vibration of Elaine's feet through the floorboards, and the weight of the long day pressing down on her shoulders, Rae did not move until she felt a drop hit the back of her wrist. She jerked upright impatiently, dashing the tears from her eyes, then dumped her grubby backpack on the bed.

Tired as she was, she knew there was no way she would fall asleep. Too much repressed inner turmoil, too many glasses of wine, too little exercise for a body accustomed to vigorous labor. She took her flashlight and her fleece pullover from the knapsack and let herself out of the inn.

Elaine had mentioned that the beach at the foot of the inn road was a public one, so Rae headed for that. She walked down the paved surface until the light over Elaine's front door was faint, and then she stood in the dark and waited for her vision to adjust.

Now was when the cost of ignoring the events of Folly began to come due. *Can't hide, can't ignore.* If it had been just one thing, she might have repressed it satisfactorily until it shrank to a manageable size. But everything piled together—finding the skeleton, reading the diary, the growing certainty of what Desmond's end had been, topped off by all kinds of unsettling feelings stirred up by the dinner with Sheriff Jerry Carmichael—was too much; Rae's skin crawled with distress and fatigue.

Since Rae was a child, her great-uncle Desmond had inhabited the recesses of her awareness. That William had disapproved of his ne'er-do-well brother was always as evident as William's disapproval of Rae herself; that alone would have been enough to make Desmond a secret companion, even without the pathos of his solitary end in the desert. Coming here as a fifty-two-year-old woman escaping personal horrors, she had begun to feel herself following in his footsteps: After all, the man must have had some reason to cut himself off from the world so emphatically. Her sympathy and admiration for his work, her curiosity about his life—and now his death—had caught her up, made her feel almost as if Desmond Newborn was the pattern after which Rae had been modeled. The older twin, as it were. Through her hands, his life's work was being reborn. Now, having read through his personal diary in growing dismay and understanding, she was coming to think that the madness in her, too, had its origin in him.

For he had been mad, on and off over the years of his journal, a madness that was oh, so very, terribly familiar to her.

When Desmond Newborn was most disturbed, he kept lists. Rae could only imagine what his actual war journal had been like, since this book began during his recovery in the early months of 1918, but the war constantly broke out in his consciousness, like a wound that continued to suppurate. Every time the infection began to heal over, he would swear that never again would he write about those terrible months, and every time, after days or weeks, the festering sore would erupt anew and plunge him back into the trenches. Again and again in the first section of the journal, the chronological progression, brief, tentative mentions of seasonal changes and the family's activities, would break off abruptly, sometimes in the middle of a sentence, and another list would begin. Page after page of tiny, precise writing, beginning with a catalogue of French towns and districts that were rich with the horror of war. Even Rae, who was no historian, recognized that Thiepval meant a river of blood, that Passchendaele translated as a desolation of foot-rotting mud, stomach-wrenching odors, and gut-clenching terror. And then the names, dear God, the names of people. They covered three sheets of the diary, the various shades of ink and sizes of nib testifying to his constant return to the pages—men's names, all marked as dead or injured, with the terse addition of how:

Tommy Smithers. Both legs gone. Dead.
Jethro Hammerley. Shrapnel in the stomach. Dead.
Willy McMasters. Left arm above the elbow. Wounded home.
Orville Tellerston. Face gone. Must be dead. Hope so.
Matthew Grinwold. Gassed. Wounded home.
James Kinkaid. Sniper bullet to the head. Dead.
Harry Butters. Shrapnel. Dead.

Lists of the dead, lists of remembered letters and packages from home (how one parcel containing socks had arrived when he had none left, the pleasure in a fruitcake, the strange and thrilling cleanness of a packet of paper), lists of birds glimpsed in rare days behind the lines, lists of books borrowed and read, page after page, some of the entries given pages of their own, others just squeezed together. A litany of the world's madness, brought together under the orderly notation of desperation. Desmond's writing in the list sections was painfully precise, his margins exact. On one page, Rae had found a brief series of dates and wounds, without names. After a moment, she had realized that they were Desmond's own injuries: Gas. Shrapnel. Trench foot. And last, in letters so exact they could have come from a penmanship chart: Sniper bullet, left shoulder.

The list of wounds was half a dozen or so pages from the beginning of the small book. He seemed to have begun the journal in winter, although the early pages bore no dates, and as time went on she could almost see him growing toward wholeness: His hand and his mind began to unclench, the penmanship became less rigid, the things he wrote shifted from list to reflection. The signs of healing began as memories often do, with a smell.

Dogwood blossoms. They have the fragrance of a woman's body. I remember lying in the medical tent, the English sister bending over me, and all I could smell was dogwood blossom.

Bacon frying downstairs. Bacon's the only meat that doesn't make my stomach heave. And chicken, so long as it's been freshly killed.

Hay being mown. In Thiepval, in the middle of a push, the sweet odor of cut hay came on the wind, stronger than blood and loose bowels, more powerful even than putrid flesh. Half my company stopped what they were doing, lowered their rifles, and raised their faces to the air. The Huns, too, paused to breathe in the farmer's work, until our officers woke to the interruption.

And reflection:

What does it mean, to lose one's mind? Where does it go? If a man is out of his mind, where is he? What is insane when the world is mad by contrast?

The descriptions of evocative scents interspersed with philosophical speculation went on for pages, followed by those of sights that meant something to Desmond—his father's library, a huge old tree on the grounds of the Boston house that Rae was startled to recognize from her own childhood, a trio of brightly dressed young women strolling through the park. Summer wore on, ending in a reference to falling leaves, and then the bitter armistice of November 1918. The war's end shook him; Christmas was a bad time. After the first of the year there was another list, a page with nothing but eight dates on it, each a week or two apart during January and February; there was no explanation of what they meant. Then the darkness seemed to reach out again for Desmond Newborn. His next entry was not for many months, not until October 24, 1919, and read in its lonely entirety:

Arrived in Omaha. Why am I here?

Sporadic entries over the next pages—dates, places, and brief pathetic phrases—chronicled the wanderer's dismal cycle of ill health alternating with aimless travel.

Until the early summer of 1921, when he wrote the following:

An old Italian in a railway yard near Tacoma told me how beautiful the San Juan Islands were. He said that when he read about God walking through the garden in the cool of the evening, it was the San Juans he pictured. I thought the substances he drank had turned his brain to porridge, but I came here to see. And he was right. God does walk here.

He went on to describe the islands, the soothing odor of the sea air, the quality of the light, and most especially the sense of hush that lay over the watery land. It was the longest entry he had written since leaving Boston, and he went on over the weeks that followed, until in June he found Sanctuary.

July 7, 1921

Paradise, on a hundred fifty acres of rock. The silence is profound. For the first time, I have found a place without artillery fire at the edges of my hearing. All the island has is the sea, and birds, and the slow speech of trees. I wired W. for the money, he wired back that he would need to see the place with his own eyes before he approved it. The gall of the man, to imagine me a child, needing his signature on a form in the bank! No, I will not have his shiny boots on my refuge.

I shall name my island Sanctuary.

The money was sent. Months, happy years of entries followed, details of the water system that set Rae to smiling, valuable descriptions of the building process, the sources for his varicolored rock, his happiness with the quality of the cement he bought from Roche Harbor. There was even a mention of the front porch he proposed to add, come the following spring.

For six years, following two and a half years of trench warfare and four more years of battles in the mind, Desmond Newborn had peace. From June 1921 until the summer of 1927, he built his house, he shaped his world, he brushed up against his neighbors in friendly distance. For six years this solitary man lived his life, held conversations with his ghosts, and only occasionally dipped into the fringes of melancholia.

Then suddenly, out of the blue, he received a letter from his brother. In the middle of August 1927, Desmond wrote in his diary:

W. writes to extend a hand of friendship. After years of silence, my brother wishes to be reconciled, and posthaste, as he is on his way west on business. I am to respond to his hotel in Chicago, to say if I am willing or no, and to suggest how he may reach me.

The temptation is great, to act as if his missive never reached me. But truth to tell, I desire greatly to tell the family that I have made something for myself, will leave something behind, even if it only be a lowly abode of wood and stone. No, I will put temptation behind me, and write to say he is welcome. Then I shall have to break off the work on the tower windows to build another chair on which my guest may rest his city suit.

Desmond's calm acceptance of the visit swiftly darkened, however, with irritation and querulous remarks about his brother that did little to hide the growing tension he was feeling. Late in the journal, three pages from his last entry, came a final list—of things needed in Roche Harbor, true, but why inscribe a shopping list in a leather journal if not for the sense of order and control it bestows on the writer?

In the middle of September, Desmond Newborn wrote what was to be his final entry:

My brother comes tomorrow, to talk me out of my folly. Let him try. Although I freely admit, to myself if none other, that the thought of seeing his face fills me with a terrible dread.

Nothing more, just an illegible scrawl that looked as if the ink had smeared. The nearest Rae could come to deciphering it was:

I have a—

Terrible dread—yes, "dread" was the word. William had inspired it in his brother at the age of—what?—forty-five, just as he had inspired it in his granddaughter until the day of his death at the age of ninety-four, following on the heels of Rae's second breakdown. He had dominated his son, crushing him into insignificance by his indifference; he had cowed his wife, Lacy, into the pale shadow Rae had known as a child; he had given Rae's mother a life of unremitting criticism until she died young to get away from it; he had bullied Rae, scorned her gender and railed against her instability. The only way Rae could escape him was to marry the first man who asked her, and move from the Boston mansion into graduate housing in California.

Everyone else had had to die to get away from William's devastating disapproval and impossible standards—Rae's mother when Rae was five, Lacy the following year, his two sisters (one never married; one had a son and fled to England, there to die in the Blitz during the Second World War).

All dead. Rae's father, William's only child, had lived for seventeen years after the old man finally expired, looking over his shoulder and preparing to cringe every hour of the day. Even after William was gone, Rae's father had never let up, never allowed anyone a glimpse inside. In all his life, the sole moment of tenderness Rae had ever seen him allow himself came bare weeks before his death, when four-year-old Bella had cajoled him into reading her a story, then fallen asleep in his lap halfway through it. Rae had happened to pass by the room, glanced in, and saw her father sitting on the sofa with his arms around his granddaughter, his lips in her curly hair, weeping. He must have been a lonely man.

When Rae had nightmares, they felt like William.

She felt now as if she was walking into one of those nightmares, as if her grandfather was sitting in his straight-backed chair behind his vast mahogany desk, his icy blue gaze fixed on her as she walked down the dark road on San Juan Island, the curl of chronic disappointment on his lips.

Terrible dread.

He was a hateful old man, yet Rae had never been able to hate him. He poisoned everything he touched other than money, but he carried with him the tragedy of Midas, who loved only one thing besides gold, and ended up killing her. Rae hated thinking of William's blood in her veins, saw every flicker of selfishness or impatience as a danger sign, wondered often if William, too, had been mad but controlled it with sheer willpower, but she could not hate him.

Every psychiatrist Rae had ever been to sooner or later focused on the "unresolved conflict" with William, but to none of them, no matter how much she loved them, could she say, "Yes, I hate my grandfather."

But dread? Oh yes. And terror and guilt and the shame of failure and . . .

Rae stumbled as her feet left the asphalt and hit rocky sand, and she continued up the dark beach, Desmond's last words in her ears and the past few days twitching like a swarm of insects beneath her skin. As she walked, the loud crunch of stones underfoot scraped at raw nerves until the edginess threatened to flower up into full-blown panic. When she finally perched on a driftwood log, her fingers plucked at her lips and her shirt buttons, her nails dug at the spongy wood and into her palms.

Terrible dread, the waves whispered to her.

Dread. Dread.

Terrible. Dread.

My brother comes (terrible dread) I admit my brother my folly talk me out of my terrible dread

Desmond's words and Desmond's bones and Desmond's bullet, Desmond's bad left arm and William's face *(dread oh terrible dread)* as the brothers rowed over the calm water to Folly, then the gouts of fire spewing from the stone towers and the fiery shock of electroconvulsive therapy and the deep urge of the fingers to draw up a list of events so as to rationalize the terrible *dreadful* events and yet the fingers' inability to be still enough to hold a pen, all welled up like water in the sculptor's pools, welled up in Rae's bones and spilled over and filled her until her thoughts were ratcheting wildly around inside her skull to escape, inside her grinning skull with her fingers digging into the skin as if fingers had any power at all against the infection of dread the dreadful infection of terror the—

A heavy foot hit the pebbles of the beach behind her, and Rae's mind exploded.

She ran blindly for the water, aware only of something big and heavy and fast and male gaining rapidly, splashing and catching at her arm until she hit out and connected with something that felt like a tree. She lunged again toward the open water and the hands were on her again, the attacker avoiding her teeth and, less successfully, her kicking shoes, until after forever she finally heard what her ears were telling her, that her assailant was repeating her name, over and over, in a loud, firm voice.

"Ms. Newborn, Rae, it's Sheriff Carmichael. Rae, it's Jerry, calm down, it's only me."

Rae went abruptly still and would have fallen into the water had his powerful hands not been holding her upright. "Jerry?"

"Yes, it's Jerry. I frightened you. I'm sorry."

"Jerry? Oh God, Jerry?" she said again, and she let herself lean forward against his chest, the only stable thing in the universe, and felt herself being wrapped in the security of muscle and bone, the smell of his masculinity, the solid thud of his heart. She drizzled tears in a disgusting manner all over his nice clean shirt, and allowed herself to be led back up the crunchy beach like a rag doll, or a child. He peeled off her jacket, replaced it with a blanket he took out of the cruiser's trunk, and sat her in the front seat with the engine on and the heater going full blast. He got in beside her, and she felt his concerned eyes on the side of her face.

"I'm really, really sorry," she told him. Her throat felt hoarse; had she been screaming? "I just don't seem to have any control these days. Other people get a little nervous—I go into full-blown panic. System failure. The hard drive crashes. A short circuit in the mechanism, whatever you want to call it. I heard you coming down the beach, and I just lost it. I hope I didn't hurt you any."

"You've got a powerful right hook, but no teeth lost. It's not your fault. If anything, it was my own stupidity—anyone who's been attacked once is bound to be a little touchy. I thought you heard me coming."

"So did Ed, until I nearly brained him with my hammer." *Maybe I should get Petra to make me a T-shirt with a warning sign that says,* BEWARE, JUMPY WOMAN, Rae thought muzzily. The heater in the car was very efficient, and the counterreaction was setting in.

"Is it just . . . what you found in the cave that's bothering you?" Jerry asked.

"Oh no, that's nothing. Not nothing, I mean, but . . . Look. Can we talk about this tomorrow?"

Even Rae heard the flat exhaustion in her voice. Jerry responded by reaching for his seat belt. He drove her back to the inn, the blowing heater drowning out words if not thoughts, and went with her to the front door, then waited until she had fumbled the key from her pocket and turned it in the lock. Once inside, she paused with her hand on the door.

"Why did you come back?"

"That can wait till tomorrow, too. I was just passing on a message, and Elaine told me you'd gone out for a walk. Figured that meant the beach, and there you were. Sleep well."

True? Or had Elaine reported her late-night excursion to him? Was Rae like some foreign irritation infecting an organism, her path easily tracked by the close-knit natives? Or was Jerry watching her closely for reasons of his own?

Or was she just too damned paranoid to be set loose on society? She shook her head in confusion, and told her escort, "Good night, Jerry."

Rae dropped her soggy clothes in a heap by the bed, and crept between the crisp sheets, naked and sandy.

Thirty-four

Letter from Rae to Dr. Roberta Hunt

May 25

Dear Roberta,

One unfortunate side effect of a spell in what you will not allow me to call the loony bin is that every time something odd happens, the ex-patient immediately sees it as portentous. Strange things must happen all the time to "normal" people, just like they happened to me before I had my psychic skin rubbed raw and became so painfully sensitive to life's careless wounds and strangeness.

Having been mentally ill, and knowing that I am, I suppose, mentally susceptible, nothing comes past me anymore that is not weighted with significance. My great-uncle Desmond's bones have turned up on the island; he too was wounded by life; does his fate have to resonate so deeply with me? Two teenage sisters disappear on the other side of the state; my granddaughter Petra wants to come to the islands; if I permit it, will she too disappear? I can make no decision without looking at it a thousand times, doubting the ability of my eyes to see hidden meanings.

It's really tiresome.

Rae

Thirty-five

The following morning, when Rae woke for the fourth or fifth time, she smelled bacon, and wondered for an instant if she had begun to suffer Desmond's hallucinations. Then she realized that she was lying between fragrant sheets on a soft mattress, and she decided the smell was no fantasy.

A rumble of voices and motion suggested that the inn's breakfast was under way. First, though, she would enjoy a true, civilized shower.

A beautiful, long, fragrant, hot shower it was, too, removing sand and salt and some of the cobwebs from her brain. She felt, as always after an episode such as that of the night before, cleansed, and when she looked in the mirror, she saw little sign of her father looking back at her. He only showed himself in her mirror when she was tired, when the slight sag of his left eyelid appeared over her own eye and the color of her irises darkened toward his true brown. Today, however, Rae saw only herself in the glass.

She dressed in work jeans and a long-sleeved T-shirt, and went down the stairs in her stockinged feet with her poor, water-stained, once-good shoes in her hand. She ducked outside to prop the damp objects in a sunny corner, then returned to the aromas of bacon and coffee.

And to Jerry Carmichael, freshly uniformed, polished of shoe and face, looking up from a half-demolished plate of food and beaming at the newcomer.

"I told Elaine that if you weren't down by the time I finished, I was taking yours as seconds."

"Thirds," a voice from the kitchen corrected. The other guests, young newlyweds, looked up from their self-absorption and smiled at Rae. She helped herself to coffee and went to sit across from Jerry, not as hungry now as she'd thought she was.

"Good morning, Sheriff," she said. He raised an eyebrow at the title, and she blushed. "Jerry."

"Mornin' yourself, *Ms.* Newborn. Rae. I hope you slept well."

"I . . . Yes. Thank you." Was she thanking him for asking, or for what he'd done the night before? And what had he done, after all, but give her a ride up from the beach after scaring her to death? Had two months of solitude made her incapable of normal, good-mannered conversation? She started again. "I slept all right, thank you, although the mattress was far too comfortable after my cot and sleeping bag." And why the hell did she feel as if she was making suggestive remarks to the man? *Grow up, Rae!* "And you?"

"I always sleep well. Not enough imagination to have insomnia, my mother used to say."

"Good. I mean, I'm glad you're rested." Before Rae could reconsider the overtones of that statement, too, her plate was set down in front of her, containing nearly as much as Carmichael's had held. She welcomed the diversion, and took up her fork.

Breakfast conversation was kept simple, since the young couple, honeymooners from Los Angeles, had also just begun their waffles. Once they had gotten past the presence of a large uniform at their table, they began to ask for suggestions of things to see, and escaped twenty minutes later with an island itinerary that would keep them busy for a week. Then Jerry took out his pen and while Rae was mopping up the last of the syrup, he wrote down the essentials of her statement. She signed it, and he suggested that they adjourn outside, to a pair of wooden chairs set on the lawn. Away from curious ears.

Rae sat down and studied a hole in the toe of her sock. "About last night," she began.

"We both said we were sorry. Maybe we should let it go at that."

"It didn't mean anything, my . . . I don't know what to call it. Tantrum? Fit?"

"Okay. But it also didn't mean nothing at all. Finding those bones would be enough to make anyone a little upset."

"Upset," Rae repeated dryly. "Right. Do you know how he died yet?"

"That bullet in his shoulder blade wasn't what killed him."

"I didn't think it was," Rae said.

The sheriff pounced on this admission. "But you did disturb the body. What did you take off it?"

If he was expecting Rae to start guiltily and turn red, he was disappointed. Rae had lied to far more subtle truth-seekers than a county sheriff; besides, she'd been expecting the question.

"I didn't take anything." She met his sharp gaze with a bland one.

"You don't deny you touched the body."

"I lifted the shirt to look at the bones."

"Why?"

"I really don't know." She changed her expression to one of puzzlement. "It just seemed necessary. To see his remains, I mean."

"And you claim you didn't take anything?"

"What was there to take? Bones and old clothes?"

After a minute he subsided, apparently satisfied.

"You sound like you're treating this as a suspicious death," she said.

"We have to."

"You don't think he was . . . murdered?" Rae was rather proud of the little squeak she gave the word.

"Any death is treated as suspicious at the beginning. But if you found a knife sticking out from between his ribs and took it away, I'd like to know."

"No knife, sorry. Say: If you're treating it like a crime scene—God, that sounds like something from television—does that mean you've got yellow tape all over and I can't go back to work?"

"Oh, no. Not much point in that."

"That's good. I've got family coming and lots to do. But look, Jerry: If it is Desmond, and if somebody did kill him, what on earth could you do about it? I know there's no statute of limitations on murder, but everyone from those days must be dead by now. Other than the satisfaction of figuring out a puzzle, is there anything you could actually do?"

Jerry sat back in his chair to think over her question.

"Only thing that comes to mind, offhand," he said eventually, "is if there was an inheritance involved. I don't know about the law back then, but these days, a person's not allowed to benefit from a crime. Which means if a boy kills his father, say, the father's estate goes to the other siblings."

"Desmond didn't have any children."

"So there are no survivors around to argue with your ownership of Folly."

"I guess not."

"You want to tell me what it is you're keeping to yourself?"

Rae frowned. There was no apparent reason why she should not tell him about the bullets, but . . . "There's nothing much. A few ideas I had, but I need to talk to my lawyer first. I think I should know the whole picture before I burden you with it."

"Burden me." The sheriff appeared caught between official disapproval and amusement, but came down on the side of humor. Rae smiled crookedly in agreement.

"I know. But you might feel like you need to do something about Desmond, even if you don't want to."

"Did *you* kill Desmond Newborn?" Jerry asked suddenly.

Rae's head snapped around so quickly she nearly bit her tongue. "Me? Of course not, you saw—"

"Then there's no reason to worry, is there? About 'burdening' me."

Rae began to protest, and then looked more closely and saw that the man was making a joke. She dutifully chuckled until, still smiling, he added, "Just don't work yourself into interfering in an investigation."

"So it is an investigation."

"Damned if I know. Depends on what the bone woman at the university says, if she can tell what killed him."

"Fine. Let me know when you hear. Now look, Jerry, you had something to say last night, too."

The big man sat forward in the creaking chair, and for a moment Rae feared he was about to reach for her hand. He did not, but at his serious expression, the breakfast began to congeal in her stomach.

"I had a call from Sam Escobar. I'm afraid your house has been broken into. On Saturday or Sunday, he's not sure which."

"Oh, God. Did they . . ." she started, then broke off. What was she going to ask? Did they trash it? Did they steal anything? Did she care? That would have been more to the point. Another world, another life.

"It doesn't sound like there was too much damage. The lock on the back door, a collection of glass things on a shelf." Rae found herself wincing: She did care. "The insurance man is going to go in and have a look, check your inventory and see what's missing. Did you have many valuables?"

"Art, mostly. If it's the glass I think it was, my husband had it insured for something like a quarter of a million." She glanced up at his stifled oath, and explained. "We didn't actually buy most of it, maybe three or four pieces out of the two dozen, but we traded, the artists and I, or I was given pieces, before they became well known. The same way with the paintings, or a lot of them, anyway. Are those all right?"

"Escobar didn't say anything about paintings. If you phone your house around ten-thirty this morning, he said he'd probably be there by then. He's going, not one of his deputies—wanted to see the damage for himself."

Rae wasn't listening. One of those glass sculptures had been a gift from Alan, bought during a trip down south to see his son, and although Alan had seen instantly that Rae was not as entranced by the frozen glass jellyfish as he was, he had continued to collect art glass for himself, and she for him. She was caught up in the vision of all those luminous, ephemeral glass shapes reduced to shards, and yes: It hurt.

"I'm sorry," Jerry said, seeing her expression.

"Do all sheriffs tell people that as often as you do?" she inquired with an effort.

"Only when—" He stopped, and it was his turn to look flustered. "Just part of the service, ma'am. Well," he said, getting to his feet. "Back to work."

"To protect and to serve," she remarked, craning her neck to look up at him. "Which reminds me: I hope your people have been keeping out of my things. One invaded house in a week is enough. Even if the other house is a tent."

"I checked last night, and I'm on my way out there now. Everything's just like you left it."

"When will they be finished?"

"The lab people should be through this afternoon. My people will wait there until they've gone."

"Good. I'll call Ed and ask him if he could take me back."

"How 'bout if I run you over? I'll have to make sure they haven't left anything behind, anyway. Might as well save Ed a trip."

"You sure? Thanks. What—four o'clock? five?"

"Five'd be better."

"I'll pick up something at the market, we can have a third-rate picnic to pay you back for the first-rate dinner last night. Unless you have other plans?"

"A picnic would be great. Five o'clock down at the harbor."

"See you then."

He left, and Rae went inside the inn to make her phone calls.

Her lawyer was not in the office. She was, in fact, already on her way out to Rae's house to meet the insurance agent. Her secretary told Rae that Pam had received the mysterious package and already arranged to messenger it to the private lab that had been recommended to her, with an ASAP request.

Rae then phoned Tamara, got the machine, and left a message saying that she just happened to be in Friday Harbor for the day and would try to call back before leaving for Folly in the afternoon.

She phoned her own number, which rang twice and then kicked into the mechanical voice of the machine, and she hung up. Try again in an hour.

Then she took a deep breath, eyeing the phone. The letter she'd had yesterday from the owner of the New York gallery was the third Gloriana had sent her in the last two months. Rae owed the woman a call. She picked up the phone and, before she could stop to reconsider, hit the numbers. Gloriana herself answered, and gushed and flustered and was so thrilled, absolutely *thrilled* to hear from her that Rae seriously considered hanging up.

"G.," she said into the spate. "G., stop, you're giving me a complex."

"Darling, never. Seriously, Rae my sweetheart, I am so very glad to hear your voice."

"You're not going to be as happy to hear what I have to say."

"Oh no. Don't tell me you're not working."

"Oh, I'm working all right, just not on anything that would interest you."

"Tell me anyway."

So Rae told her, about the island and the process of rebuilding the house, and although Gloriana's first reaction was predictable—intense disappointment that Rae would be giving the gallery nothing for many, many months into the future—her mood shifted to wistful optimism when she cornered Rae into admitting that perhaps, next year, when the house was less urgent . . .

Rae liked Gloriana, respected her, and knew that the gush was partly an act but also the way she presented her honest concern for Rae's well-being. And because she liked the woman, because Gloriana had encouraged and stood by her for so many years, Rae went on to tell her about the driftwood workbench. After a dubious hesitation ("I mean, my dear, kitsch has been in and out so many times I'm quite tired of it") Gloriana started hearing Rae's genuine interest in the piece.

When Rae finished, Gloriana was silent. Rae knew she was still on the line, because she could hear her breathing over the gallery's background music.

"What's wrong, G.? Has somebody just come in to hold the place up?"

"Would it photograph?"

"Would what photograph?"

"Your driftwood bench. Would it photograph well?"

"I suppose, if I cleared it off."

"Oh my God. You're not actually using the thing?"

"G., it's a workbench."

"Rae, you are hopeless, you really are. You'd sit in a Wright chair."

"I do, when all the comfortable chairs are taken."

"Stop, please. And stop using your workbench until we can get a picture of it."

"I have a picture of it. Why do you want it? I'm not going to take the bench off and ship it to you—it'd fall apart without the tree."

"Oh, would it? How glorious. It's symbolic, too."

"G., I'm going to hang up if you don't tell me what's going on."

"A book."

"A book. About my bench?"

"About the whole concept of Folly, my dear, from conception to completion. A great, gorgeous, limited-edition book with some stunning cover, solid wood maybe, and that luscious thick paper, the sort of book only collectors and university art departments can afford. Plus limited-edition photographs in the gallery for sale, of course, and a few small pieces if you feel up to it. With a cheaper version of the book for hoi polloi," she added, chortling with pleasure.

"G., I'm hanging up now," Rae warned her.

"But I must come and see your fabulous island, while it's still pristine. I'll get a photographer. We'll be there ASAP. How do we reach you?"

"The island is hardly pristine. There's a lot of bare soil and a huge ugly blue tarpaulin that dominates the clearing; you have to take a tattooed man's smelly boat across; and once you're on Folly there's a shower made from a bucket hanging from a tree branch and a toilet over a hole I dug myself."

A long silence followed, during which Rae wished she could have seen Gloriana's face, and eventually came the answer, coolly polite: "Oh, well, that's all right then, my dear. You let me know when you get the hot tub in."

Rae finally extricated herself from the conversation, hung up, and sat looking at Elaine's collection of porcelain dogs, thinking about how she felt. Not too bad, she decided. The conversation hadn't actually been as painful as she had anticipated, considering it was her first overture into the world of her chosen profession since the accident. The longer the wait, the bigger the step. So, the first small step had been ventured, without blood having been shed on either side. Not allowing herself to think about the book proposal just yet, but smiling to herself at the thought of Gloriana's Italian sandals stepping up to the Folly privy, Rae went upstairs to brush her teeth and push the sandy clothes back into her bag. She paid Elaine for the night's room and board with crisp bills from the ATM machine, then went back to the phone, dialed the endless string of numbers required to bill her calling card, and heard her own phone ringing again.

This time, it was picked up. Sheriff Escobar answered, asked her politely how she was, then handed the receiver over to the insurance agent, who sounded stricken—more, Rae soon decided, because of the money his company would have to fork over for a heap of useless broken glass than because the damage was so extensive. Rae breathed a sigh of relief that the paintings were intact, and a sigh of dismay at the general bashing and throwing around in her workshop, and a sigh of impatience at the mess waiting for her in the study, where, according to the agent, every file—correspondence, reviews, bills, catalogues, you name it—had been upturned, either in a search or just to make the greatest possible mess.

"Well," she cut him off, "there's not much I can do from here. Is my lawyer there yet?"

"Sure, she's right here."

There was a muffled conversation and the sounds of the phone changing hands, then a familiar voice said, "Rae?"

"Hello, Pam. I'm really sorry to drag you into this. Is it as bad as the insurance guy says?"

"It's a mess, but other than the glass there's not a lot of damage. But I'm canceling all your credit cards—you should have new ones in a week or so. And because your computer looked like it was turned on when they smashed it, you should assume that you have no secrets."

Rae didn't know that she had secrets anyway, but promised to think about what other problems might come from having her hard drive ransacked. Pam's secretary would be given the job of contacting everyone on Rae's mailing list, to see if some electronic thief was making the rounds. Pam ended by telling Rae bluntly that she'd been damned lucky it wasn't any worse, then said more immediately that the contractor would replace the locks and a security team Pam worked with was coming the next day, to look into a better alarm system.

Rae thanked her meekly, then had to ask what was chief on her mind.

"Have you heard anything from Don's lawyers?"

"Oddly enough, no. I responded to their document, of course. We'll just have to wait and see if the court wants to take it further. If it does, you might have to come down."

"So they can see I'm not raving and covered in sores?"

"Rae," Pam chided.

"Well, that's what they're after, isn't it?"

"Yes, but you don't have to be so graphic."

At that Rae could chuckle. She asked Pam to give the insurance agent an address to send his pictures and forms, told the lawyer with false regret that she could not get free just now, and hung up with the feeling that she'd gotten off light.

She then set off for the metropolis of Friday Harbor, to buy some jeans.

Jeans she found, and socks and a pair of work boots whose leather tops were not threatening to part company with their soles, and a sleeveless fleece vest, warmly red and without the glue spatters and burn holes that decorated her other vest. She had her hair cut short again, and at one o'clock she ate a sandwich in a place near the harbor and arranged to stash her bulky parcels beneath their register until five.

The historical museum was due to be open, but on her way there her eye was caught by a gallery window display of several wood pieces, bowls and a table. She paused to admire the professional use of the grain and the balance of textures, although she cast a more critical eye on the quality of the table's inlay (osage orange, redheart, and ebony, garish and lamentably clumsy), and walked on down the block. She slowed, then turned and went back. The man who was sitting the gallery that dull afternoon glanced up as she came in the door, did a double take, and shot to his feet, a look of utter amazement spreading over his clean-shaven features.

"Aren't you—omigod, you're Rae Newborn!" he declared, voice rising in disbelief. When she nodded, he sidled over to a curtained-off back room, ducked in reluctantly as if fearing to take his eyes off her, shuffled around, slammed a drawer shut, and came back into the gallery with a magazine in his hand. He thrust it at her.

"I was just reading this," he told her. "Somebody was talking about you the other day, and so I dug this out to show them and to reread it. How amazing."

Nikki Walls, Rae would have bet. The man was probably one of the infernal woman's "dozens of cousins." She took the magazine politely, glancing through the advertisements for chisels and plans for Shaker armoires until she lit on the photograph of herself, four years and a whole lot of wear and tear younger, standing next to a piece she'd won a best of show with in New York. Frankly, she couldn't imagine how this young man had recognized her. She gave him back the magazine, and he laid out the double-page spread of her workshop, all the chisels in place, works in progress arranged artfully if inconveniently across the floor, and he looked from it to her, beaming. Rae smiled back, feeling the nearly forgotten stir of being a Name. It was a small pond, but once she had enjoyed being one of its larger fish.

She let him talk about her pieces for a while, answered a couple of technical questions, and then turned the conversation to his own work. The pieces in the window were his, he admitted, and Rae went to look at them with her fingers. The man's work showed a rare sensitivity and respect for wood, and if his eye for design was untutored, that could be taught; the other was a gift. He nearly choked when she told him that she wanted to buy the applewood bowl in the window.

"Oh hey, please, I'd love to give it to you."

"Absolutely not. It's a beautiful piece, you could get three times that in San Francisco. The only thing is, I'd like you to hang on to it for me until I get a roof up. I'm living in a tent, and it would not do the bowl any good to get leaked on."

From the man's reaction, Rae knew that half the people who came in the gallery would hear the tale behind the Sold sticker the piece wore, but she found she didn't much mind.

As he was (reluctantly) making out the sales slip, he asked if, since she was here for a while, she had any plans to teach, either one-on-one or workshops.

"I hadn't thought about it," she told him, the simple truth. Teaching woodworking was far down on her list of priorities these days.

"Well, if you ever do, you'd be welcome to use my place. You could even do a residential thing—the people next door have a bunch of vacation cabins they rent out, right down on the water. And there's people all over who would kill for the chance—Anacortes, Seattle even."

She told him the same thing she'd told Gloriana in New York. "I'll think about it. No, honestly, I will. I used to enjoy teaching."

"Oh man, that'd be so awesome. I met someone who took a class with you three, four years ago. You haven't been teaching a lot lately, though, have you?"

Rae looked into his earnest and unlined young face, seeing that the news of her last two years had not penetrated the fringes of her chosen world. For which she was profoundly grateful.

"No, I've been a little out of things for a couple of years," she told him.

He nodded sagely. "Sometimes you gotta do that. Return to the well-springs, like they say."

"Right. I'll let you know about the workshop. It wouldn't be this year—my plate's pretty full. But once I get my house up, who knows?"

When she had left the gallery, Rae had to sit down for a while and think about the conversation—which, taken in conjunction with her earlier phone conversation with Gloriana, a radically different breed of gallery owner, made it appear that Rae intended to take up her chisels again, and not just to build herself a place to store books and dinner plates. This reawakened interest in her profession had taken her by surprise; she had not even suspected it was coming. Up to now, she had been going through the motions; today, for the first time, she was aware of the juices stirring again.

Life, she reflected, had a way of sneaking up on you.

Even when you didn't want it.

After a while she gathered up her scattered wits and continued on to the museum, where the woman was friendly and knowledgeable until she heard that Rae was interested in anything the museum had on Folly, at which point she put two and two together and became positively effusive and encyclopedic.

Very fortunately, Rae had a ready excuse, or the museum would have been spread in front of her feet until midnight, along with its entire staff of volunteers and their spouses and children. At twenty to five, more than two hours after she had walked in, she rose desperately to her feet, thanked the four enthusiastic amateurs who had appeared, apparently, out of the wallpaper, and bolted for the street.

Rae made for the harbor, holding before her the vision of a solitary canvas tent in a silent clearing. Her ears rang with the unceasing beat of human speech, her nerve endings quivered from the repeated goodwill of human intercourse, the back of her neck crawled with the continual presence of strangers behind her, and she felt not far from weeping with exhaustion. Near the harbor entrance she passed a telephone booth, and she had walked nearly a dozen more paces before her sense of responsibility protested loudly enough to bring her to a halt. Reluctantly, she turned back to make the promised call to Tamara. With any luck, the answering machine would pick up again.

The answering machine did not pick up; instead—a gift from the gods that went far to wipe out the effects of the day—Rae heard a beloved voice in her ear.

"Petra!" she cried. "Hello, my love. I thought you'd be out riding."

"Gran! Where are you? Did you get a phone?"

"No, afraid not—I'm over in Friday Harbor. I had some business to do here, so I thought I'd call and say hi. How are you?"

"We're all great. Well, I'm not great; I bashed my leg the other day and since I have a test tomorrow and a paper due Monday, I'm home working hard."

"Sure you are."

Petra laughed happily at her grandmother's skepticism. "Did you get my letter?"

"I did, yesterday. That's great news, that you can come play with me for a while."

"Dad says it depends on my grades—that's why I'm home working. I really am. But if they're okay, I can come, maybe even for two whole weeks!"

"And what else does it depend on? Did you and your father have a fight about this?"

"He's just so weird these days, Gran!" Petra burst out in a rare flash of petulance. "All I said was how much I missed you and how lonesome you must be, and he just went off about how irresponsible I am and everything, like I'm some kind of stoner flaking off at school. I'm getting mostly A's, Gran—what does he want?"

"Petra, sweetheart, calm down. It's okay." But Petra would not be calmed. It was difficult to comfort an upset adolescent over the phone while standing on a street corner and with no idea of the scope of the trouble, but Rae did her best. Her comfort consisted largely of listening to Petra's outpouring of resentment and indignation, grunting the occasional "uh-huh," and giving an apologetic shake of the head to a couple of people who wanted to use the phone.

At long last, Petra wound down; eventually Rae contributed the only thing she could think of that might help.

"You know, Petra, it sounds to me as if the real problem here isn't you, it's something to do with your dad. Like maybe he's got some hard worries at work, and instead of admitting it and talking about it, he just blows up."

"Yeah," said the voice on the other end of the line. "Maybe."

"Honey, you know your dad and I don't always see eye to eye," (*understatement of the year!* Rae thought) "but he loves you, and he works hard for you." (*Give him the benefit of the doubt.*) "If something's not going well at work, he wouldn't want you and your mom to know until he'd fixed it, would he? But it would make him short-tempered as a bear. You think?"

"Yeah. I guess." This time Petra sounded, not convinced perhaps, but willing to consider it.

Rae's strong impulse was to urge her granddaughter, "Don't cross your father, Petra; don't push him into a corner and make him react." But she kept her mouth shut. It would only make things worse. Instead, she asked after Petra's pony and dog, received news of a new kitten, and told Petra in response a few innocuous tidbits about the house. But not about the bones, and definitely not the bullets. They talked for a few more minutes, mostly concerning Petra's school history project on Folly, before Rae reluctantly said she had to be going, and would write soon. Petra promised the same thing, and added that she'd try her best to be patient with Daddy.

Rae hung up, smiling, if unassuaged. For twenty minutes she had been blissfully unaware of her surroundings, unplagued by itches along her spine. Now, as she set off for the harbor again, a horn blared, practically under her feet. She leapt back for the safety of the curb and knocked hard against a man; the bag in his hands flew into the gutter. He cursed under his breath and irritably refused her help in picking up the spilled contents, so Rae escaped—checking this time to see that there were no cars bearing down on her.

Her heart rose when she recognized Jerry Carmichael standing halfway along the dock. Pleasure, in part, but at this moment mostly relief.

"You look harried," he commented when she had come to a halt in front of him.

"I *feel* harried. My granddaughter's becoming a teenager and many infinitely friendly and helpful individuals have been harrying at my heels most of the day; I feel a powerful impulse to kick someone. Can we go?"

"I thought you were going to do some shopping."

"I did. Oh God, I left it in that—oh, let Ed bring it when he—oh damn! I said I was going to buy makings for a picnic. Christ. I'm sorry, Jerry, I'll have to go back up and get something."

He put out a hand. "Unlike you, I've had a nice quiet day, watching other people work. How about I go get your things and pick up our picnic, while you sit on the boat with your feet up and listen to the quiet."

Had this been an order rather than a suggestion, Rae might well have dug in her heels and turned back to the town. But again, he looked more friendly than commanding, so after a moment she nodded and let him lead her to the boat, then allowed him to walk off.

"To protect and to serve," she murmured, then went to collapse with her feet up and listen to the quiet. Of which, truth to tell, in the busy harbor there was not much.

Jerry was back in an amazingly short time—either that, or Rae, following her last two disturbed nights, had fallen asleep. He stepped onto the boat as laden with bags as a pack animal, pulled a long-necked bottle of Mexican beer out of one bag, and put the bottle down near Rae's hand without comment before leaning over to slip the ropes from their ties. When they were free, he kicked them away from the dock and went to the wheel. The engine caught; Friday Harbor fell behind them.

Ten minutes later, he glanced down at where she had been sprawled, unmoving but for the effort of opening and drinking the beer, since he'd walked away at the dock to go fetch her shopping.

"Want another?" he asked her. She shook her head wordlessly. He had opened his mouth to say something else when the radio squawked, its message unintelligible to civilian ears. He took up the handset and identified himself, and listened for a moment. His face went dark, as fearsome as if he was about to hit someone, and he slapped the throttle down to an idle so as to hear more clearly. Rae sat up, watching him. He was turned her way, but his eyes were not seeing her. At last he spoke, two curt phrases. "Hold them all," he said; then, "Twenty minutes." He replaced the handset, and his eyes focused on her.

"I'm needed on Lopez," he told her. "A girl has disappeared."

"Go," she urged.

"I can get you a ride," he started, but she was shaking her head.

"We'll worry about me later. Go."

He went. The boat flew over the surface of the water as if jets and not propellers were powering it. Rae jammed her empty bottle down between the cushions to keep it from rolling about, and worked her way over to his side.

"Do you want something to eat?"

"That would be a good idea," he acknowledged. "God knows when I'll get a chance later."

Bracing herself against the wildly bouncing motions, Rae found various containers of food, put together a thick sandwich, and took it, a pasta salad, a plastic clamshell container of deviled eggs, and two bottles of lemonade up to the wheel. He began eating the sandwich one-handed, and the eggs, while Rae dug into the container of salad with a plastic fork. When he had demolished his food, she held up the second fork questioningly, and was amused to see him open his mouth like some enormous fledgling bird. She fed the salad into his mouth, a process that seemed to entertain the recipient as much as it did the server. She went back to the bags for his chosen dessert, which turned out to be some thick and chewy cookies, and carried the box over to him. He ate three, and then they were at Lopez Island.

The sun was low behind them when they approached the ferry landing at the northern tip of the island. One ferry was nestled into the docking pad and another was lying offshore, its engines grumbling quietly. What looked like several hundred people lined the walkway and the upper levels of both boats, and Jerry put in around the corner from the ferry at the dock. He paused, one foot off the boat.

"I'm not sure—"

"Go," she interrupted. "Do your job."

He nodded, and strode away.

She followed, slowly, and joined the crowd on the landing. It took her a while to sort out fact from rumor, but one thing was sure: A fourteen-year-old girl named Caitlin Andrews had disappeared from the ferry. The girl and her parents had gotten on in Anacortes, headed for a Memorial Day boating weekend with business associates of the father, and Caitlin had wandered off while Mom and Dad had coffee in the ferry's dining area. As the boat neared Lopez, its first stop and their destination, her parents looked for her, then searched for her, to her mother's concern and the father's mounting fury. All the other Lopez-bound cars off-loaded, and Caitlin did not appear on the car deck. Caitlin was not on any car deck. Caitlin had vanished.

Boats were already searching along the ferry's wake, but with darkness coming on, they had not much time. Jerry Carmichael was speaking with the ship's personnel, and seemed to be instigating a thorough search of the ship, control room to lifeboats. After a while his voice came over the loudspeaker, asking the driver of each of the cars still on board—just the driver, please—to go and stand next to his or her vehicle, with the keys.

Time passed. The other ferry gave up and sailed away, continuing on to Shaw, Orcas, and San Juan. The next ferries chugged past without slowing. The small café at the head of the landing did a booming business in coffee and anything edible, and after a while Rae dug back into the picnic bags to make sandwiches for Jerry's deputies. By nine o'clock the sun was setting and the line of vehicles waiting to get on the ferry extended up the road and around the corner into the woods. Rae bought a cup of coffee and walked slowly past the cars and their variously irate or dozing passengers. She was still bone tired, but the jittery reaction to being around too many people had subsided. Why, she wasn't sure, because there seemed to be nearly as many people around the ferry dock as she had seen in all of Friday Harbor. Maybe it was because they were all focused on something other than Rae Newborn, woodworker and resident of Folly. Anonymity was a poor substitute for solitude, but it seemed to placate the nerves.

Anonymous she might be on Lopez Island, but hardly invisible. The people who had stuck it out, determined to get on the ferry and off the island, wandered in and out of the parked vehicles, carrying on conversations about everything from the ferry service to the local school board, perched on each other's fenders and saying "Hello" as she passed, or "How you doin'?" or "Any news?" She nodded, smiled, or shook her head, and walked on, ignoring the feeling of being watched. Of course, she *was* being watched, but only as a convenient distraction by bored individuals. That she could handle. One woman barking into her cell phone from behind the wheel of her BMW glared furiously at Rae, but then, she was glaring at everything else as well. One young man and his friends had been making inroads into a twelve-pack of beer, so that an impromptu party was starting up around them; Rae gave their truck a wide berth, head down and heart beating swiftly. They did not seem to notice her. In the next few cars, people looked to be sleeping.

The driver of one vehicle, a late-model pickup with a dozen rolls of fiberglass insulation in the back, was slumped into his seat but seemed to be staring at her intently as she strolled up the line of cars. Rae thought the man might say something as she reached his half-open window, but he merely shifted his gaze to the back of the car in front of him—embarrassed at being caught staring? Or had he realized she was not the person he thought? A hasty glance as she went past his window revealed only a bearded face with a network of lines near his eyes and a head of long, wavy hair flowing out from under a baseball cap. She flicked her eyes away before he in turn could catch her looking and continued on up the hill in the growing dusk, sipping her tepid coffee. The guy reminded her of one of her neighbors back home, she reflected idly, a man named Mac something, McArthur maybe, who lived farther up her road. A real mountain man, who did carpentry and yardwork to pay his property taxes but had little more to do with the world. From an MIA/POW sticker on his ancient Ford pickup and a couple of overheard remarks at the local market, she had decided that he was a soldier who had never really come home from the jungles of Vietnam. No doubt there were a fair few of those here on the islands as well. Although this particular man's pickup indicated a greater degree of affluence than McArthur's beat-up truck.

Fantasy, all of it, as no doubt was the feeling that he was looking at her retreating form through his rearview mirror, and again that he was watching for her when she reappeared at the top of the hill, headed back toward the water. Maybe she fulfilled some fantasy of his, a fantasy involving a tall gray-haired mountain woman. She smiled to herself, then her attention went up ahead to the beer drinkers. In her absence, however, they had attracted the notice of one of the many law enforcement personnel gathered around the ferry, and the young men stood in abashed silence as their licenses were examined. Rae stood in line to use the hard-pressed portable toilets, then went back to Jerry Carmichael's boat.

An hour later, dozing among the cushions, she was startled to hear the sudden racket of car engines starting up, one after another, and numerous voices being raised—relieved voices that told her the ferry had at last been cleared for loading. She listened to the thumps of the cars passing over the metal bridge, and went to see what was happening.

"Hey," she called to a group of boarding foot passengers. "Did they find her?"

"She's not on the boat," said a man.

"They're going to search the island," said another.

Rae pulled her jacket closer around her chest, and shivered.

Thirty-six

Rae's Journal

A house is not always a home, despite the blandishments of real estate ads.

The old saying that home is the place where "When you have to go there, they have to take you in" does not apply to all of us. Maybe it doesn't apply to most of us in this day and age. I have two houses— three if I count the Boston mansion, those vast cold hallways of my childhood home turned into a halfway house now, tenanted by a constantly shifting band of people working their way from locked ward to the freedom of their own front door keys.

None of the three contain any "they" who are required to let me in. In none of them could I find the sense of loyalty (however grudging) and permanence that is "home."

A house is just a building until it becomes a home.

But is that really so? A house is a convenient reality, but it is also a metaphor for one's self. The house stands, it looks out across the view, it runs smoothly, it is strong (or flimsy) and honest and beautiful. We are our house.

A house is a statement of belief in the future. The "House of" someone is not just the bricks and mortar, but the legacy, the inheritance, the impact the family will have on the world. We build a house because we are a family, not the other way around.

And like the human body, a locked house may feel secure, but its walls are no more impregnable than human skin. A house cannot, in the end, protect its human beings from any harm greater than rainfall. The terrible truth of the matter is, as court records and shelters for battered women tell us, for a woman, it is behind those locked doors that the greatest threat may lie.

I wonder if fourteen-year-old Caitlin Andrews heard Watchers in the hallway outside her bedroom door.

Thirty-seven

The last cars loaded onto the ferry. Rae watched their lights dip and rise as they came off the bridge, dip and rise, and made up her mind. There was no reason to delay here. She caught up her bags, leaving the ravaged scraps from the picnic, and stepped onto the dock. Striding toward her was a dark figure that could only be Jerry Carmichael. After another few steps, he saw her.

"I'm going to take the ferry back to Friday Harbor," she called out. "Ed or somebody will give me a ride to Folly." More likely she'd end up staying the night and going out in the morning, since it was nearly midnight. No matter.

"I was just coming to tell you that I'm finished here for the time being," he replied, coming to a halt in front of her. "They've decided to hand it over to the big boys, in case a lowly county sheriff messes things up, and I'm making the officer in charge nervous. So I've given my deputies their jobs and told them I'd be back in the morning."

"Which is maybe six hours off. You should catch some sleep."

"Frankly, I'd rather take you home."

Rae studied his face in the shifting light. His expression betrayed nothing, although a tautness beneath the watchful calm made her think he might be angry at something. "Okay," she agreed. "If you're not just doing it to be gallant."

"God forbid," he said, making an effort at lightness. "Sheriffs aren't allowed to be gallant. The oath of office specifically forbids it." He took

261

the bags from her hands, and stepped back to allow her to go first. This time she did so without hesitation.

Rae cast off. Carmichael reversed away from the dock, where the long-delayed ferry was also being freed from its connection with the dry land, and he took their launch in a wide circle around the churning water that the big engines were turning up.

In the darkness, and with the first urgency gone, Jerry's speed barely kept them ahead of the ferry. The night was clear and the air, even moving, no longer seemed cold. Rae sat next to where he stood peering out at the placid water.

"Can you tell me what happened?" she asked him.

"A girl by the name of Caitlin Andrews just disappeared from the boat. By the time the family realized she was missing, all the Lopez passengers were already off. It'll take a day or two to hunt them all down, see if any of them noticed anything. But she's definitely not on the boat now."

"I saw her family," Rae commented. Jerry grunted, but said nothing, and she leaned forward in an attempt to read his expression. It was too dark. "What do you mean by 'huh'? You think the family—what, they threw her off the boat? They had her in the trunk of the car? What?"

"There's nothing to think. The state guys haven't even done an interview yet, beyond the initial statement. I just didn't trust the father's attitude."

"Like he's hiding something?"

"Like he doesn't have a thing in the world to hide, all honest and up front about what a difficult child Caitlin is, how they were looking forward to a quote 'family bonding time' unquote this weekend. But he looked to me like a very worried man. Like a salesman trying to convince the world that his company's not about to fold. And he said at least three times that his daughter was a liar and a hussy."

"A hussy?"

"Sorry—my word, not his. What he said was that Caitlin is, in his word, 'impossible' and that she always wears heavy makeup and shows a lot of skin."

"Other than the skin, it sounds like my granddaughter. What did the mother have to say?"

"Not a thing. She let Dad do all the talking. However, she kept one eye on him the whole time, and she always positioned herself just behind his line of vision."

"All of which means what?"

"She's afraid of him," he said baldly. "She's more afraid of her husband than she is worried about her daughter. I think they might well find that the girl's run away from an abusive father, that the mother's terrified he'll take it out on her, and that the father's scared that the girl will talk before he can get her back under his control. That's just my take on it. I don't know what the *real* cops'll make of it."

"But why run away here? And Lopez is the first stop—how'd she get off the boat? Dive off and swim?"

"Hitched a ride with someone driving off, maybe? Hiding in the trunk? Kids that age, they don't tend to plan very thoroughly. Maybe she just couldn't take the idea of a weekend of 'bonding' under the eye of Daddy's boss, and met some other kids who agreed what a bummer it all was, then saw a chance to split with them. Who knows? If my suspicions are correct, then she'd have been better off going to the authorities back in Seattle where they live, but what fourteen-year-old believes that an adult in the school administration or social services is going to take her side and keep her father from punishing her for telling? I've seen it before. Even here on the islands."

By the grimness in his voice, the experience was close to home, more personal than professional.

They traveled on down the passage between Lopez and Shaw Islands, both of them retreating into their own thoughts. When the lights on the shores began to fall away, the sheriff spoke abruptly.

"Are you in a particular hurry to get home? I mean, I'm happy to take you now, but I was thinking of spending the night on the water and watching the sun come up. Dropping anchor off the tip of San Juan. You're welcome to join me. If you'd like."

Rae watched the light on the end of a dock go by, trying to judge her reaction. She had been thirsting for solitude, craving it as an insomniac desires the refuge of sleep, but for some reason his offer did not cause her to cringe. The presence of Jerry Carmichael, large as it was, did not demand her attention in the way others' did. He was comfortable without being dull, attentive without becoming pushy, and although she felt no particularly urgent attraction for the man, the thought of spending a night on his boat was not in the least threatening.

"Sure," she said.

Sunrise was grand, and the strong coffee Carmichael came up with even better, cupped between her hands with the fragrant steam brushing across her face. She wouldn't say that she had slept, exactly, what with the lumpy cushions and the constant shift and creak of the boat, but it had been a comforting sort of wakefulness, like being rocked in a pair of immensely strong if rather distracted arms.

They drank their coffee, and then Jerry pulled anchor and turned north for Folly.

He, at any rate, had slept well, as Rae could testify by the hours she had spent listening to his deep, slow breathing. He needed a shave and his uniform was crumpled, but inwardly he seemed calm again.

Halfway up the western length of San Juan he called in on the radio receiver. Nothing seemed to have happened during the night, the quartering of Lopez was about to begin, and his presence was not immediately required. He told the dispatcher where he was going, and hung up the radio.

"I admit I am surprised," Rae said. "I'd have thought you would want to be in the middle of the search."

"I do. It's driving me nuts, keeping my hands off it. But there are times when old rivalries and resentments get in the way, and this is one of them. I'm better off letting . . . a certain cop get things going to his own satisfaction before I move back in. He's good. It's not at all jeopardizing the girl."

Jerry Carmichael was, Rae decided, a big man in more ways than the obvious.

They flew over the calm sea with the sun at their backs, water slapping rhythmically against their hull, the wave of their passing rising high on either side. Rae was just thinking that a boat would be a fine thing to have, that there was no need to let her fear of driving a car interfere with all mechanical pleasures, when the roar of the engine cut abruptly away. The front of the boat slewed around, the prow flinging itself skyward before it dropped back down in the water. Rae grabbed at the window to keep from tumbling overboard; the launch rocked back and forth in protest.

"What—?" she started to ask; Jerry's arm came up, his finger pointing in the direction that they had been heading, now at right angles to the boat. With the engine off the only sounds were the pats of the bow wave on their sides, which quickly passed away. Rae stared in obedient befuddlement at an empty sea.

And then she saw it: a sleek dark line the height of a man, rising up from the flat waters. Its appearance was followed seconds later by a loud, sharp exhalation of air, a general impression of something massive and swift breaking the surface of the water, and a wide tail fin snapping into the air; then fin and fluke slipped back into the calm sea. It was gone, as if it had never been.

"Orca," she breathed. Jerry nodded, his eyes on the water. Thirty seconds later, the whale came up again, blew out its great explosive breath, then slipped away once more. Three times, four, closer and closer each time, and only when it surfaced and sank a bare fifty feet from their fiberglass sides did it occur to Rae that their fragile craft was directly in the way of an aquatic freight train with teeth.

No such thought occurred to Jerry. Instead, he placed his hands on her shoulders and urged her forward until her knees were touching the side wall of the boat, and then she was staring as intently as he into the gray water below. In a moment, they were visited by the fleeting passage of a huge and mysterious manifestation of the deep, a dark-and-light mass flashing through the world beneath their feet. The two humans hurried across the boat deck; Rae counted to five, and the orca rose and blew again. Then it vanished, to pass on toward the open sea.

The splendor of the creature's visitation, the power and the magic of it, left Rae speechless; she could only laugh with delight. Jerry, though, had a pronouncement: "'So is this the great and wide sea. There is that Leviathan whom thou hast made to play therein.'"

He grinned at her, started the engine, and turned the boat back north.

Rae's cove was as still as glass when they entered its green waters, the clearing beyond as calm and empty as it ever had been, with no sign of importunate uniformed invaders. And yet something was missing. Its absence left a wide beaten-down rectangle and a peculiarly raw gap in her landscape where there had been a blue monolith. She opened her mouth, but Jerry got in first.

"Oh man, I am sorry, Rae. I told them to put everything back. Looks like they forgot." He sounded not the least bit sorry as he concentrated on bringing the boat up to the dock, and Rae for a moment thought he was serious, until she caught the tiny quirk in the corner of his mouth.

She turned her back on him, crossed her arms, and made her voice as dry as dust. "And can you tell me, Sheriff Carmichael, why you found it necessary to move that great stack of lumber?"

"Why, Ms. Newborn, you might've been hiding any number of skeletons under all that wood. We didn't have any choice."

Jerry and his deputies must have spent hours, moving every scrap of wood from the place where the lumberyard had piled it on the first flat ground after the rock promontory. And for some reason, the sheriff's department had found it necessary not just to shift that hideous young mountain, but to haul it all the way across the clearing to the very foot of the stone foundations. It was a gift, saving one solitary carpenter days and days of backbreaking labor.

"You want me to have them move it back?" he asked, with mock anxiety. "I'll call them up right now, pull 'em off the search."

Rae turned to face him. "Jerry, you fool. You shouldn't have. But thank you." She stepped forward and, after the briefest hesitation, went up on her toes and kissed his stubbled cheek. Then she briskly went to find her much-traveled purchases and led the way up the dock.

She put on the big kettle so Jerry could shave and shower, and took out eggs and bread to begin breakfast. A scrap of leftover ham from their picnic the night before and a bit of stale cheese made it an omelet, and then she showed him how to hoist the water into the shower reservoir to rinse off. He had a spare uniform in the boat, and when he had finished, hair slicked, cheeks smooth, gun strapped on, nobody would have ever known how he'd spent the night.

She walked him back up to the boat, and thanked him for . . . well, everything. He stepped into the boat, she stood on her worn dock, and they looked at each other. After a minute, Jerry smiled gently and nodded, as if she had said something, then lifted his hand briefly in farewell.

Thirty-eight

Letter from Rae to Gloriana Boudreau

June 1

Dear G.,

Our phone conversation the other day was a bit inconclusive, but I've been turning it over in my mind, and as you see, I've decided to send you some photos, to give you an idea of the layout here. A couple of them might even be usable.

Do not take this as a commitment on my part. I don't know if I'm capable of taking on anything else right now, and I'm not playing coy when I say I may not be able to see it through.

No contracts, G., and NO PUBLICITY. If I hear a rumor that Rae Newborn is building a live-in sculpture on a remote island, I'll know instantly where it came from.

Furthermore, if we do this, it'll have to be one step at a time, and with the clear understanding that I am free to call a halt at any point along the way. Agreed?

If you decide to accept those unacceptable requirements, and if I'm feeling strong enough, we'll need to talk about a photographer. Jaime Brittin did a sensitive job with Cassandra a few years back, if he's available, or that guy who did the photo essay on Yosemite whose brother you knew.

You can write me at the address below—and no, I don't have a phone, or a fax or an email.

Rae

Thirty-nine

Rae was back at work long before Jerry Carmichael tied up at Lopez. Her labor went fast now, luxuriously so, with the heavy lumber at her feet instead of those three hundred long yards of hillside away. When Ed pulled in the following week, at ten o'clock in the morning on the first day of June, he was amazed to see the actual outline of a house, tying together the double towers for the first time since 1927. His shout of "Whoo-ee!" rang through the trees, startling the squirrel into a rage and bringing Rae to the front steps. They waved at each other, her brown arm and his richly colored one, and she slipped the hammer into its holster before trotting down to meet him. She was wearing shorts and a sleeveless shirt, and Ed watched her approach with appreciation. *No, not a bad-looking woman at all,* he said to himself, *and all by her lonesome out here.* He tucked his thoughts away as she approached, and held out a bag of food for her to take.

They talked about her house as she unloaded the cold stuff and the block of ice into her cooler, and she asked about his weekend and agreed that yes, she definitely had seen an increase in the number of boats.

"Yep," he remarked, "Memorial Day to Labor Day, we just sorta turn the islands over to the mainlanders, take their cash, and stand back."

"I've had two boats try to anchor in the cove, even with the new sign up."

"Put in an ice machine and a hot shower, you can make a killing," he suggested.

"I had a little different kind of killing in mind," she replied grimly. "I swear the second guy had to've been a lawyer—he stood on his deck the other night with his girlfriend, who was wearing a string bikini even though it was only about fifty degrees out, and he argued my ear off about how he'd put in here for years, had rights to continue no matter what the sign said."

"So what'd you do?" Ed looked at her slyly out of the corner of his eye as he tugged one white mustache. "Threaten him with your hammer?"

She laughed. "No, I had to resort to ruining his dirty weekend. I told him that in the future he really ought to take his used condoms and toilet paper back with him. The young woman seemed to take offense, because I heard them arguing until three in the morning and they left first thing in the morning."

Ed opened his mouth, then subsided, with a slightly abashed look on his face that made Rae suspect he'd been about to make an off-color joke.

Another day, she might have teased it out of him, even if it meant opening herself up to the assumptions behind those interested eyes of his. But she really did not want to begin a dating-and-mating ritual with Ed De la Torre, certainly not this morning, when she was feeling groggy to begin with from her arguing neighbors. At least the small but irritating outboard motor that went past at all kinds of strange and unneighborly hours hadn't then chosen today to putt by and wake her on one of its pre-dawn jaunts.

Rae reached the bottom of the shopping bags, folded them away, and then picked up the newspaper to read the headlines.

"They haven't found that girl, then?" she asked. "Caitlin Andrews?"

"Nope. Combed every inch of Lopez, had divers follow back the way the ferry came; only thing they came up with was somebody saw a girl like her talking to an older guy on the ferry just after it left Anacortes. 'Course on a busy run like that, there were at least a dozen blond teenagers on board and half the guys on the islands would count as 'older,' so it means less than nothing."

"I just wondered," she said, adding with infinite casualness, "Sheriff Carmichael was giving me a ride home from Friday Harbor when he got the call. I had to wait hours until he was free to bring me back, and I was curious how he was getting on."

"Yeah, he and the guy in charge have what you might call a history, so Carmichael turned his deputies over for the search and then did all their patrols himself."

"On what was probably the busiest weekend of the year."

"He was no doubt stretched a little thin," Ed agreed, sounding not unpleased at the thought. "We even had a couple citizen's arrests—a bar fight on Orcas that got out of hand and nobody to respond. That must've been fun. How does that work, do you know?"

Ed had been arrested and convicted at least twice that Rae knew of, but still the gleam of the amateur law enforcer shone in his eyes. Rae had to admit that she knew nothing whatsoever about the process of a citizen's arrest, and Ed moved on to philosophy (Martin Buber this time) until it was time for him to take his leave.

That explained Jerry Carmichael's absence, Rae told herself back at the building site. She'd been halfway expecting him to pull into the cove one evening, just in passing. She trimmed a length of 2x4 and set it between the studs as a fire block.

On Wednesday, Nikki Walls pulled into the cove just before midday, carrying a paper grocery bag. They met at Rae's kitchen, and Rae's mouth started watering when she saw what Nikki had brought: tomatoes, a whole basket of dark red tomatoes, firm and smooth as a milk-full breast and nearly as large. Rae cupped one in both hands and breathed in the earthy fragrance.

"Ahh," she sighed. "Man. These aren't from any grocery store."

"My sister-in-law. She raises the plants in a portable greenhouse, lifts the top off as soon as the sun is warm enough, always has the first tomatoes on the island. She grows about ten different kinds, says that when you start your garden, she can give you recommendations for varieties that do well here. And this is goat cheese from a cousin of mine on Lopez; thought you'd like to try it. And then since I was inviting myself for lunch, I brought a loaf of bread as well."

They ate the dense, still-warm, herb-laced bread smeared with the tangy white cheese and topped by drippy tomatoes. Rae had to say that she did not think she'd ever had a more perfect meal.

It was true. In recent weeks, Rae's palate had begun to awaken again. Before, food had been habit and duty; now, particularly since the dinner with Jerry Carmichael in Friday Harbor, the world of taste was waiting for her to rediscover all kinds of things. The downside was that most of the food in her pantry tasted like its containers, and she had suddenly realized that the wine she had been happily drinking, and of which she had a plentiful supply, was more suited to the cook pot than the glass.

Next time Ed came, Rae vowed, her shopping list would be more of a challenge.

The price for the lunch was giving Nikki a personal tour of the house and cave, but it was a small price. Besides which, Nikki would have talked her into the tour anyway.

The small side cave was empty now, swept clean of death's presence, and the main cavern had nothing but a crate of bottles and some rickety shelving to show that a human had ever been here. Jerry had not mentioned seeing the petroglyph of the orca and Nikki did not notice it now, probably because Rae stood in front of it holding the lamp.

"Did you ever open that bottle of wine?" Nikki asked.

"Not yet. I sent a letter to my lawyer asking her to find out what they'd be worth."

"Good idea. That's all you found here?" Nikki poked around the edges of the larger cave as if hoping for another hidden entrance.

"That's all," Rae told her. It was a flat-out lie, but she was not ready to share the contents of the diary or the strongbox with anyone, particularly a talkative woman who was related to half the local population. "I think Desmond had moved his stuff into the house by the time it burned down. This was just storage space while he was building."

Nikki nodded thoughtfully, took a last look at the crate of dust-covered bottles, and crawled out of the cave in front of Rae. The narrow path between the cave's opening and the house had been swept clean—literally—by Jerry's team, put through a sieve, and left for her at the garden site.

She and Nikki worked their way around the house, with even the sure-footed ranger bracing her left hand against the siding that Rae had nailed up along the back wall. They slithered down the hill, rounded the front tower, and walked up the steps and through the outline of the front door. Once inside, Nikki turned in a slow circle, getting a sense of the space.

The back and left-hand walls, from the fireplace all the way around to the door and incorporating the front tower, were now solidly sheathed on the outside in cedar. The remainder of the front and the eastern wall were both still skeletal, studs and headers, fire blocks and cross braces. Nikki leaned out of the framed-in window space on the east and looked down at the ground, which on this side was a good ten feet below the windowsill.

"How are you going to get the wood up on these sides?" she asked.

"Once I get the second floor framed, I'll put up some scaffolding, mount the siding from there."

"I was trying to picture you hanging out over the edge in a climbing harness or something. Not that I'd put it past you."

Rae laughed. "No, the climbing harness is for the roof." She could see the young ranger trying to determine if it was a joke.

Nikki chose to change the subject. "That's a heck of a lot of wood you moved up here."

"Actually, Jerry Carmichael and his deputies moved it up. He claimed they had to search the ground underneath it, but they were just being helpful. Incredibly so."

Nikki shot her a glance, and when she looked back at the pile of lumber, there was an unhappy little smile on the ranger's face. All she said, though, was "I think everybody's interested in seeing Folly rebuilt."

"In that case," Rae told her, "I'd better get on doing just that."

With the cage of the first-floor walls up and firm, Rae was ready to move on to the second floor. She had decided that, although her interior walls would carry a rough plaster finish, the ceilings should be wood. So she had ordered peeled cedar logs with one side milled flat, exposed beams that would support the upper floor.

Each one weighed a ton, or so her middle-aged muscles informed her. She could pick up one end without much problem, but carrying a log's full weight and lifting it over her head was more than she could manage.

Which was where primitive technology—Rae's favorite kind—came in. A block and tackle, rigged from the reinforced and braced header over the wide east window, would do most of the work for her. Once the beam was inside, she could use a manual lift, rented from the builder's supply outlet and delivered by Ed the week before, to raise it onto the upper plates. Slow and careful work, but not a risk to skull or muscle, assuming she watched what she was doing.

The first log was immense, awkward as hell, and frighteningly close to impossible to maneuver: raising it up, swinging it through the window hole, rolling and wrestling it onto the lift, and cranking it up to the upper level. The sun was low over the treetops and her muscles were trembling with stress and sweat-induced dehydration by the time the first log was in place. She slumped against the door frame and gazed up at the ropes and ladders and shims and one beautiful, honest, stripped cedar tree, lying perfect and clean against the indigo sky.

Jesus, she thought in despair; this is going to take forever. And Petra would be here in four weeks, parents in tow.

The sun rose Thursday at quarter after five; it found Rae already at work. Beam number two took less time than the first one had, and the third one was faster yet. The trick was to ignore the thuds, bashes, and scrapes of its passage and just get the damn thing up. Manhandling and mistreating wood was not a thing that came easy to Rae Newborn, but she was learning.

She broke off for a late breakfast at eight-thirty, and spent the whole meal with her eyes on the project, calculating. Then she brushed off her hands and went back to the pulley rope. The fourth log was a breeze—a stiff breeze, but it went up so smoothly she couldn't think what her problem had been. The fifth one found her so cocky that she took her eye away for a split second; the young tree slipped off its high perch and came within an inch of killing her.

The immense boom of its fall reverberated, and faded, and she was miraculously still intact. Not even a concussion, which she richly deserved for her instant of inattention; nothing more serious than the scraped shoulder she'd got jumping out of the way. Then reaction set in, and she tottered shakily over to the framed doorway and collapsed onto the step, her head between her knees, breathing shallowly. When she raised her head again, she was looking down at a veritable armada of invaders.

Rage, pure, strengthening rage brought her to her feet and filled her lungs to bellow, "This is private property, God damn it! Can't you read the damn sign?"

Occupants of two of the boats whirled to look up at the mad (certainly angry) woman of Folly, but the third and last boat, from which an anchor had just been dropped, shifted and a man came out into view, a big, smooth-shaven man in jeans and plaid shirt whom Rae had no trouble recognizing.

Jerry Carmichael. What was the man up to now? And at his shoulder the equally familiar head of red hair: Nikki Walls, wearing shorts, work boots, and a long-sleeved T-shirt.

Men, and women, too, were pouring off the boats, into dinghies, onto the dock. They looked like quitting time at a factory. They looked like the Amish community gathering to raise a barn in that Harrison Ford movie. They looked like . . .

They looked like salvation.

Rae scowled at them as they drifted up the beach, scowled at the tools and the work belts. She stayed where she was in her doorway until she was glaring down at seven grinning figures from her superior position on the upper step, staring into the eyes of three strangers, two known deputies (Bobby Gustafsen and the boy with the blushing cheeks), Nikki Walls, and Jerry Carmichael.

"What is the meaning of this?" she demanded, sounding to her own ears like an elderly schoolmarm.

Jerry answered her. "We had some free time. You have some work that needs doing. This is Kathryn, one of my deputies; Nikki's cousin Bo; and Matty, an old friend. The rest you know."

Rae looked out over the eager faces of her new neighbors, her friends and community, and she could not bring herself to say the words, "No thank you, I have to do this myself." She took a deep breath, stepped back, and, for that afternoon at any rate, the island community took control of Folly.

It was disturbing, frightening almost, the speed with which a team of eight worked. The remaining logs were up in a trice, without use of her slow equipment, hefted by large men and wrestled bare-handed into place. The tongue-and-groove cedar boards for the ceiling and the upper story's floor—kiln-dried, these, and not a warp in sight—were laid tightly onto the flat upper sides of the logs and nailed invisibly into place. Working alongside them, Rae could spot no difference between her work and theirs, not a single crack or gap.

Two ladders were fetched from the armada and siding was thrown up on the remaining first floor even as the second story was taking shape overhead. When the upper level had been framed, those walls, too, were sheathed—although Rae had to look away when the crew's two acrobats reached the precipitous southeast corner. Her team of helpers put the window holes precisely where she wanted them, they laid neat headers along the tops, they let in diagonal 1x4 braces for additional stability, and not one of the nails from their temporary blocks punched carelessly through the cedar ceiling. They squared, plumbed, and leveled as they went, they set aside studs weakened by knots to use for jacks or cripples, they even turned the boards used for the headers to avoid cupping.

In other words, they knew what they were doing.

They were there for seven and a half hours, during which time Rae's work was more that of consultant and overseer than laborer. Several times she put down her hammer to fetch cold drinks from the trio of well-iced coolers which they had also provided. She watched both as an onlooker and as a participant, saw the way the men on the team looked at Nikki, even her cousin, saw Nikki's reciprocal awareness even of the married man Bobby Gustafsen, noticed the young ranger's amusement over and acceptance of the men's response. And Rae saw also Jerry's amusement, avuncular and hearty to a degree that made her wonder if it wasn't just a bit forced.

Shortly after lunch, Rae happened to catch Nikki in the process of stripping off her long-sleeved shirt. Her hands waved over her head and her flaming hair emerged, jerking Rae vividly back to the dream she'd had of the dancing women in Folly bursting into flame. The men, too, had paused to await the appearance of Nikki's tank top, and suddenly Rae knew, with a vision so clear and precise that it could have been the catalogue photograph, what her next wood sculpture would depict: Nikki as wood nymph, emerging from the trunk of a tree, a gnarled, heavy-rooted, sea-worn trunk that would give way to clean red cedar, the sprite's arms stretched upward as if she were plunging into the air.

Rae blinked. If she ever did another sculpture. She picked up a 2x4, and the moment passed.

The afternoon drew to a close; one by one the hammers fell silent and the crew gathered down in Rae's campsite. Sweaty and tired and beers now in hand, they perched on the cedar trunk and the stump rounds to look up with the craftsman's quiet pride at what they had done.

Anchored by the two stone towers, the house stood, strong and complete even without a roof. Folly it might be, but the structure belonged in that place, facing its cove and the strait beyond, rooted in stone and grown in wood, the vision of a man, the determination of a woman, and the skill of a community gone into raising it again.

Rae had tears standing in her eyes as she thanked each of them, tears (as they thought) of joy and pleasure, but not (as she herself knew) untainted by a faint sour trace of failure.

"Jerry," she said, "could you stay for a minute? I need to talk to you."

She saw Bobby Gustafsen elbow the younger deputy, who predictably enough blushed, but she ignored the exchange. Ignored, too, the glances they gave Nikki as she gathered her tools and one of the coolers and got into cousin Bo's boat, her back resolutely turned to shore. When the sounds of the engines had died off, Rae dug two beers out of the melted ice in her own cooler and handed one to Jerry. They strolled out the promontory and settled down on a pair of sun-warmed rocks. Jerry faced the house; Rae sat looking out over the open strait.

"Was this your idea, or Nikki's?" she asked him after a while.

He did not answer immediately, and Rae knew that it was not his memory he was searching, but his understanding of the implications of her asking.

"It was Nikki's," he said. "She came to me with the suggestion, I agreed, we each rounded up a couple of others. You're angry."

"Not angry. Overwhelmed, yes. And confused, I guess, and a little bit resentful. Just a little bit. None of which sit well with grateful and over-joyed, which I am as well."

He said nothing, merely waited for her to go on.

"I think what it boils down to is, I'm not simply building a house here. I came to Folly as a kind of last stand, and building this house, with my own hands, is like building myself. If I don't do it myself, it isn't real. I don't want you to think I'm pissed off at how today went—hell, you guys saved me weeks of work—but just the way it came. Nikki's a lit-tle . . . too helpful."

Carmichael listened carefully to her explanation, frowning as he rolled the bottle back and forth between the palms of his large hands. The sleeves of his work shirt were turned up on his forearms, and he smelled like a long day of hard work. When he was sure she had finished, he gave her his side.

"I'd probably feel the same way, if I were in your shoes. Sort of like when a parent comes along and finishes up a kid's project for him, try-ing to be helpful. It's because it was Nikki, and because she is pushy, that I got involved. She just doesn't know when to stop—if it'd been up to her, you'd have your shingles, windows, and a front door up by now.

"I thought about discouraging her, or at least asking your permission. I mean, not everybody likes surprises. But in the end, I went along with her, and I'll tell you why.

"You see, here on the islands, we tend to divide into 'us' and 'them'—you're either a full-time resident who was born here, or you're a new-comer. Obviously you're an outsider, but because it's Folly we're talking about, the situation's a little different. With you it could go either way, because although you are clearly a stranger, at the same time you're a part of the islands in a way someone who just bought a piece of land to build a two-million-dollar summer house on could never be. And the people who live here would be happy to have you stay a hermit, happy if you never set foot off Folly, if they could still feel like you're one of them. Us. That's what today was about: saying, 'You are one of us, so we'll lend a hand with Folly.'"

"Or, on the other hand: 'You're one of us, *because* we lent you a hand with Folly.'"

"That too. Sometimes a family has to go that extra step, to remind one of its members that she belongs."

Rae tipped her head back to watch the sky, rose shading to indigo.

"Okay," she told him. "Just so it's only the once."

"Just the once," he promised. "If you want some help with raising the roof, you'll have to ask. And, provide dinner for the whole crew."

Rae cast a last glance at the sunset and stood up. "Dinner for one I could manage. If you don't have to rush back to the world."

"They know where to reach me," he replied. "Thanks, I'll take you up on the offer."

Forty

Rae's Journal

What is faithfulness?

I was never unfaithful to Alan. In nine years of marriage, I was never tempted beyond thought—and although a certain President admitted to having committed adultery in his mind, if we held everyone to those standards, the entire nation would end up behind bars for imagined crimes from embezzlement to mass murder.

It was a great shock when it dawned on me a short time ago that there was no longer any barrier between me and another man. I am not a married woman anymore, even though I still wear the wedding band that Alan placed on my finger ten years ago. I am perfectly free to look with speculation at a man's broad shoulders, or to kiss his mouth if I want to, or even to go to bed with him if I choose. Hell, I don't even have to worry about pregnancy now.

That was a revelation. A troubling one; scary, even.

I am feeling the same sense of adulterous betrayal to poor Folly, that I have been unfaithful to the house that Desmond set before me, letting others intrude on the solidarity of our relationship, his and mine. I made vows to this house, to have and to hold, from this time forward, till death us do part. Instead, I have allowed strangers to lay their hands on it, to shape it and somehow claim it for their own.

(God, I must be drunk. I'm certainly raving.)

278

My neighbors have intruded, yes; on the other hand, a house is married to its community, not just to its owner. And if the owner is her house, I suppose I could say that I have just consummated my relationship with my new neighbors.

Oh, God. I am raving. This is all quite insane and I am more than a little drunk. I think I must feel guilty that I've saved myself so much work. Where's my hair shirt?

Forty-one

Interested in food or not, even at the best of times Rae was no gourmet chef, and her current cuisine, coming as it did out of crates, tended toward the dried, the canned, and the instant. Still, there was plenty of it, and Jerry was too polite (and too hungry) to complain.

After they had scraped the pot and their plates, she asked him to carry the two chairs down to the beach. She followed with the dusty wine bottle she had found in the cave, a corkscrew, and her two elegant glasses.

The moon was hugely lopsided over the still waters of the cove, four days past full but still throwing distinct shadows on the beach. Rae sat with the butt of the bottle trapped between her boots and went cautiously to work with the corkscrew, going more by feel than by sight. The cork gave way slowly, crumbling slightly but emerging more or less intact. Rae undid the cork from the screw and held it under her nose, then dropped it in her shirt pocket and reached for a glass. Proper manners suggested she should offer the first glass to her guest, but she didn't want to be held responsible for poisoning the sheriff of San Juan County.

She breathed in the vapors, took a tentative sip, and rolled it across her tongue. When she did not instantly gag and spit it out, Jerry asked, "Not vinegar, then?"

She swallowed. "No, but it wouldn't make a bad marinade. Or a cleaning solution."

She held it out for him to try. When he sipped and swallowed and still kept the glass, she poured herself some in the other one, screwed the bottle down into the sand, and sat back to try it again. Yes, about the most that could be said for the substance in the bottle was that it was not vinegar. Flat, heavy, with all the nuance of a boiled shoe and possessing a distinct aftertaste of mildew; but it was not quite vinegar.

Perversely, they both drained their glasses, although the moon had heaved itself several degrees farther into the sky by the time they did so.

"It's not bad," Jerry pronounced lazily, "if you don't think of it as wine."

"If I donate it to the historical society like Nikki asked me to, they could sell it as Desmond's furniture stripper."

"It's not that bad."

"Yes it is." She got to her feet, noticing with some concern that her legs had gone numb from the knees down. Although that might have been from the six-pack the two of them had polished off before dinner. "You want some drinkable wine, or would you rather have Scotch?"

"Whatever you're having."

Scotch it was, twenty-year-old single-malt tipple, and it required several swallows to scrape the fur from their outraged tongues. The moon danced with the faint ripples in the cove, breaking up and re-forming, as the small brown bats flitted back and forth over their heads.

"Not a bad place to grow up, was it, Jerry?"

"A fine place. I missed it while I was away. Used to wake up in the barracks smelling the sea."

"Were you in Vietnam?" He would have been old enough to hit the final days of that war, Rae figured.

"Germany."

"Lucky."

"I guess. My brother went through 'Nam. Seeing what it did to him, I always felt like I'd cheated and somehow got away with a cushy couple of years. And then at the end of it they even paid for me to go to college. Survivor's guilt, you know."

Rae Newborn knew survivor's guilt very well indeed.

"Did he die, then, your brother?"

"No. Wounded once, not badly enough to get sent home. But something bad happened over there that he never got over. I never knew the details, since it never came to trial, but it was some kind of My Lai thing, involving civilians. Children died. Like I said, he never got over it. When he came home he started working with abused kids, as a way of making amends, I always thought. I don't know what he's doing now."

"Does he live around here?"

"Nobody seems to know where he lives. We get phone calls from time to time, and he sounds good, but he and my dad don't see eye to eye, so he doesn't come home much. I haven't seen him in a couple of years."

A tiny fish leapt out of the water, breaking the moon's reflection into a shower of sparkles. Rae lifted her glass, and noticed the same reflections there, dancing. Maybe it was her vision, she thought; everything seemed to be dancing more than a little. She pulled herself together. "You know, ever since I got here I seem to be running into—what's the saying? War and rumors of war. I mean, where I live, or where I used to live in California, there's military bases all over the place, weapon development companies, you name it, to say nothing of kids with guns in their hands, but other than the foreign news I'd never hear about war. And then I come here, to the most peaceful, gorgeous corner of God's green earth, and I buy a guidebook and read about places in my neighborhood called Slaughter and Victim Island and Murder Point. Bobby Gustafsen lives on Massacre Bay. Then there's the Pig War, and smugglers of everything from Chinese workers to rum and cocaine, and Al Capone–type crime lords, and now here we are talking about Vietnam. And I suppose next you're gonna tell me Nikki Walls went out with Desert Storm."

"Not Nikki, no."

She held up her hand, which seemed to wander around a little at the end of her arm under halfhearted control. "Don't tell me who it was, I don't want to know. It's all I can do to cope with Desmond Newborn, who came out here to get away from shell shock. God—there's another war."

"A pertic—party—" He was having trouble with the word. "A pretty brutal one that was, too. You must mean the First World War."

"Desmond's own. Shot, gassed, diseased, and sent home broken. Took him years before he could think straight."

"So he came here and built this place."

"Built himself." On reflection, Rae decided the observation was not as profound as it might have been. "I believe I've had too much to drink," she told her guest.

"Comes from mixing grape with grain," he agreed, sounding none too sober himself.

"Too bad I don't have any vodka—we could stir some potatoes into the pot."

Jerry thought that terribly funny, but when he caught his breath again, he said sternly, "I've got to have some coffee before I leave."

"You don't have to leave," she said without thinking. The night went suddenly still for two heartbeats, until Jerry raised himself out of his chair.

"Yes, I do," he said, and walked up to the campsite to put the kettle on.

She had not meant the offer as anything but a mooring place for his boat, the easy gesture between friends, but those two heartbeats of sharp awareness abruptly opened a door she had not known was there. And to have it so easily closed again was every bit as disconcerting as having it appear in the first place.

Had she meant more than a place to sleep? she wondered later, when the cup of coffee she had swallowed out of Jerry's pot had not gone far to counteract the alcohol. He, on the other hand, returned swiftly to efficient sobriety, gathering his things to leave. Rae listened to him coming back across the clearing, the creak of his tool belt, the rattle of the hammer in its metal rest and the tap of the various screwdrivers against each other, a musical language as comforting as a native tongue. Then without warning he was behind her chair, his left cheek brushing her hair and his voice breathing words into her right ear.

"I'll go now before one of us does something we'll both regret tomorrow. 'Night, Rae. Thanks for the dinner."

She reached out, but he was already away. She watched his ghostly progress down the beach, hearing the music of his tool belt and the thump of his boots across the dock, followed by the cough and growl of the boat engine. She lifted her face to the bowl of the sky and the dark branches framing its edges, then turned to look over her shoulder at the pale box of her suddenly expanded house, dropped so precipitately from the heavens.

How easy it would have been. A small turn of her face to his, one unambiguous word, would have been enough to change . . . everything. Most shocking of all was the realization that there was no reason that she should hold back. There was nothing holding her to faithfulness, not anymore. Even the suspicion that she found Jerry more attractive as a friend than as a lover would not have stood in the way, had he moved away from her any less quickly.

"I wouldn't have had any regrets," she told the house defiantly, and not entirely truthfully, then went with uneven dignity to her narrow bed.

Regrets were in plentiful supply the next morning, however; dry-mouthed, queasy-stomached, pounding-headed regrets. Rae groaned, squinted up at the unusually high angle of the sun hitting the canvas, groaned again. The idea of wielding a hammer today made her teeth ache.

Glass after glass of cool water, a handful of aspirin, a pot of powerful coffee, and some bread toasted over the propane stove brought her back to the brink of humanity, but the only thing she was truly happy about was that she hadn't woken to find Jerry Carmichael's humorous eyes watching her in this state. Jesus, she thought fervently. Never again.

She uncovered a pair of sunglasses, which helped, and up at the house found a billed cap one of the deputies had left behind, which when tugged down to the rim of the glasses helped a bit more.

There was no way she was going to pick up a hammer until much later in the day, if then, but there was plenty of work that did not involve loud noises and sharp jolts. Unfortunately, those jobs all required a functioning brain. Bed was attractive, with a damp cloth draped across her forehead, but she dragged on her belt and squared her shoulders. She'd just have to let her hands do what they could.

Yesterday's vast acceleration in her building's progress created a new problem—namely, that she now had a second story with no way to get to it.

Desmond's towers were stone, but the stairs themselves had been wooden. The upper windows—unfinished, according to his journal, thus open to the air—had sucked the fire up the towers as if they had been chimneys. Nothing was left inside but the mounting holes in the stone walls—now joined by one aluminum extension ladder and the smooth tree trunk that would be the stairway's central pole, both of which Jerry's muscular acrobats had dropped in before they capped the tower with an unceremonious if temporary hunk of plywood.

Rae had never built a circular stairway, but since first laying eyes on the project, coming here with Alan and Bella, she had read up on their construction, so she knew what she wanted to do. Here she would wind a wooden corkscrew, steps splaying out from the central pole with a handrail against the stones. She might do something more experimental with the other tower, but for the back one, the construction process was clear in her mind. It just needed meticulously detailed and completely accurate measurements and calculations.

Very soon, she was wondering if she wouldn't be better going back to hammering.

It was going to be like building a sailing ship inside a bottle—measure thrice, cut once—only in this case, since she would need so many identical pieces, the Friday Harbor lumber mill was doing the bulk of the cutting for her. She would, however, order the steps as triangles, and shape each one to fit into its niche between the uneven tree trunk and the still more uneven walls.

The tower's diameter, the height of the stairway, the depth and rise of each step, and the thickness of the wood all had to be factored in. Rae sweated over her drawings on through the afternoon before she finally had one that worked, and then she realized that although it was terribly elegant, it would deposit a person straight into the tower's rear wall. Back to the drawing pad.

The second time she finished her figuring, Rae stared doubtfully at the results, and finally threw the pad down in disgust. What she needed was a swim in the icy cove, as much dinner as she could face, and an early night; tomorrow she could check the calculations with a clear brain, then take up her hammer again.

But the early night did not come about. Whether it was the remnants of alcohol, or the accumulated agitation of muscles gone five days without hard labor, or the intrusion of Jerry Carmichael's humorous eyes, or just the bright moonlight against the sides of her tent, she lay awake, staring at the patterns the branches made on the canvas, moving slightly in the breeze.

About one in the morning she gave up the attempt, stepped into her sandals, and went out to sit for a while on the promontory. Two boats lay offshore, sleeping vacationers kept at bay, perhaps, by the stern No Trespassing sign. Somewhere around to the right, up the side of the island blessed with rock cliffs and a wicked reef, a familiar low engine muttered, her nocturnal neighbor. After a minute it went still, leaving Rae Newborn alone with the night.

There was a grunt close by, and she froze until the noise came again, and then she relaxed. Correction: leaving Rae Newborn alone with the night and the harbor seals.

Nine weeks she'd been here. When she arrived, she'd spent most of the time rigid with either terror or tension; gradually, with hard work, familiarity, and a spark of interest, the life of the island had taken her in, until she could understand why Desmond had called it Sanctuary. Having been forced off the island for three days, she could see more clearly than ever how essential it had become to her. The stillness that had so oppressed her in the early days now slipped into her as easily as the breath into her lungs: Where she had once felt the silence wrap her like a winding sheet, it was now a welcoming blanket.

Alone. At last.

She was even becoming accustomed to her life as a solitary, one tiny spark on a dark stage. The awareness of being alone still made her jumpy, but the knowledge that someone could be watching her out there was not as intensely threatening as it had been. How long had it been since she last imagined Watchers in the woods? And other than the night on Friday Harbor—which didn't count, she decided, because the sheriff's boots had set that one off—how long ago had her last panic attack been? Days. Weeks even. She slept badly, sure, she lost her temper, she ached for Alan and Bella and missed their presence hourly, but the pain of the loss was no longer on the edge of unbearable, tonight at any rate, and she did not feel the urge to take out the gun and hold it to her breast, or her temple.

Healing, they called it.

After a while she rose stiffly and went back to her tent, but only to gather her sleeping bag and fold up the camp cot. Still moving solely by moonlight, she carried her bedding to the house and unfolded her bed in front of the black stone fireplace, zipped the sleeping bag to her chin, and lay in her warm cocoon, listening to her house talking to itself, the ticks and creaks of the wood adjusting to its load, the brush of a branch against a wall. This was a house now, a hollow shell of walls broken by window holes; on this lower floor she could even pretend that the roof was in place. Brilliant moonlight streamed through the black rectangle of the doorway; through it she could see the silver-and-black lace of the madrone and the shimmer of the moonlit sea. It was like a stage setting, needing only the sudden, dramatic appearance of a human silhouette in the door for the play to begin. Rae smiled at the image, more fancy than threat, and after a while gave herself over to sleep.

The following day, halfway through a solid morning's work that had done much to restore the feeling that she was building this house on her own, she was startled to hear the approach of a well-known motor. For a moment she wondered if she had lost a couple of days somewhere, but decided that no, this was not Tuesday, even if that was the *Orca Queen* pulling up to her dock. She laid down her tools to see what Ed wanted.

He stepped off the boat wearing long sleeves and looking like any other weather-beaten, middle-aged longhair, the peacock glory of his skin hidden under a batik print. The shirt was the brightest thing about him, too: He appeared subdued in spirit, and bore not his customary double armload of brown paper grocery bags topped by a roguish grin but a tiny cell phone and a wary look. He held the object as if his fingers were about to crush it, and thrust it at her as if it were a bomb, or a new-born infant, palpably relieved to get rid of it before it went off. She took it and automatically held it to her ear, but the instrument was dead. When she found the switch that turned it on, the small screen informed her it was out of range. She raised an eyebrow at Ed in unspoken query.

"You're supposed to call your lawyer," Ed told her. God, Rae thought, her heart simultaneously sinking and beating faster. What now?

"It's not working," she pointed out.

"They said that if I took you out on the boat a ways, it'd come into range." He looked dubiously at the instrument, and she had to agree that something the size of two of his fingers was not likely to have a lot of power.

"Are you in a rush, Ed? Because if you're not, this would give me a chance to see if these things work here. Give me twenty minutes to gain some height in the direction of Roche Harbor. If I don't have any luck, then you can take me out on the boat. In the meantime, why don't you put on a kettle for some coffee."

"Fine with me, but she did say it was urgent. Nothing would do but I had to find somebody with a cell phone and come out right away. Said she'd pay me double."

Rae set off down the path to the garden site on the eastern side of the island, glancing down every few steps to see if the instrument was ready to talk, but nothing, not until she had run out of navigable land and was climbing up the side of Mount Desmond. Then the tiny display flickered and grudgingly admitted that it might be possible. When the reception indicator gave three bars out of a possible four, she sat down on the steep hillside and punched in the string of numbers. The phone crackled, and rang on some distant planet. Pam Church's secretary answered, Rae identified herself, and Pam herself came on the line.

"Rae, thank God. I feel like I'm trying to contact Antarctica or something. *Why* won't you get a cell phone?"

"I'm speaking from a cell phone, and you can hear how well it works."

"What?"

"What do you want?" Rae shouted into the phone.

"You sent me five *bullets,* Rae," Pamela exclaimed through the static. She might as easily have said "anthrax vials" or "live scorpions."

"You did send them to a lab?"

"But Rae, *bullets?* You know that if you have evidence of a major crime, you and I need to—"

Rae cut her off impatiently. "Pam, I may be insane, but I'm not stupid. Those bullets are seventy years old—four of them, at any rate. What did the lab say?"

"Are you absolutely sure there's no potential liability here?"

"I'm positive," Rae told her, not sure at all but unwilling to go into it.

"Okay. Well. You sent five bullets. Numbers three, four, and five all appear to be from the same weapon, which the lab thinks—"

"All three?"

"Three, four, and five, from a caliber gun out of common circulation since before the Second World War. Can you hear me? It *sounds* like you're in Antarctica."

"Just dangling halfway up a mountain."

"What was that?"

"Nothing. What else did they say?"

"There's a lot of technical information here. Do you want me to read it to you?"

"Save your throat. Why don't you overnight it—Ed can bring it when he comes back on Tuesday. What about the other two bullets?"

"The other two are from a different gun, also an older handgun. These two were too badly damaged for the lab to see any distinctive marks, but numbers four and five had a sixty percent match on the striations—I'm reading this, not exactly sure what it means—and number three, while too misshapen to retain any marks, weighs approximately the same number of grams as four and five. Is that all clear? Rae? Are you still there? Oh, damn this connection, anyway!"

Rae woke to the voice in her ear, told her lawyer she'd be in touch, and jabbed the END button on the still-squawking telephone.

It was one thing to suspect, to play with the possibilities as if she were Petra constructing one of her stories for Bella's entertainment, but in the glaring light of day—

Deep in thought, Rae turned blindly down the hill, and somehow made it back to the campsite without mishap. She found Ed drinking his ritual coffee, a pair of garish red half-glasses perched on the end of his nose and a book by a man called Spencer in his hand. He looked up as she approached, and pulled off the reading glasses.

"Any luck?" he asked. She handed him back the tiny instrument.

"Sure—all I have to do is climb to the top of the mountain. I think I'll wait to get a cell phone until the technology improves a little."

"Good idea. Can I offer you some of your own coffee?"

She took the cup he poured and allowed his conversation to beat against her ears, making responses in more or less the correct places. She even managed to pull herself together enough to give him her list of supplies and milling dimensions for her tower stairway, which would enable her to get that going a week sooner.

She barely noticed when he left. Instead, she reluctantly made her way up to the house to stand before the chip in the fireplace where twenty-two days earlier she had dug out bullet number three.

The bullets she had labeled numbers one and two were those she had pried from the wood of the front door.

Number four, which the lab had paired with number three, was the lump of lead she had taken from between the bones in the cave, the loose bullet that had been left behind when the tiny scavengers had finished their work on Desmond Newborn's remains.

Five she had shot herself into a soft log on the beach, then dug out and dropped in its bag. A bullet from the antique pistol inherited from her father, the gun with the rosewood grip that Rae had brought to the island as her own last escape.

Forty-two

Rae's Journal

June 5

I feel so peculiar, as if I am coming down with the flu—feverish, restless. Nauseated.

I guess revelation will do that to you.

When I came here, my only intention was to occupy myself with building a house. In the back of my mind was the vague hope that I might learn something about Desmond, the life that brought him here, what happened after he left this place.

I did not imagine that I would discover that he had not left at all.

Five bullets. Two of them fired from a handgun into the heavy door, by someone standing near the fireplace. From the pitted, rusty lump of metal that seventy years later made me think of an old soldier, scarred but potentially deadly.

Two, then, from Desmond's gun.

Three other bullets. All from a second revolver. One lodged in the fireplace, the second in Desmond's body, the third fired into a spongy tree trunk by me as a sample.

Three from William's gun.

And I thought I was being melodramatic, fantasizing a shootout in the cabin. Even now it feels absurd to write that sensational word. What could "shootout" have to do with William and Desmond Newborn, one brother a building tycoon, the other a holder of the Great War Croix de Guerre?

There is, however, no doubt in my mind: Desmond Newborn was killed by the gun now resting in my knapsack. Desmond Newborn was killed by his brother.

290

I imagine it happened like this:

Desmond has spent the day entertaining his brother—or rather, submitting grimly to his brother's disapproving inspection. He rows William back to Roche Harbor in the afternoon, not returning to Folly until sunset or later. Too late to do any work, too late even to bother changing out of the suit he'd put on to face William. Desmond merely takes off the jacket and the stiff collar, stirs up the fire against the cool September evening, and sits in his easy chair with a glass of whiskey, allowing the island peace to creep back in and soothe his badly shaken nerves.

He dozes in his chair. Or perhaps he rouses to cook himself a meal, or even takes a walk before returning to the hearth. In any case, the evening passes.

By the time his brother William steps back onto the shore of Folly that night, either self-rowed (in the skiff that went missing that same night, which the Journal *article attributed to the island burglar?) or brought by a hireling, Desmond is preparing for bed. His feet are bare, his suspenders looped down off his shoulders, the buttons on his good white shirt undone. He sits down before the fire with his journal, uncaps his pen to write about the day's events, but gets no further than three short words before the noise at the door has him on his feet, a soldier's instant and unthinking response.*

What did Desmond hear moments before William burst in? It may have been merely the working of the latch that he had mounted that very day, the latch I removed from the door all those years later. It had no locking mechanism; William would merely have laid his hand on it and pulled the heavy door open far enough to fire around it. Did he catch Desmond in the act of going for his own gun? One of William's shots went wild and buried itself in the fireplace. Others may have missed their mark as well, but one did not. It struck Desmond dead center, passing through the unbuttoned shirt to sink into his lower left abdomen: There were no holes in the shirt itself.

Desmond had his own gun by now and returned fire. Did he know who his attacker was? Had he perhaps looked into William's eyes in that last moment? In any case, he fired back in the direction of the dark outside his door. Two of his bullets hit the door—entering the wood at different angles, perhaps because it was pushed open by the impact of the first shot. Bitter irony: Desmond's attacker protected by the defensive thickness of the builder's own front door. I imagine William beat a hasty retreat into the night— uninjured, as far as I know. No neighbors heard the sounds, since the same orientation that baffles phone reception on Folly would have channeled the echoes of gunshot off in the direction of distant Vancouver Island.

Desmond abandoned his gun (which was empty when I dug it up), and his uncapped pen had flown away with his first lunge, but he managed either to retrieve or to retain his diary, and thrust it into his breast pocket. He crawled through his secret door, bleeding terribly, knowing all too well what such a wound meant. He made it through the woodshed and into the cave, where I believe the end must have come fairly soon; there was no sign of any first-aid attempt, no indication that he had even tried to stanch the wound. By the position of the skeleton, Desmond just put his right hand inside his shirt, rested his head back against the wall, and died.

The house, meanwhile, was burning. Accident—an oil lamp knocked to flames by a stray bullet or Desmond's dive across the room? Or deliberate effort? I can't imagine that Desmond showed William his secret escape route, which meant that William (God, I can't believe I'm writing this—William! Grandfather!) would have believed that setting the house on fire would either destroy its occupant or drive Desmond out into vulnerability. In either case, Folly and its owner were wiped out. William Newborn left the island, sinking or taking his brother's rowing skiff with him to introduce the possibility of Desmond's escape, and he went home to Boston, inventing a letter two years later, but never saying a word of the truth to anyone.

Fantasy? No doubt, but how else to explain the facts? My grandfather's gun killed Desmond Newborn.

But why? Granted, even as an old man Grandfather was a furious man, fueled by resentments and the supreme joy of doing his enemies in the eye. The only thing that really mattered to him was the acquisition and maintenance of power, chiefly through wealth. Work, friendships, even family left him cold: Supreme authority, over all he surveyed, was what really mattered. He would have sold his only child, my father, had the offer come in high enough.

Could the shooting have been a money dispute gone bad? Desmond demanding his portion of their inheritance, and William losing his temper?

I do not know. All I am sure of is, the scenario in my mind is very clear.

My grandfather murdered his brother, the brother whose handiwork I have come here to lift up again.

Part Four

RAISING THE
ROOF BEAM

A simple plan, carefully worked out, and a bare minimum of outside help. Elegant, is what they called it. And when The Thief goes missing, or turns up drowned, no one will be too surprised.

Forty-three

In less than a month, Rae would have houseguests—whether she had a house or not. She had water and a rudimentary shower, she had walls that were raw and unfinished but of sufficient solidity to reassure city dwellers, and she had a capacious privy, the use of which would no doubt be good for her guests' spiritual development.

Three things she needed, though, before her daughter and son-in-law arrived to entrust the sole surviving member of the family's next generation to the madwoman's mercies: a roof, more seating, and a way to hide the cave.

The chairs in a pinch she could always buy from Friday Harbor or fashion from stumps, but the roof was urgent for everyone's physical comfort, and concealing the cave was every bit as important for her psychological comfort. Why, she did not exactly know, but the idea of Don Collins poking disdainfully into the cave where Desmond had died filled her with revulsion.

During the days, she tackled the roof. Because she had no photograph of the inside of the house, she had no way of knowing how Desmond had supported his gable roof, but she doubted, considering the building sensibilities of his age, that he had done anything with the upper floor but finish it with a triangular attic space above for future storage.

Rae, however, craved height and light in her upstairs room. She would keep the ceiling open to the rafters and put a (historically inaccurate) window into the south-facing gable wall. Therefore her wood counted, needed to be beautiful as well as structural: cedar again.

It was a chore getting all the lumber up and through the wide upper east window, but it was her only choice. Standing outside, she would work the rope up the pulley, lifting two or three boards at a time, each bundle bumping and teetering its way up the house's outside wall. Then she would go inside, climb the ladder in the tower, and swing the boards onto the floor.

Except the ridge beam. That came up not in a bundle, but by itself, thirty-two feet of rich, fragrant, native Washington State red cedar six inches thick and eighteen wide, six hundred pounds of tree. The stripped cedar logs she had lifted were toothpicks by comparison. The entire house groaned when the pulley took on the weight, and the beam crept up the wall, one terrifying millimeter at a time.

When at last, cursed at, cajoled, and sweated over, the roof beam lay threaded across the sills of the upstairs window frames, Rae allowed herself a whoop of triumph. All those lists, all those drawings, the endless calculations of weight and height and angles, all the compulsive, emotionally draining paperwork that had been taken by all as a symptom of Rae's mental imbalance, all that lengthy battle for the right to try doing this was justified, vindicated by the presence of a massive slab of lumber lying at rest seventeen feet off the ground.

Not that it was in place. The remaining ten feet would be every bit as arduous, but that would involve propping and bracing first one end, then the other: like building the pyramids, not impossible if one took it slow.

And Rae took it slow, and safe. To the top of the existing headers inched the great beam, then into the air with a series of enormously sturdy temporary braces. Once it was floating in the air, Rae could start cutting and fastening down the rafters.

Ed came, found her dangling among the 2x10s, and departed without his coffee and conversation. Nikki appeared briefly with vegetables from a relative's garden. The sun shone, the wind blew, and Rae raised up the bones of her roof.

Then on the eighth day, the roof's framework was finished. A web of cedar lay suspended over the entire house: the massive red authority of the center beam, bearing down; the rafters that held it, looking delicate by comparison, stretching out to transfer the weight onto walls and thence to bedrock; the collar ties that linked each rafter pair into a flat A, ties whose fibers were slack for the last time before the supports came out, the weight came down, and their long lives of tension began. Locked together like a skeletal rib cage, ready to receive the thing that was the ultimate purpose of shelter, a roof. Compression: tension. All Rae needed to do was remove the temporary braces that held the great beam in place, and her house would be, if not covered, then certainly enclosed.

First, though, she would placate the spirits. She climbed down the tower ladder and stood on her front steps, surveying her choices.

Through the ages, particularly in northern Europe, it was traditional to mount a branch when a structure's high point was reached, a sacrifice to the spirits of the trees that had given their lives for human shelter. Properly speaking, the roof tree should be either cedar, which grew all around her tent, or fir, which stood nearby. Those were, after all, the woods she had used in the house. However, Rae found herself eyeing the madrone that overshadowed her workbench, the tree at whose base lay the ashes of Alan and Bella, a tree that for seventy-two days had been absorbing their molecules into its roots and leaves. The madrone's outer skin was shedding vigorously now, rich brown flakes against the smooth, fresh, pale green inner bark. More and more over the past weeks, Rae had felt like that inner bark, shedding the rough outer protection until she stood, smooth and naked and fresh and serene.

Foolishness, she mocked herself. Nonetheless, it was to the madrone that she moved, and with a brief inner apology, it was one of the madrone's small branches that she cut off with her folding knife. She carried the branch to the house, climbing front steps and tower ladder and second-story ladder until she was standing at the very height of the roof, her head even with the bare, fire-scarred tops of the towers. There she nailed the wide-leafed branch.

The view was astounding, on a clear afternoon such as this. She felt that she could see halfway to Japan, that San Francisco had to be just against the horizon. Vancouver Island stood to one side, the mountainous Olympic peninsula below, mainland Washington to her left. Sailboats had been scattered across the blue water for her pleasure, their sails tipped with the breeze. The dark bulk of a cargo ship made for the Pacific; closer in, a turmoil of white spray and dark flecks, the whole less than the size of her thumbnail at arm's length, marked the passage of a pod of Dall's porpoises, teasing along in front of a motorboat. Over the past two months, she had grown to know the regulars, animal and human. The *kathunk* sound of one of her less technologically sophisticated neighbors making a weekly trip into the market, the powerful thrum of another neighbor who went past at water-skiing speed whether he was pulling someone or not, a vacationing teak sailboat that had been around for the last few days and that had more than once prompted her to pull out her binoculars in envy. There were a couple of black inflatables in the neighborhood, one of which she had decided was the middle-of-the-night disturber-of-the-peace. That boatman had been away for a while, although she had heard the motor again Saturday just before dawn. Seasonal birds came and sometimes went on, and the orcas, too, seemed to have a pattern that she vowed to begin noting down one of these days. Unlike the floatplanes that swept past at unpredictable times, day and night, carrying those residents too impatient or important for water travel. And then as Rae stood there supervising the varied elements of her watery community, her right arm crooked around the roof beam and her boots balanced on the sill plates twenty feet above solid rock, another boat rounded the end of San Juan Island, scudding rapidly in a direct line for her cove, white spray flying up from its bow. She knew the boat long before she could make out the man at its helm.

Jerry Carmichael had not been back to the island since the framing crew had swarmed in and transformed her house, eight days earlier. Rae could soon hear his motor above the movement of air and branch; from her godlike perch, unseen and unsuspected, she watched him tie up and step onto her dock. He had a thick dark bottle in one hand and a grocery bag with flowers sticking out of the top in the other. Smiling, Rae lowered herself down to the floor and took up her hammer, and set about freeing her roof beam from its supports.

In a few minutes, drawn by the sound of hammering, Jerry emerged up the ladder from the tower. He was still carrying the bottle, but had exchanged the bag for Rae's two elegant wineglasses, which looked small between the fingers of his hand. He stopped just inside the room, in the corner where the black stones of the fireplace met the orange stones of the tower, to watch her work.

Temporary supporting nails screamed their withdrawal from the floorboards, chocks and shims were bashed out of the way, and then the front support wobbled free. Rae caught it and gathered up the pieces, dumping them with all the other rubbish against the empty opening of the south tower. Then she took the hammer to the back brace, which was now bearing most of the weight. Rae slammed the tool against the base of the support, again and again, feeling the blows all along the length of her body, just as the entire house was doing. The bones of her feet and the skin of her scalp, the cedar beneath her boots and the two figurines deep in the foundation below all shuddered with the harsh, joyful reverberations of steel against wood. The support gave minutely, then shifted visibly, then more, until finally with one great blow she was catching the boards to keep them from crashing to the floor. She and Jerry stood still, heads tilted, listening.

Not a sound, not a creak or a groan from the neatly aligned pairs of rafters that stretched from roof beam to walls, distributing the weight of that young tree without a murmur, pulled taut against the collar ties, compression and tension working together in beauty.

The cork popped loudly, and Jerry caught the foam in the two glasses. She dragged the now-useless wood over to the discard pile, slid the hammer into its loop against her thigh, and went over to take the glass of champagne from her visitor. He held up his glass to her in a wordless toast, and then his eyes went up to the massive beam over their heads.

"How the hell did you get that up by yourself?" he asked.

"A step at a time, Jerry. One small step at a time."

He crossed the airy room to the south window and stood admiring the view. "Bobby told me you looked to be nearly finished framing. I figured that called for a celebration."

"Champagne and flowers."

"And dinner. I know you eat meat."

She sipped from her glass and pushed away the uncharitable niggle of resentment, that Deputy Gustafsen had been keeping an eye on her, and incidentally the progress of her work, and further, that Jerry Carmichael had decided that mere completion was not celebration enough. *Damn it,* Rae scolded herself, *you are impossible to please,* and held out her glass for a refill.

She was feeling easier about his presence by the time they went down to the campsite.

Jerry had brought steaks, thick and marbled with fat. He had also brought the expertise to cook them, so while Rae looked about for something to hold the grocery-store flowers, he laid logs and kindling in her fire pit and told her about his week. Like old friends, Rae thought with amusement, although she'd met him less than two months before.

"We finally figured out how that Andrews girl got off the ferry," he was telling her. "She must've gone under her own power, though, so she's a runaway now, not a kidnap victim, no matter what the father says. She was driven off the ferry in a pickup truck, either hunched down on the floor under a blanket or in a tool compartment across the back. Just drove right off while her parents were standing there tapping their feet and waiting for her to show up at the car. Fifth or sixth car off was the pickup, and you know what the driver did then? He went up around the corner, turned into the park road, circled around, and got back in line for the ferry. The same ferry, heading west. We didn't even think to look in the line of cars waiting to get on, for Christ sake."

"So what was it, a boyfriend?"

"Some scruffy-looking older guy. As far as anyone knows, Caitlin didn't have any older friends, much less boyfriends. But did you hear the kicker? About the mother?"

"No, what happened to her?"

"Last week, on Friday, the mother disappeared, too." He sounded, incredibly enough, amused, as if this was someone's clever trick.

Rae sat forward in the canvas chair and stared at his profile. "You don't sound terribly worried about it, Jerry."

"I'd say the only thing to worry about is if the two of them come home. See, the wife sent a letter, saying that she and Caitlin had taken their passports and fled the country, to get away from the husband. They couldn't go at the same time because the father was always watching, so she waited a couple of days till he was fully occupied with the hunt, and then she pretended to collapse. She spent the next seven days, while he thought she was in bed weeping, out selling or pawning every last little thing she could pry loose from the house. At the end of it she stripped the checking and savings and took off. She's riding the underground railway now, and good luck to them both."

"Seems a little extreme. I mean, why didn't she just file for divorce?"

Jerry, hunkered down out of the rising smoke from the fire, grimaced. "From what I've been told, it was one of those cases of a guy with enough weight to make sure that complaints and reports found cracks to fall into. The wife—Rebecca's her name—had a history of emotional problems; she'd never have got custody of the kid, would've been lucky to get visiting rights. And as for alimony, don't make me laugh."

"So now she and the girl have to disappear," Rae said.

"Until Caitlin turns eighteen."

"That doesn't seem right."

"Was it Shakespeare who said, 'The law's an ass'?"

"Dickens, I think. That's an odd thing for a lawman to admit, Jerry."

"I see it from the inside, Rae. It's getting better—I do honestly believe that—but there are still plenty of big, unfair holes waiting to swallow up the innocent."

"Don't I know it. I could have bought a house with what I've paid out to my lawyer over the last year."

It was said spontaneously, but the instant it left her mouth Rae knew that it had also been deliberate. She did not know for certain why Jerry Carmichael continued to drop by Folly, but if it was, in fact, something more than mere neighborliness on his part, she wanted all her cards laid on the table from the beginning. Or most of her cards. The Conversation, in fact. Complaining about lawyers had been an invitation for Jerry to take a step into her life; he did not hesitate.

"Legal problems, huh?"

She took a breath, let it out carefully. "My son-in-law, Don Collins, is trying to get me declared mentally incompetent."

The big sheriff gaped, and then guffawed as if she'd made the world's funniest joke. Only when he realized that she was not laughing herself did he swivel on his heel to stare up at her.

"You're not serious? God. I'm sorry—for laughing, I mean. I—"

"Don't apologize, Jerry, for heaven's sake. It's the nicest thing anyone's done for a long time, in fact, treating my instability as a joke."

"But you are serious," he said, still doubtful.

"Jerry, you knew I'd been in a mental hospital."

"Yeah, but you're cured, right?"

"What's 'cured'? Jerry, look. There are some people who are so stable you could build an office block on top of them—no self-doubt, no neurotic tendencies, not so much as a psychosomatic illness all their life. At the other end of the scale are the flat-out psychotics—delusional, violent, self-destructive, uncontrollable even with heavy medication. Most people spend their lives somewhere between the two extremes, functioning well most of the time, dipping into neurotic or even

psychotic behavior under stress or hormones or the phase of the moon—
no one really knows, although most mental illnesses seem to be about one
part chemistry to four or five parts circumstance. Schizophrenia, like you
said your cousin has, is a little different, but you probably know that."

"Yeah, I remember."

"I have been, at different times in my life, severely depressed, suici-
dal, and even delusional. My postpartum depression after my daughter
Tamara was born nearly killed me. When my husband and other daughter died eighteen months ago, I ended up in a locked ward after another
suicide attempt. Basically, Jerry, Don has a point: My foundations are
not very stable. Don't build a house on me." It was a small joke, but it
was also a warning, and Jerry Carmichael heard it clearly.

"But you were also attacked," he noted, as if she might have forgotten.

"I was so wrapped up in my depression and my delusions that I forgot the world is a dangerous place, yes."

"So you're saying it's your fault you were attacked."

"Not my fault, no, but—"

"But you feel like maybe it was."

"I suppose I do," she replied slowly.

"Because you were delusional?"

"Because I was out of control."

"Not violent?"

"No."

"Hearing voices?"

"Yes. And movement, and footsteps, and—"

"Why are you so sure those were delusions?" he asked calmly, and
Rae gaped at him, as stunned and breathless as if he'd punched her in the
stomach.

"But . . . they were," she said stupidly.

"Were they different somehow from real noises, or was it you that felt
different because of the state you were in?"

"I . . . Jesus, Jerry, I don't know. But look, the sheriff and his deputy
came up several times, and there was nothing there. I *was* hearing things.
And," she added suddenly as the thought came to her, "why are you asking me this? Because if you're trying to convince yourself and me that
I wasn't stark raving nuts just because in the end two guys actually
attacked me, I'm sorry, but I was."

He picked up her iron fireplace tool and poked irritably at the burning wood before blurting out, "Somebody's been calling around the island about you. Asking where you are, when you're coming back."

"Well, a lot of people know I'm here, but don't know exactly where. The woman whose gallery I sell through in New York, for example. A couple of friends. My wood man in California."

"A gallery . . . oh, right. I didn't know they sold furniture in galleries."

"My kind of furniture they do," Rae said, and added with asperity, "I make furniture that wins awards and sells for a lot of money. I'm really very well known."

They both heard the plaintive protest in her voice, but Rae chuckled first.

"So there," she told him. "Look, are you planning on cooking those steaks? 'Cause in another minute I'm going to eat mine raw."

Their actions turned to the preparation and then consumption of food, but their thoughts were fixed on Jerry's news. Once the peaceable hiatus of the meal was over, Rae turned back to what he had told her.

"Are you trying to frighten me?"

"By suggesting that someone's looking for you? Someone who may or may not have attacked you in California last year?"

"Yeah."

"I suppose I am."

"Shit, Jerry, thanks a lot." She got up and began to slam dishes into the plastic dishpan, not a satisfying noise.

"I'm just suggesting that you—"

"Might come and stay with you?"

"No, actually I was going to suggest Nikki, or her aunt's inn."

Rae just snorted.

"Only at night. One of us, or Ed, could run you over during the day."

"No."

"Rae—"

"No! No. Nobody's after me, nobody's coming out to Folly to attack me. I told you, Jerry, this is my last stand. If I can't make it here, I'll—" *Shoot myself,* she did not say. "I won't make it anywhere."

"I understand," Jerry said after a long minute of watching her furious back. It might, Rae thought, even have been true. "Keep your handgun with you," he said abruptly.

At that she did turn around. "Aren't you going to ask me if I have a permit?"

"I'd rather know if you have bullets."

"I do." Five now, which would not stop a charging grizzly but would no doubt send a hired attacker fleeing. *Like William, into the night,* her treacherous mind noted. "I also have the flare gun that you sent with Nikki. Now: You want some coffee?"

"Are you changing the subject?"

"Yes, damn it, I'm changing the subject."

"Then yes, I'd love some coffee."

The mood had changed, the growing tendrils of mutual awareness hacked off at the root. As he left, the launch motor seemed to fire unevenly, as if in displaced frustration. Rae retrieved the pistol and the flare gun from the locked box in her tent, and vowed to keep them both at arm's reach at all times. She would be responsible for her own protection.

Forty-four

Desmond Newborn's Journal

I clear ground, stripped to the waist on all but the coldest morning, and meditate on the nature of fear.

The link between the two activities may sound unlikely to the civilian ear, but any front-line soldier knows well the logic of it. Green troops only panic and flee if they are allowed to rest in their advancement, given time to think about the approaching sounds of battle. Any sergeant knows that assigning the body a task, no matter how small, distracts the mind from its dread and allows the unseasoned soldier to learn how to master himself. If the task can be both mindless and physically demanding, so much the better.

For fear can be mastered; more, it can be used. In one small step, terror transforms into rage, and rage is as powerful a weapon as anything a man's hands might grasp.

However, rage exacts a price from a man's life force. When I came back from France, I felt as if the core of me had been emptied out, as if I were one of those ancient, center-dead trees, huge of girth but possessed of scarcely enough life to maintain a handful of leaves at the ends of its barren branches. Cut me down, and a person would have found a circle of wood surrounding a great hollowness.

When life began to return, it was as painful as blood penetrating a dead limb. Many times, I wished devoutly to die. I was instead husbanded back to craggy life, and promptly misused my strength. It was terror, though, not guilt that drove me out onto the road, cold, sweating fear that would have rooted me to the spot like a frightened rabbit had I not kept moving, fear that I both embrace and keep at bay here on Sanctuary.

Keeping the terror at bay absorbs all of my limited energy. If I work to exhaustion, dig and haul until the ache in my left shoulder fills my universe, then I am granted sleep; but if I quit for the day merely pleasantly tired, I am sure to wake at night with a scream clenched between my teeth.

This preoccupation with my internal demons seems to have rendered any degree of social intercourse almost beyond my capabilities. No sooner did I move onto the island than my mind lapsed into a near-animal state. For weeks now I have found words difficult to retrieve and to use around others. I grunt at my grocer, I point and scribble my order, I nod and duck my head and smile like an imbecile. Indeed, I should not be surprised if my neighbors believe me to be mentally deficient.

I tell myself it is the long accumulation of terror, that like a poison takes time to work its way out of the body. There are things the human eye was never meant to see, the spilled viscera of the human spirit. There are things the human mind and body were never meant to do—easy murder, casual betrayal, the theft of what is most precious.

So I grunt, and put out a few stunted leaves at the ends of my branches, and spend my days sweating hard and meditating on the nature of fear.

Forty-five

In the days that followed, Rae applied herself to the roof, nailing boards across the rafters with a climbing harness securely around her waist. It was hot, tedious work and she was grateful when the fog lingered or the clouds blew over, grateful but equally worried that a summer rainstorm would catch her unprepared.

Early in the mornings, however, and last thing during the lengthening evenings of summer, Rae went to the back of the house to rebuild Desmond's woodshed, the structure that would hide the cave once again.

That job went fast, once she had brought the lumber over, and was so cool and undemanding compared with the roof that it felt like a holiday entertainment. Sophisticated joinery, she had decided, was a luxury she could ill afford on a woodshed no one would see. The notches Desmond had chipped out of the rock face fit her supports adequately, and she even used plywood for the floor.

The only tricky part was hiding the small door from the house into the shed. The door's edges she placed behind studs and its top behind a fire block, so that all she had to do was whittle a latch for the back of the left-hand stud that fastened with a sliver of wood—which, because it could only be worked from inside, did not compromise the security of the house. She tapped the sliver into place and stood back. From two feet away, it just looked like a rough spot in the wood; when she hammered a casual eightpenny nail up on the bare stud above it and draped her carpenter's belt over it, the door became invisible.

Then she went inside the shed and repeated the process to make the door to the cave, at the far back of the shelter, invisible as well. Unless a person knew it was there, that door, too, looked like part of a wall. And finally, for the large external opening used for filling the space with wood, Rae spent an evening fashioning a wooden latch that could be worked from either side, both as a source of amusement and for the security of knowing that her house would have a back exit.

Then she returned to her roof.

The roofing paper went down the first day of summer, a cold and gloomy, fog-bound morning that kept her firmly tethered to the climbing harness lest her foot hit a damp patch on the sloping surface. It was with a heartfelt sigh of relief that she let herself back onto the solid ground inside, unbuckled the harness (which pinched and chafed like a cross between a rock climber's rig and a chastity belt), and flung the contraption onto the growing pile of discards blocking the empty front tower. The roofing paper would keep out the rain for a while, and she was seriously leaning toward hiring a team of professionals to put on the shingles.

Ten days until the first of July, when Tamara, Don, and Petra were due to arrive, and Rae could not bring herself to spend the time constructing rough benches for their comfort. Instead, she took out the dauntingly lengthy list she would put in Ed's hands the following day and wrote down (underneath such unusual requests as a battery-powered camp light and four six-packs of Heineken) "six folding wood-and-canvas director's chairs." They were ugly and flimsy, but they would keep her guests' bottoms off the ground. She could always use them for firewood when her guests had departed.

She glanced over the list, wondering what gaping hole in her provisions she had overlooked. She had written Petra to bring any "personal items" she might need, and hoped the girl would realize that tampons and Clearasil didn't grow on trees. Toilet paper: check; an extra flashlight: check; a couple more beach towels: check. Rae's eyes traveled down the list, caught on an item that had gone onto it following a warm-afternoon visit to the privy, and she took the pen and scratched it out. An aerosol spray can of air freshener in the woods was too absurd to contemplate.

Rae anchored the list back under its rock, satisfied. Her family's rear ends would be cushioned by nice clean canvas. Hell, with that many chairs she could throw a party. So now, instead of constructing some rough imitation furniture, she could begin her stairway.

She had been hungry to do so ever since Ed had brought that tower of thick cedar triangles milled for her in Friday Harbor. Rough, dull, and crudely sawn, they were pure potential, awaiting their magical transformation. When she had first stacked them up in the house she had not been able to resist licking her thumb and wetting the dry wood into color: orange, like the freshly scrubbed stone walls of the tower, like the morning light that would pour down the stairway from the high windows.

It made her warm just thinking about it.

Jerry Carmichael had come by twice since the night she had finished the roof framing. His first visit had been to reassure himself that she was well and untroubled by visitors, and to reassure her that the various law enforcement personnel had been alerted to keep an eye on Folly; if this did not exactly fill Folly's resident with enthusiasm, she did not mention it to him. The second visit was more of the same, with two additional pieces of news: one, that the forensic anthropologist was working on Desmond, and two, that whoever had been phoning around in search of her had stopped doing so. Rae seized on this as an encouraging sign, doggedly ignoring Jerry's uncertainty. Jerry's day off was Thursday, three days from now. He'd said he would be there in the morning with tool belt and steaks. She still was not sure just what his attentions meant, whether he was being a friend, or doing his job with a fanatic's scrupulousness, or whether he was, in fact, romantically interested. She found this last proposition the least likely. She was, after all, at least six or eight years older than he was and no prize, in her body or her mind. Furthermore, she could not fail to notice his disinclination to take advantage of the various openings that had come up. The ambivalence could not be allowed to persist for much longer, that she knew. Still, puzzling as his trips to Folly might be, she did enjoy his presence. His willingness to spend his precious day off with her was a piece of knowledge that Rae tried not to take out and think about too much, for fear that too much handling would either wear it out or chase it away.

In any case, first the stairway.

Because the wood had come to her more or less shaped to size, most of the work would be delicate—trimming the shapes to fit between the stones and the center pole, chiseling away at the bottom surfaces so the metal supports were flush with the wood. For the first time in weeks, Rae took up the box that she had built many long years before to hold her woodworking tools; she carried it to the house, humming quietly.

She wrestled with the ladder that had been left in the tower, cursing under her breath the harsh intractability of aluminum until she had it on the ground outside, and then set about bracing the wooden center pole so it stood upright and equidistant from the walls, cursing out loud the clumsy persistence of wood. At long last, the pole was upright to her satisfaction. She brushed off her hands and went over to her beloved toolbox, squatting down to thumb open the hand-forged latch and pull back the pieced exotics that made up the lid. She frowned, and a sensation of cold began to spread out from the pit of her stomach as she cast about for an explanation of what she was seeing.

As a woodworker, Rae Newborn was the most methodical of women. An outsider might find her shop a jumble of crudely sawn wood, abandoned tools, and half-completed pieces, but Rae knew instantly where everything was, could feel in a moment when something had been moved.

Something had been moved.

The toolbox was a product of her own hands, a piece of equipment both practical and decorative, just like the furniture she made. It had been constructed with a specific set of tools in mind: Japanese chisels made by families that had forged swords for warriors since the fifteenth century, a wooden mallet that she wore out and had to replace every few years, an antique folding measure of brass and ivory that Alan had given her one Christmas—these and other tools that her fingers knew and found without the consultation of her eyes.

And the tray that formed the top layer was turned the wrong way around. The front left corner of the tray was where her fine-grit touch-up sharpening stone lived, but instead of that oily black square, the front left corner was now occupied by the wickedly sharp blade of the one-inch Takahashi chisel, normally in the upper right. If she'd gone to pick up the stone without looking, as she often did, she'd have sliced off the end of her thumb.

Could she possibly have put the upper tray back the wrong way? While she was tired, distracted enough that her hands forgot a movement they had performed a thousand times? When had she last opened the box, anyway? Building the driftwood workbench, she'd taken out a medium-sized V-shaped chisel from the bottom layer to run the strip of inlay up one leg, then put it back—and there it was, undisturbed in its niche with all its brothers. Since then, she had not had reason to use fine tools, but . . . wait. Eight, nine days ago—a couple of nights anyway after the celebratory steak dinner with Jerry Carmichael, she had wiped them all down with a lightly oiled rag so the sea air would not get its rusty teeth into their vulnerable steel. She'd had a drink with dinner, and another one afterward, and had, she recalled, been thinking about Jerry as she sat on the tent floor and wiped her tools—but no, she did not think that she could have dumped the top layer of the box down the wrong way. Blind drunk, inflamed with passion, or stark staring delusional, Rae's hands would have replaced the upper tray of the toolbox they had made with the sharpening stone in the front left corner. She could not imagine otherwise.

Which meant that someone had been going through her possessions. The was-it-a-footprint up near the spring back in April had been bad enough; this time it was as if Crusoe had discovered Friday asleep in his bed.

Rae lifted the upper tray and righted it, then closed the box, latched it shut, and got to her feet. Her hammer came into her hand, and she paced up and down the bare wooden room clutching it, not knowing if she should be angry or frightened or both. She paced and swung the heavy tool back and forth with such force that it would have threatened her kneecap, had its presence and its weight not been such a natural part of her grip.

A stranger, or a nosy acquaintance? She couldn't even decide which would be worse, or how to ask Jerry if he had— Or Nikki! Now there was something she could imagine: curious Nikki, slightly and unwillingly jealous of Jerry's affections, finding an excuse to go through Rae's possessions.

Slow down, she warned herself, coming to a standstill in front of the tower entrance. *You cleaned the tools a little more than a week ago, and you haven't been off the island since then. You've been right here, hammering furiously away. It had to have been someone sneaking inside while you were busy on the roof. Or in the woodshed behind the house.*

Most likely it was when she was inside the shed: On the roof she'd have seen anything moving in the cove or the clearing, and she'd only begun working inside the house itself this morning.

Jerry had said he knew no more than a couple of idiots—wild kids, it sounded like—who would even attempt to get at the island other than up from the cove. This might have been an exaggeration, however; certainly sneaking up to the camp through the trees while Rae was working would hold much less risk of being seen than a stroll down the promontory in full view.

Rae abruptly realized that she was stomping up and down again, swinging twenty-one ounces of steel furiously at the end of her arm as if looking for someone to hit with the thing. She held the clawed head up in front of her curiously, and it occurred to her how odd it was that anger could be antithetical to insanity. Psychotics acting out their imbalance might join the two definitions of "mad," but in truth, indignation, righteous or otherwise, was sometimes just what a disturbed person needed to restore a strong sense of identity and entitlement.

Better to *get* mad than *be* mad, you might say.

And, Rae realized, she was indeed angry.

Angry enough to march halfway down the hill before it struck her that she might have even better cause to be afraid. The revelation came in Jerry Carmichael's voice, a question she had struggled to push away ever since he had asked it.

"Why are you so sure those were delusions?"

Rae faltered, nearly tripped over her suddenly frozen feet, and then tucked her head down and scurried on to the tent, falling breathlessly through the flap door and going not to the various places that might have been picked over by an intruder, but to the pistol that lay on the table in her tent, the pistol that she had vowed to keep close at hand and forgotten in her delusion that Folly was a safe refuge. Fingers shaking, she checked to see that all five bullets were in the chambers and snapped it shut again. The click seemed very loud, and she glanced rapidly between the door and the screen window, ready for battle.

The most threatening thing that appeared was a blue jay, and although Rae winced at its squawk, she was by then sitting on the edge of her cot, the gun clasped in both hands.

There was Nikki's flare gun, too, she reassured herself. Come on: No one was going to attack her smack in the middle of a summer's day in a heavily populated watery playground. She knew without going to the promontory that there would be half a dozen boats—sail, motor, and paddle-powered—within shouting distance. Several times a day, boats or dinghies ventured into the open end of the cove in hopes that the No Trespassing sign did not mean them, only retreating when they saw clear signs of habitation. Ironic, perhaps, for a hermit to find safety in numbers, but there it was.

Still, from here on out, she would keep the gun with her, wearing it on her carpenter's belt with all the other tools. Maybe not stuck openly into the hammer holster, but if she wrapped its handle in a rag and pushed it into one of the belt's two big nail pouches, the weapon would look innocuous enough, one more lumpy object on a tool belt. She tried it, hated it, didn't know how long she could bear having the thing riding against her belly, but its weight was, she had to admit, reassuring.

Then she turned to a careful scrutiny of the tent. There were any number of incongruities that might have resulted from a stranger's search of her possessions; however, all of them could as readily have been due to her own carelessness. She was nowhere near as scrupulous with socks as she was with chisels, so that finding a pair of underwear among the T-shirts and Petra's last letter in with the receipts from the builder's supply proved nothing.

Calmer now, she went back up to her stairway—albeit with her hand resting on the nail pouch near the butt of the gun, and her eyes probing the bushes. A hundred times during the afternoon she froze at what she was doing to listen for sounds, got up half of those hundred times to check the window and door openings, but there was never anything there that shouldn't have been, except once a couple of kids on an inflatable dinghy with a motor, who saw her in the doorway and putted away back out of the cove.

After a couple of hours, she quit work in disgust. She was so jumpy she'd come close to ruining one perfectly good step, and she was exhausted in a way she hadn't been since her early dirt-hauling days. She halfway wished that Jerry was coming tonight, then she was equally glad he was not: Rae was old enough to know that a Jerry Carmichael with his protective feathers ruffled was a problem she did not need. And in this mood, she was almost sure to end up going to bed with him—something else she was not at all sure she wanted.

No: What she needed was not a protective male, but a restoration of her own sense of security.

If she'd learned nothing else over the past two years, she had absorbed one painful lesson: There is no such thing as safety; there is only strength.

Forty-six

Desmond Newborn's Journal

November 11, 1922

Armistice Day. A noisy storm played over the islands the other night, and for the first time in seven years, the thunder was not a bombardment, the lightning over the horizon not some poor bastards up the line getting it. Thank you, God, for this favor.

I have been on Sanctuary for a year and five months, and still live in a rough shack. I have begun my foundations, but they have long months to go. The better part of this year I spent ranging through the islands in my rowing skiff, searching out the right stones with which to build my house. The natives find me amusing. They wave as I pass and they nudge each other good-naturedly when I enter the grocery store, but I respond in kind, with words few but friendly, so they think me harmless, if colorful.

The beach on Lopez that I discovered last spring has proven an almost limitless source of perfect stones, although, in the nature of perfect things, one must dig deep for them. I have overturned the entire beach from one end to the other three times now, and will return again in the spring. Fortunately, there was a lad who lives nearby with a stout motorboat, who for a small fee saves me from the worst of my labors. Rowing a heavily laden skiff even with the tide is no easy matter; if I am caught on the water at the turn, the situation rapidly ceases to amuse.

I have discovered a small cavern immediately behind where I am laying my foundations. It seems to me to have been used by my Indian predecessors on the island, but I do not think they would object to my making use of it. The place is snug and dry: a secure dugout that even a direct shell would find hard to collapse.

I shelter in the cave sometimes when the weather is inclement, and I seem to feel around me the men who came before, companions strangely dressed and murmuring in incomprehensible tongues.

What would they think, if they were to notice me sitting among them? What tales would I tell, were I to be transported back to their company? That they as a people have all but died off? That their shell middens are more prominent than they are? That nothing is left of them in these islands but their shades?

And what if I were to find myself similarly confronted by a strangely dressed man from the future, telling me tales of how I too have died unmourned, forgotten but for the stone midden I left behind? No heir, no friends, no great public foundation to mark my passing, nothing more than the ripples of a stone in water or the outline of a whale carved in the wall.

And yet, surely the earth holds far too many men who would Make their Mark, who would Change the World? Am I wrong to think that some of us ought to pass through the world more quietly?

Forty-seven

Tuesday came, nine days short of The Arrival, and while the morning mist still lay on the water, a boat pulled into the cove. The boat was not Ed's, and the man who jumped onto the dock holding the boat's rope was not bearing groceries. Nor did he start up toward the clearing, but rather stood waiting for her to come down. Jerry's face looked . . . official. Not grim, just watchful and concerned.

"What's wrong?" Rae asked when she was standing in front of him.

"I'm having a call patched through on the radio. You want to get on board and take it?"

The hell with this, was all that flashed through her mind: *I really am going to have to make some kind of phone arrangement so the rest of humanity doesn't need to act as my damn messenger boy.*

"Hello?" she asked the device.

"Good morning, Ms. Newborn, this is Sheriff Escobar. How you doing?"

"I *was* doing fine. Why do I think that's about to change?"

"I've got two men here I'd like you to look at. Could you possibly get on a plane and come in for a lineup?"

"What, today?"

"I can't hold 'em beyond tomorrow without charging them," he said, and that was all he said. Rae could hear him waiting through the crackling that came across the receiver while she stood on Jerry's gently rocking boat and stared at the dials and gauges. Of all the things Rae did not want to do nine days before her family descended on her, leaving the islands to go to a crowded airport full of other anxious people, then closing herself into a plane, all for the purpose of looking at two men she probably couldn't identify (and with the result of stirring up all kinds of unwelcome memories if she could), was fairly high on the list.

However, she owed Sam Escobar, owed him for his persistence and his honesty, for his patience with a woman who heard bumps in the night, owed him for the kindness with which he had tried to coax a terrified and obviously unbalanced victim out from behind her paper-strewn sofa.

"I'll be there," she told him.

"Thank you."

She heard relief in his voice—too much relief, perhaps. "Don't you have anything to charge them with other than my identification?"

"Yes, but they'd be bailed before dark, and gone. If you can ID these two, we have a chance to hold on to them."

"All right. But I have to tell you, I may not remember their faces. It's been a long year and a half."

"All we can do is try," he said crisply. "Let me know when you're getting in—I'll have someone meet you at the airport."

Jerry seemed pleased that she was going, which Rae took as an indication of his relief that she and her problems were going to be out of his jurisdiction, if only temporarily. Policing a spread-apart county couldn't be an easy task, she reflected. She thought about telling him what she had found in her toolbox, even though it would underscore his conviction that she was in some kind of danger, but he was already in motion, and so, it appeared, was she.

"I can get you on a two-thirty flight out of Seattle, if you can get ready in twenty minutes. They'll hold the Anacortes ferry. That'd get you to San Jose before five-thirty."

She didn't ask how he knew the schedules so well, just nodded her agreement and turned on her heel to throw some things into the knapsack. Telling him about the toolbox could wait.

When she reached down to unbuckle her tool belt, she stopped: the gun. She couldn't possibly take it on the plane; on the other hand, she didn't want to leave it in the tent, even inside the locked trunk. Rae snatched up the flannel-wrapped object and trotted up the hill to the house, paused to pick up the precious box of woodworking tools (the only thing of real value on the island since Desmond's journal and strongbox had gone into the Friday Harbor bank) and took gun and box through the woodshed into the cave. She left them just inside the cave's entrance, and secured both invisible doors on her way out.

Jerry was in the boat, on the radio making her travel arrangements. She ducked into the tent and threw off her dirty work clothes, grabbing up a wrinkled shirt and trousers, exchanging mud-caked boots for city shoes and rummaging through her stored clothes until she found a linen blazer. If she was going to hang around a jail, she'd look like a lawyer, not a suspect. The jacket was rumpled beyond fashion and tighter than she remembered across her shoulders, but it would have to do. Rae took a last look around, dropped the bedside clock and her journal into the knapsack, then zipped and tied shut the windows and door and hurried to join Jerry on the boat.

Conversation was virtually impossible over the motor. In Friday Harbor he eased the boat up to a dock near the ferry, where Bobby Gustafsen, wearing his deputy's uniform, stood waiting. Bobby caught the boat's rope, gave Rae a shy grin and Jerry a set of keys, and then stepped onto the boat in Jerry's place. She and the sheriff scurried up and over the bridge onto the ferry, which immediately cast off and lumbered out into the channel between San Juan and Shaw. Still on Jerry's heels, Rae went up some stairs and through some doors, and then they were in the shipboard cafeteria with the smell of French roast coffee and maple syrup. She dropped into a seat, ears ringing and nerves jangled, grateful that for the next hour at least she would not be rushing anywhere. Jerry went over to the food line and came back with a trayful of things wrapped in cellophane. He dug in; she sipped her coffee.

"I take it you're driving me to the airport?" she asked.

"If that's all right," he said, looking suddenly doubtful around his sandwich.

"It's fine," then, "I'm grateful," she amended. "I'd just think you had things to do. Sheriffing about."

"Let Bobby be in charge. He loves it. And what's the point in being the sheriff if I can't move things around to let me spend a few hours with a woman I—" He halted, and changed it to, "—with a friend."

Rae smiled ruefully. "So I didn't manage to scare you off with all that truth telling?"

"Were you trying to?"

"Might be a good idea, if I could," she told him, and reflected that it would all be much simpler if she could decide how she felt about this relationship.

"Sorry. No can do."

"Just . . . keep your eyes open, okay? With me?"

"Always do."

Which reminded her. "Jerry, I need to tell you that it's possible someone's been going through my tools, sometime in the last week."

His eyebrows came together in a frown. "Is something missing?"

"No, just part of my toolbox got moved around, but I don't know when. And it could have been just my own absentmindedness."

"But you don't think it was," he said. It was not a question.

"Honestly? With that toolbox? No."

They looked at each other over the plastic table, oblivious to the magnificent scenery rolling past the big windows. "What are we going to do about this?" he said at last.

"Well," she said. "It's possible that if these two guys I'm going to look at were the ones who attacked me last year, they'll be able to explain what's going on now."

"And if not?"

"If not, we'll have to think about it."

They both thought about it a great deal over the next three days, beginning with Rae on the airplane south and Jerry in the car heading back north and then west. Rae also thought about the way Jerry had sat behind the wheel of his official car at the airport drop-off, eyeing the masses of people, and, with a sort of "Oh, the hell with it" shrug, leaned over and kissed her. When Rae had surfaced, flustered beyond words, she halfway expected an audience, but the only one openly watching was the pretty cop on duty, who nudged her hat brim up with one finger, a gesture like a salute, then moved off down the line.

Rae had grabbed her knapsack out of the backseat and looked over the top of the car at the big man in the uniform, who had, if nothing else, taken her mind off her apprehension about being shut in a plane with strangers.

"You look great," he told her. She glanced down at herself in surprise, and then, hesitantly, returned his grin.

"So do you," she admitted, and went to catch her plane.

The woman at the check-in counter took one look at Rae's taut features and said she'd be happy to trade the forward aisle seat that Jerry's travel agent had booked for a window seat in the absolute last row on the plane. Rae marched to the gate, head down and teeth gritted, and sat in a corner with her back against the wall. She was the last passenger to board, and settled into her seat, light-headed with relief. All those people, and not one had grabbed her from behind.

For two hours her spine ceased its crawling; although she kept a wary eye on every person going to and from the toilet, at least her nerves did not imagine that a hand could come through the wall at her. On the ground at San Jose, she again waited until everyone but the flight attendants were off before she picked up her knapsack and scurried to the door.

To her surprise, the person looking toward the gate with the worried, "Did she miss the plane?" expression was wearing not a sheriff's department uniform, but a brief red leather skirt and a suede jacket: Pam Church. The lawyer's face cleared when she saw Rae, and she gave her a quick embrace and a peck on the cheek.

The lawyer's first words were a near-duplicate of Jerry's last. "God, woman, you look superb."

Again Rae glanced at her undistinguished and unkempt clothes, but Pamela shook her head.

"No, I mean *you*. You look like you've spent the last three months at a health spa, pumping iron and sitting on the beach. Brown and muscular."

"I don't know about pumping iron, but I've shifted a hell of a lot of wood and nails."

"Whatever it is, it suits you. You need a manicure, of course, but your hands have looked like that ever since I've known you. Is that all you have?" She gestured at Rae's disreputable knapsack.

"That's it," Rae told her.

During the drive to the county jail, over the mountain highway that was home and not home, they caught up on a lot of business and a little personal news, which had always been the balance in their relationship. Traffic was heavy going over the hill as it was smack in the middle of commute hour, but Pamela did not seem worried about the delay.

"Sheriff Escobar said he'd wait for you," she told Rae.

"Are you coming in?"

"If you want me to. If not, I'll drop you there, and we can get together tomorrow for a proper going-over. You're not going back to Seattle tonight, I hope?"

"Oh no. As long as I'm here, I'll stay a couple of days, take care of business, dust the plants, water the shelves."

"Um. Would you like to stay with me? I have an extra room; I'd be more than happy to have you."

"No, I'm fine."

"I just hate to think of you all alone in that big house," the lawyer said cautiously.

"I'm staying with a friend tonight—my wood man, Vivian Masters. He's driving me up to the house tomorrow, and maybe I'll stay on then. I'll see how it feels."

"Well, the offer stands."

"Thank you," Rae said. "I appreciate it." She did, too.

Then they were at the jail, and Pam was looking at her doubtfully and saying that maybe she'd come in after all, and then there was a uniform that was like Jerry's but different and much smaller, and a lot of coming and going and delay and doors opening and closing until finally Rae was in a room with Sheriff Escobar and a couple others and she was looking through the mirror at a line of complete strangers. Half a dozen stocky, dark-haired men, with absolutely nothing to distinguish one from the next. They all looked like thugs, although she was dimly aware that they used police personnel to fill out the ranks of a lineup.

"Are both of the men here?" she asked the sheriff, trying not to sound panicky.

"Only one. We'll do a second lineup with another group."

"I just don't know."

"Take your time. Ignore the clothes; think about what part of their faces you saw. You want me to have them turn?"

"I guess."

The line of men dutifully shuffled to face right, then left, and at the final shift of position Rae stiffened.

"Something?" the sheriff asked.

"The fourth one. Could you have him come up and sort of, well, grimace?"

He gave the order to the lineup, and one by one the men came up to the glass, bared their teeth as if checking for stuck spinach, and went back into line. The fourth such grimace sent a jolt through Rae that turned her bowels to ice water.

"That's him," she stammered. "Look, can I use the toilet?"

"Do you identify one of these men, Ms. Newborn? For the record."

"Number four. He's the one who threw me off the road. He had a mustache then. Look, I really need—"

She was whisked away. When she returned, feeling unnaturally empty, a different group of men stood on the other side of the mirror, shifting restlessly at the delay. All were taller than those in the first lineup, and blond-haired, and she waited fearfully for another twist of recognition while they turned from one side to another. Nothing.

"It could be number two," she had to say finally. "But it could be number two's brother, as well. I'm sorry, I can't be anywhere near as certain about this one."

The sheriff did not seem unduly worried about it, and when they had finished the paperwork, Rae looked over at him.

"I didn't pick out two policemen, did I?"

"Oh, no, you most certainly did not. And don't you worry about the second one—we've got something to work on him with now."

"They haven't said anything about who hired them? If anyone?"

"Not yet. But if you want to phone me tomorrow, I'll tell you what I can."

"What about my house being broken into? Did these guys do that, too?"

"I'm afraid they couldn't have. Both of them were in jail when that happened—an alibi that's hard to break. We'll ask them, of course, if maybe they mentioned to somebody that the house might be empty, but somehow I don't think so. Other than the deliberate damage, the break-in itself looked pretty smooth. Maybe not professional, since nothing much was missing, but from a cooler head than these two. You going up there, while you're here?"

"I'm meeting my lawyer there tomorrow, to see if I find anything she and the insurance man missed."

"Let me know if you do. Now, can I get you a ride somewhere? Arrange some dinner?"

"I have someone expecting me, thanks, but if someone could give me a lift across town, it'd be a help."

The someone expecting Rae was her tree merchant and importer of exotic hardwood, Vivian Masters, a sawyer with the name of an English aristocrat, the build of an Olympic weight lifter, the voice of an Australian drover, and the hands of a Dutch diamond cutter. Vivian had been Rae's partner in craft for more than a dozen years before the accident. When she had phoned him from the airport in Seattle to tell him she was coming down and would want to drop by the shop, he had shouted with pleasure, and insisted that she stay with him and his lover (who Rae knew by long experience would be tall, intense, probably bearded, possibly foreign, and lamentably temporary).

When she stepped out of the official car at Vivian's door, he burst from the shop at a run. Arms like steel bands wrapped around her rib cage, a grip that would have triggered a panicky struggle for escape had it been any man in the world other than Vivian. Him she hugged back with equal fervency, her arms around his neck, her chin resting on his hair, as they rocked with the pleasure of seeing each other. Then the wood merchant thrust her at arm's length and declared how positively buff she was, and how the hell was she, anyway, she looked good enough to eat. Rae looked over her shoulder at the bemused driver and waved good-bye, then strolled into Vivian's yard with her arm over his shoulder, his arm around her waist.

Vivian lived, literally, over the shop, which might have had something to do with his various lovers' disinclination to become permanent, but when Rae walked through his shop door she felt her lungs instantly expand, followed a moment later by her soul. The fragrance of a hundred woods filled the air, the distilled essences of topsoils stretching from Borneo to Nicaragua. Two years had passed since Rae last set foot in Vivian's warehouse, and the instantly remembered visceral magnificence of the air caught her unawares. She felt dizzy, frightened and intoxicated simultaneously. She had to sit down, and was aware of tears trembling in her eyes, and of Vivian bending over her in concern.

"I'm okay," she reassured him. "I'd just forgotten."

He straightened to his full five foot five, sawdust-clogged blond Afro and all, and turned to survey his wooden kingdom. "I know. When I'm gone for a while and come back, the bloody place does the same thing to me."

"It's . . . primeval."

He shot her a look that was pure joy. "Shit oh dear, girl, it's fine to see you. Come in, have a drink. Have ten drinks. Let's get smashed to the eyelids and talk about wood and trees and curse the fucking gallery owners. But first you have to meet Jordan. Jor!" he bellowed hugely up the stairway that led to his living quarters. He continued talking as they went up. "I can't believe you two've never met, like my left hand not knowing my right, but I guess it was that Christmas—oh, Christ Almighty." Vivian turned on the narrow stairway to look into Rae's eyes, his voice gone suddenly soft. "What a terrible time that was. I never told you. When I talked to you, coupla days after the funeral, I knew damn well you were goin' through hell up in that house of yours, but you told me you wanted to be alone. I knew I should've gone and snatched you up and brought you here, even then I knew it, and instead of that I let you talk me into leaving you be and just dove in head over heels with Jordan, like some demented teenager with his balls on fire. I was a fucking idiot and—"

She impulsively took his face in her hands and gave him a quick kiss on the lips. "You're not an idiot, and honestly? Nothing you could have done would have made a speck of difference. Even if I'd let you come near, that kind of breakdown is like a broken leg or an earthquake—friends can't make it heal any faster or stop any sooner."

"Yeah," he said in his Aussie drawl, "but mebbe I wouldn't've felt like such a shit."

A voice came down the stairs. "You notice that his primary concern in the matter is the problem of being stuck with a feeling of guilt?"

"A' course," Vivian retorted, instantly happy again. "You don't think I'd worry myself about a mad sheila like Rae, do you? Rae—Jordan Benedict. Jordan my love, this is the other woman in my life. You have to adore her, I order you to, she's a genius."

Rae had never seen Vivian quite so manically Australian before, and it occurred to her that, unlikely as it might be, the man was nervous. The proximity of the mentally ill had that effect on people, but she wondered if in this case it might not be something else. Such as the man in the doorway above them, a man who had survived eighteen months with Vivian Masters (whose relationships had never gone more than four in all the time she'd known him), a man who did, granted, have a beard, but who was neither foreign nor tall, and more comfortable than intense.

His handshake was strong but not assertive, and if he was troubled by Rae as rival—a rival, moreover, who had been smooching Vivian on the stairs—it did not show.

"Hello," he said. He had a book in his left hand, one finger marking his place.

"Good to meet you."

Vivian had pushed past them and was already in the apartment, shouting over the clatter of beer bottles. "Have a beer, Rae? Go and dump your clobber—you know where your room is—and then we'll eat. Here, try this little brewery up in Marin, daft name but paradise in a bottle. Say, you haven't turned into a vegetarian or some crap?"

"No, I eat anything."

"That's a relief. Seems like everybody I know's sworn off meat or drink or both. Don't know how they bloody expect—"

"Vivian." The wood man and his client both stopped what they were doing to look at the source of that gentle, authoritative voice. When he had their full attention, Jordan continued. "I do adore her, Vivian. I recognize her genius. And I'm very happy to share your life with the Other Woman. So would you stop racketing around like a frog in a frying pan? Just calm down. Everything's fine."

Vivian's jaw dropped, then snapped up into a crooked grin. He beamed at Rae, kissed Jordan, and wordlessly went back into the kitchen. Looking calmer. Rae met the man's eyes, saw the depth of affection and humor there, and felt like kissing him herself.

Rae slipped into the evening with the ease of a fish entering its native pool. The meal had been cooked by Vivian, who rarely bothered but when he did always created some culinary echo of himself—blunt, muscular, and full of unexpected subtleties. He couldn't have followed a recipe if his life depended on it, but he stormed around and tossed together unlikely ingredients that worked. Tonight's was vaguely Middle Eastern in flavor, with touches of Japan and New England.

When they had eaten, Vivian shooed Jordan out of the kitchen and handed Rae a dishcloth.

"Final papers," Jordan explained with an apologetic smile as he allowed himself to be pushed out. "Grades are due."

"I'll bring you a coffee when we're done washing up," Vivian shouted after him, and rolled up his sleeves.

"Jordan teaches?" Rae asked.

"At the uni. Part-time, so far—Shakespearean lit and creative writing. He never met Alan," he added, knowing what she wanted to ask. "He's a writer—his first novel's coming out in the fall. Real highbrow stuff, boy growing up in a small town."

Rae made the appropriate noises of interest, but her mind was not on Jordan Benedict's literary future. After a minute, Vivian dropped the sponge in the soapy water and turned to plant his back against the sink.

"What is the matter?"

"I'm sorry, Viv, I'm not being a very good guest, am I?"

"Sod that. What's wrong?"

"I saw the men who attacked me, this afternoon. Stood on the other side of a one-way mirror not four feet from . . . oh Christ, Viv, it was like a nightmare. I honestly expected his hand to come through the glass at me. It's—I mean, it's okay, I'm glad they caught them, but it's left me—"

He seized her shoulders with his wet hands, marched her over to a chair, pushed her into it, then went to the cabinet and poured her a large slug of expensive brandy.

"Drink that." He stood over her until she had swigged half of it, then he nodded. "Nothing like booze for the shakes. Now, tell me everything."

Rae told him, if not everything, at least a clear outline of the last months. He went back to the dishes, and when he had stacked the last pan on the stove, he filled the coffeemaker, then set out cups and a jug of milk. She finished her story about the time the coffeemaker stopped spluttering. Vivian took a cup to Jordan, and when he came back, he poured enough brandy into theirs to dilute the mixture to room temperature.

"You're working now?" he asked, an apparent non sequitur. "Not just the bloody four-by-twos?"

"Gloriana has some idea of the house as subject of a book of photographs. I told her I'd think about it."

"Tell her you'll do it. Do anything. Work, and love—they're what keep anyone from running off the rails."

"You're more firmly on the track than I've ever seen you, Vivian. Jordan's a sweetheart."

"Jor's a bloody wonder. The best thing that ever happened to me. And you—you gonna find someone in those islands of yours?"

It was said as a jest, but Rae hesitated a split second too long with the memory of Jerry's hard mouth on hers before laughing her response. Vivian was on it in an instant.

"You have found someone! Why, you beaut, tell Uncle Viv all."

"No, I haven't found anyone. How could I? I'm a hermit; the only man I see is the aging hippie who brings me groceries. But I'll tell you, he's worth a minute's fantasy, this guy. He's like something out of a Jimmy Buffett song, and he's got these incredible tattoos . . ."

Ed and his skin sidetracked Vivian, and as he refilled their cups, not bothering with the coffee this time, he told her about this tattooed boy he'd once known. The subject drifted safely away from Rae's love life.

The level in the bottle went down, and they moved into the comfort of the living room, where Vivian lit a fire with wood scraps from the shop below. She asked him about recent acquisitions; he told her a few tall tales about the wood trade.

"You wrote me about a piece of burl," she suddenly remembered. "I don't think I even wrote you back, did I?"

"You did not."

"Do you still have it? Let me see it."

"Not tonight. But let me tell you how it came to me," and he was off again, the only man who could make buying and selling dead trees sound like piracy on the high seas.

It was pure pleasure listening to him, watching his eyes gleam like black diamonds. It was even a pleasure, if a bittersweet one, when Jordan came in and joined the conversation for a while before wandering off to bed. She watched him go, unaware of the look on her face, somewhere between wistful and yearning.

"So," Vivian said in a brook-no-nonsense voice when they were alone again. "What's this about you and some bloke?"

"It's nothing, Viv. There's just . . . the sheriff up there seems to have a thing for me."

"Anything wrong with him?"

"Not a thing. He's a few years younger, but not much, and a really nice guy."

"Uh-oh."

"Don't be rude. Alan was nice."

"Alan was a lot of things, but I don't think 'nice' would've been your first word in describing him. What's your sheriff's name?"

"Jerry Carmichael. He's six two, lots of muscle, lived on the islands his whole life. Good sense of humor, sensitive without being sickening about it. He's even a good listener; do you know how few men are good at listening?"

"So what kind of a tree would he be?"

"What kind of— Oh, right. Let me see." Rae had nearly forgotten Vivian's old game, typing people as trees. Vivian himself was clearly a eucalyptus: thirsty Australian native; bending to a certain point and beyond that terribly brittle; unworkably hard when dry; going up in flames at the merest spark. Alan had been bamboo—flexible looking, steel at the core— and Rae, Vivian had once let slip, was one of those Monterey Pines hanging on to the cliff face near the sea, battling the elements but tough and with roots deep in the unfriendly ground. "Jerry's a cedar, I think. Straight, strong, solid, both soft and impervious. Plus that, he smells good." Rae suddenly blushed, and Vivian crowed with laughter.

"Gotcha! So what's he like in bed?"

"Vivian! Alan died less than two years ago. I've known Jerry two months, met him maybe half a dozen times. Though I will admit, he's not bad at kissing."

"'Not bad'? Ah, Rae, come on now."

"What? Damn it, what's wrong with him?" Having been not at all sure she wanted Jerry, she now found herself fully prepared to defend the man against her old friend's scorn.

"Since when is an okay nice guy good enough for you? After Alan, I'd've thought—"

"Don't." Rae was suddenly enraged. "Don't you go there, Vivian. Alan was once in a lifetime."

"You think I don't know that? I knew you before, and during, and now after Alan. I know you well enough to tell you that if you can't have that, you're better just sticking to your work."

Rae gaped at him, incredulous. "You, of all people, say that."

"Too right, me of all people." Vivian was angry now as well, and not just at her attack. "I've spent my life not knowing, and now I do, I see why it was you lit up like a bloody floodlight when you met Alan Beauchamp. Chemistry, electricity—shit, I don't know what it is. But I do know that you'd be a pinheaded moron to take another man into your bed if you didn't have some of that going. You'd kill him dead, with Alan always lying there between you."

"Vivian, you're talking nonsense."

He slammed down his cup so violently it shattered. The smell of spilled brandy filled the air, but Vivian ignored it, ignored the blood running down his finger and the damage being done to the table's finish. He grabbed Rae's arm and hauled her to her feet.

"Come 'ere." He dove for the door, and Rae had no choice but to follow, wondering what the hell this was about. She found him standing in the center of the shop, between a stack of rough-cut oak boards and a shapeless mass nearly the size of a small car draped in a canvas tarp.

"Look at those," he ordered, pointing at the boards.

She looked. "Okay. Very nice." Nothing spectacular, but oak was always an appealing wood, even without a quirk to it.

"Now look at this, and tell me I'm talking nonsense."

He whipped the tarp off the mass with the air of a conjuror, and stood back.

The walnut burl was, at first glance, simply an ugly, ungainly, dense lump of vegetable matter. An untrained eye might have considered it worthy of a bonfire.

Rae's eye saw instantly that this was indeed something special. What had Vivian said in his letter? Just Rae's kind of thing, he'd called it: dark and twisted and completely impossible. She was aware of Vivian's watching her, peering into her face as she bent down to study the twist of grain, running speculative fingertips over the grotesque surface.

"You feel it," he declared triumphantly.

"Vivian, you're a genius."

"Chemistry, God damn it. That stuff there's nice." He cocked his thumb dismissively at the milled lumber. "This"—he slapped the burl—"this bloody beaut's why we both work with goddamn dead trees. And you want to tell me you can go back to that?"

She followed his pointing finger to the boards, which were, in truth, perfectly . . . nice.

"How do you know, Viv? Just because a fabulous piece of wood like this is something you're instantly sure of doesn't mean there aren't other pieces you haven't had to think about first. Since we seem to be stuck on this damned metaphor. How many times have you brought me a piece and said, 'I don't know about this one, Rae'?" She imitated his Australian drawl, which drew a reluctant smile from him.

When he answered, however, he was dead serious. "So how *do* you know, Rae? When I brought you that filthy piece of half-rotted maple that'd been in somebody's basement for ninety years and you made that incredible twisty piece with the ebony drawers, how did you know it was worth bothering with? I'll tell you. It was in your bones. Wasn't it? You felt in your bones there was something great there. So tell me, Rae Newborn: What do your bones tell you about your nice sheriff?"

She picked at the frayed side of the burl for a minute, and then blew out a breath. "I hate you, Vivian."

"Nah. You love me."

"That too."

"Trust your bones, Rae. Trust your bloody bones."

But that night she lay staring at the ceiling, wondering how she could know what her bones thought when the rest of her was so distracted by the memory of Jerry's arms and mouth.

Forty-eight

Desmond Newborn's Journal

October 1, 1926

The poet has declared, No man is an island.

Having resided now for five years on an island among islands, I have to say that the statement is truer here than any other place I have known.

Recluses there are here aplenty, misanthropes or men running from something. Eccentrics abound—the Scotsman rumored to be building an authentic Scottish castle to the north of me, the Oxford graduate explorer and big-game hunter of the last century who seldom wore shoes, and a hundred others.

Each soul here occupies his island home, cut off by a stretch of cold, treacherous water from the warmth of his neighbor's hearth. Even on the more populous of islands, even on those large enough to have a center where the sea is unseen, the resident is never unaware of the salt water just beyond his door.

This knowledge of how alone and endangered we all are is the very thing that binds us together. Only during the war did I find such easy friendships, such ready willingness to lend a hand or a shoulder. On the mainland we pass by our neighbor's drive with nary a glance; here, we peer and crane, to reassure ourselves that all is well with him. On dry land, neighbors argue over fence lines and border encroachments; here, the sea between us, while not precisely an enemy, is never to be trusted with the safety of a child or a neighbor. We know the danger around us; we know who we can trust.

Here, all men are islands, linked by the touch of the sea. That which divides us is what brings us together.

Forty-nine

Vivian was right, Rae decided: If she couldn't have love then work was the best. Friends, and work: the flexing of expert muscles, the shared vocabulary of a passion; the rediscovery of who she had been, what she would be again. And if Rae had drunk far too much the night before, at least the expensive brandy was gentle to her head, and she rose in the morning not suffering too badly.

When Vivian's two assistants came in they wheeled the burl over to the light, and all four woodworkers spent a tense couple of hours arguing about which cut would give them the best grain. Chalk marks were made and rubbed out, half a ton of gnarled, unprepossessing tree trunk was pushed and prodded, and finally the remnant of a living thing, a sapling when Elizabeth Tudor took the throne, was fed into Vivian's enormous saw. They stood tensely, oblivious of the terrible noise, until the sawn slab was separated. Four faces relaxed in the pleasure of the texture and the shape.

Rae circled the slab of wood, already planning how she would work around the incursion of pith in the center, admiring the precision of the cut Vivian had chosen.

"You were right," she told him. "It's absolutely gorgeous."

"I'm always right." He was not talking only about wood.

"You're the man," she agreed.

When they had brushed the sawdust from their hair, Rae and the sawyer climbed into Vivian's ancient Audi and headed up into the hills to Rae's house. Pam Church was meeting them there, and Rae had offered to catch a ride with her instead, but Vivian came from a family of lawyers and did not really believe that a person could be friends with one. Rae did not insist: The more warm bodies she had with her in the house, the better.

The amazing thing, she thought an hour later when she stood beside the car in the redwood-scented quiet, was how little it had changed. Aside from the shiny new electronic security panel on the wall next to the front door, she might have walked away yesterday. Bella might be peeking out of the upper window, Alan sitting at his desk grading papers.

Even her shop was a land of ghosts, the big power machines brooding under their covers, the stacked lumber airing on the heavy shelves, row after row of hand tools gathering dust. She had already told Vivian that she would not be spending the night at her house, if he didn't mind her using his as a hotel; walking through the house with him at her side, she was glad she had done so. Everywhere Rae could feel the faint outlines of Watchers, waiting in the dark spaces among the trees.

While Rae and Pam were occupied with the claims forms and the accumulated bills for house and taxes, Vivian retreated to Rae's shop, where he set about furiously oiling everything in sight against the incursion of rust. When she stuck her head in some time later, he was fussing with the wood, rearranging and turning it, muttering curses under his breath.

Rae left him there, and went through the downstairs rooms with Pam to see if the insurance man had missed any damage or theft. The dust sheets had been taken from the furniture, folded neatly in a tall stack now but showing signs of wear: The top one had been ripped and trampled. Bare wires marked the stereo system; the television set and all its attachments were stripped, the silver cabinet empty. Rae was relieved to find little pure destruction beyond the glass collection, which had been carefully swept up into cartons as if she might want to save it. She pulled open one of the boxes and glanced in at the sparkling fragments, then closed it again sadly. Alan would have wept. Something in the frozen motion and elegance of glass had spoken to him more deeply than it did to Rae, and it was for his pleasure that she grieved over all that once-molten beauty now ground to dust. Still, the invader had not touched the art on the walls, either not knowing its value or realizing the difficulties of unloading Picasso sketches and Modernist prints. Her much-loved and painstakingly assembled collection of furniture—Maloof and Stickley chairs, a Morris settle, an antique apothecary's chest from Japan—was also intact, aside from an ugly bash in a Medieval English trestle table where one of the heavier vases had landed on its way to destruction.

Alan's study, on the other hand, was heartbreaking. The invader appeared to have systematically upended entire file cabinets, strewn about the notes for articles Alan had planned to write, and flung into the air reviews, photographs (*So much for finding that negative of Desmond that Nikki wanted* flickered irrelevantly through Rae's mind), and correspondence dating back twenty years. Alan had kept a display of Bella's drawings tacked to a corkboard beside his desk; the board had been ripped from the wall and stomped, by careless or angry boots, the drawings shredded. When Pam turned around from her contemplation of the computer remnants, she found Rae on her knees, a mutilated drawing in her hands and tears on her face. Pam swore under her breath, and waded over to Rae.

"I'm sorry, Rae, I should have tidied those up. Stupid of me to let you see them."

"I have all the best ones," Rae told her as she allowed the lawyer to pull her to her feet. She surrendered the torn drawing of Petra's horse, watched Pam smooth it out and slide its ragged halves into a drawer, and then looked back at the totality of the destruction and asked in despair, "What was he looking for?"

"Whatever it was, either he didn't find it, or else he did and wanted to hide the fact. Come on, let's get out of here," Pam urged.

Rae followed her back to the kitchen, and started to search through cabinets for the makings of coffee.

"About Don," Pam began.

"Oh, fuck Don," Rae responded.

"No thanks."

"What's he done now?" Rae asked, slamming one cabinet door and jerking open another.

"Nothing, actually. I haven't heard from his lawyers in a couple of weeks."

"Did you expect to?"

"Sure. I fired back a powerhouse of a response, no holds barred, a real don't-fuck-with-me document. I thought it might at least get a letter in reply."

"Maybe you scared the hell out of them, they're withdrawing." Pam just snorted. "Or maybe they sent Don a bill and when he couldn't pay it, fired him."

"Lawyers don't fire clients," Pam responded automatically.

"That was an attempt at humor, Pam." Rae moved on to the next cabinet.

"Rae, we have to talk about him."

"Why, Pam? I'm not just being frivolous: Is there any point in expending more energy talking about Don Collins? Either he continues with the case or he doesn't, the ball's in his court. Hey, here's some coffee. Do you suppose it's still drinkable?" The cupboards were a weird mixture of the utterly familiar and the completely foreign. Rae picked up a box of herbal relaxing tea, its box thick with cheery platitudes, and wondered if it was something Tamara had brought when she came to clean the place up, or if she herself had bought it during the dark time: herbs to keep the Watchers at bay?

"Rae, I do not think that Don has a chance of actually winning this, but he has put together a serious case and he has an aggressive law firm. If he can get his wife to testify that your state of mind remains disturbed, he may well convince a judge to place a hold on what you're allowed to do with your money. He wouldn't win, but you could be tied up in court for years."

Rae was more concerned with what lay beyond the case, and thought the silence from Don's lawyers distinctly ominous. But since she did not know what could be done to avert whatever Don had in mind, she would not go into the possibilities with Pam. The ball truly was in his court; Rae would just have to pretend the silence was encouraging instead of like some jungle movie with the drums falling still. "Then I'll just have to look absolutely boring and sane. Call me Ms. Prozac. I told you they're coming to visit me, didn't I?"

"Who?" Pam sounded alarmed. "Don and Tamara? No, you most certainly did not."

"Petra wants to come stay with me for a week, so they're bringing her."

"And when is this little confrontation to take place?"

"There won't be any confrontation. We're far too well bred for that, didn't you know? A week from tomorrow. On the first."

"Of July? Jesus, woman, are you nuts?"

Rae stared at her furious lawyer, and began to laugh, a bit wildly. "Of course I'm nuts, you idiot—what do you think all this has been about?"

"Oh, shut up," Pam snapped. "You know what I mean. Look, you have to cancel. It'd be just asking for trouble, inviting Don into your front yard just when this legal action is under way."

"I don't have a front yard."

"Rae!"

"Sorry, I'm sorry. Okay, I admit a visit with Don there is going to be really, really uncomfortable, but assuming I refrain from braining him with a two-by, I can't see that his coming or not is going to make any difference. I live on Folly, I'm not going to deny that. Some people might think that it's a nutty place to live, but my house is coming along, it's going to be a nice, conventional building—well, more or less. At any rate, it has straight walls and level floors and insulation, and it'll have a real roof before too long. I have a water supply. It's even fairly compliant with the state building code. Would an insane woman worry about the building code?"

"What's a two-by?"

"A two-by-four. You know, construction lumber? God, you're ignorant."

"I'm a lawyer, not a contractor, what do I know from lumber?"

"And what do I know from law? Pam, if you're flat out telling me not to have any contact with Petra or her parents, I'm sorry, but I can't do that. Contact with my granddaughter is what this is all about, remember? If there are specific things I ought to do or not do, say or not say, let me know and I'll try my very best to follow your orders. Otherwise, we'll have to let the courts muddle along until they throw it out. It might even work out for the best. I mean, Don's probably hoping that while he's there he'll spot something or I'll let something slip that he can use as evidence, but what about when I don't? And surely having them leave Petra with me indicates a strong degree of trust? How could they claim I'm dangerous if they feel she's safe alone with me? Look, I'm even making friends up there—that must count for something. The park ranger and the sheriff stop by all the time." Maybe Ed was not the best person to offer as a character witness, Rae reflected.

"The sheriff?"

"He's always dropping by. Brings me flowers. And steaks. Once he brought a bottle of champagne."

"Really?"

"It's very rude to sound surprised, Pam."

"Sorry," the lawyer said, sounding more curious than apologetic. "It's just that I can't imagine you with anyone but Alan."

"I'm not with anyone but Alan. We're not having an affair. We're not going to have an affair. There's no . . . chemistry."

"Then why are you smirking?" the suspicious lawyer asked.

"Just a private joke. But Jerry is very smart, good-looking, nice sense of humor, stable as a mountain, so he'd make an ideal character witness. And the ranger is the most gorgeous woman you ever set eyes on. If we had a jury trial, between the two of them, all twelve jurors would be drooling."

This seemed to please Pam considerably more than Rae's straight walls and water supply. Now there was a picture, Rae reflected: her cedar tree of a sheriff in uniform, testifying with calm and complete authority. And Nikki—if she was a tree, she'd be a—what? Something rare and exotic that was deviously hard to work, with lots of splintery bits to get under your skin but absolutely gorgeous when you'd finished. And Ed? Hmm. Ed was a cipher. A tree whose appearance gave no clue about its wood inside. Tamara was a fine, hard-working shade tree with rot at its base, and Don was without a doubt not a tree but poison oak, insidious, all-pervasive, and bringing a person out in blisters by mere proximity.

Rae shook off her thoughts. Abandoning the coffee, which smelled even more rancid than the swill she'd been given by Escobar, Rae stood up and told Pam she thought she'd go upstairs for a look.

"I'll come with you."

"No, I'd rather be alone. To say good-bye. Or something."

Halfway up the stairway, Rae paused: Five years ago, her hands had refinished the oak she stood on, wood that bore the memory of Alan and Bella's feet, father's like daughter's so often bare, going up to bedrooms and television room, down to the breakfast table and the family hearth. The *pat pat pat* of Bella's ghostly feet ran past Rae in the hallway, to precede her to the room Rae had shared with Alan with its big bed that had welcomed the day-old Bella home, the big bed where, often as not, Bella came to cuddle in the mornings, the bed where Rae and Alan had slept and talked and loved. Rae walked through the room, past the naked mattress, to push back the glass door to the balcony. She breathed in the dusty tang of the redwoods and sat down in the dirty wooden chair where she had sat so many mornings, looking out over a hillside that was somehow not as familiar as it had been, her ears seeking out the trickle of the tiny stream that Bella had dammed and fished and splashed in.

Home.

And yet, not home. While she was here, Alan and Bella were no longer the static, frozen mental images that she had encased in her memory. They moved and breathed here, but only as echoes (*Mommy!*) of her life with them. With their odors still buried in the folded blankets and their voices playing the air around her, Rae came face-to-face with the knowledge that, in spite of everything, she had moved on; they had died and she had not—and more than merely being alive, she had grown and she had changed, so that she was no longer the person who had flourished in this place. She still loved those two as she would never love another; she would never cease to mourn them, but she finally had to admit that losing them had not brought about the world's end. Whether or not she would ever live between these walls again was an open question, but if she did, it would be as a different Rae Newborn.

One other thing Rae knew, there in the chair with the ghost of a husband sliding back the glass door, planting a stubbly kiss on the back of her neck in his morning greeting, putting a steaming cup of tea on the chair's wide arm, knew suddenly and with all the clarity of a voice speaking in her ear: The gun that she had cradled to her breast, the smooth wooden grip, the cool steel, the sweetly seductive bullets, would remain unused; the pistol that had killed Desmond Newborn would not be turned against his great-niece as well.

"I miss you, Alan," she said into the air. "I love you. Take care of Bella."

Then she closed and locked the sliding door, and went downstairs to tell her companions that she was ready to leave.

She and Vivian returned to his house, to the rich odors and provocative shapes. He had suggested asking a few of Rae's close friends over for an informal meal that evening, and she had agreed, but the early exhilaration of her return could not hold out against the grind of unfinished business, during the afternoon and the following morning. Jail visits and phone calls, legal papers and good friends with a surfeit of joy and worry in their eyes; far, far too many people altogether, for a woman accustomed to solitude. She tucked the hours with Vivian's wood into her memory, and got on with the rest of it. By the third day, she was more than ready to leave.

She crawled into the plane's back-row seat, too tired for nerves, and kept her eyes closed for the entire trip. The small connecting plane bounced and rattled and touched down onto San Juan Island just before dusk. Ed met her in an equally rattly pickup truck, transferred her onto the *Orca Queen,* and took her out to Folly. He spoke so little, she wondered if she had done something to offend him—or maybe he was just intimidated by her linen-jacketed transformation from builder to imitation lawyer. In either case, she did not feel up to asking him, and although she offered coffee, she did not argue when he turned it down.

"I will walk you up to the tent, though," he said.

"No, no, I'm fine."

"You don't have a flashlight."

"It's plenty light enough. The moon's up, and I'm used to walking around in the dark. Don't worry about me."

"Well, if you say so." He held the boat against the dock until she was safely on shore, and then allowed it to drift free. "Good to have you back, Mizz Newborn." Not "Rae," she noted.

"Thank you, Ed. See you Tuesday."

The lights receded, the engine noise faded. Rae climbed onto the promontory, dropped her knapsack at her feet, and raised her face to the night. She hadn't seen stars for four days, wouldn't have known if the moon had fallen from the sky, and every cell in her body told her she'd been breathing other people's exhalations for far too long. Even the silence here was different. It comforted, like a friend who didn't demand conversation. Unlike the silence surrounding Don Collins and his damnable court case, a silence that reminded her of Desmond's description of no-man's-land, straining for the sounds of a sneaking enemy. She should have instructed Pam to pursue it—pursue him—and find out just what he was up to. This was no time to play aloof, not with Don himself about to arrive.

Or maybe not. Maybe it was best to ignore the whole thing. Yes, things did go away on their own, sometimes.

She exhaled, rubbed her fingers through her cropped hair, stretched luxuriously, and then glanced at the dark sailboat lying offshore. The hell with them, she decided, and stripped off for a brief and icy nude swim in the cove.

She dressed and laid a fire, but before it was going fully she went up to the house. The bare clean walls echoed her footsteps, and the fragrance greeted her like a friend. The building lay in stasis, the stack of cedar triangles for the stairs where she had abandoned them on Tuesday morning, her tool belt on its nail over the secret door. The hammer brushed her arm as she went by to retrieve her gun from its hiding place. The cave's air felt dry enough against her face, so she left the toolbox with its beautiful chisels where it was, and shoved the gun into the front pocket of her hooded sweatshirt. It dragged down like some leaden marsupial baby, but it made her feel safer against the rustles of the night.

The fire was going well when she got back to the campsite, sparks rising into the darkness, and she heated and ate a can of beans and some limp vegetables. She took the kettle from the hottest part of the fire and poured the water over a teabag in her mug, turned off the lamp to keep the flocks of moths from getting any thicker, and was just sitting down again when she heard the unmistakable rhythmic scrunch of footsteps approaching—and not from the beach, either, but from the hillside behind the tent. The mug of tea flew into the air as Rae lunged for the fallen cedar, scrambling over in a desperate effort of clumsy limbs, fighting to free the gun from its confining pocket.

The footsteps came closer, matter-of-fact footsteps with nothing stealthy about them, which was in itself terrifying. Half a dozen steps more, and they rounded the tent, and there they stopped. Rae squinted past the rising sparks at the indistinct shape—and there was actually someone there, someone *was* there, an indistinct but solid figure taller than the side wall of the tent. The only thing about the intruder that Rae could see clearly were a pair of male hands, held forward so they were in the light, long fingers spread wide and palms angled outward in a declaration of peace.

"I have a gun," she choked out.

"I know," said a voice, and something about the intonation, combined with the shape of his hands, gave her pause. The gun drooped slightly as she raised her head up to see past the fallen tree.

"Jerry?" she asked uncertainly.

"No," the ghostly figure replied. "It's Alan."

Fifty

Desmond Newborn's Journal

June 6, 1925

At long last, the walls of my house have begun to rise up above the stones. And yet they bring me no small degree of sorrow, that walls are necessary at all. On a night like tonight, I should like to leave my house open to the breezes and the birds, to allow the moon's great light to shine freely beneath the merest shadow of the roof.

However, the crows and the raccoons would rob me blind, and after four years here, the endless, nerve-racking feeling of vulnerability that comes of constant exposure, of sitting on a dark shore beneath a solitary light, grows no less wearisome.

Fifty-one

Afterward, Rae could never quite believe that she hadn't just shot him where he stood. Certainly the electrical reaction of that name among all others fizzing through her should by all rights have jerked her already twitchy finger tight against the steel tongue of the trigger. It would not have taken much of a pull. Instead, she froze, unbreathing and unblinking behind her fallen tree, staring across the leaping fire at the two wide-stretched hands, and then her heart gave a convulsive thud and time began to run again.

"I could shoot you right there," she found herself saying, as if the words might take the place of the actual deed.

The man's fingers spread a fraction of an inch wider. "Please don't," he said.

For some reason, that response brought Rae up short. After a minute, she cleared her throat, which felt inexplicably raw.

"Why shouldn't I?"

"Because I came to talk to you, unarmed, openly. I even waited until you had your gun with you. It hardly seems fair that you'd then use it on me."

His voice was low and melodious, his words reasonable, his tone, incredibly enough, humorous, and Rae was opening her mouth to tell him to step forward into the light when a horrible thought occurred to her: If he knew about her gun, then he could have laid hands on it. Trying to keep one eye on him while she was peering into the opened chamber left her vulnerable, but he stayed where he was, and all five bullets nestled securely in their spaces, untampered with as far as she could tell. She was tempted to fire one round into the night, just to be sure, but there were too many innocent people out there.

"Come forward so I can see you," she ordered, her voice none too firm.

He edged up until she could make out the features of a tall, slim, wide-shouldered man in his fifties whose face had the vulnerable look of some-one who had recently shaved off a beard. His short hair was newly cut as well, and for some reason looked as if he had normally worn it longer—perhaps because the drawn, almost ascetic lines of his face called for the frame of hair waving to below the ears. It seemed an oddly romantic image, for there was nothing particularly saintly about the rest of the intruder. He wore a faded plaid shirt under a short denim jacket, dark jeans that needed a wash, and stained hiking boots. No jewelry, not even a watch. His hands stayed up, fingers splayed, motionless as the rest of him under her gaze.

The naked skin of his face was the only remotely vulnerable thing about the man. His brown eyes were impassive—remarkably calm for a man with a gun pointing at him. Almost as if he were the armed one here. If he had come to kill her, she thought, he would do it efficiently; she wouldn't get beaten up and raped first.

Cheerful idea. Her gaze went back to his face; it reminded her vaguely of someone she knew.

"Who are you?"

"My name is Allen Carmichael."

"Alan—Are you related to Jerry?"

"He's my brother."

A few—a very few—things came together in her mind. "You're the brother who disappeared. He told me about you."

"Oh yeah? And what did he tell you?"

A faint sardonic shading to the question stung Rae into bluntness.

"Among other things that you'd never gotten over Vietnam."

"Vietnam was one of those things that proved hard to get over, all right. Some of us have had to settle for working around it instead."

"Are you Alan A-L-A-N?" she asked suddenly. That close a similarity really would be too much to bear.

"A-double L-E-N," he said, to her relief. Then he asked, "You were close to someone with the same name, weren't you?"

Suspicion flared again and the gun went back up. "How did you know that? Have you been in my things?"

To Rae's astonishment, the man threw back his head and laughed, a deep-throated, full-bellied guffaw. It was the most amazing thing he'd done so far, and truth to tell, she was sorry when a moment later he caught himself and raised his hands again.

"When you first got here," he explained, "I was up on the hillside trying to figure out what the hell you were doing here, and I leaned against a dead branch. You must have heard, because you picked up a piece of firewood and threw it in my direction and then you started shouting— at me. 'Allen, you son-of-a-bitch,' on and on. You were furious, which I couldn't figure out, and you knew my name—that really freaked me. I decided later that I must have heard you wrong, but at the time, I tell you, it had me worried. And then tonight when I said my name, you reacted so strongly, 'Allen' itself must mean something to you."

A brief silence fell across the fire pit. "My husband's name was Alan," Rae told him. "He died."

"Ah," he said, and then, in a different voice, "Oh. So tonight, when I told you my name, you must have thought . . . Christ, it's a wonder you didn't blow me away."

"What are you doing here?"

"That's what I wanted to talk to you about. Can I sit down? My arms are getting tired."

She thought about it, then said, "Sit down on that chair, in the light where I can see you."

"I'd rather not be too close to the fire, if you don't mind. If anyone came into the cove and spotted me, you might have problems explaining this. That could disrupt the plans of a lot of good people."

She should have insisted; after all, she had the gun, and he was on her property, a potential threat. But what in her youth she would have called the man's "vibes" did not raise her hackles. For a reason she could not have begun to explain, it seemed natural to nod and say, "All right, but sit at the edge of the light, so I can see you."

Moving deliberately, the tall man picked up the chair Rae had been about to sit in several minutes earlier and moved it back from the light. He stepped forward, hesitated, bent down to retrieve her fallen tea mug and place it on a nearby stump-table, then sat down. When his hands were resting, clearly visible, on the chair's wooden arms, Rae swung her leg over the tree trunk and dropped to the ground in front of it, her back to the bark. The firelight touched his nose and mouth, and she suddenly knew where she had seen him before, why his face seemed to require more hair.

"You were in the pickup, waiting in line for the ferry the night . . ."

She paused, and went on more slowly. "The night the Andrews girl disappeared."

"Damn," he said, his monk's features relaxing into a rueful smile. "I knew you'd made me then. I should have pulled my hat down and pretended to be asleep, but I saw you coming up the road and, well, I couldn't help trying to get a closer look at my landlady."

Rae narrowed her eyes and adjusted her grip around the gun. "Would you care to explain that statement?"

"I live here. On Folly. Not all the time, just a few days here and there, and I'll admit I've never put the address on my driver's license, but for the last eight years this has been what I think of as home."

"But . . . where?"

"A cave, on the other side of the island. A small cave, just above sea level but it's dry and warm enough, and not far from fresh water. Pretty basic shelter, little more than a hole in the earth, but it's actually comforting that way."

"And where do you live when you're not in the cave?" she asked. *Why are you interested?* she asked herself. *Because damn it, this is an interesting man,* came the response.

"Wherever work calls me. Los Angeles. Denver. Spokane. Last month, by mere coincidence, work called me here. As it has a handful of times in the past. And that's why I'm talking to you now, because having you here on the island changes things. It would be difficult for you to plead ignorance, if I were caught here. You could be considered an accomplice. Now, if you chose to take the risk, that would be a different matter, but I can't allow you to be made vulnerable in ignorance."

"You're doing something illegal on Folly," Rae said. "Smuggling. What is it—drugs? guns? Freon?"

"Freon?"

"I understand there's a lot of money in smuggling the stuff."

"Freon. Live and learn. No, what I smuggle may be technically against various laws, but it's not for money, and it's never in my opinion immoral. I smuggle people."

"People? People as in criminals, or people as in illegal immigrants?"

"I'll take the fact that you differentiate between the two as an encouraging sign." This time his smile was crooked, almost boyish, and something deep inside her flipped right over: That was Alan's smile. "No, people as in abused children and wives who are in danger. People as in underground railway."

"Caitlin Andrews—you *did* take her off that ferry."

"And I kept her here for nine interminable days until her mother could join us. Poor kid—she was so sick and tired of my music collection by the end of it. Anyway, the two of them stayed together in the cave for a night, then I passed them on north."

"Jerry thought it was something like that."

"My brother?" He sounded alarmed.

"He figured it out, from the parents' reactions and then the girl's mother disappearing like that. He even used the same term: 'underground railway.' He was sympathetic. At least, he didn't seem to think anyone ought to search too hard for them."

"Interesting," he mused. "Still, Jerry's a cop, through and through, and if he came across this section of the railroad, he could do a lot of damage. And that's why I'm here now. If you feel you need to tell him, please, say so now. If you are uncomfortable about any of this, just tell me and I'll remove myself from the island. I know you're close to Jerry, and it's not fair to ask you to keep something like this from him. If you're having a relationship with him, just say the word and I'll be gone."

"I'm not."

"But he comes here."

"Jerry's a friend. And you say he figures things out, but I'd say that when it comes to personal relationships, he's a bit of a dunce. You know Nikki Walls? Of course you do, you were married to her . . . sister, was it?"

He did not answer, just asked, "Is Jerry interested in Nikki?"

"Well, no, but—" Rae stopped. Was any of this his business? Or was he simply maneuvering to get her guard down, and then—what? If he wanted to attack her, why wait until she had a gun in her hand? Something else that he had said then registered in her mind.

"Spokane. Two girls disappeared there."

"Ellie and Joanna Rugeley."

"Your work?"

"Mine and others'."

"Why?"

"Their mother was dead. The father was raping them. They had an aunt in Europe who wanted them. I helped them reach her."

Four simple declarative sentences; two lives snatched out of hell. If she could believe him. "Do you have any proof?"

"Of what? That the bastard was abusing them, or that I helped them get out?"

"That the girls reached their aunt."

"Ah," he said, understanding what she was asking. "And proof that Caitlin and Rebecca are together, and alive."

"Yes."

"Of course I do. Believe me, I document everything, cover my ass every step of the way. Signed letters from friends, neighbors, and teachers, statements by their doctors, tape recordings of what goes on in the house when the doors are shut, videos if I have them. And afterward, I get dated proof that they're still alive a couple of weeks later. I don't know if the letter from Caitlin and Rebecca has arrived yet, but I have one from Eleanor and Joanna. You may have read about Joanna writing a friend to say they'd both run away? That's part of the process, taking the heat off. They wrote at the same time to me, for my records. I could show you their letter, but I keep everything in Seattle. We'd have to go there."

"So you don't have anything here that would make me believe that you didn't . . . kill those girls." Rae braced herself for some reaction, from outrage to violence, but there was none. He remained as he had been all along, serious and watchful.

"Nope, not here. I don't keep any evidence at all on the island, nothing that could be traced. You never know when some kid'll stumble onto the cave. Not worth the risk."

His final word hung in the air between them. They looked across the fire at each other while Rae tried to decide what to do. Allen Carmichael was a self-confessed criminal, a large male trespasser who had stepped out of the darkness into her life, and every bit of good sense yelled at her that she ought somehow to tie him to a tree and hand him over to his brother.

However, good sense had never been Rae's strongest point. And she could hear Vivian in her ear, dead serious under his humor: *Trust your bones, Rae.*

Her bones, she knew, should be quaking. A woman who couldn't walk through a nice, safe, crowded airport without being certain that someone was about to attack her, a woman with vivid memories of what solitary places could hold, what strangers could do—she should have been on the edge of sheer terror. What was wrong with her well-oiled panic mechanism? She ought to get up and race for the promontory, shrieking and rousing the sailboat and everybody else for miles; instead, the gun in her hand was feeling less and less necessary, her position hunched up beside the fallen cedar more and more ridiculous. Her bones were telling her that Allen

Carmichael was exactly what he said. Her bones were saying she should offer him a drink. Her bones were tired of sitting on the hard ground.

Hell. Every important decision she'd ever made had been utterly irrational. Falling in love with Alan, having Bella, turning to woodworking, coming to Folly—all irresponsible, all transforming. Why not one more, knowing it might be her last? *Trust your bones, Rae.*

Rae removed her finger from the trigger guard of the old revolver and pushed the weapon back into her sweatshirt pocket. With the motion, her—what? Guest? Tenant? Resident serial killer?—relaxed more fully into his chair, and when she was on her feet again, she saw that the smile now reached his eyes.

"Do you want a drink?" she asked him.

"I'd love one."

"Wine, beer, or Scotch? They're all warm, I'm afraid."

"A beer, thanks—or no; I'll have a proper drink with you. A small Scotch."

She poured two, and settled into the chair across from him. Carmichael held up his glass to her, and said, "To sanctuary."

"To Sanctuary," she repeated. They both took a swallow, as if sealing a pact.

"I'm curious," he said, stretching his legs out to the fire. "Tell me about my brother and Nikki."

"There's nothing to tell, really. As I read it, Jerry's enough of a gentleman to think that because he's known Nikki since she was a kid, and because she could have pretty much any man on the islands, his being fifteen years older than she is leaves him out of the running."

"Jerry is a fool," he agreed. He took a sip from his glass, rolling it around his tongue in pleasure.

"Nikki'll have him in the end, I think. He needs someone he can feel he's protecting."

"But I saw him bring you flowers," the sheriff's brother protested, without thinking.

Rae went still as suspicion returned, nibbling around the edges of her mind. "You do watch me, don't you?"

"No. Not you. But I do always check for visitors in the cove before I take my boat out, and I happened to see him the other night, sitting here with a fresh bunch of store-bought flowers on the table. I do not watch you, not since the first days."

Rae wasn't sure it was the entire truth he was telling, but remarkably enough, her nerves did not react to the thought of those eyes on her from the hill above. She could read no threat in Allen Carmichael's eyes, no judgment even, just a great deal of understanding. She suddenly thought, He must be very good with frightened children and . . . and with those women for whom men were generally threatening.

"Tell me what you do, exactly."

"What, in vanishing people?"

"Yes, your organization. Does it have a name?"

"No name, no real organization in the sense of a public face. It's mostly women," he explained, "helping other women get away from impossible and often dangerous situations. But sometimes a man is needed, for muscle or distraction or just to act like a husband where the police aren't looking for a couple. And sometimes we have to put clients on ice for a few days, vanish them off the face of the earth. That's where I come in. I vanish them, until the search cools off and we can put them on the next stage."

"How on earth did you get involved with it?"

The dark eyes dropped to the glass in his hands; Rae remembered Jerry saying something about an incident in Vietnam. "That's okay," she said. "You don't have to tell me."

"A person's experiences transform them," Carmichael began, as if she hadn't spoken and he had merely been pulling together his thoughts. "Literally change the structure of the brain. In my case, a single experience during the war stripped my brain down and rebuilt it, completely. It was what the papers label an 'atrocity.' A bunch of scared, angry boys with M16s in their hands were pushed to the breaking point and turned on the nearest convenient target, which happened to be a civilian village. Forty-three innocent people died, women and children and old people. I could have prevented it, if I'd been paying attention, but I wasn't. I didn't.

"They haunt me," he said simply. "Especially the little kids. I hear their voices—some of them were still alive when I entered the village. And, to make a very long and convoluted story short, after I returned home, I eventually discovered that the only way I could sleep at night was if I spent the day in the service of children."

Rae could find no reply to that. He raised his eyes to hers, and smiled at what he saw. "Don't look like that, for heaven's sake. I have a purpose to life, a job that matters and that I do well. How many people do you know who can say that?"

"Your calling," she murmured. "A quest." Why did images of monastic discipline and knighthood's nobilities surround this tired, dusty-looking man?

"I don't know if I'd go so far as that," he replied. "To tell you God's honest truth, I sometimes think I do it just because I'm a troublemaker, and I really, really like getting away with things."

He had a gorgeous laugh, deep and full and infectious.

"And here I thought it was the younger brother who was supposed to be the rebel against the older," she commented.

"Yeah, me and Jerry . . . I tell you, I'd just decided to come clean with you on Tuesday morning when who should I spy but my little brother, come to spirit you away? I was sure he'd found me and was getting you out of the way before they brought up the troops and the bloodhounds, but the troops never landed."

"No, I had to go to California for a few days on another matter."

"I figured you wouldn't be gone long, once I saw the way you left things."

"It was you who searched my tent, wasn't it? Before that—a couple of weeks ago."

"Your tent was searched?" Carmichael leaned forward sharply, squinting to see her face. "When?"

"Sometime between when I finished framing the roof—the night you saw Jerry here with the flowers—and the day before I left for California."

"Sorry, it wasn't me. I did have a quick glance through when you first came, for which I apologize, but I've had my hands full since then. Must've been some kids off the boats. I've chased two sets of them away the last few days, making ghost noises. Which reminds me—don't be surprised if you hear rumors that Folly's haunted."

More and more, Rae was beginning to mistrust her memory. She had been sloppy and left the toolbox tray the wrong way around, that was all. She stretched out an arm for the bottle and replenished their glasses.

"How did you find the cave?" she asked. "Your cave. I didn't see it when I went around the island."

"I discovered the opening when I was a kid—used to sail all around these islands—but it's obvious that other people have used it over the years. Smugglers, rumrunners. It's tucked in behind a small rock spit, with trees down to the ground, not far from the waterfall. I've encouraged the tree branches to grow down to cover it, but it's hard to see even without that, and nearly impossible to get into except at low tide."

"Are you the idiot who wrecked his boat?"

"What?"

She laughed, and then laughed again at the sound. She felt as if her skin had suddenly taken wing. She felt like a winter-dead tree bursting into full flower. She felt . . . she felt at ease. And not only because of the alcohol. "Jerry told me that he'd only known two idiots who would have tried to get onto Folly except through the cove, and one of those wrecked his boat trying."

"Hell no—I was the one who made it. In fact, that was the day I found the cave, when I was rescuing Jerry. *He* was the idiot who wrecked his boat on the reef. Dad was furious."

"What a pity I can't give him a hard time about that."

"You could always have heard it from someone else. It was common knowledge when we were kids. Not the cave, of course."

"You really keep people there?" Desmond might have found the little cave behind the house a cozy retreat in stormy weather, but she wouldn't care to spend many hours cooped up there.

"It's actually fairly comfortable. Some of the older kids call it the hobbit hole, and the younger ones seem to think it's where Rabbit lives in *Winnie-the-Pooh*. Teenage girls have the hardest time with it at first— no hair dryer or Internet. I have a collection of posters they can put up— that helps, and every CD you can think of. I go through a ton of batteries for the CD players."

"Low tide," she said suddenly. "I've heard you going in and out at low tide. You have a black inflatable."

He looked chagrined. "I *knew* you'd seen me. Sooner or later you'd have found me out."

"Without a boat of my own, it would have been difficult. Would you like another drink?" Both glasses were empty.

"Better not. Two's more than I usually have in a day."

"Coffee, then? You know, I really don't know if I can call you . . . that name. It's just too weird for me."

"A lot of people call me Mike, from my last name."

"Mike. Michael okay?"

"Sure. And I would kill for a cup of coffee. It's one of the things I can't risk, down in the cave. Any odor that stands out against the smell of seaweed, I have to avoid."

As Rae was filling the kettle, she suddenly chuckled. "You know the joke about Adam naming the animals?" Allen/Michael shook his head. "Well, it's not really very funny. But anyway, Adam is sitting there in the

Garden of Eden naming the animals. God's bringing each one and Adam takes a look and says, 'I'll call this one a *parrot,* and that one's a *tiger,* the next one's called a *giraffe.*' God is waiting for Adam to find Eve, you see, to choose another creature he wants to spend his life with, and Adam just keeps on inventing these names—*porcupine, cat, rhinoceros.* So the day's wearing on, God is getting a little impatient, and Adam's names are getting more and more outlandish—*guppy,* he says, *platypus, hippopotamus*—and finally God's getting tired of the whole thing, and when He brings in this weird-looking animal and Adam says, '*Aardvark,*' God just explodes. 'Why on earth are you giving My creatures these bizarre names?' He shouts. 'No one will ever respect an animal with a name like aardvark.' 'Well,' says Adam, who's pretty fed up with the whole thing himself, having spent the day expecting a wife and getting all these damned animals instead, 'what would You name it?' And God says, 'How about Mike?'"

Rae looked at Allen and Allen looked at Rae, and Allen spoke first, his face straight but twitching. "You're absolutely right. The joke's not really very funny."

They collapsed simultaneously into howls of laughter, sweeping away the last dregs of tension.

"No," Rae admitted eventually, "but it's appropriate." She turned to pour the steaming water onto the coffee grounds, and the aroma filled the air.

"So what, you want to call me Aardvark?"

"Now there's a thought," she replied. "What do you take in your—"

But he was not to get any coffee that night. A powerful engine that neither of them had noticed was coming into the cove; the sound cut through the easy camaraderie like an axe. There was a quick scurry from the other side of the fire pit, and Rae turned to find Allen Carmichael vanished into thin air; only the gentle rising of the canvas seat betrayed his existence. For the first time, Rae called his name; the sound of footsteps on the other side of the tent halted.

"Look," she said to the shadows, "you're welcome to use the cave, and anything else on the island you need. I won't say anything to your brother. In fact, let me know if I can help, if you need money or something."

"Thank you," came his low voice. "I'll be gone for a couple of weeks. I'll let you know when I get back."

"Good luck," she told the tent wall.

"Hide the glass I was using," he ordered, and with a scrabble of his boots on the hillside, Folly's ghost was gone.

Vibram soles, she noted to herself. She missed him already.

She picked up his glass from the tree-stump table and put it on the ground behind the corner of the tent, then lit the lamp again. As she walked down to the dock with it to see what had brought Jerry Carmichael to her island at eleven-thirty at night, she found she was humming. It took her a moment to identify the tune, and when she did, she shook her head at herself: "Someone to Watch Over Me" . . .

At least Jerry hadn't brought flowers. And he was in uniform, although it was clear even by the light of a kerosene lamp that his clothing lacked its customary crisp polish.

"You look like you've had a long day," she told him.

"Very long. Sorry it's so late—I took a chance you'd still be up, and when I saw your fire going I thought it'd be okay. Bobby Gustafsen decided to break up a fight by himself last night, got stabbed in the arm. He'll be fine, but I got the call at two in the morning, and that's when my day began. So yeah, it's been a long one." He collapsed into the chair that his brother had just so hastily vacated. The frame gave an alarming creak, but he stretched out his long legs toward the fire with a sigh, making himself at home. "Is that coffee I smell?"

Startled, Rae glanced at the cooktop where the French press pot stood, its plunger still waiting. There were two cups next to it, but since there were three more lined up behind them, the intended use was not too glaring.

"I felt like a cup," she told him.

"Looks like you felt like a whole pot."

"Well, you know how it is, you get in the habit of making certain quantities of things. My grandmother was incapable of making less than a gallon of potato salad, even when it was just for her and her husband." *You're babbling, Rae,* she cautioned herself sternly. "Sorry, but I don't have any milk."

"I'll have some sugar, if you have any. For the energy."

She handed him the tight-lidded tin of sugar and a clean spoon. "If you've had such a long day, what couldn't wait until tomorrow?"

"I had a call this evening. Sam Escobar charged the two men you identified, and they've confessed."

"Oh, God, Jerry. What a relief. Oh, thank you for coming to tell me. Both of them?"

"Both. And—maybe you should sit down for a minute."

"Why? What is it?" He just looked pointedly at the chair until she plunked down onto it, then he went on.

"It wasn't just the assault."

"What do you mean? What else was there?" She was going to strangle him in a minute, if he didn't start talking.

"Remember when you told me that you'd been hallucinating noises outside your house?"

"And you said how did I know they were hallucinations, and I told you I knew."

"Well, maybe some of them were. But it was also these two. They'd been hanging around your place for a couple of weeks."

"Hanging arou—you mean, around the house itself? Jesus, how creepy! But why?"

"That was what they were paid for, not the attempted . . . assault. To harass you at night, every night, till you were going nuts."

"It sure as hell worked," Rae said, barely aware of what she was saying.

"I'm afraid, however, that they couldn't identify the man who hired them. He reached them at a bar phone, and he'd call them the same way every couple of days. They'd tell him what they'd done, what you were doing; he'd give them orders on what to do next. He paid them in cash, envelopes dropped and picked up, so they never even saw him. They stayed in a motel near the freeway, slept days, drove out and parked in a back road the guy told them about, hiked over the ridge to your house. In the dark—one of them was fed up with that side of it, and was about to quit when the voice on the phone told them they could finish up the job in one more trip."

He was watching her closely to gauge her reaction; but the possibilities this revelation opened up were too enormous to grasp all at once. She felt a moan building in her throat, swallowed it down, and asked a more or less random question that might have concerned someone else entirely.

"What . . . what exactly did he tell them to do then?"

"They were to hurt you, but not badly, and it wasn't to look like you'd been beaten up, but maybe like you fell down. Mostly he wanted them to frighten you. Terrify you. That's what he was after."

Not to rape me? she thought.

Were there no imaginary Watchers, then? Rae asked herself in wonder. *None at all? My Watchers and the two men on the road that day, one and* *the same, equally real and solid? <u>All</u> the Watching eyes and the footsteps? All that time, in the house, along the road, in the night . . . ?*

No, she decided, reluctant but sure. *Uh-uh; not possible.*

"He paid them two thousand bucks each," Jerry went on. "He promised them double that, but he never called back with the directions for picking up the last payment. Escobar's trying to work backward to find how the guy got ahold of them in the first place, how he knew they'd be willing. It's going to take a while."

It was going to take a while for Rae to work out the meaning of this to her, as well. One thing she knew, though, beyond a doubt: Some of those Watchers had indeed been no more corporeal than the shift of synapses in her brain. But to think that there were other, actual live bodies tapping on her windows and walking across her deck . . . After the initial shock, she began to feel giddy with relief. She was not insane—or yes, she was, but perhaps not as dreadfully out of touch with reality as she and everyone else had assumed.

The sheriff was staring at her with an expectant and worried expression; Rae roused herself. "Sorry, what did you just say, Jerry?"

"I said, we have to face the fact that the man behind this is still out there. I think you should move into Roche Harbor for a while, at night anyway."

She scrubbed at her numb face for a minute, then looked up at him. "Are you saying that as a sheriff, or as a friend?"

He opened his mouth to answer, then paused. When he started to speak again, Rae could see what his answer was going to be, by the abashed look he wore.

"I guess I just don't like the idea of your being out here all alone."

"In other words, there's no reason to believe that this nameless . . . what do you call it? Stalker? That he hasn't crawled back into his hole? Are people on San Juan still getting phone calls asking about me?"

"No, not in a couple of weeks."

"And there's no rumors about people asking for thugs-for-hire in a bar on Orcas, no sudden appearance of strange men with ominous bulges under their left arms?"

"It's not funny, Rae. Don't joke about it."

She suddenly felt unutterably weary, as though the last three days had turned into a steamroller that was in the process of slowly running her down. Airports filled with strangers and the close-up face of a would-be rapist, a smashed house and a smuggler of abused children, to be crazy and then not crazy—one more thing, and her brain would explode. "What else can I do, Jerry? What the fuck else can I do? We've been through all this before. You've got no evidence there's anyone out there, have you? Jerry, I've been dealing with bumps in the night since you were playing with cap guns. I can't handle someone else's paranoia as well as my own." *Go away, Jerry,* she thought. *Leave me alone.* She wanted nothing but to sleep for a week, even if some faceless Watcher crept up and murdered her while she slept. "Unless you're keeping something from me, it sounds suspiciously like paranoia."

"No," the sheriff admitted. "I don't have any evidence that you have an active stalker."

The defeat in his voice roused her. "Jerry, you could well be right. There could be someone after me. Like the old saying goes, just because you're paranoid doesn't mean the world isn't out to get you." *God, Rae, you're just full of awful jokes tonight.* "If you come up with something firm, I promise I'll listen. Hell, I probably won't sleep for a week anyway, and we'll be lucky if I don't shoot off the flare gun every ten minutes. But as far as my safety goes, I'm better off here than in Roche Harbor. You yourself said it's nearly impossible to sneak up on me here." *And Petra's safety?* her treacherous mind asked. She refused to think about that.

"Okay," he said, throwing up his hands. "But we're going to step up surveillance, so don't be surprised if you see a lot of county boats around and get buzzed by floatplanes from time to time."

"Fine. Whatever you like. And, Jerry? Thanks. You're a friend."

She had intended nothing more than a heartfelt thank-you, and that was precisely what Jerry heard: nothing more. He rose heavily to his feet and gazed down at her, his half-shadowed face looking older than that of his brother.

A day ago, she might well have reached for him, might have taken him to bed, good sense be damned; tonight he was a friend, and nothing more.

Rae saw his hurt. On top of his long day and her refusal to be coddled, she couldn't bear leaving it at that; she blurted out the first impulsive thing that came to mind.

"Nikki loves you, Jerry."

The big man reared back, as startled as if she had jumped at him.

Rae blundered on, laying it on thick. "Age doesn't matter, Jerry. Previous family ties shouldn't stand in the way. She needs you, and she really, really loves you. It's hurting her that you don't see it. And Caleb adores you. Give it a chance."

His mouth opened and closed a few times, with no sound. The poor man didn't know what hit him, Rae saw; his only response was to turn and retreat back to his boat, leaving Rae to her revelations.

Which was worse: imaginary Watchers or real ones? Knowing that at least some of the bumps in the night had been real was both vastly reassuring and frankly terrifying. Any number of times during the night she found herself wishing that Jerry had just cuffed her to his boat and dragged her off the island.

On the other hand, her knowledge did not actually change anything. She had known for a while that someone had been out to harass her, she just hadn't known the scope of that harassment. And she still had no doubt that some of her demons were imaginary, even if others were not. So although things were different, things were also much the same. And she still had just as much work to get through as she had before Jerry arrived with his earthshaking tidbit.

Seven days now before the descent of her daughter's sharp-eyed, suspicious, and litigious family, and Rae threw herself into her labors. She kept the eyes in the back of her head fully open at all times, she slept fitfully, aware of every crackle and creak, and she never left her gun farther away than the bedside table next to her pillow. Engines approached with regularity, planes dipped overhead. It didn't take long to figure out that only some of those vehicles were owned by the county, and the thought that she had been made a ward of the entire population infuriated her, until Jerry, on one of his near-daily visits, assured her that those in the know were few and discreet. After that, she tried her best to ignore the mechanical intrusions, or sang aloud the old song that had come to mind following Allen's visit—except that, with the boats and planes, the words "watch over me" took on a strong flavor of irony.

Jerry and Nikki came to see her on Monday, bringing Caleb with them, now that school was out for the summer. Rae said nothing about the coincidence of the sheriff and ranger's having a day off together but, watching closely, she caught subtle changes in the glances Jerry cast on Nikki—he was less certain of himself, almost shy. She allowed her visitors to help out by building a shower cubicle from odd bits of wood and helping her connect the propane water heater to the shower line, then she sent them on their way. Later that night, glowing and content after a deliciously hot shower, Rae sat on her beach and listened to the neighbors across the strait drumming up the full moon. How long would it be before Nikki had Jerry Carmichael drumming with the others on that beach?

On Tuesday night, Rae finished her stairway. It was rough still—bare feet would not be a good idea in any part of the house—and it lacked a handrail, but it was sturdy, and it had the bones of beauty. Rae's two floors were now linked.

Finally, on Thursday morning, the day of reckoning dawned. Several fretful hours later, Ed De la Torre arrived to take Rae to Friday Harbor.

All the way over, two refrains throbbed through her mind. The phrases from Desmond's diary—*My brother comes tomorrow . . . the thought of seeing his face*—alternated with Pam Church's: *Are you nuts? Asking for trouble.* Over and over again. Ed spoke little, sensing her turmoil if not fully understanding its source. Her face was shuttered, and she would only pray it remained that way when Don came off the ferry *(seeing his face . . . terrible dread)*. For everyone's sake, she had to stay calm and aloof when she clasped the snake to her metaphorical bosom.

She and Ed were half an hour early at the town. Rae hung around the terminus and nervously drank bad coffee until the ferry docked; then she grimly went forward to meet the Collins family on the pedestrian bridge. Petra was dressed in full-flowering grunge, from black-dyed hair to black-painted fingernails, but she flung her arms around Rae as if she were a gingham-clad child of six. Tamara presented her mother with a cool cheek, and shifted her suitcase into the other hand. Rae looked back up the walkway.

"Where's Don?" she asked, when it became obvious they weren't waiting for a third passenger.

"It's a long story," Tamara said with a glance at Petra.

Rae took the hint and subsided, but it was with a stir of hope in her heart that she escorted her daughter and granddaughter to Ed's waiting boat, and to Folly Island.

Fifty-two

Desmond Newborn's Journal

May 29, 1927

A roof, boys, a roof! With the closing in of the roof over my head it all comes full circle. I have fashioned myself a cave, I have made a shelter of stone and tree that both protects me and cuts me off from the firmament of the heavens. I stand apart from God's other creatures; I am a man again, a member (however solitary) of the community of house dwellers, no longer a creature of the woods and hills. I sit by my fire and warm my stockinged toes with no concern for rain dripping down the back of my neck, and I laugh at the misery of the lesser creatures outside my door.

This untoward happiness makes me uneasy. The soldier who lets his guard down is the soldier who gets a bullet between the eyes. Even behind the front there are unexploded shells, buildings waiting to collapse, booby-trapped rooms.

But I will push the unease away, because I am safely wrapped in stone and wood. I have rejoined the human race, and I find myself looking around for companionship, thinking: I need to hold a party.

Fifty-three

Tamara stepped off Ed's boat onto the uneven planks of the dock and cast her habitually disapproving gaze up at the tired and sunburnt canvas tent, the six shiny new canvas-and-wood chairs arranged in a circle around the grimy fire pit, and the raw and idiosyncratic house going up in the background. For the first time in the rushed week since she had staggered off the little plane on the San Juan airstrip, Rae was grateful that she'd been forced to spend three days in California. Those few hours with Vivian among the wood had proved more valuable than six months of psychotherapy in restoring Rae's sense of worth and identity. She was not this young woman's unbalanced mother, she was not a mental patient, she was not an attempted suicide and a twice-bereft widow and the victim of a vicious attack; she was Rae Newborn, a strong woman with bad times and good in her past, determined that there would be good times yet to come. She caught up Tamara's large suitcase and carried it easily along the promontory to the tent. Petra followed them, sullen still in her mother's presence, while Ed deposited the bag of fresh vegetables, milk, and a block of ice on the dock, then slipped away as silently as his engines would allow.

Petra headed for the building site. Rae dumped Tamara's luggage on the foot of one of the two cots she had borrowed, which alongside hers (for Petra's use, Rae having planned on sleeping up in the house during the invasion) took up most of the floor in the tent. Petra's had a sleeping bag; the other two were made up with clean sheets.

"I borrowed these for you and Don," she told Tamara. "If he's not coming, I could either sleep here, or take one cot out so you and Petra could have more floor space."

"We're getting a divorce." Tamara said it bluntly, looking at the fresh sheets, at the storage boxes jammed into the corner, at anything but her mother. "He moved out a month ago. Just before Memorial Day weekend."

"A *month* ago? But . . ."

"I know, I should have told you. I threw him out a couple of days after I wrote telling you we were coming. We had a fight about it that didn't seem to end, and then I found out about . . . I asked Petra not to tell you about it. I wanted to do it myself."

A *month*. Rae wanted to scream at the top of her lungs, a wordless roar of frustration and relief, could feel it building, and struggled to keep it down. *She threw the bastard out an entire month ago—all that time of straining to hear the enemy sneaking up and fretting about where Don and his fucking court case were going to pop up next, a whole month getting ready to look into his smiling face and getting my teeth ready to smile back, all of that month completely unnecessary, as if there hadn't been enough stress, as if I—* Rae fought back the furious recriminations with an effort that made her shudder. But once she had, she could finally see Tamara, see the heartbreak on her daughter's face, and she could be a mother again. She stepped forward and silently wrapped her work-hardened arms around her daughter, a thing she had not been able to do since her daughter was Petra's age. For an instant Tamara stiffened, and then she gave way and began, painfully and piteously, to sob. A few minutes later Petra looked in the door. Rae met her eyes, and after a moment the spiky-haired, Doc Martens–wearing, black-clad girl pushed her way through the mosquito netting and came up to her mother and grandmother. Rae opened her arm and pulled her in, and they stood in a huddle, three women weeping.

Tamara was the first to break away, looking miserable and blotchy but relieved that the worst was over. Petra pulled back, her heavy eye makeup halfway down her face, and searched for a box of tissues. Rae, on the other hand, was finding it hard not to burst into song.

There were a lot of unanswered questions, however, and over the course of the long and unreal day, Rae tried to get them answered.

It was Don's affair that struck the final blow, Tamara confided when Petra was safely out of earshot on the beach in a bikini (a black one). She had put up with business practices that threatened the family's financial and legal future, she had managed to overlook his tirades against Petra's appearance, friends, and work habits, she had even forgiven the two occasions on which he lost control and hit her—Tamara, never Petra—but she could not forgive him for sleeping with his personal assistant.

There was a lot more to it than that, of course; once the flood of catharsis was loosed, it took a while to reach its end. And with Tamara, who all her life had flat out refused the possibility that she might benefit from therapy, it all had to gush forth at once. Her manifold guilts were laid bare: taking Don's side against Rae even when she knew Rae was right; withholding Petra when she knew full well that Petra was all Rae had left; even her shame at not having loved Alan as freely as he deserved. And eventually, with a bemused Rae stepping for a change into the role of counselor, the ugliest, hardest little truths at the bottom of it all began to work their way into the light.

How although Tamara had loved her half-sister Bella, at the same time she had deeply resented her, because Rae loved the child so easily, and because Rae had chosen Alan over Tamara's own father, David. How she had kept Petra from Rae because of that resentment. How when Bella died, Tamara secretly hated Rae for failing to turn to her, for reaching past her to seize on Petra.

And buried deepest of all, a bitter confession that needed alcohol to prime it: Tamara's lifelong guilt over her own birth. Intellectually, Tamara knew that she had not caused Rae to go crazy that first time; she had read enough about mood disorders over the years to know the biochemical inevitability of depression. Nonetheless, her heart was convinced that it was her fault. After all, David, David's mother, and Tamara's great-grandfather William had all told her at one time or another that her mother had been fine until her birth. How could she help believing that Rae had exchanged her sanity for her daughter's life?

Rae sat with her daughter, and rocked her and cried with her, bitterly cursing all those members of the family, cursing herself as well for not seeing, despite fifty-two years' intimate experience with the mechanics of guilt and the failures of love, that Tamara had taken it all on herself. How could she have been so blind, not to realize what was happening with her own daughter? If Rae herself still harbored vague feelings of responsibility for *her* mother's death—and that of cancer, when Rae was five years old—how could Tamara not blame herself for Rae's mental disintegration, when it occurred nearly simultaneously with Tamara's birth?

God, Rae groaned to herself; the cycle was never-ending.

No conclusions could be reached, not in a single afternoon of tears. Not in a week, even. All Rae could do was hold Tamara as much as Tamara would allow. All Rae could hope for was to lay the first corner-stone of a foundation, a base on which the future could be built. All Rae could do was to tell her daughter that she loved her.

It made for a long morning and an even longer afternoon, with many repetitions and stumbling confessions and an apparently endless stream of tears. Rae listened, and murmured reassurances, and patted her daughter, and forced her to eat some lunch, until finally she began to cast around for distractions. She was not Tamara's therapist, and even if she were, one fifty-minute hour was usually a day's limit; this session had gone past four hours. At the next pause Rae interjected a gentle inquiry about the monies that she had arranged through Pam Church to be dis-tributed between the three members of the Collins family. Tamara's face twisted in a look of bitter satisfaction.

"We got the letter from your lawyer the day after I threw Don out."

Tamara went on at some length about her pleasure in telling her hus-band that he would be receiving no more of his mother-in-law's money, but Rae heard less than half of it. Don had known for a month that he no longer had any legal claim on the Newborn estate, yet less than three weeks ago someone had been calling around the islands in an attempt to find her, and it was after that that her tent had been invaded. Finally she shook her head. Jerry was wrong; Jerry was speaking personally, as a man, not a sheriff. Coincidence happened. Some trespassing kids, look-ing for cash or a stash, that was all.

The sun traveled across the sky, Petra turned herself over twice and applied sunscreen once, Tamara continued to pour out the years of repressed indignation, and Rae began to long for the saw and hammer; even the brutal labor of excavation started to seem attractive.

By half past three she'd had enough. She got stiffly to her feet (canvas chairs were not intended for long sessions) and asked Tamara if she wouldn't like to see the house. Tamara looked startled, having clearly for-gotten her mother's preoccupation for the last months, then dried her eyes. She looked awful, and Rae decided it was well past time to bring the session to an end.

"I forgot to tell you," she said, "I invited a couple of friends to join us for dinner. The local sheriff and a park ranger. I thought you might like to see who your mother's been hanging around with." Rae had originally invited them to provide support in the face of her son-in-law; now the guests would function as another but equally valuable kind of interruption. "Hey, Petra! You want a tour of the house?"

The teenager eyed her mother with a wariness that ill concealed her concern, and shrugged to indicate a general state of disinterest; nonetheless, she was on her feet in seconds, with the sandy towel wrapped around her waist like a sarong. Tamara automatically ordered her to put on her shoes, and Petra equally automatically started to bristle, but when Rae actually agreed with her daughter, explaining that building sites tended to collect a lot of sharp objects, Petra subsided, digging a pair of rubber flip-flops out of her pack. They weren't exactly what Rae had in mind, but she would compromise this time.

They started at the workbench, where Rae showed them the old black-and-white photograph of Desmond's home tacked to the tree. Looking back and forth between picture and reality, she had to admit she had a ways to go. Her towers looked particularly sad, capped as they were by hunks of plywood in place of Desmond's neat shingle cones.

"There's some things I'm willing to leave to experts, and that roof is going to be one of them," Rae told them. Petra looked mildly disappointed, Tamara approving, and they went up to look the house over.

It was highly satisfying to have an audience, even an uneducated and not terribly responsive one. And because most of what she had done up to now was simply reproducing Desmond's genius, and Rae believed in giving credit where it was due, she could praise and brag with no fear of vanity. She had already decided not to tell them about the bones she'd found: time enough for that disturbing knowledge.

Two other things she kept to herself: the access door beside the fireplace, invisible but for the splinter latch behind her hanging tool belt, and the one into the subfloor crawl space, hidden beneath an ancient and filthy scrap of carpeting to keep curious adolescents from venturing under the house to see Desmond's Native American mortar—and the figures it held. She led them proudly up her new stairway to let them admire the view. Tamara then retreated to the tent with a cool wet cloth across her swollen eyes while Rae and Petra swam in the cove and then laid the fire for the steaks Jerry was bringing.

The two upholders of law and order on the islands arrived in Jerry's boat just after six, Caleb in tow. Rae strode down both to meet her guests and to convey a quick warning to the adults over the child's fiery head.

"I haven't told my daughter and granddaughter about the s-k-e-l-e-t-o-n," she spelled out. "And, I just found out that my daughter is divorcing her husband, so walk carefully around that topic as well."

With that Petra came onto the dock, no doubt at her mother's urging, with an offer to carry something. Jerry shook her hand and then placed a white bakery box in it, with a caution that it should not be tipped, and introductions were made there and at the fire. Nikki, at her most cheerful, took up the conversational ball and ran with it while Jerry occupied himself at the cook fire, a red-and-white-check apron over his clean blue shirt. Rae listened to the conversation with half an ear, the rest of her mind occupied with the problem of Don Collins. Should she be concerned for the safety of her daughter and granddaughter? Was there any unequivocal evidence that someone was laying siege to Folly?

None at all. Jerry Carmichael's mother-hen nervousness was contagious. *Enjoy the party, Rae,* she exhorted herself. *Quit fretting about the Watchers in the woods and pay attention to the rare pleasure of friends and family.*

All in all, the evening was not as awkward as it might have been. Tamara even came out of herself to flirt mildly with Jerry, to the well-concealed amusement of Nikki Walls, and they all ate far too much. Rae and Nikki did the dishes while the shadows grew long and Jerry talked to Tamara and Petra, Caleb nestled into his lap. When Rae glanced over at the fire pit, she was amused to see Petra sitting with her Doc Martens outstretched, propped on the rock ring in a position identical to Jerry's—although she lacked a sleeping child draped over her chest. Rae finished drying the dishes, tossed the towel over its branch to air, and crossed to the fire; before she could sit down, Jerry got to his feet and asked if he could have a word. Caleb stirred in sleepy protest as Jerry transferred him into his mother's arms, where he settled instantly with small childish sleep-noises.

Rae walked with Jerry down to the beach, glowing still in the last rays of sunlight. Jerry scooped up a handful of flattish stones and proceeded to skip them over the smooth face of the cove waters.

"Escobar phoned to say one of the guys he's charged is pleading guilty, and the other one will go to trial. You'll have to go testify for that in a few months."

"I thought I might."

"Also, something else came up in questioning them. Apparently one of the guys thinks the man who hired them may have been trying to drive you to suicide."

That was a jolt. Jerry felt her go still, and his big hand sought out her shoulder, a gesture clearly visible to the three variously speculating women near the fire.

"I guess I was assuming he only wanted me to be crazy," she told him in a small voice.

"Do you have that kind of an enemy?"

Rae turned slightly so that her back was to the campfire, as if Tamara might be able to read from her face what she was about to say. Jerry's hand fell away, but he remained close, his upper arm brushing her shoulder. "I have that kind of a son-in-law," she told him. "Or I thought so until today."

"Son-in-law. You mean Tamara's—"

"Don Collins. He's greedy, he's crooked, and he's always in a tight place financially. But I just found out that they've been separated for nearly a month and that Tamara's filed for divorce, so he surely can't expect to inherit anything now. If it was him, I'm safe."

"Did you tell Escobar about this? Has he talked to Collins?"

"I told him in a general sort of a way, at the time." Although that had been in the weeks after the attack, when Rae as a witness had left much to be desired.

"I think I should make sure he's seen the possibility."

"Maybe . . . oh, hell. Have him get in touch with my lawyer. She knows my whole history with Don."

"Will she give it out?"

"I'll write her a letter, asking her to open her files. You could witness the letter—that ought to make it legal."

"Do it tonight. If Collins had anything to do with hiring those two, he'd most likely have phone records, cash withdrawals, that kind of thing."

The sun dropped behind the heights of Vancouver Island; Rae dry-washed her tired face. "This is going to be hard on Petra."

"Harder on her if he'd managed to injure you. Though how he thought he could make you commit suicide, I can't imagine. Sounds like a bad thriller."

At that, Rae turned to stare at him, incredulous. "What are you talking about? He very nearly did."

"Oh, Rae, come on. You had a breakdown. Hardly surprising, under the circ—"

She thrust her left arm under his nose, forcing him to look at the scars. She tapped at the highest one, the pinkest and freshest of the three. "*That* was serious, Jerry. Five more minutes to myself, and I wouldn't be standing here." She watched his face, seeing the realization and the fleeting twist of revulsion. When she was certain he had understood, she added, "Depression kills, Jerry. It doesn't take much of a nudge."

"I, um . . . I didn't really think . . ."

"I know. I'll go write that letter now."

She went through the campsite and into the tent, where she took out her pad and a pen. On the canvas wall above the desk she had fastened Caleb's drawing of Rae with the twenty-three crabs at her stick feet, the only piece of decoration in the place. The artist himself had wakened from his nap and was chattering with Petra, a bittersweet reminder of long overheard conversations between the girl and Bella. Rae listened for a minute to Caleb's serious lecture on the life and habits of the hermit crab, then went back to the letter. When she had signed it, she called Jerry in to sign as well. He read the few lines, scribbled his name, and folded the document into a pocket.

Then it was time for the San Juan natives to leave—Jerry distracted, Nikki curious, Caleb alone lighthearted. Rae and Petra waved them off at the dock, and walked through the midsummer's evening to join Tamara at the fire.

Tamara stayed only two nights. On the Friday, the three Newborn women ate blueberry pancakes and then went for a hike up Mount Desmond, diverting on the way back to dabble in the tepid spring-fed pool (where Petra discovered both salamanders and dragonflies). On the way downhill they picked a giant bouquet of paintbrush and brodiaea and a few late blossoms of Nootka rose. They went for a swim in the icy cove—even Tamara, who was trying hard—and in the evening Ed came to taxi them to Roche Harbor for dinner. They spotted a distant orca on the way over, ate a satisfying meal, watched the sundown ceremony in the boat harbor (complete with salute from the miniature cannon), went back to play a few surprisingly congenial hands of poker in front of the fire (Tamara really was trying), and went to their cots content.

Then on Saturday morning, Tamara abruptly announced that she had decided to leave, ostensibly to avoid the rush of Sunday traffic. Rae suspected that there were other, more important reasons, from the discomfort of the living quarters and the dearth of Tamara-style entertainment to Petra's reflexive and unceasing prickliness around her mother, to say nothing of Tamara's embarrassment over having broken down in front of Rae. Mostly, Rae thought, Tamara was feeling the need to draw back and recoup. She'd obviously faced as much as she could bear for the moment. Rae was satisfied—more than that, she was optimistic in a way she hadn't been for a long, long time when it came to Tamara. Their relationship was by no means healed, and it remained to be seen just how far Tamara would be willing—or able—to allow it to change. But it was a first crack in the façade, and on the dock she met Rae's embrace with a stiff hesitation followed by a long, tight hug and a quick turn away to the boat.

Whatever the reasons for her early departure, now that Tamara had been reassured as to her mother's mental state and her daughter's safety, she was ready to escape.

The trouble was, escape from Folly was no simple matter. Fortunately, Tamara had brought a cell phone for Petra's use, or Rae would have been reduced to flagging down a passing sailboat to get Tamara a ride. It might actually have been easier to flag down a boat, since using the phone involved a hike even farther up Mount Desmond than the first time Rae had sought a signal. But in the end, Ed was summoned. He arrived two hours later looking not at all pleased at the prospect of being trapped on a boat with Tamara Collins, even for the short run to Friday Harbor. Rae thanked him, often and vigorously, until Ed relented with a rueful half-smile and said he'd see her Tuesday.

Rae and Petra stood shoulder to shoulder on the undulating boat dock. Tamara's retreating spine was stiff again, but Rae thought it not quite as unyielding as it had been the last time Ed De la Torre had taken her away from the island, three months before on the eve of April Fools'. And this time Tamara turned before the boat reached the point, turned around and waved at them. The two generations on the shore waved back in farewell.

Then the *Orca Queen* was gone, and it seemed the most natural thing in the world for Rae to wrap her arms around Petra. They held each other as they had not while Tamara was there to look on, their only motion the slow rise and dip of the boards beneath their feet. After a delicious interval, Rae spoke.

"I'm not going to be able to rest my chin on your head for much longer."

"I'm the eighth-tallest person in my school, including the teachers."

"I hope you don't mind being tall."

"No, I like it. I want to get to six feet."

They separated then, to move along the dock and up the ridge of the promontory. Petra looked over her shoulder in the direction of San Juan.

"I hope she'll be okay," Petra said.

"She'll be fine. You'll be home in a week and a half."

"It's just that Mom really needs someone around to take care of."

"She'll have to make do with the horses and dogs."

"And the cats."

"And the cats, of course." Rae saw the child glance again out to sea, and asked gently, "Do you want to talk about it?"

"Maybe later. It's all kind of a relief, you know? Not that I want them to get a . . . a divorce or anything, but at least it's all out in the open. I mean, man, for about three weeks it was like you can feel that there's something about to hit you, and you wait and wait with your teeth all clenched and when it finally comes it's a relief, that you're still walking around and it didn't hurt as bad as you thought it would. You know?"

"I know."

"But, Gran, you're really looking great."

"I'm feeling well."

"I mean it. You look—beautiful."

Rae laughed. "Oh come on, Petra, you need your eyes examined."

"You do. Not like an actress or anything, but like a . . . a statue maybe. Like, 'I am woman. I am strong.'"

"You know that song?" Rae asked in surprise.

"That's a song?"

"Once upon a time, when we were all burning our bras."

Ancient history not being Petra's immediate interest, the child let it go. "Anyway, I'm glad to see you looking so good. I was real worried when we left you here. You looked kind of sick."

In more ways than one, Rae commented internally. "I wasn't in very good shape, you're right. Of course, the rain that day didn't help much. But this place has been good for me. A thousand times better than I could have hoped. When I got here, it was still halfway winter, so I've been able to watch the island come to life around me. I guess the sap's been rising in me, too."

The analogy did not make a lot of sense to Petra. Rae diverted her with a question. "So, what do you want to do?"

"Don't you have to get back to work?"

"I think I could afford to goof off another half-day."

"Well, if you're sure, could we go up to the spring again?"

This time, they wore swimsuits under their shorts. Rae plugged off the water inlet and she and Petra lay in the warmer waters of the upper pond, drifting into each other and the mossy banks and gazing up at the trees and the sky and the visiting life of the island. They saw the dragonfly again, to Petra's joy, and discovered a number of slim, moist, earth-colored newts.

Rae assembled cheese sandwiches for their late lunch. When they had eaten, she turned to Petra and said, "Would you like to see Desmond's secret cave?"

Rae's two invisible doors earned her Petra's ultimate encomium, "Cool!" but the cave itself rendered her granddaughter speechless, awestruck by the sheer romance of the thing. Rae said nothing yet about Desmond's bones, not even when the girl crawled across the stains on the floor in the side cave, looking around. They continued on to the main cave, and Petra gave the moldering shelves the merest glance, preferring to stand silently before the rear wall and wait for the next drip to gather, appear, elongate, fatten, and finally tremble free from the rocky point to *plink* into the tiny pool on the floor.

"Can you drink that?" she wanted to know.

"I haven't had it tested, but I should think it's safe enough."

After a minute Petra squatted down and swished her fingers in the water, then held them up to dab the drips onto her tongue.

"I wonder if there could be another cave underneath this one?" she asked in a dreamy voice. "I mean, the water must be going somewhere, or the cave would've filled up, even with that slow a drip. Don't you think?"

"The water's getting out somehow, that's for sure. I just figured it was seeping back into the sandstone, but I suppose there could be another cave down there."

The girl was obviously taken by the idea of caves atop caves, worlds within worlds.

"I want to be a writer," she said abruptly, her back to Rae and her face in the lamp's shadow.

"Do you?" Rae answered. "I think you'd be good at it. I remember all those stories you used to tell Bella."

"Mom says I'll starve to death."

"What kind of writing?" Rae asked, stepping firmly around the question of Tamara's judgment.

"Fantasy, science fiction, that kind of stuff. I really like the idea of caves for that. You know, like what if under here was a huge cave filled with diamonds and things, sparkling in the torchlight, and a whole city of people? They have a queen, and—" Petra stopped abruptly, becoming aware that she had an adult audience. Rae responded as if she had not noticed.

"I've never read much science fiction," she told her granddaughter. "Never read much fiction at all, for that matter. My imagination seems to be wired into my senses too firmly, which may be why I'm a craftsman rather than a pure artist. Your way of imagining things isn't tied down like mine. You'll probably be a fine writer."

Now the embarrassment was from educated praise instead of inadvertent revelation, and it drove Petra briskly to her feet. She took a last look around the cave as if to point out how cramped and musty and dull it really was, and then turned back toward the entrance, her mask of disdain firmly in place. It made her look like her mother, although their coloring was entirely different.

The mask slipped again when Rae stopped her to point out the petroglyph of the breaching orca, halfway up the wall. They had to put out one of the lights to get the shadows to fall right, and then it leapt into view, as clear as if the artist had rubbed pigment into it. Petra went soft again, and one hand came out, then hesitated.

"Can I touch it?"

"It's carved into the stone—you'd have to bash it with a hammer to do any damage."

Petra's fingers, strong and brown from long hours grasping reins, tipped by nails bitten short and painted a purple so dark it looked black, lowered delicately onto the incised image. She was not aware of holding her breath as she traced the arching figure, its swirl of pattern and the strong triangular fin, but Rae heard the faint sigh of satisfaction the child let out when her hand came away.

"Desmond wouldn't have done that, would he?" Petra asked. It startled Rae, hearing the intimately known name coming from another's mouth. Petra seemed already to think of him as a personal acquaintance.

"No. That's a Native American design—the people who hunted and fished these islands before the white man came. Some Salish or Nanaimo or Lummi probably got stuck here one stormy day with nothing better to do."

Petra thought for a moment, and then she switched her flashlight back on and directed it upward. There on the low ceiling was a black discoloration, clear sign of the smoke from an ages-old torch.

"Aren't you the clever one!" Rae exclaimed.

Petra ducked her head and her flashlight, and they left the cave.

Once they were out in the daylight, doors secured behind them and the sun dappling through the leaves above the campsite, Rae told her the rest of it, how she had found the bones she assumed to be those of Desmond Newborn.

She did not tell Petra the whole story—the bullet, the fire, and her private conclusions about what had happened. That, she decided, was too much family burden for a thirteen-year-old to carry. And because Desmond's end was inseparable from what had gone before, she also kept secret the journal, the strongbox of mementos, and the locket. When the girl was eighteen, perhaps.

Then, to drive away the cold ghostly bones from Petra's imagination, Rae tossed her a pair of leather gloves and put her to work.

Fifty-four

Desmond Newborn's Journal

September 12, 1927

Mere months ago I lightheartedly proposed to myself the idea of a house-warming party, to which I imagined inviting all the kind and disparate souls who have nurtured me in my quest and helped me regain a few shreds of human dignity. From the bank manager to the ironmonger, the powerful magnate of the Roche Harbor quarries to the lady who bakes my bread, I imagined them all gathered beneath my new roof, unlikely companions, the initial discomfort of their distinct stations in life melting under the warm unlikeliness of the event. Alcohol, too, might lend its hand.

And then my brother wrote to say that he was coming, and a heaviness began to settle in, as the air grows close before a storm, as the Front went profoundly still just before a push.

I find myself listening, as one listened out into no-man's-land in the dark of night, when placed in a far distant post, waiting for the movement of a German raiding party: Every small breath of wind through the wheat seems designed to conceal the enemy, every distant rattle of their Maxim guns timed to hide the rattle of the crawling men's equipment, every cloud across the slim moon placed there to obscure the movement of grasses. You remove your steel helmet so the roots of your hair can help listen to the dark, your very skin shudders at the rustle of a nearby rat, and if the man at your side has to stifle a cough, God help him. Here, I do not know what I am straining so to hear, just that the heavy air demands that I freeze and stare out into the distance, sweating and breathless.

I force myself to move; that is the only way to conquer the urge to bolt. And so I build and finish my front door, a door more suited to a besieged castle than an island shack, and I mount it with three immensely stout hinges fashioned by the man who sold me this piece of God's earth, my friend and benefactor Thomas Carmichael on Orcas Island—although as yet the door swings free, for I will not receive his latch until I row across to Roche Harbor tomorrow.

It is, I say so myself, a good house. It sits well on the land, for all that it is odd, like its builder, although a little more flamboyant and considerably more robust. Just to see it, standing up the hill from its small harbor, lends a man strength of spirit. To walk through it, to stand upon its floorboards and look through its windows, steadies a man and calms the urge to listen with every pore for the creeping enemy.

Yet he is merely my brother. Three years the elder and disapproving of all he surveys, but what of that? The island is mine, the house as well; W.'s pale gaze cannot harm them.

My brother comes tomorrow, to talk me out of my folly. Let him try. Although I freely admit, to myself if none other, that the thought of seeing his face fills me with a terrible dread.

Fifty-five

In the wake of hard work, fresh air, a substantial dinner, and the absence of her mother's eye, Petra went to bed early and fell instantly to sleep. Rae sat by the last glow of the fire, listening to Petra's endearingly child-like snores mingling with the night. The moon was five days past full but the clear sky made it remarkably bright; the waves were high on the beach and receding.

Rae poured herself a glass of Scotch and took it down to the promontory. She felt restless, although she could not have said why. The moon, perhaps, and the nervous chittering of the high water retreating from wet rocks, to say nothing of the accumulated stresses of the last month pulling at her, stresses that ranged from the unforeseen reawakening of many kinds of life forces simultaneously to the heavy responsibility of a sleeping child, and taking in along the way murdered skeletons, familial revelations, the faces of her attackers, three cartons of shattered glass beauty, interesting ghosts, the crippling secret guilts of a daughter, and the rebirth of her life as a woodworker. Her flesh crawled, as if the soft night were studded with unfriendly, even malevolent eyes, watching her every movement. She rested her hand on the pocket of her sweatshirt from time to time, to reassure herself with the bulk of the pistol inside.

She sat as far as she could from the dark fringe of trees around the camp-site, out on the farthest point of the promontory, settled on a flat rock with her knees drawn up to her chest. The Scotch helped calm the shivers along her arms and shoulders, and reduced the twitches up the back of her neck.

However, drink also lowered her resistance to the sensation of unheard voices in the bone behind her ears, a faint hissing pulse of sound that seemed, as always, to hold words that she had to strain to hear.

But she would not strain to render sense out of voices that were nothing more than the breeze in the trees and the blood in her veins. Petra required Rae's full and capable presence. If it meant another dip into full-blown madness and voices at the end of the girl's visit, well, she would deal with it, but not now. She drank her Scotch and watched the shadowy boats lying off her shore, rocking gently with the tide. The rapidly expanding population of the holiday weekend, she told herself; the low conversations she imagined could well be coming from them. Mosquitoes whined, and after a while, she went to bed.

Lying on the cot, inside her canvas walls, Rae's unease only grew. She was excruciatingly conscious of the net window above Petra's limp form, of the loose flap of the door across from her feet, of the flimsy canvas, just inches from her hand and hip, requiring only a sharp knife to enable an arm to reach in and grab. It was irrational, it was anxiety and not fear, but she began to feel as if the night air were a blanket laid over her face, and she was sweating far more freely than the cool air would justify. She lay rigid, heart pounding and breath uneven, fighting against a panic attack that she could not walk off for fear of disturbing Petra and which refused to fade on its own. She was not far removed from whimpering in the back of her throat when Petra turned over and spoke.

"Are you okay?"

Rae hadn't realized the child was awake. *How long had the child been lying there listening to her grandmother's labored breathing?* Rae swung her legs over the side of the creaking cot and rubbed her face.

"Yes, sweetheart, I just can't sleep. I'm sorry to wake you."

"You didn't. I had a dream, about a bunch of orcas, playing and fighting in a tangle under the water, and one of them swam right past where I was standing. It was beautiful, with a sort of white patch when it went by, but kinda scary, too. That's what woke me up."

"You know, I actually saw an orca do that, not too long ago," Rae told her. "When I was out on Jerry Carmichael's boat. It went right underneath us. It was magical."

"I liked Jerry," noted Petra, distracted momentarily from the topic of her dream.

"He's a nice man."

"Is he, like, a boyfriend or something?"

"Just a friend. I think he and Nikki are about to get together."

"Nikki's gorgeous, isn't she?"

"She is indeed," Rae agreed.

"I guess it must be hard, after . . . I mean, you loved Alan a lot."

Ah, thought Rae, *the things that can be spoken of in the safety of darkness.* "Yes, I did. And yes, it is hard. Very few men would have any idea of what they'd be getting into."

Petra thought about this for a minute, then retreated back to her dream. "What do you suppose it means when you dream about orcas?"

"What does it mean to you?"

"God, Gran," Petra complained in disgust, "you sound just like my shrink."

Rae laughed. "Sorry. But really, you can't just go and tell someone what their dream means without at least asking them what they think."

"I guess. The shrink would probably say it had something to do with 'adolescent sexuality,'" Petra said grimly. "They're big on 'adolescent sexuality' and horses. Like that's the only reason I like to ride."

"Since you started riding when you were five I'd agree it's probably not quite that simple, but everyone expects psychologists to know the answers, and they sometimes fall into the trap themselves. Dream interpretation has been around for thousands of years. It's even in the Old Testament. If you want my opinion, I'd say that the person who carved the orca up in the cave would think that your dream was a spirit visitation. It sounded like a friendly one."

"It was, I suppose. But big, and strong."

"Spirits are powerful. That's what makes them scary. Even the beneficial ones."

"My spirit, huh?" Petra said, sounding impressed despite an attempt at scorn.

"Your totem animal. Go back to sleep, Petra."

"Would you mind if . . . Sometimes when I can't go back to sleep at home, I go outside for a while. To talk to the horses, you know? Can I go out for a few minutes? I promise I won't go far."

A cold trickle crept into Rae's heart at this echo of her own young self, walking the Boston house and grounds while the world slept, and she made a firm vow to speak to Dr. Hunt about the child. In the meantime, however, she kept her voice even.

"Feel free. Actually, I was wondering if you'd feel more"—not "safe"; no reason to suggest dangers if the child didn't feel them—"comfortable if we carried our beds up and camped out in the house. It's pretty bare, but it's friendly."

That last word slipped out past the censor, but Petra did not seem to notice.

"Sure," she said. "I'd like to sleep in your house. It smells good in there."

"It does, doesn't it? Okay, stick on some shoes," Rae said, already on her feet doing just that. "You know how to fold the cot? Do you need a flashlight?"

"It looks pretty bright out there."

"It is. Bring one anyway; you might want it." With her back to Petra, Rae slipped the revolver out from under her pillow into the knapsack, along with the flare gun, and added a bottle of water and some crackers in case Petra got hungry during the night. She noticed the cell phone Tamara had pointedly left behind, and dutifully dropped that in as well.

On their way up the hill, encumbered by rattling cot and an armload of sleeping bag and pillow, stumbling over the uneven ground in the gray half-light, Petra giggled, and the half-panicky retreat from the tent was instantly transformed into a childish prank, something girls might do at a slumber party. It was a sensation Rae had not felt for many a long year, and she was vaguely aware of the unlikeliness of a fifty-two-year-old grandmother and her thirteen-year-old offspring reduced to helpless giggles, but she truly did not care. They wrestled their burdens up the winding stairway, and Rae helped Petra set up her cot next to the black chimneypiece, taking a spot near the window for herself.

Petra, despite her protestations of habitual insomnia, was asleep again in minutes.

Rae woke with a start. It was nowhere near dawn, although the moonlight that streamed through the framed window hole had traveled across the floor while she slept and was now set to creep up the wall. The night was absolutely still; Petra's slow breathing was the only sound. Even the voices in Rae's head had fallen silent again.

So what had woken her?

She lay in the warm cocoon of her half-zipped bag, waiting for the sound to repeat itself, expecting the cry of a night bird or the scrabble of tiny nocturnal claws on her roof, even the breathy exhalation of a passing orca.

Nothing came.

There had been a noise, of that she was certain. Petra had the big flashlight on the floor under her cot, but Rae reached down to her knapsack to fish out the smaller one. Her hand found the revolver instead.

The moment she felt it, sliding cool and heavy into the palm of her hand, Rae's mind acknowledged that she was frightened. Moving with infinite caution against the creaks of the wooden cot, she eased her feet to the floor and padded silently across the rough boards to the window. She stood to one side of the rough opening, the sweetness of new-sawn fir in her nostrils, and looked across the clearing from her bird's-eye perch to the promontory and the open waters beyond.

The world was without motion. The tide was nearing its turn, and the earlier slow roll of the water and the accompanying dark-light shift of the offshore boats had ceased. The landscape resembled a badly faded black-and-white photograph, pale shapes against darker shadow. The lack of any intermediate grays rendered familiar objects into things that the eye could only identify by filling in the blanks: The tent Rae knew because it was in its place and the sharp edges of its top defined it, but two thirds of it was in shadow, and the side walls might have been nonexistent. A vertical gleam Rae's eyes read as the coffeemaker, moonlight reflecting off its curved glass, but if it had been across the clearing, she would never have known what it was. An oddly shaped pale patch bisected by dark lines, she eventually decided, was one of the white canvas-seated chairs, the shadowy upright obscuring parts of the pale fabric.

Some things, though, were transformed into otherworldly imports, alien offerings on a familiar shore. A round black patch the size of a turkey platter lay surrounded by clear, pale rock, where Rae could not recall an indentation. A shape with the outline of a squatting leprechaun occupied the corner of the faintly glowing fire pit, and farther down, where the brief pale flashes of wavelet met the overall gleam of the wet shore, a large black circle lay, like a gateway to another world. For a moment Rae smiled, thinking of offering it to the budding writer behind her as the midnight entrance to her magical cave city, and then her smile faded as she racked her brain to remember what object there on the shore would fill an oval space of maybe seven feet by four. There were no boulders on that part of the beach, no tide pools retained by the porous rock and sand.

Then a movement caught her eye in all that stillness, a brief flicker of dark against light. She waited to see if it was the raccoon that stopped by to rattle her food safe or one of the tiny black-tailed deer that swam between the islands. The movement was not repeated, for so long that Rae was thinking her visitor had gone around the front of the tent and disappeared into the trees, and then on the far side of the tent a nudge of shadow was cast by a matching round of something light, before it, too, was gone again.

Whatever was moving around out there, it was nearly as tall as her tent. Rae's gut turned to ice, her armpits started sweating, but her immediate thought, strangely enough, was of a bear. The idea may have been inspired by her earlier suspicions of raccoon and deer, but even as her mind pictured the huge animal, even as she was simultaneously wondering if there were bear on the islands and waiting for the rip of claw on canvas while she was sorting through what she might use to block the stairway against its advance, another part of her mind was laying out another, far darker and more terrifying picture.

There's a man down there.

All that, from half-seen motion to sure knowledge, took perhaps three seconds; immediately on its heels, and before fear could flower, her desperate mind threw up another possibility.

The last time a strange figure had edged into her firelight, it had been a man saddled with an undertaking both illegal and noble. Allen—she was becoming reconciled to the possibility of that name—had said he would be gone for two weeks, but perhaps he had returned early, and had come looking for her.

The sharply defined corner of the tent seemed to quiver slightly, as Rae pictured the man below drawing back the tent flap. She was not prepared for the short burst of light that flared in the perfect shape of a tent and then as quickly was gone, leaving her with a ghostly square imprinted on her retinas. She stifled a gasp at the sudden brightness and blinked to clear her vision.

If it was Allen Carmichael, he would know her habits well enough to figure that, unless she was off the island, she would be in the house. To get here he would have either to cross the moonlit clearing or take a wide and circuitous path halfway up the mountain and down the trees on the eastern side of the rock face.

If it was Allen Carmichael.

Anyway, would Allen, knowing Rae had a gun, not call out a warning? But if it was not him?

And then Rae confronted the cold, terrifying fact that in trying to convince everyone else of her staid normality, she might have been gambling with her granddaughter's life.

Drawing back from the window, Rae circled around until nylon brushed the side of her foot. Taking her eyes off the tent for a bare instant, she ducked down and snatched up her knapsack, then stood up quickly to watch the hillside for movement while her fingers searched through the contents. The first thing to reach her hand was Tamara's cell phone. She pulled it out and turned it on, cradling it to her chest to stifle the beep, then glanced at the display. Out of range. She dropped it in the pocket of her shorts anyway, thinking that she and Petra might hike high enough to get clear access to the transmitters, and then she put her hand back in the knapsack to retrieve the plastic box containing the flare gun. Fumbling with the unfamiliar shapes and trying not to take her eyes from the clearing, she got it loaded and went back to her position at the window. She was too charged with adrenaline to be concerned with appearances, but she was briefly aware that she must look quite mad, a barefoot woman in T-shirt and shorts, hair on end, a gun in each hand. Petra snored softly from the dark recesses of the room.

She waited, growing more tense by the second. Had he crossed the clearing while she was looking away? Was it Allen? Or Jerry, come back for some reason—and if so, was she about to blow the sheriff's head off? Could it have been Don that she saw—Don acting not out of greed this time but revenge, or Don with a clever plan, Don confident that he could pick off Rae and leave Petra unharmed? Oh, Christ—was that a noise she heard downstairs? Moving feet? Keep her eyes on the tent, or the stairway?

Then movement again by the tent, and a figure stepped forward. Impossible to tell in the ambiguous light, but it looked closer to Jerry's height than his brother's. What if it was only a passing boater, searching for aid in a medical emergency—but no, an honest person would have started calling out before his feet hit the shore. With that thought, Rae's eyes flickered to the odd oval shape on the beach, and knew in an instant what it was: a rubber inflatable, black as the water, like Allen Carmichael's only smaller, silently rowed and drawn up on her shore. Rae's grip tightened on both guns, the old pistol in her right hand and the flare gun in her left, and she silently urged the intruder to come into the light. Or to walk to his boat and row away—but that was too much to hope for.

Be Allen, she prayed. *Be Jerry. Be that obnoxious lawyer I threw out of my cove, be anyone but the faceless voice that sent the invaders to my home, my delusions given substance, my imaginary invaders who are currently sitting in the county jail. Be a child or a lost scuba diver or—*

The man's face seemed to tilt into a full oval as the moon struck it, and he looked up at the house, seemingly straight at Rae. She tried to open her throat, to call a last hopeful "Allen?" And then all sound, all breath, froze within her.

The man picking his way up the hill was taller than Rae. He wore his hair in a close crop of curls, had a neatly trimmed beard shadowing the edge of his jaw, and a pair of wire-framed spectacles glinted light from his eyes. It was a face Rae had sat across the table from for nine years, a face Rae had drawn often and sculpted twice, a face (minus the glasses) she had woken up to on more than three thousand mornings of her life, a face she had kissed and caressed and mourned with a grief that came close to killing her, a face atop a body whose movement did not seize her with such a sense of familiarity.

"Alan?" she whispered, and then took a step forward directly into the moonlight to lean out of the window frame and say aloud, "Alan?"

The man looked up and saw her clearly, and then his right arm came up and all her recognition, all the wonder and hope and the impossible joy that had begun to dawn were sucked up in an instant, back into a hole and gone. The man's arm held a gun; Alan with a gun in his hand was simply unthinkable; therefore the man was not Alan.

The pistol she had in her hand went off an instant after his, and whereas his shot hit the siding (another generation of bullets in the woodwork, Rae registered wildly), her bullet happened to strike the ground not far from his legs before ricocheting noisily into the night. She had not been aiming, had no time to think of aiming, but her lucky shot sent him leaping backward into the darkness near the tent.

Not Alan, not a friend, Rae thought, and then she was hurrying across the room to hush the terrified Petra. She stuck the pistol in her waistband and clapped her free hand across the child's mouth, whispering harshly in her ear, "Petra, stop it! You have to be quiet, please, Petra."

The girl regained control quickly and sat, trembling but silent. Rae bent forward and let her hand slide over to cup the side of Petra's head comfortingly.

"Petra, there's a man out there with a gun." A statement, alas, that any school-aged child would understand and respond to. "I've got a gun, too, but we have to go hide in Desmond's cave until he goes. Come on."

The discarded tools and roofing materials still lay in a pile, barring access to the gaping doorway of the empty front tower; Rae now flung aside the scraps of wood and tools until her fingers found the climbing harness, thrown there after the roof was finished. She crossed the room again, grabbed Petra's arm, and hurried her over to the rear tower.

"The top of the woodshed's about ten feet down from the tower windows," she whispered in the girl's ear. "It slopes, so don't move away until I can show you where to go. Do you want me to tie the harness around you, or can you hang on to it while I lower you down? You can't make any noise at all."

"I can hold it," Petra whispered back. Rae gave her granddaughter's shoulder an encouraging squeeze before she placed the anchoring loop in the girl's strong hands. Then she helped her up to the bare stones of the tower's empty window frame and, bracing herself against the wall to counteract the girl's weight, slowly lowered her down. The instant the rope went slack, Rae yanked it up. This time she stepped into the harness and buckled it on with frantic fingers (*Was that a noise coming up the stairs?*), then swung her legs over the tower's window frame, looped the end of the rope around the eight inches of stone that separated this window opening from the next, and took hold of the rope.

And paused. Shoot the flare gun now, while she had the chance? Or keep quiet until Petra was safe, then shoot it off? If the man below saw a flare go up, which way would he run—to his boat and escape, or to the house and attack?

She couldn't risk it. Get Petra hidden first; that had to be her priority. Rae took a firm grip on the rope and eased herself out into the black pit on the north wall of the house.

She was not altogether certain the stonework would hold, being built for the straight load of gravity and not the sideways strain of a rope with the weight of a grown woman on it, but it did not give way, and in seconds Petra was patting her grandmother's descending legs. Once on the shed roof, Rae yanked the rope free, balled it up and stuffed it into the waist of the harness, then felt her way across the woodshed, Petra following cautiously. At the far end, Rae slithered off to the ground below, helped Petra down, and worked the hand-carved catch by feel before lifting her granddaughter into the black void beyond.

She pulled the door shut behind them, whispering at Petra to stay put while she went to get the lamp from the cave, then groped her way blindly through the depths of the shed, cursing the splinters in her bare knees, cursing herself for bringing both guns and a useless cell phone but no flashlight. When she reached the spot where she knew the door had to be, she whispered a reassurance to the girl, fifteen feet away but a mile off in the pitch dark, and then, relying on memory alone, bent to let her fingertips work the hidden catch.

She jabbed the locking splinter up under her fingernail, but after that it did not take much fiddling. The door opened, the cool cave air was on her face, and in an instant she had light, and Petra, and the door shut behind them. Safe.

Rae stripped off the damnable climbing harness and slumped back against the wall until she became aware that Petra had crawled into the side cave and was curled against the wall in an unconscious imitation of Desmond Newborn's final position. Her young face was pinched with fear, and she trembled as if from cold. Rae crawled in next to her and gathered the child into her arms. Petra buried her face in Rae's shoulder and shook soundlessly, as aware as her grandmother that it was far from over. Rae stroked the child's hair rhythmically, murmuring a seamless string of meaningless phrases.

In the meantime, her mind was racing. Measure twice, cut once—only this time it was not a piece of lumber she was risking, but her granddaughter's life. And her own, which over the past weeks she had come to value once more. She had made a mistake in leaving the flashlight behind; she had made a risky choice in opting for silent escape; they could afford no more mistakes or risks. She had to be clearheaded.

The tools at hand were: a handgun, which now held four bullets; a flare gun and three flares; a kerosene lamp with five or six hours' worth of fuel, more if they kept it burning low; seven dusty wine bottles filled with near-vinegar; a freestanding shelf unit of spongy wood; a drip of water every minute or so; a climbing harness and rope; and whatever Petra had in her pockets. Rae asked her, and came up with a crumpled tissue, a broken seashell, and some black-purple lipstick.

Rae grimaced, and then her eyes lit on the other thing she had left in the cave, the only thing of real value she had brought with her to the island, deposited here to keep it safe from marauding trespassers: her toolbox with the Japanese chisels.

And, Rae reminded herself, they had their own minds and muscles. Not that she was about to launch a frontal attack on an armed man, but she might be able to go around him. Allen Carmichael had said something about soldiers who couldn't get over Vietnam having found ways to go around. Maybe she and Petra, too, could circle around the enemy until help arrived. (Surely someone would investigate that pair of gunshots they'd just loosed? Why, it was possible that even now, some irate tourist with an in-range cell phone was complaining to the local emergency dispatcher about the wild and irresponsible natives . . .)

Rae pulled her thoughts back together to the tools they had, the skills they possessed.

Sharp tools and wood; mallet and chisels. Those were what she knew, the core of Rae Newborn's identity. They were the key.

She smoothed her granddaughter's arm with her hand and thought her options over, measuring twice, three times, before moving to cut. And when she had done so, she sat up and told Petra what they were going to do. Well, mostly what Rae was going to do, since Petra would remain in the cave. But, with the gun.

"I need to go and set off a flare," Rae ended by saying, for the third time. "You and I are going to hide in here until help comes. The man won't stick around once the flare goes up, but I need you to sit here and let me back in when I knock." She broke open the garish plastic flare gun, dropped the cartridge into place, and snapped it shut again.

"But who *is* he?" Petra wailed. "What does he want?"

It was asked with no more expectation of an answer than any victim's cry of Why me? However, Rae knew it was no random sociopath out in the darkness, knew in fact who it had to be. And once the man's identity was known, everything else fell into place.

"I think the man out there is Alan's son. His name is Rory—you've never met him. He and Alan didn't see much of each other. I saw him out there: He looks too much like Alan to be a stranger." For a moment Rae paused, hit afresh by the shock of seeing her dead husband walking up the hill in the moonlight. "It must have something to do with money."

She watched Petra struggle with the idea, watched the puzzlement and glimmer of relief dawn on the young face, and moved to crush it brutally. "Rory's trying to kill me, Petra. I have no doubt he'll kill you, too, if he finds you here. If he breaks down that door, you're going to have to shoot him." Rae's heart cried out at the effect that statement was going to have on the child's mind, but there was no way around it. "It would be awful, to do such a thing; it's terrible even to ask you to think about it. If I could pretend everything was going to be okay, I would, but that would be dangerous for both of us. Rory came here to kill me. If he breaks down the door, aim carefully and get him first."

Petra had actually shot a gun before, Don's belief in the necessity for family self-defense overcoming Tamara's distaste for the activity, and the child quickly saw how the old revolver worked. She could use the weapon, but Rae was not at all certain that she would, not with a human target. However, Rae didn't see what more she could do to encourage her. She hugged Petra, then went over to the toolbox, took out the one-inch flat chisel and the smallest V-shaped one, plus the wooden mallet, and closed and latched the top of the box.

Then she went over the whole thing one last time with Petra. Not that there was much to it aside from: When I've gone, latch the door and sit with the gun in your hand and the lamp shining on the entrance, and wait for me to go shoot up a flare, after which I'll tap three times for you to open up. And for God's sake be careful not to let the lamp spill.

She kissed Petra again and hugged her hard. "Don't worry if it takes me a while. I'll have to make sure he's nowhere around first. You can do this, Petra, my little rock. We'll get out of this okay."

Measure twice, cut once ran through her head in a maniacal loop as she crawled out of Desmond's side cave and down the entranceway to let herself out into the woodshed. The protective whisper of the lamp vanished with the door; she waited to hear Petra slide the inside lock before going cautiously down the rough wood to the door leading out.

There she took several deep breaths. He would have heard her. Rory would be standing right outside the woodshed door, gun in hand, waiting for her to open up. She put the fingers of her left hand on the two-way latch and eased it back.

It let off a treacherous *click*, and she made a face, then pushed the door open.

The narrow space between house and rock was every bit as black as the interior of the woodshed. It could have held ten men, with bazookas. Beyond the corner of the house, however, the hillside was light, and the narrow swath of sky so brightly lit, the stars were dim. Rae leaned the right side of her body out the door, pointed her hand up at the sky, and pulled the trigger.

With the sound of a clap, the flare *whoosh*ed up, clearing the house and trees, dropping into a slight curve that put it out of sight over the house. She knew it was there, though, because the stars suddenly faded a few degrees more. Tearing her eyes from the sky, she tore the hot cartridge from the gun, slammed in another, and sent it, too, winging skyward.

Then she closed the door and locked it the only way she could, by taking her mallet and driving the beautiful tempered steel of her precious Japanese chisel through the wood and into the floor to wedge it shut. Two hard blows, and the razor-sharp tool had the door secure against anything short of a battering ram. She patted around for the smaller chisel, and shuffled over to the other hidden door.

The doubled point of the honed steel V sliced through the cedar boards with barely a whisper. Had Rory been standing just inside the hidden door he might have heard something, but not otherwise. Rae dug around with the chisel until a slight change in the pressure of the cut told her she had broken through. She laid the tool down and put her eye to the hole.

At first, all she saw was the pale rectangle that was the front door space, slightly overshadowed by an uneven shape that, after a minute, she identified as a portion of her tool belt, inches away, the twin fingers of the hammer claw just below eye level. Then she felt movement, an unaccustomed shivering through the bones of her house, somewhere out of sight. She peered to the side, and suddenly a light entered the room from the direction of the tower, a light and a pair of legs.

He walked in front of the fireplace, playing the beam up and down the fitted boards. The flashlight was in his left hand, and for an instant the light caught the shape he carried in his right: his gun, looking a far more dangerous weapon than the one Petra was clutching, back in the cave. No doubt this one had more than four shots in it as well. When he reached the west wall he continued around the perimeter of the room, searching, she thought, for the source of those two claps and the chisel-driving thuds, but he could not tell where they came from. He circled back to the stairway, pausing there, and then a dark shape startled Rae by flying, batlike, across her line of sight to land with a plop: the square of ratty carpeting that she'd laid down to hide the crawl space door. She and Petra had rumpled it, passing over it in the dark with their cots and sleeping bags; maybe he thought they were hiding underneath it. He hunkered down to examine the trapdoor's edges.

The flashlight illuminated his features clearly now, and Rae had to wonder if he had grown the beard and chosen those glasses in a deliberate imitation or a subconscious one, still on some level seeking the approval of a father alienated long before. It hardly mattered: Despite the uncanny physical resemblance, with that expression on his face, he looked no more like Alan than Petra did.

A thin breeze was blowing through the hole straight against her eyeball, making her eye water. The flashlight beam came up and Rae jerked back, blinking away the dazzle, hearing his boots approaching the fireplace, directly up to the hidden entrance, stopping so close that, but for a one-inch layer of cedar, she could have reached out and touched his boot. She fumbled frantically to load the third shell into the flare gun before the small door crashed open. There was a bump against the stud on the other side of the wall, a rattle and a bump, and then she had the gun snapped shut over its cartridge and was holding it out in both hands, ready to fire it straight into his face. But the door did not burst open. After a last rattle she heard footsteps—half a dozen retreating footsteps, then silence.

Rae swallowed convulsively and lowered the gun. After a minute, she wiped her mouth with unsteady fingers, then leaned forward again, to put her eye gingerly to the hole.

He was back at the subfloor access, kneeling with his back to her, the gun lying on the floor beside his knee. She thought he might be about to risk a look under the house, even knowing that his prey had a gun, but then his body shifted and his right arm rose out of the flashlight's beam, a motion Rae knew instantly, having performed it so many thousands of times over recent weeks. The arm fell, the hammer—*her* hammer; oh, that utter *bastard*!—drove into a nail, a dozen or more times. He tossed her beloved tool to one side with casual scorn and got to his feet, picking up flashlight and gun. He had nailed the crawl space door shut, assuming that she was hiding down there. He'd been upstairs, he knew that she—and another, there being two cots—had been there, but he had also seen the drop out of the tower window and concluded that a middle-aged woman could not have managed the jump to the woodshed without giving herself away. Where else could they be but under the floor? (Rae was visited briefly by a vision of the two wooden figures and their murderous spearhead, watching over the empty space.)

And with that, he left the house, flicking off the flashlight he carried and pausing at the doorway to let his eyes adjust to the darkness outside.

Rae knew he would see the flares the instant he stepped out. It was amazing he had missed the light and sound of their passing, but he must have already been making his way down the tower stairway, and heard only her final thuds.

If he had any wits at all, he would fling himself onto his black rubber dinghy and make for his boat at all speed, then weigh anchor and slip away before someone turned up to investigate the two lights hanging over the island. Rae prayed for his sense of self-preservation, urged him soundlessly to flee, to run away and live to kill another day. An eternity passed, with no darkening of the light rectangle of doorway, but before she could begin to relax, before the first threads of relief could take hold, he was back.

He came up the front steps in a hurry and stopped there, an object outlined in his hand that Rae despaired at, although she had known since he nailed the trapdoor shut that it would appear, had suspected it would come to this for what seemed like hours now. The feeling settled over her that she had lived with the inevitability of this moment from the very beginning, long weeks before, when she had freed the first charred wooden remnants of Desmond's house from the vines; known that it would come to this.

A full kerosene lamp thrown into a wooden structure.

Rory Beauchamp and William Newborn were in no way related, except under the skin. When faced with armed foes locked in a building, you don't go in after them, you burn them out. Or up. Rory was doing it thoroughly, taking the lamp apart to sprinkle the kerosene where it could do the most harm.

Rae knew she had one sensible chance: to retrieve Petra and escape through the woodshed, up the rocky hillside and into the trees. The fire would be seen for miles, even at four in the morning; the phone in her pocket would come alive; Rory would not hang around.

But she couldn't do it. In an agony of conflicting loyalties, Rae peered through her tiny hole at the figure hurrying to destroy her house, Desmond's house, intent on his puddles and the way the flames would feed into her walls, and she was simply unable to stand back and let him do it. If she failed, Petra would still be terrified at the sound of flames, but she would be safe. There was air enough in the cave and its entrance was sheltered on three sides by rock; by the time the slow-burning plywood of the woodshed had caught, the fire department would be here, and find her. Petra was safe.

Without further thought, Rae's hands picked up the slim chisel, screwed it into the narrow gap between door and siding, and leaned hard against the handle. The beautiful steel bowed; the invisible wood fastener held. Rae shoved with all her weight, grunting with the effort. The chisel gave slightly, resisted a moment longer, and suddenly the wood splintered and broke. The door slapped open into her knee and Rae's knuckles smashed themselves bloody against the rough siding, but without waiting for the brain's instructions her legs were already up and carrying her forward through the opening. Her invader, the destroyer, was standing in the doorway now, as William before him had stood; he was turning with a box of matches in his hands when Rae, still half crouched, reached the middle of the room.

Her hand swept down and caught up the abandoned hammer, the tool that had been the beginning of everything in her life, and as she did so her husband's son suddenly realized she was there. The unlit matches spilled to the steps as he grabbed for the gun in his belt, and the gun came around at the same moment that twenty-one ounces of drop-forged steel with a handle carved of Honduran mahogany left Rae's palm.

The hammer took him in the face. His hand convulsed briefly on the pistol, and lead brushed past Rae's scalp to slap safely into the beams behind her, but Rory was tumbling backward, unconscious before the back of his head cracked against the rocky hillside.

She retrieved her hammer and stood over him with it, panting hard and fighting the urge to shriek like a banshee and either bash him again or kick him all the way into the waves, but her feet were bare, her hammer too precious, and her rage too short-lived. She settled instead for pulling the loaded flare gun from the waistband of her shorts and aiming it straight at his darkly bloodied face. Her finger twitched, and then she raised the gun to the heavens and squeezed; the third flare exploded upward to join its fading brothers.

Rae did not know how long she sat on the bottom step with the hammer beside her, watching over the unconscious figure, before she heard Petra's voice—not more than a minute or two, she decided later, since the last flare was still sputtering overhead.

"Gran?" came the whisper, so high-pitched it ended in a squeak.

Rae stood quickly. "I'm here, sweetheart. It's finished—everything's okay. You wait there." The house reeked of kerosene, horribly dangerous to the least spark (had that bullet hit the stones . . .), and she scurried across the room to the access door, folded herself through, and closed it behind her. Petra flung herself at Rae, sobbing out her relief at last. Rae held her close and rocked her like a baby, taking comfort as much as giving it, until eventually her granddaughter's fear loosed a few notches.

She nuzzled the child's unkempt hair, and ventured humor. "Were you Petra-fied, my love?"

As she had hoped, the child snorted involuntarily at the bad joke, and although she then hugged Rae all the tighter, Rae thought that the immediate reaction had passed. "Okay," she said. "It's nearly over now. We'll have to go around the house to get to the tent—the lamp spilled inside the house and it really stinks in there. So it looks like you get to go barefoot on the island after all, in spite of your mother's wishes."

"A lamp?"

"Kerosene, yes." With any luck, the child would assume it to be an accidental spill.

"But what happened?" Petra wailed. "I waited and waited and then I thought I heard shooting, and then nothing happened for the longest time and—"

"I know, love, I was coming back for you. That was him shooting, but all he hit was the ceiling. I knocked him on the head. He's out cold, and I took his gun."

"But if he wakes up—"

"Petra, it's okay. He doesn't have a gun, he's hurt, and the police will be here any minute. Come on, let's go."

The girl clung to her as they picked their way down the steep slope and circled the tower. The first intimations of dawn were bringing light to the eastern sky. It seemed years since the sunset.

At the tent they retrieved flashlight and shoes. Rae took a kitchen knife to her clothesline and bundled it up into her pocket, then picked up two saucepans.

"I'm going to tie him in case he wakes up," she said, handing the pans to Petra. "I need you to go to the end of the promontory and make a lot of noise. I can't believe anyone could sleep through gunshots and flares, but you've got to make sure—create enough of a racket to make them come to the decks of their fancy boats and ask what the hell you're doing, okay? Bang and crash and shout as loud as you can. I'll join you there."

Petra took their only remaining flashlight.

Rae went cautiously up the hill, gun in hand, not at all sure Rory wasn't going to leap at her as she approached. He did not. It looked, in truth, as if he would not be leaping at anyone for a long time. Still, Rae nervously bound his feet together, cut the line, then held his hands together to bind those as well. They were twitching, and small moaning noises were coming out of his throat. She could see his outline now, and in a few minutes, his face. He was wearing a plaid shirt—another imitation of Alan—and his glasses were smashed on the rocks. With a start, Rae realized that his eyes were not only open, but looking straight at her. She stepped back hastily; he did not move.

"Rory? Can you hear me?" There was no response, but looking into his eyes, she thought he was aware. "Rory, do you know who I am?"

Ten minutes earlier she would not have seen the brief spasm of disgust that passed over his battered face, but now it was light enough. She took it as answer, and squatted down at his side. Petra's saucepans clanged once, tentatively, and then again with more conviction, and soon she was bashing and shouting at the top of her young lungs. Rae smiled involuntarily, and Rory's eyes became slits.

If he was sufficiently aware to notice her expression, then he could answer a few questions, she decided. "You paid those two bastards to attack me, didn't you? Did you know they're in jail?" She waited in vain for a response. "Did you actually tell them to rape me, or was that their own decision?"

"Who gives a shit?" he muttered. *Oh, Alan,* her heart cried; *thank God you're not here to see this.*

"It's you that's been phoning around the islands? And searched my tent two weeks ago?"

"Had to be sure." His words were slurred from the damage done by her hammer, but she could understand them. She also heard clearly that there was no regret in his voice; if anything, there was pride.

"Does that also mean you broke into my house? Trashed the place looking for where I'd gone?"

"Found you."

"Oh yes, you're a clever boy, all right. But why smash all Alan's glass?"

That got a reaction. Rory convulsed and Rae fell over backward onto her rear end as she scrabbled uphill with both feet to get away from him. He lay back impotently.

"He loved that shit," he snarled. "I was with him when he bought one, stupid bastard, drooling over it like it was a Rembrandt or something. Five hundred bucks for a fucking paperweight. A present for you. And then when he left, he gave me a lousy hundred bucks. Pissed me off. So I broke 'em."

It was a statement vastly more revealing than he could have known. When Rae first saw who it was, she had assumed it was all about money; no doubt Rory believed it was, too. But what she heard was far more raw and visceral than any drive for hard cash: Alan had loved the glass, so Rory would smash it. Alan had loved Rae: Rory would drive her mad, beat her up by proxy, provoke her to suicide.

Alan had loved Bella, too. If Bella had survived the accident, what would Rory have done? Rae pictured the savaged corkboard and ripped drawings in Alan's study, and knew that this man would have done more to their daughter than steal an antique silver rattle from her crib.

Alan had done everything he could for his son, but the boy was just a black hole that even a father's love could not fill. Rae flashed back to the strange dream she'd had, with Rory and Don standing over a baby's crib, pulling off one mask after another, but she refused to think about that now: She might pity Rory Beauchamp; if she thought about it, she might even understand what had led him to this point, but not now. And she would never feel sorry enough to grieve for him. He had tried to hurt Petra; for that he would pay.

The sun was rising now, the very tops of the cedars turning golden with the first light of the new day; she and Rory could see each other clearly. To be sure, she went forward until his face was at arm's length from hers. She was aware of the approach of a familiar boat engine, heard, too, the change in Petra's frantic noisemaking, but she wanted to kick this man before Jerry got to him. Kick him hard, where it would hurt him the most: in his pride.

"Your father wasn't the stupidest bastard in his family. You know what you'd have got if you sold those glass pieces instead of breaking them? At least a couple hundred thousand dollars. And all those paintings and lithographs on the walls that you just ignored? Even on the black market, they'd have put another, oh, half, three quarters of a million in your pocket." He winced at each blow. Rae watched with pleasure, and prepared the final kick. "And you didn't even think to look for a safe. Talk about stupid."

She turned and walked away, leaving him for Jerry Carmichael.

Part Five

HOUSE-
WARMING

Fifty-six

Rae Newborn stood with her boots on the island's rocky promontory, holding in her hands the box that Ed De la Torre had brought her two days before. She had saved it for tonight, the autumn equinox, although she was not quite sure why. Because it felt right, she supposed, and that was reason enough.

Seventy-two years and ten days after his death, on a warm September evening, Desmond Newborn was about to come home for good. Not that she could be positive just which day was the anniversary of his death, how long he had waited in his cave for the end to take him, but it hardly mattered now. Today was the equinox, halfway between midsummer and the winter solstice, and today she would scatter his ashes.

"Your towers finally have windows in them, Desmond," she told his spirit. "The roof is shingled. And my front door looks just like yours. Folly is a shell, but it's secure. I'm going to stay here over the winter, working on the inside." And after that . . . well, who knew?

"There's going to be a book about you, Desmond. Maybe not everything about you—I'll have to think about that—but all about Folly, and how you built it, and how I restored it. The photographer brought me some of his pictures—there's a magnificent one of the beach over on Lopez where you gathered a lot of your stones. It's going to be a spectacular book. And your great-great-great-niece Petra is going to help me with the words. My granddaughter wants to be a writer. You'd be so proud of her."

She stopped, hearing the sound of footsteps coming up the promontory after her. In a minute, the man whose name she was getting used to was standing behind her. He smelled of coffee.

"I'm going to have to stop carrying on these conversations with Desmond," she said, without turning to face him. "People are going to think I'm a little unbalanced."

"They wouldn't dare," Allen said.

The growl of a boat opening throttle as it came free from the Roche Harbor restrictions reached her ears, and she knew her companion would be eyeing it carefully, ready to fade away if it came too close. It was like living with a ghost when Allen was here, his habitual disinclination to be seen causing him to vanish at the hint of an intruder. Sometimes Rae found herself talking to empty air.

He was a ghost in other ways as well. The overlay of his name on her tongue, once jarring, was beginning to feel oddly inevitable, as if the syllables denoted a relationship rather than a distinct person. It was not that he filled the Alan-shaped hole in her life, exactly, but he did take over some of that same space. He was unlike Alan in all ways but the key ones at the centers of their beings, and that core similarity allowed the one man to overlap and merge with the other. Which was the ghost was not always clear to her, and Rae knew full well that it was more than a little weird, and probably unhealthy as well. She just couldn't bring herself to worry about it.

The boat moved off, and he settled down at her side. An oak, she thought, in Vivian's tree game. Scarred and fire-girt, bent by forces that would have had lesser trees flat. The only oak she'd ever met.

"Allen?"

"Mm?"

"I've decided to go to California next month. I need to clear out Alan's clothes, give Bella's toys to the local shelter, do something about my workshop. I'll be gone two or three weeks."

"You feel ready for that?"

"I do."

"I'm glad. I'm supposed to go to Europe for a week or two myself, to set up a link with a group there. Around the tenth."

"Then I'll aim for the same date." Allen would not stay in the house while she was away. Folly might be considered haunted, but ghosts did not generally light fires and cook themselves meals.

Satisfied, Rae worked open the top of the box, then eased her way down the boulders to the water. There was an odd shimmer to its surface tonight, a seasonal bioluminescence due to some kind of plankton. When she sprinkled the ashes, they flowered and glowed briefly where they landed.

When the box was half empty, she closed it, then climbed back up to sit beside the island's ghost. The rest of the ashes she planned to divide in the morning: half beneath the madrone tree, heavy now with clusters of red berries, the remainder in the spring's lower pool among the ferns and the salamanders.

When the glow had subsided and the sun was fully gone, they walked back together to the house. It smelled still of raw plaster, although the air no longer felt damp with it. She waited until Allen had drawn the curtains before she lit the lamps.

Gloriana's photographer, Jaime Brittin, had spent the day on Folly. It was his second trip to record the house's progress, following a preliminary session in late July, and he had left the table in the middle of the room—a slab of Vivian's walnut burl—piled high with a wild assortment of photographs: old black-and-white portraits and her crude snapshots mixed up with his sleek July studies that looked ready for framing on Gloriana's gallery walls. Lying on top of one stack was the bashed-up strongbox, which Rae had brought out after the photographer left, to give Desmond's journal to Allen.

She sat down in one of the frayed canvas camp chairs and began to gather together the photos while Allen stirred up the fire in the black fireplace and went to the liquor cabinet (a plastic milk crate) to pour them each a glass of wine.

"Did you finish reading the journal?" she asked him.

"I did. Are you going to use it in the book?"

"I haven't decided yet."

"You should. It's very moving. Amazing how like Vietnam that war seems to have been, except their mud was cold."

The house warmed rapidly, now that the windows were in and the door was secure, and Rae shrugged out of her jacket, then draped it over the back of the chair.

"What did you say to the photographer, when he was posing you on the front steps with the door latch in your hand?" Allen asked.

"You were watching?"

"Of course I was watching. You said something to him that made him nearly drop his camera."

"Oh yes," she said with a smile. "He wanted a modern duplicate of the picture of Desmond as one of the book's echoes, so I told him, 'If someone bursts in tonight and shoots me, I'm going to be really upset.' Of course, poor Jaime had no idea what I was talking about." Allen laughed and Rae joined him, but she glanced uneasily over at the door as well. Allen, sensitive always to the fears of others, put down his glass and went to turn the bolt.

He came back to the fire and picked up the small leather book, thumbing through the pages of a man's life.

"I wonder what that final entry was going to be," he mused. "'I have a' something."

"Ah," said Rae. His head came up at the sound. "That's the reason why I'm hesitating about using the journal in the book. Here, I'll show you."

She sorted through the photos and extracted several, then laid them out on the floor in front of the hearth like some exotic game of solitaire. Allen watched over her shoulder as Rae identified each subject for him.

The first was an enlargement of the old photograph of Desmond on his steps. Either as a result of superior equipment or through surreptitious retouching, the latch was now clear in his hand. His face remained half shaded: one dark eye, dark hair falling against one pale cheek, dark jacket with a smudge of light dust on one sleeve.

Below it she laid two others, William and Lacy, taken from the family albums by Tamara: William on the left at the age of seventy—hawklike face, thin mouth, eyes like a pair of ice chips—Lacy on the right looking as if she might burst like a balloon under one glance of her husband's eyes. The picture showed her as a young woman, very beautiful in her Edwardian ruffles and Gibson girl hair. Her skin was pale, the texture of a flower petal that would bruise at a touch, and her eyes, too, though nicely shaped, would have benefited from a judicious application of Petra's makeup. Since in the early years of the century no proper lady would have thought of such a thing, in the picture they looked almost as pale as her skin.

Then beneath those two photos Rae placed a snapshot of her parents: her father dark and shadowy, as befitted a man who had spent his life in the shadow of his father; her mother, before she became sick, a classic blond California beauty of the Forties.

As the fourth and bottom row, Rae set down a picture of herself, in which Jaime had contrived to find a trace of beauty, even mystery, in a tall graying woman with a hammer in her hand.

Finally, she reached for the metal strongbox and took out the gold locket with the two locks of hair. She opened it, and arranged the golden clamshell at the place where Desmond's photograph met those of William and Lacy. The brown curl and the blond were slightly tangled, but Rae made no attempt to separate them. Then she removed the box's other, odder contents. The assorted objects that she had thought might be mementos—twigs, shell, and pebble; concert program, button, ribbon, and tassel—she arranged to the right of the photographs. Last, she took the diary from Allen, leafed through to find Desmond's careful notation of eight unexplained dates scattered through the first two months of 1919. She laid the diary below the mementos, then sat back against Allen's knees.

"What do you see?" she asked.

It took him only moments. "Damn," he exclaimed, sitting up abruptly. "You think that explains it?"

"I think so, yes." Rae picked up the photographs of Desmond and her father, leaving the rest where they lay. "I think that when my father was about seven years old, it occurred to William that the boy's eyes were not going to grow any lighter. He thought back to the boy's birth date, and to nine months before, and he arranged a trip out west to see his little brother's island.

"On that visit, he just happened to show his brother a picture of Lacy and her son, and Desmond saw instantly what it meant. But because Desmond was a soldier at heart, true and straightforward, he couldn't see what lay behind the picture. Or rather, what lay behind his being shown the picture."

Eight dates; eight odd souvenirs.

"That night, he sat down to write about it in his journal—I found an uncapped pen in the debris under the house, right in front of the fireplace where his chair was—but before he could get his discovery down, his brother came back in and killed him. In revenge. William was always big on revenge, and on the sanctity of his possessions.

"What Desmond sat down to write was: 'I have a son.'"

Rae looked from one picture to the other, then picked up her own brown-eyed photograph and inserted it between them. She even had the same generous mouth.

"Desmond Newborn was not my father's uncle," she told her island's ghost. "Desmond Newborn was his father. My grandfather."

"Your island is well named, "Allen replied after a minute.

Rae smiled, sadly, and dropped her head back against his supporting knees. "Newborn's Folly."

Allen laid a hand on her hair, and gently corrected her. "Newborn's Sanctuary."

About the Author

LAURIE R. KING lives with her family in the hills above Monterey Bay in northern California. Her background includes such diverse interests as Old Testament theology and construction work, and she has been writing crime fiction since 1987. The winner of both the Edgar and the John Creasey Awards for Best First Novel for *A Grave Talent,* the debut of the Kate Martinelli series, she is also the author of five mysteries in the Mary Russell series, including *The Beekeeper's Apprentice,* and most recently, *O Jerusalem,* as well as a thriller, *A Darker Place.* Her website address is laurierking.com.

mys

King, Laurie R.

Folly.

¢

$23.95